# THE UNEXPECTED DIVA

# THE
# UNEXPECTED
# DIVA

*A Novel*

❧

Tiffany L. Warren

WILLIAM MORROW
*An Imprint of HarperCollinsPublishers*

THE UNEXPECTED DIVA. Copyright © 2025 by Tiffany L. Warren. All rights reserved. Printed in the United States of America. No part of this book may be used or reproduced in any manner whatsoever without written permission except in the case of brief quotations embodied in critical articles and reviews. For information, address HarperCollins Publishers, 195 Broadway, New York, NY 10007.

HarperCollins books may be purchased for educational, business, or sales promotional use. For information, please email the Special Markets Department at SPsales@harpercollins.com.

FIRST EDITION

*Interior text designed by Diahann Sturge-Campbell*

Library of Congress Cataloging-in-Publication Data has been applied for.

ISBN 978-0-06-332213-4

24 25 26 27 28 LBC 5 4 3 2 1

*For every diva . . . may you discover your gift and savor your applause.*

# THE UNEXPECTED DIVA

# CHAPTER ONE

*Philadelphia, Pennsylvania*
*February 1850*

*Come home. STOP. Quickly. STOP.*

*I* have been clutching this telegram since I received it two weeks ago. The paper is wrinkled and sweat-stained now from my nervous hands. There are no details as to why I should rush home from my precious singing lessons in Buffalo—the ones Miss Lizbeth procured for me on the strength of a favor from a friend. The lessons that are mostly unavailable in my hometown because I am Black.

Yet, no matter how necessary my lessons are, I booked passage on the first steamship I could take out of Buffalo Harbor to Erie, Pennsylvania. Then three days in a packet boat down the Erie Extension Canal until now.

My knee bounces along with my trembling hands as I peer out the tiny grime-encrusted window of the covered carriage. This is the final mode of transport to take me to the only mother I've ever known, but the driver does not appear to be in any rush.

More than anything, my worry stems from the fact that this telegram came not from Miss Lizbeth herself, but from her nurse, Sarah. When I departed for my lessons six months ago, Miss Lizbeth was in her regular state of frailty—she is nearly one hundred years old, after all—but she was not sick. Every morning she rose early to have our tea and biscuits ready before I was dressed. She could send her own telegram before I left home for my lessons.

"Here is the address," I say to the driver, who has nearly passed our brownstone.

The carriage halts so suddenly that I must stretch my arms forward to keep from being thrown from the seat. If I was a slender girl, I would have been. I give silent praise for my heavy bones and healthy appetite.

Of course, my dear friend Lucien is waiting for me in front of our three-story brownstone on Mulberry Street. I had sent word of my travel before boarding the stagecoach, but there was no way of knowing when I would arrive. He could have been standing here for hours, dressed in his church jacket and pants, his smile stretching from one ear to the other.

Lucien is tall and wiry, with sandpaper-colored skin and a friendly disposition. His kind nature makes up what he lacks in looks. Separately, his features aren't ghastly: large, wide-set eyes, a broad and flat nose that takes up too much space, and thick, heavy lips that he can never seem to properly moisturize—they're either too moist from his licking them or too dry from the elements. The collection of these features is not quite what most women consider handsome, but with his physique, chiseled from hard work, and a little confidence, he could still manage to turn many heads. Unfortunately, confidence is not something Lucien possesses, and he tends to slouch, making himself smaller.

Lucien rushes forward to take my bag and help me down the two steps, making me feel like a lady for a change.

"Lucien," I say while he encircles me with his arms. "Have you spoken to Miss Lizbeth?"

"She is not well, Eliza. It's good that you're home." I hear the concern in his tone, and it makes me feel anxious to see Miss Lizbeth.

Not wanting to go inside to Miss Lizbeth with a melancholy expression, I hold back my flood of emotions. I know how old she is. Perhaps I shouldn't have gone so far away to take my lessons.

"It isn't your fault." Lucien consoles me as if reading my thoughts. "The doctor says it's pneumonia. She's taken to her bed."

"And have you seen her? Talked to her?"

Lucien takes my arm with his free hand and helps me up the snow-and-slush-covered stairs. I am grateful for this, because the wind is whipping so that I've already stumbled twice since climbing out of the carriage. It is late February, and winter is still in charge of the weather. The winds are blustery, the skies overcast, and the cold chills to the bone.

"I have not seen her," Lucien laments. "Sarah keeps her hidden away from the world, or maybe just from me."

I believe this. While Sarah is an excellent nurse, she is not as fond of Black people as Miss Lizbeth, although she would never say as much around the other Quaker members of our closely knit community. I have seen her cast envious glances in my direction, especially once I entered adulthood. Perhaps I was less threatening to her as a little girl, and as a former slave. But at twenty-six, and with Miss Lizbeth still doting on me as if she gave birth to me herself, I may be a problem for Sarah. She would probably do away with me if she could, so I am sure she has no use for Lucien.

I use my key to open the door and am overwhelmed by the odor of sickness. The brownstone smells of medicine and decay. Of a long life nearing its end.

"Lucien, will you take my bags to my room? I want to go directly in to see Miss Lizbeth."

Sarah emerges from Miss Lizbeth's bedroom with her lips pressed together in a grim expression. She looks neither happy nor surprised to see me, but I stretch my arms toward her anyway. She barely embraces me, and there is no love in the motion.

"Miss Elizabeth is resting," Sarah says coldly. "You will have to visit with her later."

"I will sit next to her while she sleeps." I push past Sarah to open the door. "Excuse me, please."

Sarah narrows her eyes but does not object. She knows better than to do that. I may be Black, but I am still her employer's daughter.

Though I try to be as quiet as possible, Miss Lizbeth's eyes flutter open when I close the door behind me. A weak smile teases her lips, and I force myself to smile back.

"Eliza, you're home." Her voice is dry and raspy and barely above a whisper, but I can still hear her joy at seeing me. She pats the chair at her bedside. "Come and sit. Tell me about your lessons."

I fight back tears at her wasted state. She looks so tiny in her sleeping dress. Mostly she seems old and tired. Though she's been in the winter of her life since I was born, she's never appeared so frail. Miss Lizbeth has always been full of vigor. This pneumonia has stolen that from her.

I sit and fold my hands across my lap, the way Miss Lizbeth taught me. Even with her education on etiquette, I am never sure how I will be judged by even the friendliest of white people. I know that my robust size and my very dark complexion cause some to believe I am a brute, no matter how genteel my behavior.

"Lucien asks about you," I say, not wanting to remind her of the lessons that kept me far away when she fell ill.

Miss Lizbeth opens her mouth to speak, but she is overcome by a fit of coughing. She reaches for the glass of water on her nightstand, and I rush to hand it to her. Luckily, she is propped up on a mound of pillows and able to drink without incident.

"Why hasn't he visited? I would've enjoyed seeing him over these past few months."

"And he you. But Sarah would not allow it."

Miss Lizbeth's eyebrows shoot up at this offense. "Sarah does not allow or disallow anything in my home. I will speak to her."

"No need," I say, taking the glass of water from Miss Lizbeth and returning it to its place on the nightstand. "I am here now, and so Lucien will get an audience."

"No need to be so proper, my dear. You are home," she says, patting my hand and calming me. "Lucien will visit, and we will laugh as we always do."

"We will, but first we have to get you better."

Miss Lizbeth's heavy sigh does not match her smile, but I wait for her to elaborate. "I just bet Lucien was waiting for you when the carriage arrived, wasn't he?"

So we're not going to discuss her health. Or her getting better. There is a sinking feeling in my belly. A person cannot live forever, but I cannot fathom my world without Miss Lizbeth.

"He was. He is such a loyal friend to me. Always there when I need him."

"Well, he desires more than friendship. You know that."

I look away from Miss Lizbeth's knowing gaze. This is a difficult subject for me. Everyone believes that Lucien wants to court me, but I don't have the same feelings for him. I also do not have any other men inquiring after me, so there's a small voice inside me that nags at me not to discourage Lucien so hastily. "He has not said as much, and I will not broach the topic myself. I quite enjoy our friendship."

"Lucien never changes. He is a good man." Even in her whispery voice, I can hear the compassion Miss Lizbeth has for Lucien.

"I do enjoy his company, but I sometimes fear there's an additional motivation for his attentions. I don't know what will become of us if he makes these motivations plain."

There are times when I let myself dream of something more than a life with a husband and children. But then other times I think I might welcome the security of a marriage, because what choice is there, really, other than spinsterhood?

Still other times I wonder if it's the idea of marriage that gives me pause or if it's Lucien. Because would I want children and a quiet life if it was with someone *other* than Lucien? Someone who makes my toes tingle, if that is a possibility? I have never felt tingling with Lucien.

"To anyone with eyes, his motivations are plain," Miss Lizbeth says knowingly.

I no longer wish to speak of this. Not today. Today, I care only about spending time with Miss Lizbeth.

"I don't know about Lucien, but I do know I'd like to tell you about my lessons."

Miss Lizbeth closes her eyes for a long moment, hopefully accepting my hint that I'd like to turn our attentions somewhere other than Lucien, at least for now.

After coughing for an extended amount of time, she finally croaks, "And I want to hear about your lessons. How is Bella?"

I cannot think about Miss Bella without wanting to adjust my posture and breathe from my diaphragm. The tiny Italian woman is well into her eighties but has the energy of a woman decades younger. Even miles away, I can almost hear her cane tapping in my head, keeping the tempo as I sing.

Bella is short for Isabella Antonacci. She moved to America as a young woman. Her story changes almost every time I ask, but from what I gather, she had a promising career ahead of her as a prima donna and was trained by her cousin Tonio, who was a composer and one of the last castrati—young men who were castrated at an early age to preserve their soprano or contralto voices for the stage.

She says her career was ruined, and she hints at the reason, but I can never quite pin down the exact story. I believe it had to do with her exquisite beauty. If the portraits hanging in her studio are accurate depictions, she was stunning, with lush dark hair, blue eyes, full lips, and a buxom figure.

"Miss Bella is as fiery as ever," I say. "Still teaching her young students too."

"The small children? Is she mad?" Miss Lizbeth manages to sound amused between a few weaker coughs.

Weak not because there's less congestion, for I can still hear the loud rattle, but I think perhaps she's growing even more tired. I hate to leave her side, but I may need to heed Sarah's advice and allow her to rest.

"Miss Bella says she will continue to teach them singing and Italian as long as she has the energy. But lately she has started to use her walking stick all the time."

Miss Lizbeth now simply shakes her head in wonder. She motions to her tumbler of water, and I quickly give her a drink. Some of the water dribbles onto her nightgown, and she does not look refreshed, but she gives a tiny smile that makes her look peaceful.

"Show me what you've learned," she asks.

"Well, I am learning an aria, but I don't think it's good enough yet."

"I'm sure it is better than you think. Learning from Bella is the next best thing to being educated in Europe. She may even be better. Let me hear it."

Another soft smile and a hand squeeze are all the encouragement I need. I push away the thought that this may be the last time I sing for Miss Lizbeth, but her chest continues to rattle with every breath, and the pale wrinkled hand that covers mine has lost its vigor.

I swallow to moisten my throat. It isn't enough, but I will not sing in full voice, and I will pull back on the high notes—things my teacher has instilled in me, things I didn't know to do before. Miss Bella says my voice, my range, will not last forever and that I must do all I can to preserve it.

Miss Lizbeth shudders when I open my mouth to sing the first melancholy note. This aria, from *La sonnambula*, is a sad one, perfect for this occasion.

All the grief I feel at the thought of losing Miss Lizbeth comes rushing out over the notes as I sing the words. My parents, formerly owned by Miss Lizbeth, but now manumitted, went to the freed slave colony in West Africa called Liberia, along with my two sisters, when I was seven years old. Miss Lizbeth told me that my father had been brought over on a slave ship when he was a boy of about twelve years old, only a few years before the slave trade ended for good, and it had always been his dream to see Africa again. But my mother was born in America—a Seminole woman.

They'd left me behind in America, because when it was time for the ship to leave for Liberia in 1831, I had just recovered from a terrible fever, and the doctor did not believe I would survive the voyage. My mother could not stay behind if she wanted freedom. The only way the court would agree to the terms of the manumission was if the entire group boarded the ship and left America, never to return.

So Miss Lizbeth promised to take me back to Philadelphia with her and educate me. Because I was only seven, and sickly, perhaps no one considered me a threat, and I was allowed to stay.

Of course, I don't recall any of this. This story was told and retold to me over the years, by Miss Lizbeth. And with every retelling, she adds or subtracts a detail or two. Like the last time, she remembered that there were eighteen people in total who left the plantation in Natchez to board the brig *Criterion* to travel to Liberia.

What I remember of my parents and sisters is in bits and pieces. My mother's soothing voice and her long, heavy hair that she wore in a braid that went past her bottom. I recall her being much shorter than my father, and his laugh echoes in my memories. It was loud and booming and seemed to go on forever once he got going.

The memories of my sisters are even cloudier. Brown faces, chubby hands, and more laughter. That is all.

I never questioned their decision to leave me behind until now, because when Miss Lizbeth dies, I will have no protector.

Of course, I will have Lucien, who may have his heart set on marriage and family. He would perhaps relish being able to step in to protect me, but that protection would accompany his promise of forever. Only Miss Lizbeth's love comes without strings.

Tears stream down Miss Lizbeth's face as I hit the last note and perfectly trill as Miss Bella has taught me. The aria, while melancholy, is beautiful and haunting.

"The words," Miss Lizbeth says after another coughing fit, "what do they mean?"

"I'm sure my Italian pronunciations are imperfect, but it begins with *I had not thought I would see you, dear flowers, perished so soon.* That is the translation."

"I wouldn't know if it was correct or not, since I don't speak Italian."

We both laugh, though singing the words properly is part of my education. Miss Bella teaches me more than the rudiments of singing. She also teaches me how to stand, how to hold my hands, and how to look elegant and gracious while making my voice accomplish nearly impossible feats. And, of course, she tries her best to teach me Italian, so that if I become a prima donna one day, I will be able to visit Italy and learn from greater teachers than herself.

"Miss Bella says I should honor and cherish each syllable," I explain. "But it's so hard, because I only know some of the words until I hear the translation. In Italian they are mostly sounds with music notes attached."

"I have confidence in you, my dear Eliza. You will learn as much as you can from Bella, and then you can receive more training in Europe."

"You are surer of these things than I am, Miss Lizbeth. Please do not leave me. I am not ready to be in this world without you."

There. I've spoken the words in my heart. I am afraid of what comes next without her.

"Everyone, everything is temporary. But when we're gone, we must leave the world better than when we entered it, yes?"

I muster a smile. Miss Lizbeth has always been a fearless woman who has long navigated this world without a husband or protector, though she was married twice.

"And when I am gone, you will cleave unto Mary. She will be a comfort for you." Miss Lizbeth delivers her words with certainty and finality. She hates hysterics.

But my mind reels.

"I am not ready for instructions on what to do after you're gone. I do not wish to think about that."

"But you must think about these things. I don't have much time left." This is punctuated with a hacking cough that does nothing to clear the moist sounds in Miss Lizbeth's chest. I pretend not to notice the blood-tinged spittle at the corners of her dry lips.

"You have had illnesses before, and you have recovered."

"This one will finish me, and you are what I leave behind," Miss Lizbeth says. "You must pursue your gift."

What a heavy burden to lay at my feet when she will not be here to see me endure the suffering that is sure to come with this pursuit. How can I be the thing she leaves behind? I am her namesake, and it is true that she has nurtured and cared for me my entire life, but she cannot bequeath unto me the one thing that will make cultivating this gift possible.

"Pursue singing as a profession?" I ask the question, because the Society of Friends does not encourage singing or the arts in general.

"Why not?" Miss Lizbeth scoffs.

"The Friends . . ."

One side of Miss Lizbeth's mouth rises in her familiar lopsided grin. "Come now, Eliza. Don't you try to convince me that you will follow the Quaker way of life when I'm gone. I can barely get you to visit the meetings. You and Mary have your Baptist church."

"We do."

"And last I checked, the Baptists are quite fond of music and singing."

"Yes, but I am"—I search my mind for the word that will best fit this sentiment—"limited."

Miss Lizbeth shakes her head. An adamant no. "You are *gifted*."

"Yes, but there are limits to what I can achieve. I am too dark to be seen as delicate in this world. People don't expect beautiful music to come from my mouth. They must always be convinced. I must always prove myself." My explanation is rambling and emotional, but she must listen to me.

Though it seems as if it should be impossible for her to do so, Miss Lizbeth rises from her mound of pillows. She grips my hand with a strength that she doesn't appear to have, and she gazes directly into my eyes.

"Believe this. Every gift comes from God. Promise me you won't waste it."

"I—"

Miss Lizbeth's frail body shakes with terrifying coughs. What little color remains drains from her face as more blood trickles from the corners of her mouth. I try not to scream, but I do let out a yelp that brings Sarah bursting into the room. She pushes me away from the bedside.

"Eliza, she must rest," Sarah hisses. "Can't you see that with your own eyes?"

I grit my teeth but allow Sarah space to do her work. Miss Lizbeth might be her charge, but she is my guardian, and she is slipping away.

"Promise me, Eliza," Miss Lizbeth whispers as Sarah gently lowers her head back onto the rearranged pillows.

"I promise."

Miss Lizbeth's eyes close as I give my uncertain response, and she falls into a restless sleep. Her body shudders with every rattling breath. Though I am unsure about where this gift will lead me, I am certain that Miss Lizbeth will not be here to witness the outcome.

Sarah tucks the blankets high around her neck, though it looks uncomfortable, and then turns to glare at me.

"I told you she was tired, but you disturbed and excited her," she says in a tone that is not only unpleasant but disrespectful as well.

She does not deserve an answer, so I don't give her one. Sarah resumes her station next to Miss Lizbeth's bedside, and I leave the room.

Lucien is waiting outside the door, with his hat in his hand, a look of worry on his face. Seeing his concern unleashes my flood of tears. I allow him to wrap me in the warmth of his strong, muscled arms, no matter how he may interpret my closeness. If nothing else, I feel safe with Lucien. I look up at his face, his smooth skin and kind eyes, feeling sorrowful that I don't have an attraction to him. And as I gaze, I question if I could ever feel those deeper things for him.

"It won't be long," I say, after abruptly pulling away from the hug when Lucien tried to hold on a little longer than was welcome. "She can barely breathe without coughing, and there is blood in her spittle."

"She has lived a good, long life. Don't be sad."

But it is more concern and trepidation that I feel than sadness. I have made a promise to Miss Lizbeth, and I am bound by duty and by love to honor it. More than this, I want to believe in the greatness that Miss Lizbeth sees in me. Instead of marrying—no matter how much Lucien desires it—I will continue my lessons and see what unfolds.

Hopefully, my friendship with Lucien will survive unscathed even if I don't want to bear his children and cook his meals. There are, after all, many women in Philadelphia who can do these things for him.

I am the only woman I know, however, who can sing *La sonnambula*.

# CHAPTER TWO

$\mathcal{A}$fter seeing my dear Miss Lizbeth in such a state of deterioration, I must find a way to lift my spirits. So I send word to my sister, Mary, to meet me at the home of Miss Ophelia Price, our neighbor and friend. Ophelia is a widow and very wealthy, but as unassuming as a pauper.

Mary waits for me in front of Ophelia's brownstone, her dainty foot tapping with impatience. Everything about Mary is doll-like, from her big, bright eyes with heavy lashes and nose that comes to a point instead of spreading wide like mine, to hair that is as fine as silk. But the most stunning part of her face is her smooth brown skin. It is so perfect that I have witnessed people reach their hands toward her face to touch and make sure it's real.

I call Mary my sister, although our bond is by spirit and not by blood. Even though Miss Lizbeth hadn't been Mary's mistress, she had taken Mary in for a time when she'd escaped from a plantation in Mississippi on the Underground Railroad, and had contributed to her schooling out of dedication to her abolitionist cause. Perhaps she'd thought Mary would be a good companion for me, because I had none, and she was right.

But Mary was only in school for two years before she met Isaiah when she was sixteen. She'd married him without hesitation, with everyone's blessing, and with me as her young bridesmaid.

I cannot recall the number of times I have compared myself to Mary or judged my own features against her flawless perfection. It is not fair to either of us for me to do this, but when life is made easier or more difficult based on one's looks, it is impossible not to pay attention to the differences.

Mary is a perfect beauty, so it's no surprise that Isaiah allowed her to sneak out of their boutique to come visit with me. He rarely tells Mary no. One bat of her lashes, and he melts.

One would think that, since I asked Mary to use her feminine wiles to escape the rest of her workday, I at least could've shown up on time. But slipping away from Lucien had proved harder than I anticipated. He'd wanted to talk about his plans for his summer garden.

I approach Mary with a smile and outstretched arms—two things she cannot resist. Her frown evaporates as she gives me the warmest of hugs.

"What took you so long? Isaiah has given me three hours to visit with you, and then I must return. We have a large order of shirts from a wealthy gentleman who sets sail the day after next. Isaiah has already decided how to spend his money, so it will be best for us to complete the work, don't you think?"

"Yes, and please thank Isaiah for me."

"Isaiah says you can thank him by baking one of those delicious apple pies you keep promising."

"That's too easy. Consider it baked."

Ophelia's front door opens, and the scent of pastries wafts out ahead of the plump yet curvaceous woman. She waves from the top of her stairs.

"Are you two coming inside or standing out here in the cold? I just took fresh tea cakes out of the oven."

Mary and I rush up the stairs and follow Ophelia inside through her cramped foyer. The home isn't in disarray, it's just full of eccentric trinkets from Ophelia's travels. A peacock's feather here, an Indian tapestry there. Woven baskets from bushwomen in Africa and teapots from China. Ophelia has been everywhere her dead husband's money can carry her.

Ophelia, much like Miss Lizbeth, associates herself with the Society of Friends, without being in full fellowship. Both women choose the pieces of the religion that they agree with, like abolition and equality, and reject the parts that don't suit them. Such autonomy and boldness is rare even for white women, but their wealth and generosity allow them to move in these spaces without harsh judgment.

There *is* judgment, though, mostly from Quaker women who don't think Ophelia or Miss Lizbeth are proper. There are rarely invitations for either of them to tea or other engagements. So they entertain how they see fit. Even if that includes hosting two Black women who love music and tea cakes.

"How is Miss Lizbeth?" Ophelia asks. "I visited her a few days ago, and she could barely get through a sentence without coughing."

"She is the same, if not worse."

"Well, we will pray for her and leave it to God."

Ophelia calling for prayer and putting things in God's hands is far from a platitude. She spent her years before marriage as a nurse and has seen Miss Lizbeth's state. If her recommendation is prayer, things are bleaker than I thought.

"Mary, is Isaiah still treating you well?"

Mary glances at me out of the corner of her eye, and we share a grin. Ophelia always asks this, every time we visit, because Ophelia's brother Henry is smitten with Mary. At the sign of any trouble between Mary and her splendid husband, both Ophelia and Henry are ready to rescue her. And even though it isn't legal for Henry to marry her, he jokes that he'll take her to Europe, where she will live with servants and wealth beyond her imagination.

"He is," Mary says. "And he sends his regards."

"Humph."

Mary closes her eyes, and her shoulders shake with silent laughter. Ophelia is used to getting the things she wants and so is her brother.

Mary's refusal to be wooed presents an ever-present challenge to them both.

"Ladies, follow me," Ophelia says as she struts down a decorated hallway. For the moment, it seems she's abandoned her thoughts of having Mary as a sister-in-law. "I have our tea service set up in the parlor. I am eager to hear what Eliza has learned in Buffalo."

"Eliza doesn't need lessons," Mary says. "She opens her mouth and entire songs just flow right off her tongue. I wish I had a fraction of her gift. I would always be singing."

"Her voice is amazing," Ophelia says, "but Bella is a master of the vocal arts. Eliza couldn't have a better tutor."

Walking several paces ahead of me and Mary, Ophelia throws open the double doors of her parlor. The last bit of afternoon sunlight spills into the hallway, illuminating the artwork on the walls. Beautiful paintings of African men, women, and children adorn the left side, and a painting of an Indian chief decorates the right. Walking through this hall reminds me of my parents. I wonder if they look as regal as the people on Ophelia's walls.

Every time Mary and I visit, she shows us something new. I want to gasp as we step into the spacious and airy room, but I hold it in and wait for Ophelia to tell us about her new treasure. I know there's a story of how the white pianoforte has made its way into Ophelia's brownstone.

"Darlings, will you look at this beauty." Ophelia gestures joyously as she almost sings the words. "A solid marble pianoforte, with ivory keys carved from elephant tusks. Come and listen to me play."

"I have never seen anything like this in Philadelphia," Mary says. "You must have found this in Europe."

"Oh yes, of course. It was crafted by an Italian sculptor who creates musical instruments instead of the busts and statues of famous men."

Ophelia, grand in everything she does, takes a seat at the pianoforte, stretches her arms high, and wiggles her fingers.

"What shall I play, darlings?" she asks, although I am sure she does not care one bit about our musical tastes.

Mary helps herself to tea and cakes and sits on a beautifully embroidered chaise. Not very hungry after dining with Lucien, I choose instead to further inspect this lovely instrument. It almost looks too precious to play.

Ophelia closes her brightly painted eyelids as if it will help her choose her musical selection. I marvel at the translucence of her skin and the blue veins at her temple that aren't covered by a thick layer of powder. I am most amazed that she took such time to paint herself for a visit from me and Mary. I am drab in comparison.

I also examine her hair, an intricate cascading pin curl creation. I believe it is a wig, but I cannot be sure. My own heavy and thick hair is braided and pinned into a neat bun at the nape of my neck—the way it is always styled. I wonder if I could try something like Ophelia's. Miss Lizbeth would laugh at these musings and tell me to wear my hair however I please. But Ophelia's is a style that commands attention, and I'm afraid enough attention is drawn to me by my size alone.

Ophelia begins to play the opening bars of a song I know well. "When Stars Are in the Quiet Skies" is one of the first songs I learned while studying with Miss Bella. It is a ballad with a simple yet soothing melody.

"Sing with me, Eliza," Ophelia says, with her eyes now fixed to the sheet music in front of her. "You know this one, don't you?"

"We'd just like to hear you play, isn't that right, Mary?"

I glance over at Mary, hoping for help, but she munches her tea cake and grins. There's no way my only partially trained voice can compare to this instrument, and I don't want to embarrass myself trying.

Mary tilts her head and dabs the sides of her mouth with a napkin. "I love the way you sing this song, Eliza."

"Now we have a majority," Ophelia says. "Join me before my fingers tire of playing."

In my bedroom or in the garden when I am alone, I like to sing this song in my full soprano, but I did not run scales this morning. So I'll need to start in the low register to warm my voice.

"'When stars are in the quiet skies, then most I long for thee.'"

Ophelia's eyes widen, and Mary's head snaps up in awe when they hear my rich, deep baritone. Bella tells me that she has never taught a woman with notes as low as mine. I can go deeper still into the low bass typically heard only from men.

"'All my love lies hushed in light, beneath the heaven of thine.'" As I finish the first verse, my vocal cords feel alive and ready now to reach heights after climbing from the deepest depths.

"'There is an hour when angels keep familiar watch on men. When coarser souls are wrapped in sleep, sweet spirit, meet me then.'"

In the second verse, which I sing in my middle, most comfortable range, the poor lovesick soul who wrote these words pines for their lover in the middle of the night. "'And in that mystic hour it seems thou should'st be ever at my side.'"

The sound of the pianoforte matching the tone and intensity of my singing is what stirs emotion in me, not the lyrics. For I have never known a love like this.

I cannot imagine lying awake at night wishing a lover was by my side. Does such love exist beyond the words of a song? Mary tells me it does, indeed. Perhaps I will experience that one day, but it has not happened yet.

A part of me fears that this sort of love is reserved for youth. And though I am not old, my adulthood did not blossom or bloom. It simply appeared. One day I was a little girl, playing with flowers in our garden, and the next I was a sturdy woman who would make some man a capable and reliable wife. It would have been nice to have more time to be that carefree girl instead of fretting, like Mary is doing right now, over the time that she spends away from her husband's side.

On the third and final verse, I bring the full power of my soprano. Ophelia hardly breathes as her fingers glide over the pianoforte, climbing the notes with me. The intensity of sound coming from the pianoforte matches my voice. Or is my voice matching the pianoforte? I am not sure, but I do know I would like to command both instruments. Pianoforte and my voice. Then the passion in both will come from the depths of my own soul.

I sing the words, "'The thoughts of thee too sacred are for daylight's common beam. I can but know thee as my star, my angel and my dream.'"

I wish to know a love that consumes me this way. Or to have a man be obsessed with me to the point where his thoughts of me are too sacred. But I do not think it is possible for the likes of me. What man has ever written such a song about a sturdy and reliable woman?

# CHAPTER THREE

*July 1850*

*I* feel outside myself as I stand before the roomful of Miss Lizbeth's friends and admirers as they give thanks for her life. Miss Lizbeth was old when I was born, so perhaps I should have always planned for the day I'd be without her. She raised me to be independent, self-sufficient, and brave, but I am none of those things today.

Even though Miss Lizbeth was not officially a member of the Society of Friends, this feels like a Quaker funeral. No one is dressed in black; the only tears being shed are mine, and Black and white people sit side by side as if we don't live in a country where people who look like me are enslaved.

I dab my eyes and take a deep, cleansing breath. The Quakers in the audience may not wish to hear me sing at this solemn occasion, but because I know Miss Lizbeth would want it, I am going to sing if my nerves and emotions will allow it. The non-Quakers sit in expectation of greatness. Wanting to hear from the daughter whom Miss Lizbeth raised and bragged about, because they are celebrating Miss Lizbeth's accomplishments and I am one of them.

I don't know if they do it purposely, attributing my intelligence and talent to Miss Lizbeth's rearing. In theory, these folk believe in the equality of Black people. They help slaves to freedom, hide them in their homes, and then give them jobs once they've escaped. Everyone in this room claims to share those beliefs.

But their true feelings come out sometimes, in their surprise at mundane things like the fact that I am literate. Or when my singing teacher, Miss Bella, marvels at my ability to sing arias in Italian even though I am still learning the language. White people never marvel at excellence in one another.

The occasion is far from mournful, but my grief is evident as I sing "Rock of Ages." I chose it because the words speak to me. My voice trembles at first, but after the first few words, my deep tenor notes get stronger, and my delivery is more like what I've heard when attending my Baptist church with Mary or visiting Lucien's AME church. There is no accompaniment, so my sorrowful voice is the only sound in the otherwise silent room.

When I'm done singing, I float back to my seat in the front row, wishing the room wasn't so silent, because then my quiet sobs wouldn't seem so loud. Mary sits to the right of me, and though she loved Miss Lizbeth as much as everyone else, she doesn't drop a tear. She is strong for me.

The time seems to drag on as various community members and friends say wonderful things about Miss Lizbeth's generosity and character, many of them including stories about how from the time I was a little girl I was always at her side. All these things are true, but the words do not take away the aching in my heart, or the fear of what happens next.

After the service has ended, Lucien stands next to me with his hand pressing my elbow, steadying me, as well-wishers greet me and extend their condolences. I smile and nod, feeling a need to escape the room and knowing it isn't possible.

Nurse Sarah approaches me, accompanied by a middle-aged white couple. Sarah's face is tear-streaked like my own, but the two strangers look neither sad nor friendly. The woman wears a silk-and-lace gown, with a hoopskirt and petticoats. The lace umbrella on her arm completes her Southern mistress look. It is out of place here, with our simple attire, but she doesn't seem to care. In fact, she peers down her nose at me, making me feel slightly threatened. Lucien grips my elbow tighter, as if he also feels what I feel.

"Eliza, I want to introduce you to Miss Greenfield's niece, Carlotta Briggs, and her husband, Armand," Sarah says. "They've come all the way from Mississippi to pay their respects."

Carlotta's eyes sweep from my face down to my feet. It feels like an assessment. And then, after rudely gawking at me, she turns her attention back to Sarah.

"We were under the impression that Aunt Elizabeth had freed all her slaves when she moved to Philadelphia," Carlotta says in an exacting, businesslike manner. "Are there more than this one?"

"She did free the people who were enslaved by her husband," I snap, with intentional disdain.

Carlotta narrows her eyes at me, as if she did not expect me to respond to her rude inquiry. As she looks at Sarah for an explanation, a low rumble of fury begins in the pit of my stomach. The southern drawl and pronunciation of her words is full of contempt for me, and maybe even for Miss Lizbeth—her supposed aunt.

"I was under the impression that Miss Lizbeth had no family besides myself. No one ever visited her," I continue, before Sarah has a chance to explain anything.

"You forget yourself, girl," Carlotta snaps, her words a warning that while she can speak to me with demeaning generalizations and insults, I cannot respond in kind.

Lucien's hand again tightens on my elbow, reminding me that everywhere is not like our close-knit Philadelphia community, and that it is never safe for a Black woman, whether she's been manumitted or not, to sass a white woman. Perhaps Miss Lizbeth raised me too free and too sheltered. I have not been subjected to many of the offenses I hear about from my Black friends, but I should pretend to know better.

I should remember to know better.

"Mrs. Briggs, Eliza is not enslaved here," Sarah says, sounding as irritated as I am, though probably more from the insult to Miss Lizbeth's character (she'd loathe being mistaken for a current slaveholder) than out of loyalty to me.

"Please forgive us," Armand says. "My wife is simply trying to ascertain the breadth of the estate. We are here on behalf of the family's interests. We will discuss this later, after the funeral services."

The family's interests. The family that Miss Lizbeth had no ties to, nor any respect for as they are plantation owners in the Deep South. The family who also declared that Miss Lizbeth was simply overcome by grief at the loss of her husband when she freed the people she'd owned and moved to Philadelphia. This family didn't know Miss Lizbeth, and now after all these years they want to come and plunder the fortune she's left behind.

Armand whisks Carlotta away from me, and Sarah scurries after them. I am grateful for Lucien's steadying presence as the fury continues to churn in my stomach. To wonder if I am a slave and part of the spoils of an estate is more than infuriating, though.

It is terrifying.

I struggle to blink back tears, as I am approached by another white woman I don't know. Instead of mourner's black, she wears a plain brown dress nearly the same shade as her dark curls that are parted down the middle and pinned on either side. The first thing I notice about her face is the strong bridge of her nose, which does not detract from her looks but downplays the angelic nature of her mouth and dimpled chin. Unlike Carlotta's, her face is kind and full of compassion. I am tired of greeting people, but I try my best to return her smile.

She gently places her hand over mine. "I just had to speak to you, Eliza. Your voice is remarkable. I have heard singers here and in Europe, and your voice is easily the most outstanding I've ever heard."

"Thank you. Were you a friend of Miss Lizbeth's?"

"Oh, not quite a friend, but we have similar interests and I greatly admired her. My name is Harriet Beecher Stowe. I am not a Quaker, but my husband and I do support Mrs. Greenfield's abolitionist work. I'm a writer, among other things."

I wonder what the other things are. As she speaks, I notice there is a youthfulness about Mrs. Stowe, but she manages to still look matronly and settled. It is of interest to me—a married white woman describing herself as a writer. Most of the married women I know refer to themselves as wives, yet this woman mentions both husband and vocation.

"It's a pleasure to meet you, Mrs. Stowe."

"Please, call me Harriet. If you ever find yourself in need of anything, allow me to be a resource to you. I've left my address in the guest book."

"Thank you."

"I fully expect to hear more from you, dear. You are simply phenomenal."

"Thank you."

Lucien chuckles as Harriet rushes off to say hello to a group of women having a lively conversation. Across the room, Mary motions with her head toward the door, so I leave Lucien to whatever has tickled him to get some air. I feel as if I might perish in this stuffy meetinghouse.

I step outside into the stifling heat as the sun blazes from a cloudless sky. Since my tears have slowed for the moment, I use Lucien's handkerchief to fan myself. Miss Lizbeth will be buried in a quiet ceremony in the morning, so as soon as these people disperse, I will be able to go home.

Mary appears at my side, seeming even more tiny standing next to me. With her petite figure and delicate beauty, she's such a contrast to my short but robust body and plain face. Physically, we make an odd pair, but in spirit we are sisters.

"It seems as if this day will never end." My words rush out on a weary exhale.

Mary links her arm into mine and pats my hand. No words are necessary, and the fact that she knows this is the reason our friendship bond runs so deep.

"I hope Isaiah is okay," I say as I feel a tiny bead of sweat pool between my breasts. "He must be fretting with Emma. She's more than a handful."

"Well, it is just fine for him to have a turn for a change," Mary says with a mischievous grin. "Maybe he will appreciate me more after spending the day with her."

This gets a genuine and hearty laugh from me. The first I've had in days. It is not possible for Isaiah to appreciate Mary any more than he does. She is cherished beyond measure, and unlike how I feel about Lucien's possible affection, Mary loves it.

"Who were the fine Southerners who accosted you with Nurse Sarah?" Mary asks. "They didn't much look like they belonged here."

"They did not belong anywhere other than a cotton plantation. They say they are Miss Lizbeth's family members, but she's never talked about the family she left behind, other than to say that they were slavers."

Mary leans in closer. "Folks always come out the woodwork when a rich person dies," she whispers.

This is true, but I wished they'd come to see about Miss Lizbeth when she was alive. I wonder if she ever missed her family, or if they rejected her because they despised her abolitionist work.

"I must get back to Isaiah," Mary says. "I will visit later."

"Well, at least I have Lucien."

"He's your favorite anyway," Mary jokes.

I shake my head and laugh. "When did I say that?"

Mary kisses both my cheeks as she leaves me with Lucien, who has joined me on the sidewalk outside the chapel, and she pats him on the back as she walks past.

"Why are you so amused?" I ask Lucien.

His sheepish grin spreads as he puts my arm through his. "Oh, that. Well, I was waiting for you to say something more to that white woman than thank you."

"Which white woman?" I ask.

"The last one. The writer."

"Oh. Mrs. Beecher Stowe."

"Yes, her."

"Well . . ." I respond with a grin of my own. "She was showering me with accolades."

"Was she now?" Lucien's head dips in an exaggerated nod as his upper lip trembles, on the cusp of laughter.

I swat playfully at the arm connected to mine. For a moment, this feels like any other afternoon when Lucien would walk me from church or Mary's house. We've never had trouble with laughter. We find the same kinds of things humorous, and we know how to tease each other without hard feelings.

"It's just practice," I retort. "For when I am the lead in an Italian opera."

Lucien pauses as if considering this. "Then perhaps we should work on your conversation skills if you are going to take up performing."

This response pulls me out of my brief jovial mood. I pull my arm from his grip and drop it to my side, breaking the connection.

"'If'? I plan to return to my studies as soon as we've settled Miss Lizbeth's estate. The question isn't if I am going to take up performing. It is when."

Lucien turns my body to face him and takes both my hands in his. "I thought the performing was Miss Lizbeth's idea."

"No, it was God's idea, giving me a voice like this."

"I just thought you loved singing in church."

"Why would I limit myself to church? I can make enough money to sustain myself."

"God gave you a voice, but he didn't make you white." Lucien drags his gaze away from me as he says this.

"Because I'm a Black woman, I cannot make money singing?"

"Why do you need to make money singing?" Lucien's eyes meet mine again, and they plead with me to feel differently. "I could take care of you."

He's said it now, and it cannot be unsaid.

"What if I don't want to be taken care of?" I snatch my hands out of his, wanting to escape again.

"What woman doesn't want to be taken care of, Eliza?"

And now *I* look away, unable to meet Lucien's intense gaze. Because he's right. What woman doesn't want the life that he's offering? Outside of Lucien, I've never had another man show any interest. I'm someone an older widower might marry to take care of his children, clean his home, and cook his food. Except Lucien is offering to save me from this fate. He offers his love and security, unconditionally, with or without complete reciprocation. But if I were to bind myself in a marriage, it would have to be for a different kind of love. The burning and consuming kind. That is the only thing that could pull me away from singing.

I do not have that kind of love for Lucien.

"My dear Eliza," Lucien says, sounding defeated, "I always thought you and I would marry one day."

If Lucien would just let me make it through this day before he plans my next one, I could breathe. The only mother I've ever known is gone, and all he can think about is making me his wife.

"Lucien, I cannot think about this right now."

"These days, it's all I think about. I dream of a future with you. Of taking long walks by the river, picnics, and sharing meals in our own home. I dream of our life together."

But this is not *my* dream. Lucien works hard, is a loyal friend, and is there when I need a heavy item lifted or a strong arm to guide me over a puddle or crack in the cobbled streets. Though his friendship is pure, and I have affection for him, there is nothing about Lucien that fills me with longing.

There isn't ice at my core in place of a heart. I would be open to breathlessness or pining after my lover in the middle of the night. I keep waiting for these feelings to emerge with Lucien, but they have not, no matter how consistent and reliable he may be.

And the culmination of Lucien's dream—a house full of children with wet noses and eyes—does not sound pleasant at all. It sounds like a nightmare.

* * *

IMPATIENCE THREATENS TO expose a crack in my usually calm demeanor as I sit in a large leather armchair in the office of Mr. Howell, who has served as Miss Lizbeth's lawyer for the past twenty years, since the passing of his father, Mr. Howell Sr. Because it's being held the day after Miss Lizbeth's funeral, this meeting is supposed to be quick and painless. He had already informed me that Miss Lizbeth had left me an inheritance. It wasn't news to me; I'd known it was coming. Miss Lizbeth had promised that she'd always take care of me.

Mr. Howell appears nervous, however, making me think that the meeting may not be as painless as I thought. He shuffles papers left, then right, and finally makes a small pile in front of him on the desk.

"It feels like you are stalling, sir," I say. There is no reason to be formal with Mr. Howell. He was Miss Lizbeth's lawyer but also a friend. He spent countless afternoons sharing tea and sandwiches in Miss Lizbeth's drawing room.

"You're right about the stalling." Mr. Howell's tone is dry and somber. Not a good omen.

Because I don't believe I can say anything now without sounding alarmed, I sit with my hands clasped. Waiting.

"I will start with the good news," Mr. Howell finally continues, after more paper shuffling. "Miss Greenfield left you a substantial inheritance. You are to receive one hundred seventy-seven dollars a year. Once the initial payment of five hundred dollars is made five days after the estate is settled, you will receive each annual payment on January third of every year. Also, she has left you the house on Mulberry Street, with all its contents."

One hundred seventy-seven dollars a year. A fortune! I didn't expect it to be this much. She has provided for me, so that if I don't want to, I never have to marry.

"Lastly, there is a sum of one thousand five hundred dollars that is set aside for your mother, Anna Greenfield, if she would ever like to return from Liberia," Mr. Howell says, still in his ominous tone. "If she does not claim those funds, they will be given to you as well."

"Has there been any recent correspondence from my mother?"

"In the first year, after the group sailed to Liberia, your mother sent several letters. Those were mostly tragic, I'm afraid."

I close my eyes as I nod in the affirmative. I know of these letters. Miss Lizbeth shared them with me when I was old enough to start asking questions about my family, and old enough to understand their fates.

That first year in Liberia was extremely difficult for the eighteen people Miss Lizbeth manumitted. They'd all survived the voyage, but many of them contracted what my mother had called African fever in her letters. My father and sisters included. I do not know what became of them, because, as far as I knew, the letters stopped.

"Miss Lizbeth shared letters from when they first made it ashore, but I am speaking of more recent years."

Mr. Howell shakes his head. "If there were any such letters in Miss Lizbeth's personal papers, I would not be at liberty to share them."

My heart races, as I ease to the edge of my chair. "But this is my family we are speaking about. If they are alive and well, I would like to know."

"They may not be. Miss Lizbeth left money for only your mother to return to America. She did not leave funds for your father or sisters."

And now my heart sinks, although Miss Lizbeth never gave me any hope that they were alive, since she didn't have much hope herself. Not after the trials many of the settlers in Liberia had with sickness and even the simplest things like trying to grow food. But no news was always better than a definitive answer.

Perhaps Miss Lizbeth had received news regarding their fates and hadn't told me. Or maybe she'd corresponded more recently with my mother than I knew about. But why would Miss Lizbeth not tell me about that communication?

"The provision in the will is open-ended," Mr. Howell continues nonchalantly, as if he had not just planted seeds in my mind suggesting duplicity on Miss Lizbeth's part. "If your mother doesn't claim the money to return to America in a reasonable amount of time, then it is to be given to you."

"Who is to determine what is reasonable?" I ask in an almost frantic tone. "You? How long will you wait? Will you try to find her? How will she even know Miss Lizbeth has passed away?"

Mr. Howell exhales wearily, but I am confused by his weariness. I am only beginning to pester him about this. There are more questions, and I'm afraid they all deserve answers.

"All right. Then, if you cannot share the letters, can you at least give me an address for her in Liberia? I'd like to write her myself."

"She did not respond to the last few letters that Miss Greenfield sent. And this was only a year ago. That is when she added the codicil to her will. To provide for your mother if she ever resurfaces."

"Well, if she comes forward and claims her portion of the estate," I say, frustrated tears now spilling involuntarily, "please let her know that I would like to see her, Mr. Howell. You can do that, can't you?"

THE UNEXPECTED DIVA 🕮 31

"If she comes forward, I will pass on your message," Mr. Howell agrees. "Yes, I can do that."

Mr. Howell gives me a handkerchief to wipe my tears. I feel like an orphan all over again, even though my mother might be alive. Because knowing that she may be out there somewhere and not accessible to me is a cruelty.

"There is more," Mr. Howell says, sounding even more ominous than before.

Yes. He had said there was bad news, but what could be worse than what he's said about my mother? I cannot form words, so I motion with my hand for him to continue.

"Armand and Carlotta Briggs have contested the will, stating that they are next of kin."

"Is that claim seen as valid?" I ask, feeling my sadness melt away and the fury return.

"Mr. and Mrs. Briggs feel disinherited. They did not receive anything from the estate. Miss Greenfield left money to the many causes she held dear."

"Well, what does this mean for me? I need resources. I have no way of maintaining the brownstone without finances."

Mr. Howell clears his throat—stalling again. "Until the estate is settled, I'm afraid you'll have to move out of the Mulberry Street house."

"I've never lived anywhere else. And it belongs to me now, does it not? It's my home!"

"Yes, yes, I know, Eliza," he says with the first hint of compassion. "I hate that this is happening. It's not what Miss Greenfield would have wanted. She went to great lengths to make sure you were provided for."

"So they would see me turned out onto the street?"

"It isn't just your inheritance they are contesting, Eliza. It's the entire will. She left sizable resources to me and several other trustees to care for her interests and to ensure things are executed to her specifications."

"But I am the only one who will not have a home as a result of their interference."

Mr. Howell drops his head, unable to meet my gaze. I wonder how hard he will pursue justice on my behalf. It would be much easier for him to wash his hands of me and this situation. I can only hope that his loyalty to Miss Lizbeth endures even though she's gone on to glory.

"I'm sure I can arrange for you to lodge with some friends until this is all sorted."

I have no doubt that Mary would make a place for me in her home if I asked, but with Isaiah and their child, it is already full. There is no way I would ask this of her.

"What will happen to the brownstone while the judge hears this ridiculous objection?" The panic in my tone has been replaced by righteous indignation.

"Out of the funds from the estate, I will pay all taxes and send a caretaker to see to any repairs or upgrades."

"It doesn't make sense that I can't live there. Even if, heaven forbid, we do not prevail, what is the harm in me staying there now?"

I rage at the foolishness of it all. That these two people who've come out of the shadows, who, if they *are* family, never once visited while Miss Lizbeth was ailing and never came to spend a holiday with her, are able to halt the execution of her will. And only by virtue of their whiteness.

"It is the house they are after more than anything, and they have specifically made the request to the judge that you not be allowed to occupy it until the matter is settled," he says, every syllable sounding apologetic. And he should be apologizing. He was put in place to protect Miss Lizbeth's interests, and he has failed.

"And the judge thought that was a reasonable request?"

Mr. Howell sighs with apparent frustration. But he cannot be more frustrated than I am.

"I am sure that if you were a white woman, he would have found that request unreasonable."

I know the reason for all this is the color of my skin, but I did not think Mr. Howell would admit it. Hearing him say this out loud when he certainly didn't have to makes me think that perhaps Mr. Howell isn't hiding other things from me. Particularly, facts about my mother.

"How long do I have before I need to move?"

My asking this is not resignation, but today I am weary, and there is nothing that can be done for now.

"You have a week," Mr. Howell says, his tone full of remorse. "I'm sorry. I wish I could give you better news, but I will fight for your inheritance. You'll have it. It will just take some time."

Time is a commodity I do not have, now that I am at the mercy of the courts and the Briggs. These are exactly the kinds of unfortunate circumstances that force women to bind to men they don't love.

"A week."

Finally, my stoic façade crumbles, and the tears course down my face in rivers. The weeping doesn't help, and in a week, I cannot plan or strategize. I am a woman . . . a Black woman, alone, with no resources. There is only time enough for a miracle.

"Eliza, let me find you employment and lodging," Mr. Howell pleads. "Miss Greenfield would have wanted me to help you on your way. I know you have helped care for children in the past—"

"Have you heard me sing, Mr. Howell?" I ask, while dabbing at my tears and willing them to stop.

Mr. Howell jerks back in his chair. Is it shock I see on his face? Had he expected me just to say yes to his offer of domestic work?

"I have. In fact, you did a lovely job at the funeral. I've never heard a more stirring rendition of 'Rock of Ages.'"

"Then you must know that my goal is to study singing in France or Italy. Miss Lizbeth and I had planned for this before she died."

"The governess work would be temporary. Until we sort out your inheritance. Will you trust me?"

I close my eyes and nod as a wave of sadness engulfs me. There is not much I can do to ensure that this departure from my dreams is temporary. Some would scoff at the idea of my aspirations and chide me for grudgingly accepting this help.

Mr. Howell seems relieved, but I feel no respite. Only anxiety at what may befall me without the protector I had in Miss Lizbeth. All my life, I have been shielded from the cruel realities of being a Black woman. My protector was a wealthy white woman with the entire world in the palm of her hand. She begged for nothing and was respected wherever she went.

She gave me her name, Elizabeth T. Greenfield. The *T* stands for my father's name, Taylor, but the surname was Miss Lizbeth's. She could give me her name, but she could not, however, bestow upon me the privilege of her skin. The mother who gave birth to me had white and Indian blood flowing through her veins, but I am the color of coal, like my African father.

My promise to Miss Lizbeth weighs heavily on my heart. But before promises, I must address my needs. Meals in my belly, a roof over my head, clothing on my body, and shoes on my feet.

Promises can come later. Much later. After I can endure an entire day and night without weeping.

# CHAPTER FOUR

*T*wo sounds echo through the Mulberry Street brownstone I have called home since I was five years old: my heeled boots clacking against the hardwood floors and my voice as I sing the aria from *La sonnambula*. The one I sang to Miss Lizbeth as she lay fighting for her life.

Quite unsuccessfully, I try to lift my own spirits before the ladies from my Baptist church arrive. Some of them attended the Quaker funeral, but Mary has warned me that they plan to descend upon me with the full force of their love and kitchens today. Although I would normally decline such a huge outpouring of charity, after talking to Mr. Howell yesterday, I need and welcome them.

I walk down the hall leading to Miss Lizbeth's first-floor bedroom and stop in front of the door. There is stillness here in this space, so I stop singing and rest in it for a moment. Since Miss Lizbeth died peacefully, I hope to feel some of that calming spirit.

I ease open the door to her bedroom and step inside. Now that it is sterile-smelling and pristine, with no trace of her sickness lingering, I take in what will be some of my last moments with her treasured belongings until my inheritance is settled.

With my eyes closed and my breathing slow and measured, if I concentrate hard enough, I can almost hear Miss Lizbeth's laugh. I pick up a golden jar from the dresser and open the top. Her favorite facial cream. I inhale deeply its lavender scent. I smile as I remember her advice.

*Eliza, there is nothing worse than a dry and withered old woman. We cannot control the withering, but we can control the dryness.*

Things will never be the same now that Miss Lizbeth is gone, but in addition to my pursuit of the stage, she's left me with an additional passion. Now I wish, more than ever, to be reunited with my mother, and any others of my family who may be alive in Liberia.

Just as I feel myself about to break down into a puddle of weeping yet again, I hear the door knocker signaling that the church ladies have arrived. For a moment, I regret agreeing to this, customary or not. I would rather climb into Miss Lizbeth's bed, snuggle down into her blankets, and remember all the times we sat and talked. But I must be the hostess, even though I am the one grieving.

Before opening the door, I can hear the chatter of familiar voices outside on the stoop. A bevy of church mothers and sisters, all determined to lighten my load, at least in the kitchen, with their casseroles, stews, cakes, pies, and platters of meat. Despite my now being alone, they've undoubtedly made enough to share with one another, as funeral repasts in this circle are social events like any other gathering of friends.

Mary is at the head of the group of ladies when I open the door. The conversation dies down, as I assume they want to assess my mood. I've been an attendee at these gatherings before. Sometimes they are merry remembrances, and other times they are tear-filled and mournful. I suppose today's event will fall somewhere in the middle. Miss Lizbeth lived longer than most, so her life is one to be celebrated. But my current desperate circumstances don't give rise to joyousness.

Mary wraps her arms around me and hugs me tightly, not waiting for me to signal one mood or the other. "Don't worry, sister. Everyone is here to help."

The swarm of about ten women nod and vocalize their agreement. Their sympathetic looks tell me that Mary has shared more of my plight than I would have wanted her to, but I cannot be cross with her when I have such dire needs. With less than a week to vacate my home and no more than twenty dollars to my name, this is no time for privacy or pride.

Several of the ladies bustle past, arms laden with pots and bowls, down the hall, and to the kitchen. The scents that waft behind them remind me that I haven't eaten, causing my stomach to grumble and lurch. I have not thought of preparing a meal today and cannot think of the last time I've eaten. I suppose that is one of the reasons for these gatherings. People who are grieving cannot be trusted to take care of themselves.

The ladies who don't crowd the kitchen set platters of breads and cakes on the coffee tables and credenzas in the living room. After their quick moment of silence while Mary and I embraced, their chatter had resumed. This flurry of activity is somewhat unsettling, so I take a piece of Mother Gullat's lemon pound cake (my favorite) and ease down onto the sofa.

Mary sits next to me, holding a sugar cookie in a napkin. "What will you do, Eliza?"

"I had hoped to resume my lessons."

"In Buffalo?" Mary's eyes stretch wide and her voice cracks, causing several of the older church mothers to look in her direction. "How on earth will you manage that without your inheritance?"

I nervously take a bite of pound cake and chew it a few times more than necessary before swallowing. I didn't think I would have to defend my plans to Mary of all people.

"Well, I may have to find work. There are some families I know in Buffalo."

Mary glances across the room at Mother Kelley, who is the leader of the church ladies. She is full of wisdom and wit. Mother Kelley slowly waddles over on her cane, peering at me through her clouded yet compassion-filled eyes. Her firmly pressed-together lips tell me she has already made up her mind about my situation.

"Eliza, do you really think now is the time to be talking about singing lessons?" Mother Kelley asks as she struggles to sit on the other side of me. It takes her a moment to get settled—her wide hips and mine don't leave room for anyone except tiny Mary.

"The Lord blessed you with this voice," she continues as she takes my hand in hers and squeezes it lovingly, "and you can use it for His glory."

The amen corner starts to amen-ing, and Mary gives me an apologetic look because she started this. For the first of what I am sure will be countless occasions, I long for the support of Miss Lizbeth.

"Mother Kelley, I intend to sing onstage." I am resolute yet respectful.

Mother Kelley looks down at the wrinkled and veiny hand that covers mine and lets out a weary sigh. Then she gazes back up at me, teary-eyed and pleading. "Baby, that ain't a life for *us*."

*Us*.

This is the education Miss Lizbeth neglected to provide. And these are the truths these ladies want to remind me about. The pound cake in my stomach sits heavy like stone, no longer a comfort.

"Now, I know you are excellent at baking, and children seem to take to you," Mother Kelley says thoughtfully.

"Deacon Odom inquired about her a week ago if my memory serves me," Mother Eloise Benson adds from across the room as she brushes crumbs from her lap onto Miss Lizbeth's beautiful rug.

My eyes settle on the crumbs, hoping she doesn't grind them into the delicate fibers with her boots, because I will sweep them up later. My thoughts need to go anywhere else but to a life with the widower Deacon Odom and his house full of unruly boys.

Someone knocks at the front door, undoubtedly more of the women from Shiloh Baptist with more pots, more pans, and more lessons about life's harsh realities. I quickly stand to answer the door. Perhaps if I can quickly get through greeting everyone and accepting their condolences then I can go back to relishing the final moments in my home.

But Mary leaps up too. "Sister, don't trouble yourself. Rest. I will take care of that for you."

I ease back down onto the couch, but with the church mothers' gazes fixed on me, waiting for my response, I do not consider it rest.

"Is Deacon Odom looking for a governess? I hadn't heard that," I say to Mother Eloise as I absentmindedly take another slice of cake. "His boys do not heed me when he does bring them to Sunday school, so I don't think I'm the right selection."

Of course, I know their implication is for more than employment with Deacon Odom. And they know I know. The shrewd glances that pass between them tell me as much.

"Eliza."

I look up at the sound of Mary's nervous-sounding voice. And then I scramble to my feet at the reason.

Lucien's mother, Mrs. Sadie Brown, stands in the doorway flanked by her two oldest daughters, Caroline Brown Feathers and Beatrice Brown Pickens. They're three shorter, rounder, more feminine versions of Lucien. Sandpaper-colored, wiry, and well-built just like him. At least the women in the Brown family have softer facial features. They have the same nose, but narrower, and identical almond-shaped eyes. Beatrice is blessed with the most striking dark lashes, giving her a sweet and demure look that I'm sure was helpful in landing her a husband.

Standing in front of the three women, who appear to be on a mission, I wish I could shrink myself the way Lucien does when he's around white men.

"Hello, Eliza," Mrs. Brown says as she takes both of my hands in hers and squeezes them gently. "We are here to offer our condolences on the loss of your benefactor, the late Mrs. Greenfield."

"Thank you."

The words and sentiment are welcome and appropriate, but they feel impersonal coming from the woman I've known since I was fourteen years old. Since Miss Lizbeth sent me to a summer youth camp at Mother Bethel AME and Lucien and I befriended each other. But that's how Mrs. Brown always is, especially regarding me: cold and impersonal.

There is something that bothers her about our friendship, although I don't know what it could be. When I met Lucien, he was sitting on the back pew of the church alone, stewing, while everyone else was having a good time chatting and socializing. It was my first time at the church, and I didn't know anyone, but I suspected that he was one of those young people who stayed on the outside of things.

My suspicions were confirmed when the boys and girls separated for their own sessions, and the girls gave their opinions about the boys. The words used to describe Lucien were "strange," "peculiar," and "odd," while they thought his older brothers were "dreamy." Their disdain for him is what made me open up to his friendship.

Unlike Sadie, Beatrice gives me a warm hug. "We're all here for you, Eliza. Not just Lucien."

"We might as well be your sisters," Caroline adds as she gives me a smile and an arm squeeze, "as much as we share Lucien with you."

"He was always there whenever Miss Lizbeth or I needed him," I say. "I'm sure he's going to miss her too, so please make sure to take him some of this cake."

Both of Lucien's sisters seem to find this as hilarious as I intended, but Mrs. Brown does not join in the mirth. She also has not let go of my hand. I look down at where she still has me gripped tightly.

"Eliza," she whispers, "is there somewhere we might speak privately for a moment?"

She slowly loosens her grip as I lead her to Miss Lizbeth's study. The room is rather stuffy and warm, because the windows haven't been opened in days. Immediately, sweat beads gather on my brow, and I wish I had a handkerchief to dab my forehead. But not Mrs. Brown. She's too sophisticated to sweat.

"I'm sorry it's so hot in here," I say. "We are closing the town house for when I leave."

Mrs. Brown closes her eyes and shakes her head. "It's a shame what's happening with your inheritance, Eliza. I pray things are settled soon."

"Please pray harder," I say sadly.

Mrs. Brown turns my body to face her and gives me the most serious and imploring gaze. Her look is unsettling.

"What is it, Mrs. Brown. What's wrong?"

"I wanted to talk to you, Eliza, because my son is planning on asking if he may court you, and I don't want him to be hurt." Her words sound like a warning.

"Any man who seeks the hand of a lady takes the chance of rejection," I say, treading carefully.

Perhaps I did not tread carefully enough, because it seems that any compassion she might have had for me has evaporated. The grip on my arms tightens, and her nails dig into my skin.

"My son has had stars in his eyes for you for years. Do not ask me why. There are much better choices. Young debutantes who did not originate on plantations in Mississippi."

I try to ignore the spray of spittle on my cheek. My upper lip trembles with anger, but I hold my emotions in check.

"I am not ashamed of my origins."

"But you dismiss my son as if you are too good for him," she hisses. "Perhaps it was your former owner who put those thoughts into your head."

This explains her coldness toward me. It is the opposite of what she says. She thinks her son is too good for me because I was once enslaved. Even though I cannot remember those days of my infancy in Mississippi, the stain is still there.

Because she is my elder, and Miss Lizbeth would not want me to disrespect her, and because Lucien is my friend, and she is his mother, I hold my peace.

"Lucien is my friend, and I care for him. I do not think I am better than he is."

"He is my son, and *I* care for him." Her tone softens, and her grip loosens. "If this inheritance goes unsettled, you will have nothing, but if he chooses you, we will welcome you into our family, despite your . . . origins."

"But shouldn't I be in love with Lucien?"

"That has nothing to do with this conversation, Eliza."

Mrs. Brown pulls on her collar as if she's suddenly realized the temperature in the room. She takes a handkerchief from her bag and dabs at her face.

"Consider what I've said, Eliza. There are not many options for penniless Black women. And my son is offering you a wonderful and honorable solution."

"Lucien is very honorable, yes, but this may be settled soon, and I will be on my way to Europe for more singing lessons. With the amount of money Miss Lizbeth has left me, I will be quite wealthy."

I know that this is in poor taste, and that Miss Lizbeth has raised me to never flaunt the things I have. She was very generous with her fortune, which was not all accumulated through scrupulous means. Neither of her husbands was a man of virtue.

Mrs. Brown snaps her handkerchief back into her bag and looks up at me with shock. Probably from my lack of manners and not out of jealousy of my inheritance. The Browns' shipping business is very successful, and they are landowners. She and her children lack nothing.

"What is it they say, Eliza, about a bird in the hand?" Mrs. Brown asks curtly, not giving me a chance to respond as she turns to exit the room.

I follow closely behind, but Mrs. Brown has gathered her daughters and is ready to leave by the time I make it back to the sitting room. Caroline and Beatrice rush to give me goodbye hugs, and I hug them back, giving no clue of any cross words between me and their mother. She is too much of a lady to let on in front of these women that I have offended her, but at home, I'm sure she's going to call me every name but a child of God.

"Have a good afternoon, ladies," Mrs. Brown says as she floats out with her two daughters in tow as abruptly as she floated in.

After seeing them out, I step back into the sitting room to several sets of eyes staring directly at me. They continue to follow me to my seat on the sofa. I take yet another slice of cake from the coffee table.

"I suppose she couldn't trouble herself to tarry too long with us Baptists," Mother Kelley says. "They must've been having tea down at the AME fellowship hall."

Some of the other ladies laugh, but I do not. Mrs. Brown's words echo in my head, and I can't shut them out. Lucien is *a bird in the hand*. And I don't know if there is anything waiting for me in the bush. There could be an inheritance. Or there could be Deacon Odom and his hellions. Or worse, Armand and Carlotta waiting to whisk me back to a plantation as part of their spoils.

Mary rejoins me at my side. Then she takes the piece of cake from my trembling hands and puts it back on the coffee table. My nerves are finished for today, and I wish that everyone would leave, but perhaps this is the time when I need them most.

"What did she say that has you so rattled?" Mary whispers.

"Lucien wishes to court me. Marry me."

She places a calming and steadying hand at the small of my back. "But you already knew Lucien's wishes. He told you this on the day of the funeral."

"Yes, but not formally, and his mother was not involved, and then I didn't have to leave my home in a week. Last week I had a choice. Today, I'm not so sure I do."

My breaths are rapid and shallow, and now my dress feels too tight though I am not wearing a corset. I close my eyes to try to stop the room from spinning. But my world is spinning, and everything is left in the hands of providence and prayer.

"You *still* have a choice."

"Do I? Not if I must leave in less than a week. Not if I am not to have my inheritance."

The other ladies in the room quietly observe me fall to pieces, but I do not care. Am I not supposed to be falling apart? Isn't this why they're here?

Mary pulls me to my feet. "Excuse us for a moment, everyone."

I don't give her any objection as she guides me upstairs to my bedroom and closes the door behind us. It is a bit cooler here, because it is on the shaded side of the house and has windows on both sides letting in a breeze in the afternoon.

I plop down onto my bed and am overcome by emotion. This is not supposed to be my life. Miss Lizbeth had laid out careful plans. I'd done everything she wanted me to do. I'd studied. I'd learned. I am ready.

And to have it swept away like this and replaced with this thing that I don't want. This man whom I don't love. This dream that does not belong to me.

I cannot breathe.

Mary lies down next to me and enfolds me in her arms. "Let it out, Eliza."

And I do. I wail and scream and cry to heaven. Perhaps Miss Lizbeth can hear my tortured sobs and beseech the Lord on my behalf, because I feel forsaken. What does this mean to have a gift that I cannot pursue?

Just one day ago, before Mr. Howell destroyed all the hope I had left, I had a plan. I was going to see it through to completion no matter the odds. And now? I have absolutely no idea what comes next.

# CHAPTER FIVE

*August 1851*

One day I am going to learn to stop speaking ill of providence and prayer, because both came to my rescue right before I was forced to leave my home. They came by way of my neighbor Miss Ophelia Price. She offered me both a room and an opportunity to continue my musical education with private instruction on pianoforte and guitar. She also introduced me to a family, the Howards, who split time between their homes in Buffalo and Philadelphia and need a tutor for their two daughters while they are here.

So the problems of shelter and the continued pursuit of my music while I await the release of my inheritance are solved—for now. But there is another issue at hand for which I don't quite have a resolution.

"I took the liberty of pruning Miss Lizbeth's rosebushes," Lucien says as he clumsily sips tea from Miss Ophelia's dainty teacup. "Mr. Howell said he appreciates me participating in the upkeep of the property."

Lucien is the issue. The bird in the hand. He and this courtship are like a woodpecker on the side of a house. A tapping, annoying thing that won't move, growing louder until it causes the vein at one's temple to throb. That is Lucien. An annoying, rapping, tapping bird in the hand.

He sits across from me in Miss Ophelia's sitting room, a formal guest, with her a respectful distance away in the next room. An official chaperoned visit, in our official agreed-upon courtship.

Just as Mrs. Brown had predicted, Lucien hadn't wasted any time asking me, and because I'd said yes, he'd indulged my request for a lengthy courtship while I studied musical instruments. We have crossed a year of courting, so I know a marriage proposal is imminent, but I hope to be able to delay him further with a long engagement.

I don't feel too bad about this procrastination on my part. He is free to end it anytime he wishes, though, contrary to what Mrs. Brown says, he does not have a line of debutantes clamoring to be his bride. Even with his means and pedigree, in his circle, Lucien isn't anyone's first choice. But he does have more choices than I do when it comes to marriage, so if anyone should be concerned about letting the bird out of their hand, it is me.

Still, I cannot bring myself to fully commit. Because I know the moment Mr. Howell tells me my inheritance has become unencumbered, I will be planning my voyage to Europe.

I swallow the rest of the tea in my cup in an unladylike gulp and stand to pour another. But first I pour one for Lucien. He gives a hopeful smile at this, although it is not a sign of domestication, only an indication of good manners.

"I'm sure Mr. Howell is thrilled about your gardening, since you don't charge anything," I say to Lucien with a chuckle as I drop three cubes of sugar into his tea. "He does have a groundskeeper in his employ."

"Thank you, my love," he says as he takes the cup from my hand. "His groundskeeper doesn't know a weed from a rosebush. He's already ruined the ones in the back of the house."

He has recently started these escalating endearments, trying them on for size in conversation, perhaps trying to gauge my reaction. I do not react poorly, because I know he loves me, but he must notice that I never reciprocate. I never call him "darling" or "dear." Never "my Lucien." It is always "Lucien." Only Lucien.

I drop my sugar cubes into the tea and cut a slice of the apple pie I baked. Lucien has already had two slices and holds up a hand to stop me when I offer him a third. I don't mind baking for Lucien when he asks. Since I haven't yet given him my hand in marriage or babies, the least I can do is give him a baked good every now and then. But I bake tasty treats for all my dear friends.

"You may be tending roses for naught." I slump back into my chair, suddenly not feeling in the mood for tea, pie, or courting as I think about the meeting I had yesterday with Mr. Howell.

"So you didn't receive good news? The case is not progressing well?"

"It seems that there are many points of Miss Lizbeth's will that are being hotly contested. Of course, my portion, but there is a very large sum being left to her four trustees that is also of concern to Miss Lizbeth's long-lost family."

Lucien's eyebrows lift in surprise. "Mr. Howell shared this with you?"

"I asked him to let me read some of the court documents. Perhaps he didn't think I would understand them, or maybe he thought I should be aware so that I would know he was fighting for his own interests as well."

"A large sum for trustees? Outside of the typical fees?"

"Yes, ten thousand dollars apiece."

"Well, if I was her family, I would contest that amount as well. Doesn't that seem a bit odd to you? Do you think Mr. Howell and his colleagues would defraud an old woman?"

I don't know how to explain Miss Lizbeth's eccentric lifestyle to Lucien. It wouldn't make sense to him how she lived on her own terms but, as a woman moving through the world, needed men to do her bidding exactly the way she wanted it done. Even after she was gone to glory. And to ensure that her wishes were followed, she left the four trustees richly rewarded.

"No, I don't believe that, Lucien." I try not to sound exasperated when I say this, but I am not sure if I'm successful. "She also left one thousand dollars to the Philadelphia Female Anti-Slavery Society. This is who she was."

"Oh, that society is all my mother can talk about these days. She and my sisters go to every meeting."

"Yes, I know. I have seen her many times."

"Wonderful. Maybe this is work that you and my mother can do together. A way to find common ground," he offers thoughtfully. "I'd love to see you two become better friends."

"I don't know about friends, Lucien. But common ground is possible."

And now there is a look of confusion on Lucien's face. I take a sip of my tea while I try to think of a way to explain. The ladies of the anti-slavery society are a mix of Quakers and free Black women, and all are welcome who believe in the cause.

But I have found that some of the Black women there are much like Lucien's mother. They believe in the work, but since I began my life on a plantation, I *am* the work. I am evidence of all their charitable ideals. They believe I have a place in society, just not their society. Those few snooty, awful women are the ones I try to avoid, and I certainly am not interested in their friendship.

"I'm sorry to hear that," Lucien says, sounding truly sad about it. "Although, I'm hopeful regardless."

Isn't he hopeful about everything? Is it hope or delusion that drives him?

"Well, she'll be happy to hear that Hattie Purvis asked me to sing at a gathering she's hosting next month to kick off the planning of the anti-slavery fair."

A huge smile spreads across Lucien's face. "She'll be tickled about this. I can't wait to share the news. At the home on Lombard Street?"

"Not on Lombard. Things have been very difficult for the Purvis family. Too much violent talk of late. Did you hear they purchased farmland out in Byberry?"

"Did they? And things continue there?"

I nod. The *things* Lucien refers to are the movements of enslaved folks on the Underground Railroad.

"What will you sing?" he asks. "Something inspirational? A church hymn?"

"Well, I thought I'd start with something upbeat like 'Home Sweet Home.' You know? Something to really get everyone in the mood to have a great discussion. And then . . . Wait. Why are you looking at me like that?"

Lucien looks like he's on the verge of laughter. He leans forward in his seat with one arm resting on his thigh, and he cradles his head in his hand. But it's the smirk on his face that makes me think he's found humor in my words.

"I find it so amusing how you light up when you start talking about music. No matter what the conversation is about, you're going to get excited."

"Is that a bad thing?"

"No, it's not." Lucien sighs and leans back in his chair, his amusement fading. "I would just like to see you get excited about other things as well."

"Come and listen to me sing, Lucien," I say as I stand and cross the room, offering him my extended hand. "I've taught myself the accompaniment on pianoforte."

"Is that so?"

"Mmm-hmm, and I am rather good."

Lucien laughs as he takes my hand and rises. "And a little bit over-confident, perhaps?"

"Hmmm . . . Let me know what you think about that after you hear me perform."

Lucien follows me into Miss Ophelia's music room, where she's given me free rein to use any instrument I'd like. I tend to stay mostly on the pianoforte and guitar, which I've spent the most time learning and practicing, because the tones of those two instruments complement my voice best.

I point to a chair where Lucien can sit and observe, while I take my seat on the piano bench. "Home Sweet Home" is a simple tune that doesn't require me to warm up. It's one of those popular songs that people sing along to at parties, but the upbeat tempo helps my fingers become more agile on the pianoforte. It's better practice than scales.

I play the introduction, and Lucien bobs his head. "That's nice already," he says.

"'Mid pleasures and palaces though we may roam,'" I sing, "'be it ever so humble, there's no place like home.'"

The irony of this first verse is not lost on me, lodging in my neighbor's home while mine is two doors down. I miss the sanctity and security of my own brownstone. I look down at the piano keys to keep Lucien from seeing the tears that pool in my eyes while playing this happy tune.

"'A charm from the skies seems to hallow us there, which seek through the world is ne'er met with elsewhere. Home, home, sweet home. There's no place like home. There's no place like home.'" My voice croaks out the last few words, and when my eyes meet Lucien's, I cannot make out his thoughts.

"That was lovely, Eliza," he says while giving an enthusiastic round of applause. "If you sing that for the ladies' society, they will ask you to sing for every meeting."

"Say that loud enough to reach heaven," I say, gazing directly at him now so that he can see that my mood has shifted from joy to sadness. I cannot tell whether he's noticed. "That's the plan, of course, to allow wealthy women of influence to hear my voice and invite me out for engagements."

"In their homes?"

I flinch with offense at the incredulity in his tone.

"Their homes, their weddings, their churches, their balls, wherever there is a fee to be paid for services."

Before there was talk of marriage, when we were young, we used to fancy these kinds of dreams without judgment or ridicule. Now my childhood friend has been replaced by the aspiring-husband version of Lucien. A man like his father who believes women should be in a well-protected home rearing a brood of children.

Lucien walks over to the pianoforte and examines the intricately carved keys, and I shrink away from his touch when his hand comes close. *This* he does notice. He grimaces. "You intend to sustain yourself with the kindness of influential women?" he asks, full of derision and disbelief.

"Influential women have influential husbands who can book theaters and concert halls, Lucien. When the wives tell their husbands that they want to hear me in concert, their husbands will listen."

"I think you're overestimating the amount of attention husbands pay to the chatter of wives."

"I would think, if I had a husband, I would want one much like Robert Purvis."

These words seem to hit Lucien hard, but I do not care about my scathing tone. He stumbles backward a few steps. "Is that so? In what way?"

I close the top of the pianoforte and caress the smooth marble. "He and his wife are co-laborers in the anti-slavery movement. He listens to what Hattie says and supports it. He doesn't think it's only chatter."

"You have no idea what goes on inside the walls of their home."

"That is true. But if he didn't support her, she wouldn't be holding meetings in her home, raising money, attending rallies in other cities, all while they have children. I have heard him speak of her with admiration and pride."

For a long moment, Lucien remains silent. He paces the room, brooding, as if trying to think of a response. But I don't want him to try to think of anything. A courtship isn't supposed to be this hard. It is a ruse that will perhaps one day be the end of our friendship, but I still engage in the charade.

It is only fear that makes me do so. Fear of being alone and unprotected when I am in dire need of protection.

Last year Congress signed the Fugitive Slave Law, which states that slave catchers may come north and demand that those who have escaped to freedom be turned over to them and placed back into captivity. But they are not only targeting the ones who have escaped. Free Black people are being kidnapped into slavery, especially ones without families and people to vouch for them. So I cannot be alone in this world.

Today, I am free. I have papers that say I am. I have no one whom I must call master or mistress.

But what about tomorrow, or the next day? This is as uncertain as my claim to Miss Lizbeth's fortune. Things written down on paper and in ledgers and sworn before lawyers and in courts can be contested and protested before more lawyers, in different courts. Systems created by white people for white people, with my freedom not being of primary concern.

And so, while I dream of and pursue a life of singing onstage, I must also face the possibility that it may never happen. And if I cannot achieve notoriety, if I cannot be known as a famous singer, then could someone kidnap me and sell me into bondage?

There are whispers of disappearances. People who mostly wouldn't be missed. Those who exist on the outside of things. Orphans, prostitutes, beggars. But there is strength in numbers. In families. And this is something Lucien's love offers me, even if I do not feel the same about him.

"If—no—when I have a wife," Lucien says, finally breaking his silence, squaring his shoulders as if in opposition to any opinions I may have formed about him, "I would hope that she would understand that I love her with every fiber of my being, and that everything I do would be for the betterment of our family."

He does not wait for my response, and I don't want to admit how relieved I feel about that, not even to myself. But for now, with no inheritance, and not yet enough resources saved to return to Buffalo or journey farther onto Europe, the ruse continues.

# CHAPTER SIX

$\mathcal{F}$or my whole life, until now, birthdays came and went without much fuss. And it never bothered me that they were quiet affairs. Being the only child of an eccentric, wealthy white woman had enough of its own charm without adding on extravagant birthday celebrations.

But this year, my twenty-seventh, Lucien has gone overboard in trying to make me feel special. He brought flowers over first thing in the morning, which tickled Miss Ophelia. And now he's collected me for an elaborate dinner party at his family's home.

I am seated at the head of a long dining table—the seat of the birthday honoree, I suppose—and Lucien is on my left side. Lucien's mother, Mrs. Brown, is opposite me at the other head seat and flanked by the fertile sisters, Caroline and Patience, and their husbands. The younger sisters help the staff with serving the food, while brothers Bowman and Paul sit next to Lucien. The entire family is coiffed, regal, and dressed in formal attire.

I am overwhelmed by the sheer volume of them.

One bright spot in this unwelcome gathering is that Mary is also here with Isaiah, Emma, and little Mary, whom we call Minnie. I am glad Lucien invited them here, since this celebration, however unwelcome, is for me. I do wish Mary was seated closer instead of at the other end of the table with her family. I could use her good humor to push away my melancholy thoughts.

It seems odd that I should be so ill-tempered on my birthday, but it's only because I know how this evening will culminate. Lucien has

THE UNEXPECTED DIVA ❧ 55

been hinting all week how things are going to be different after my birthday. And how we're going to have decisions to make.

This can mean only one thing. He's planning on making his marriage proposal tonight after a little over one year of courtship. And my hands are tied. I will have to accept.

I take a bite of the meat pie on the plate in front of me and struggle to return the family's gleeful expressions. Surely, they are in on the surprise, the way they all keep sneaking furtive glances in my direction. I wish there was a way for me to speed the passage of time. To get through the dinner and the agonizing conversation to the part where I say yes to the ruination of my life.

Instead of conversing with Lucien's family, I give myself a reprieve by enjoying the splendor of this home. Mrs. Brown spared none of her late husband's hard-earned wealth in decorating. From the French-inspired furniture pieces to the silk floral arrangements in ornate vases that look like they belong in a palace, everything appears to have been carefully chosen. It reminds me of the care Miss Lizbeth took in decorating our brownstone. Nothing was ever left to chance. My nostrils flare at the thought of strangers coming into our home, mishandling our precious items, and assessing them for profit.

No longer feeling very hungry, I push the plate away from me.

"Lucien tells me you've scored a coveted invitation to sing at the planning meeting for the anti-slavery fair," Caroline says, to Mrs. Brown's apparent consternation, as the older woman scowls at her daughter. Caroline ignores her. "What a coup."

"It is nothing all that special," Mrs. Brown says indignantly. "They live out in the country, for God's sakes."

Caroline cackles, while Beatrice covers her mouth with a hand to hide her laughter. "Mother is cross because she volunteered to assist with the anti-slavery fair and Hattie told her that her attendance was assistance enough."

"That is *not* what she said," Mrs. Brown hisses. "She said that she had all the help she needs, and that this kind of thing is really young woman's work."

Caroline's laughter continues, and poor Beatrice finally gives in to hers. I think the younger girls know better than to have a joke at their mother's expense, and so do I. Mary stares at me with wide eyes, probably wondering what is going on and how she should react. Hopefully, she'll follow my lead.

"Well, it should be nice," I say. "It's been a while since I had a new audience outside of church members."

"You tutor two little girls, is that right?" Beatrice asks. "Do you teach them music?"

"Yes, I teach them sight-reading and a bit on the pianoforte," I explain, feeling myself become engaged now that they're talking about something that interests me. "I am a beginner on that myself, but what I teach them reinforces my own lessons, so it is a victory for all."

"That is a good thing," ruggedly handsome brother Bowman says. "A woman with a vocation is a blessing, I believe."

From his end of the table, Isaiah lifts his cup in agreement, then kisses Mary's cheek. "I agree," he says. "Having Mary at my side in our shop is certainly the answer to a prayer."

From the corner of my eye, I see Lucien fidget in his seat. He grunts under his breath and makes a little snorting sound. Clearly, he doesn't agree with Bowman and Isaiah, and everyone at the table can see his discomfort.

"While a woman having a vocation might be a blessing, it is not, in my opinion, a necessity." Lucien's words are sharp and brusque, and he folds his arms across his chest to let me and everyone else know that it is his final word on the subject.

I do not speak my peace. I will not embarrass Lucien in front of his brothers by arguing with him. But I do close my eyes and give a heavy sigh, and maybe that is communication enough.

"Anyway, Eliza doesn't need to work for anyone anymore," Lucien declares.

My eyes pop back open, and I draw in a sharp breath.

"And why is that, Lucien?" Mrs. Brown asks, her previous embarrassment seemingly forgotten, because now she wears a pleased and expectant grin.

"Because tonight, in front of my most cherished family, and in front of God . . ."

Here it comes.

". . . it is the perfect time for me to formally ask for Eliza's hand in marriage. We have courted for a little over a year, and the next step for us is to start our own precious family. I believe Miss Lizbeth always hoped we would marry."

He places a small golden ring in my trembling hand, and then closes my hand into a fist around it. Isn't the ring supposed to be offered to the woman for her to accept? Isn't it supposed to be my choice?

I cannot look up at him. I just stare at my fist as it clutches the hard metal. I should probably be looking at Lucien. And saying yes.

Both Lucien's brothers jump up from their seats and cheer. I do look up now. Mrs. Brown and the fertile sisters give smiles of approval. Mrs. Brown may not care for my origins, but I suppose she approves of her son finally getting a bride. Especially when that bride has somehow managed an invitation to Hattie Purvis's home.

"So, are you joining the family?" the oldest brother, Paul, asks with a hopeful grin on his face and a gleam in his eyes.

The sound I make is a mumbled something or other. Not quite a yes. Something audible yet indecipherable.

"Is that a yes?" Lucien asks me with a chuckle. Then he looks at his brothers and the rest of the waiting family. "Of course, it's a yes!"

The flurry of congratulations that ensues overcomes me until I can hardly breathe. I can hold a note for nearly thirty seconds, so there is no problem with my lungs. But this feels like an attack from

Lucien. Because I didn't say yes. Of course, I *must* say yes. But I haven't. Not yet.

With trembling hands and unsteady legs, I stand with no other thought but to flee. To slow this moment to a halt. Everything is moving too quickly.

"I—I am feeling lightheaded. Please excuse me for a moment."

The words have barely fallen from my lips before I scurry away from the table with Mary at my heels. I rush into Mrs. Brown's parlor, and Mary slides in before I can close the door behind me.

"I can't do this!" I wail as I sink onto a love seat so pristine, it probably is not normally used for sitting.

Mary is eerily quiet, and she never minces words. She closes the space between us and offers an embroidered handkerchief. With its ornate stitching, it's almost too beautiful to use to dab my tears.

"Tell me what you're thinking, Mary." My voice is shaky, because I am hardly breathing, but I need her to say something.

Mary starts with a long, heavy groan. This does not bode well for her message, but maybe it is something I need to hear.

"Lucien is a good man, Eliza, and he's already been waiting for so long."

"I know that Lucien is good. His goodness is what makes this so hard. He's good, and strong, and a hard worker."

Mary sits next to me on the love seat and takes my hand. "So don't break his heart by being so difficult. Do you intend on rearing other people's children forever? Do you not want your own? Lucien is offering you a wonderful life."

Her definition and my definition of *wonderful* are not the same, but I don't want to insult the life that she and her husband have built. It is a good life for them and for Lucien. But I can't be sure if it will be a good life for me when I don't love Lucien the way she loves Isaiah.

Mary can only see this through the perspective of what she has with her husband. And maybe because she escaped the horrors of a plantation and being raped by her master's son, her life with her husband is perfection. For *her*. Even a loveless marriage with a man like Lucien would have been better than what she'd faced in Mississippi.

"Mary, you know my dream. You know what I want to do. If I could sing onstage as my vocation, then I wouldn't have to marry Lucien."

Mary's eyebrows form a deep frown. "That can't be the reason you want to turn down Lucien's marriage proposal. I thought it was because you don't truly love him, or because you were afraid he doesn't love you. Or, holy hell, Eliza, because you hate his mother. Not because you want to be a singer."

"Miss Lizbeth thought I could, Mary. She even made me promise before she died to try."

"If she were alive to sponsor you, I would agree with this idea. But you no longer even know if you have a home or inheritance." Her tone is shrill and sharp, cutting the air like a blade. "And Miss Lizbeth is no longer here to provide a safe place to land when—if you fall."

"What if I don't fall? What if I soar?"

Her body slumps with an exasperated exhale. "Oh, Eliza. Sometimes I think you believe you *are* a white woman instead of having just been raised by one."

Mary's words are nothing short of devastating. I thought she believed in this dream with me. She had been my first fan, sitting in the front pew at church every time I sang. Rising to her feet first and clapping the longest, even if my voice cracked or I stumbled on a lyric. In the summer, before she was married, she'd sat on the edge of my bed waiting while I ran scales when she'd wanted to go out walking to catch a glimpse of Isaiah.

But now she's telling me to abandon everything I've worked for to marry a man she knows I care for only as a friend. I know all the practical reasons I should say yes to Lucien, but I need just one person—my best friend, my sister—to believe in my heart's desire with me.

"It's a child's dream," Mary says, softer now that tears pool in my eyes. "Now that we are grown, we must put away childish things."

Perhaps, if I am meant to pursue my dream, I am meant to do it without friends or family. Miss Lizbeth is gone. Lucien and Mary have turned their backs on me. Am I to walk into the promised land without anyone who is familiar and true? Or is this land flowing with milk and honey too far for me to reach alone?

The bird in the hand has put a ring in my hand. And now all I must do is say yes.

I dab my eyes dry and slowly rise. "Let's go back to the dining room," I say. "I don't want Lucien to worry."

Mary grabs hold of my arm as I take a few purposeful strides toward the door. I close my eyes, but I do not look back at her. Our conversation is over. She has spoken what was in her heart, and I have listened.

"Please don't be cross with me, Eliza," Mary says to my back. "I never want there to be distance between us."

I turn slowly to answer her. "There is no distance."

This is the first time I've ever lied to my sister. There is now a chasm between us.

"I just want you to be well," she says. Her voice is sweet and sincere, but I only partially receive the message.

"And I will be."

"So, you are accepting Lucien's proposal, then?"

Done with this conversation, I spin on one heel and march into the dining room. This time Mary follows, but at her own, slower pace. Lucien's family did not miss a beat and have continued on to the next course in my birthday dinner. Lobster bisque, my favorite soup.

Everyone is eating except Lucien, whose now ashen face has a somber expression. He knows me well enough to know that my hesitation is not a good sign. I am not a fickle woman.

My hand lightly grazes his back as I sit, and he jumps, but then looks up at me with hope in his eyes. I wonder if he can read the desperation in mine.

"Yes, Lucien," I whisper. "I accept your proposal."

There is surprise and then relief in Lucien's expression. He takes my still-clenched fist and pries my fingers away from the ring, then places it on my finger. When he then raises my hand to his lips, there seems to be a collective exhale around the table. They were all held in suspense, and his one action has communicated that all is well.

"We must start planning right away. You two have dawdled long enough," Mrs. Brown says joyously from her end of the table. "I love planning weddings. And since poor Eliza is motherless, I get to be mother of the bride and mother of the groom."

"I am not motherless." My voice barely rises above a whisper, but it is loud enough to be heard by everyone at the table.

Mrs. Brown chuckles nervously. "I didn't mean to offend you, dear, but Mrs. Greenfield has passed on to glory. God rest her soul. We will honor her during your ceremony."

"We will, but I do not mean Miss Lizbeth."

Lucien's head turns slowly toward me, his face full of questions. I have not discussed my mother with him or the possibility that she may be alive and may want to come back to America.

"Surely you don't mean your birth mother from the plantation." The disdain with which Mrs. Brown says *plantation* would make one think she wasn't less than one and a half generations removed from enslavement herself.

"That is who I mean. My mother, Anna Greenfield, has been writing to Miss Lizbeth since she boarded the ship to Liberia," I explain. "Miss Lizbeth left money for her in her will in case she ever wanted to return."

"I wouldn't be surprised if she wanted to come back," Lucien says, as if he knows my mother personally. "I have heard it isn't always easy for those born on American soil to make their way in Liberia.

They are not always accepted, especially when they had a wealthy sponsor to make things easy for them."

"Well, you must write to her, then," Mary says, with excitement in her eyes. "Won't that be a lovely reunion to have her at the wedding? How old were you the last time you saw her?"

"I was seven years old."

Although the thought of seeing my mother again is the only thing that can warm my heart about this wedding, the glance that I see pass between Lucien and his mother chills me to the bone. I leave out the fact that I have no way of knowing how to contact my mother right now. I'd like to hear Lucien's thoughts on the matter.

"Will that be a problem?" I ask Lucien. I want to make it plain that I saw him look at his mother, and that I want to know what it meant.

"Well . . ."

"It will take weeks for a letter to reach your mother if it ever did reach her in the first place," Mrs. Brown says, quickly interrupting the hesitant Lucien. "And then it would take weeks for you to get a response. Then you would have to send for her, and it would take weeks for her to arrive."

"I don't see why these weeks would be at issue," I say plainly, now finding my full and robust voice. "It's not as if we will be holding a wedding this year. At the soonest, we won't be exchanging vows until next spring. That should be plenty of time for us to contact her and for her to make the voyage if she so chooses."

"Isn't your inheritance being withheld?" Isaiah asks, although it is none of his affair. "Is Miss Lizbeth's allowance for her return fare being withheld also? Isn't that—"

Isaiah's voice jerks to a stop midsentence. Likely, Mary kicks him under the table or elbows him in the ribs to get him to be quiet. I approve of either action.

"Yes, Isaiah," Mrs. Brown says, peering knowingly at Mary. "It is expensive. That is what you were about to ask, wasn't it? It is an expensive ticket. One that my son cannot afford while planning to pay for a wedding and starting a family."

Mrs. Brown and I stare at Lucien. It seems we are both waiting for a response.

"Eliza, my love, that does seem like a great expense. Perhaps we can delay a reunion until we are settled into our home."

I pull my gaze from Lucien's face and rest it upon Mrs. Brown. As I expected, she wears a smug expression. A winning expression.

"At any rate," Mrs. Brown says, her tone triumphant, "after the marriage, it will be up to Lucien to decide the distribution of any of the family's resources, including any funds that may come to Eliza in her inheritance. My dearly departed husband always made sure we had everything we needed, God rest his soul."

Underneath the table, where no one can see, I snatch my hand from Lucien's. The ring on my finger suddenly feels heavy. I stare straight ahead, seething, but he glances at me with a look of concern. He should be worried.

Is this what marriage will be like? A mother and son conspiring against me and the desires of my heart? I cannot sing. I cannot have my mother. And it sounds like if my inheritance is ever released by the courts, then it will be Lucien's to dispense as he sees fit.

Then what can I have? A houseful of children whom I do not wish to bear and a husband whom I do not love? And a mother-in-law to bask in the glory of it all?

This cannot be the future that Miss Lizbeth had in mind for her only daughter. And it is not the future I envision for myself. Hopefully, my inheritance is untangled before this fateful day. Mr. Howell and the judge can rescue me with a swift judgment, so that I will not have to marry Lucien. If not, I pray that providence—and a little planning—grants a way of escape.

# CHAPTER SEVEN

$\mathscr{I}$ know that Mr. Howell is surprised to see me in his office so soon after our last meeting, but things have changed. These new developments with Lucien and the engagement have caused a sense of urgency regarding other matters. Especially Lucien and his mother's disdain concerning my mother in Liberia and their clear indifference to assisting me in bringing her home.

"Eliza, I'm afraid I don't have anything new to report," Mr. Howell says as I sit perched in my usual position in the leather chair in front of his expansive desk, "but I have heard that congratulations are in order. Lucien Brown is a fine man. Mrs. Greenfield would have been delighted."

"Thank you, Mr. Howell. That is part of the reason I've come to visit you today."

"Oh?"

I take a deep breath to try to steel myself against any refusal or denial of my request. After our last discussion on this subject, I'm not that optimistic about a favorable response, but I must try.

"I'd like to revisit our conversation about my mother. Anna Greenfield."

Mr. Howell begins to shift uncomfortably in his chair. But I ignore this and continue to press forward.

"If she has expressed a desire to return to America, I would love for her to be present at my wedding," I explain. "Mrs. Brown has referred to me as motherless, and I am not an orphan. My parents may still be living."

"I do not have any information to share about your parents, Eliza."

"Except that you do," I press. "You said there were letters that stopped a few years ago. Miss Lizbeth left funds for my mother's return."

Mr. Howell gives a frustrated sigh. "Perhaps I shouldn't have told you about the letters or what was in the will, because I am not authorized to take action on either of those."

"I understand. But can you mail a letter to her for me? I would like her to know that I am well and that I am getting married. And that I would love for her to be here, and that she is welcome to live with me if she wants to come home."

"Eliza . . ."

"What is the problem with that, Mr. Howell? I understand there is a cost associated with the voyage, but perhaps I can do something to earn the fare. Fifteen hundred dollars is a fortune and far above the price of a ship's cabin. I'm aware that she may have to take one ship from Africa to Europe, and then come to America—"

"It is more complicated than ship fare," Mr. Howell says while wringing his hands.

"There is nothing complicated about mailing a letter, Mr. Howell," I say, with sarcasm punctuating every word. "You place the folded sheets in an envelope. Then you write the address on the outside and affix postage—"

"Eliza! There are very powerful people in this country who do not believe in the manumission of slaves. The whole idea of sending them to Liberia was born because many white men got the idea that too many free Black folk milling around was not a good thing. That they might get the idea to take revenge against their former captors. Their manumission was contingent upon them getting on that ship and sailing to Africa."

"I know that, Mr. Howell."

"So then you are aware of the odds we're up against here," he says, his voice calming from his previous frantic tirade.

"Are you saying it's impossible to bring my mother home?"

"I'm saying that, even if she is alive, and that if I knew how to find her, and that if she wanted to come back here, it would take an enormous amount of influence, power, and time to get her back."

Now it occurs to me, the reason Miss Lizbeth structured her will the way she did is because she was never one to leave things to providence and prayer. A brilliant woman. Always strategic.

"And that is why Miss Lizbeth left a fortune for this to happen."

"Yes, that is precisely why."

This knowledge of my mother's possible discontent being in Africa coupled with my loneliness without Miss Lizbeth have become a heavy burden. And Mr. Howell has done nothing to lighten the load. To the contrary, he's made matters worse.

"I believe that maybe it was God's will for you to be left behind in Mrs. Greenfield's care," Mr. Howell says thoughtfully. "Look at you! Educated, talented, moving among the wealthy circles of free Black people in Philadelphia. Eliza, your mother would be proud of you."

I swallow a lump that forms in my throat and will myself not to start bawling. I am sick of crying. It seems my eyes are raw from tears falling every day for one reason or another.

"You should plan your wedding," Mr. Howell continues, in a passionate and caring tone, "continue the abolitionist work both you and Mrs. Greenfield were involved in, and be an exceptional person. That is what everyone wants."

"But if I can help my mother, I want to do so."

"If your mother had wanted your help, she could've written to *you*. You had the same address as Mrs. Greenfield. I think she wanted you to be free to spread your wings, and not miss the mother who'd left you behind."

My sigh is deep and mournful. Maybe he's right. My mother knew Miss Lizbeth was an old woman when she left me.

And I know she loved me. I remember her hair, because I was always in her arms. My little fat fingers would wrap around the long strands and pull. And she never seemed to grow tired of it. I remember this about her. And her voice. Never loud or demanding or cross. Always soothing.

"I suppose that is all, then, Mr. Howell. You'll contact me when there is another hearing on the inheritance?"

"Yes. I'm sorry I could not help you more."

I rise and give a curt nod. "I'm sorry as well."

"I hope to receive an invitation to the wedding. It sounds like Mrs. Brown is planning a very large affair."

"That she is. I'm sure she is going to invite half of Philadelphia, so I don't doubt you'll be in the number."

I make my way to the door, swallowing repeatedly to remove the copper taste of bile from my mouth. But it's not the thought of the wedding that's making me ill; it's the idea of never being reunited with my mother, because my heart had become set on it.

Maybe I will not abandon the idea completely. Mr. Howell said it would take time, influence, and power to get her home. Well, I've got nothing but time. And perhaps I can become a person of great influence and power.

But how will I manage to do that while being Lucien's wife?

* * *

SINCE I AM NOW Lucien's fiancée, we decide to make the PFASS anti-slavery fair meeting our first social outing as an engaged couple. Well, Lucien and Mrs. Brown decide. I am not consulted on the matter. But, I suppose, consultation or not, there was no way around it, since Lucien is our transportation to Byberry, in his covered carriage.

We leave right after breakfast so that Lucien won't have to deal with the hottest sun on his face as he drives, but it is already humid on this late-summer September day. I pile into the back of the carriage with Mrs. Brown, Caroline, and Beatrice, while Lucien and Caroline's husband, Silas, climb in the front. Beatrice's husband found some excuse not to join us, but she doesn't seem to mind. Neither do I. The two of them bicker constantly about one thing or another. Or maybe it's just the same argument repeatedly. Either way, it's insufferable.

"My Lord, it's hot out here," Mrs. Brown says as she tries to fan herself with a handkerchief she's pulled from her bosom.

Caroline shakes her head and laughs. "Mother, if you hadn't worn your corset so tight, maybe you wouldn't be so hot."

"Hush now. You should've pulled yours a little tighter," Mrs. Brown retorts. "Everyone knows a lady's dress needs proper lines."

"Doesn't a lady need to be able to breathe?" Beatrice asks, giggling with Caroline.

I sit quietly, even though I feel Caroline and Beatrice are always egging me on and inviting me to join in the teasing of their mother. Sitting next to me in the carriage, Beatrice keeps grabbing on to my arm every time she laughs, but I sit as still as a marble statue.

It would be nice to join in their comradery, but ever since Mrs. Brown reminded me of my origins, I have tried to steer clear of her bad side. I don't want to give her the opportunity to remind me of how I am not good enough for her son.

"Maybe I should've worn a Sunday church frock like Eliza," Mrs. Brown says as she takes in my plain dress with a look of aloofness. "Would you two have been happy then?"

"I'm wearing a simple church frock because I cannot sing in a corset," I explain, feeling the need to at least defend myself. "It's too constricting."

"See," Beatrice says, barely containing her giggles and grabbing me yet again. "Breathing is required for singing. And staying alive."

"Most of the Quaker ladies don't even wear these fancy dresses, Mother. I hate that I let you talk me into it. You always make us stand out from everyone else." I can hear the exasperation in Caroline's voice, but she is a grown woman. I would wear what I want.

"Is that such a bad thing? To stand out?" Mrs. Brown asks as she dabs a bit of perspiration from her bosom. Heaven forbid she glisten like an actual human. "I'd much rather that than to fade into the background."

She looks at me when she says this. It is one thing to be invited by her daughters to tease Mrs. Brown, but when she is prodding me herself . . . Well, my self-control has its limits sometimes, but I do not allow myself to lose my composure this morning.

"I know a time when Eliza should stand out for certain. On her wedding day," Beatrice says. "I can't wait to curl all this hair."

"It truly is a waste what you do with all that beautiful, heavy hair, Eliza," Caroline says, then slowly kisses the back of her teeth like an older woman. "I'd let it cascade down my back and wear a flower behind my ear."

"You would not," Mrs. Brown scoffs. "You'd look like a whore. Thank God Eliza has enough sense to pin it up. It might be nice to pin curl it for the wedding, though. If we add some lovely beaded pearl pins, it'll be perfect for a winter wedding."

"We're going to be married in the spring at the earliest," I say directly, not wanting to leave this up for discussion. We hadn't decided upon an exact date, but I know Mrs. Brown has already had conversations with Lucien.

"What's wrong with a winter wedding?" Beatrice asks. "We could even wear Christmas colors."

"No. I don't think I'd like to share my anniversary celebrations every year with the holidays," I say, interrupting Beatrice's musing.

"What's the rush, Mother?" Caroline asks. "I would hate to have their wedding day ruined by a snowstorm. That would be tragic."

"They've been dawdling," Mrs. Brown grumbles.

"I think a year's courtship and a less-than-a-year-long engagement are perfectly acceptable," I say matter-of-factly. "The only time a couple needs to rush things along is if there have been unwholesome activities. And there have not been between Lucien and I."

Mrs. Brown and I lock gazes. Of course, I know the reason she wants to hurry things along. She wants to guarantee that her son will have command of my considerable inheritance when it finally becomes available.

"Well, now that Lucien is engaged, no one is asking questions any longer about what he intends to do with himself, Mother. That is a good thing," Caroline says. "Perhaps you can have an engagement party for them over the holidays. Will that scratch your planning itch for a while?"

"We might as well begin planning the wedding," Mrs. Brown says. "I'll call in my dressmaker from Baltimore."

"No need. Mary will make my gown," I say. "She's been sewing for me for years."

Mrs. Brown's lower jaw shifts from side to side in the most exasperated way that I almost burst into laughter. I am not trying to annoy her, but she keeps making declarations that I wouldn't agree with even if I wanted this wedding.

"What are you going to sing today?" Beatrice asks, completely changing the subject, probably not wanting to see her mother explode before we arrive in Byberry. That's fine. I'm not particularly interested in Mrs. Brown exploding either.

"I think I'll let it be a surprise."

"A surprise?" Mrs. Brown asks. "Well, remember that you are now representing the Brown family and Lucien. Do not embarrass us."

"Ignore her, truly," Beatrice says. "You will not embarrass me no matter what you sing."

"Please forgive our mother," Caroline says.

"Do not apologize for me. I mean exactly what I say. I have spent my entire adult life building this family's name," Mrs. Brown says in response to Caroline, but directing all her words to me. "I built your father's business. He may have done the hauling, but I did the thinking behind every decision that was made. I welcome you to my family, Eliza. But it is *my* family. Do you understand this?"

"I understand."

My response is due to respect for her age and the friendship that I have with her son. It is not a sign of submission to her will. My question is, if the Browns are *her* family, can they also be *my* family? Is there room for us both?

I ponder that question for the rest of the ride to Byberry, while mother and daughters fuss about things I find trivial and unimportant. If it wasn't so hot, I think I would've preferred riding outside with Lucien.

Although we left early, it looks as though most everyone has already arrived at the newly constructed Byberry Hall by the time we get there. The hall is right next to the Byberry Friends Meeting and a two-hour carriage ride from the heart of Philadelphia, making it far removed from the mobs that had chased the Purvis family away from Lombard Street. This new location only serves the abolitionist movement more, at least when we move fugitives from southern plantations north to Canada.

The fair meetings always start with the women's official business, and then end with the men joining in for laughter and socializing. I'd never much participated in the social part before. Mostly because Miss Lizbeth preferred to leave immediately following the official business. Every now and then, Mary and I would linger and pick up a tidbit here and there, but once she married Isaiah, Mary had no time to attend the meetings at all.

Lucien comes to help us get out of the carriage. He goes to reach for me first, but Mrs. Brown gives him a glare, so he changes his mind and reaches for her. I shake my head and refuse his offer of assistance when it's my turn and make my way down the carriage step on my own. Silas helps the sisters.

"It looks like the men are over there in that barn," Lucien says. "I'm assuming they've got food and lemonade."

"And nothing any stronger than that," Silas says with a disappointed frown.

He is a man who likes a strong ale, and he knows an afternoon and evening hosted by a group of women, half of them Quakers, isn't going to get him anything in the way of spirits. Poor Lucien. Silas is going to be grumpy on the ride back home.

Caroline, Beatrice, and I follow Mrs. Brown into Byberry Hall. The two daughters are close behind their mother, their matching corseted gowns quite the spectacle in comparison to my simple attire. But I am content to let them be spectacular without me.

The meeting has already started when we walk in, so, thank goodness, Mrs. Brown does not get the opportunity to draw too much attention to herself. She chooses the first available table, and we sit with her. It is near the back of the large open hall, but still some of the ladies turn to look at us as we get settled.

Mrs. Lucretia Mott, one of the founders of the Female Anti-Slavery Society, sits at the table next to us. A tiny, pleasant-looking woman, wearing her customary white bonnet and gauze shawl, she modestly blends in with the rest of the ladies. She started her abolition work as a younger woman, and now, in her late fifties, her hair has started to gray at the temples and she's less energetic, though her impact as a Quaker minister and leader is legendary. And while she's as active as ever in the abolition work, she's turned over most of the running of meetings like this to Hattie Purvis and the other younger women. She glances over at me and smiles, and I return the gesture.

Mrs. Brown sees this interaction and sneers. Good Lord, this woman is a ball of jealousy. As a show of goodwill, I'll try to introduce them later if I can. I do not want Lucien's mother to be my enemy in case I do have to marry him.

In the front of the room, a very charismatic Hattie Purvis shows items donated for the anti-slavery fair. Although she's a mother of six children, she doesn't look drab or haggard. Quite the opposite. She's lovely, with smooth brown skin that's dark in comparison to her husband's, who could easily pass for white and is often confused for a white man when in the company of his Quaker contemporaries. Her hair is parted down the middle with curls framing her face on either side, and the back pinned in a neat bun at the nape of her neck. But more noteworthy than her looks is her energetic mannerisms and spirited nature. She holds up two wooden sticks from the table in front of her.

"These items, I'm told," she says in a feisty voice that reaches clear to the back of the hall, "are rulers formed from a tree under which George Fox preached. Yes, *that* George Fox. The founder of the Society of Friends. Now, I know these are bound to fetch us quite a pretty penny at the fair. They are worth at least four hundred dollars."

There are excited squeals and shouts from the ladies in the room, because that kind of windfall could do so much to help the cause. PFASS doesn't only help fugitives to escape to Canada. For any Black person who settles in Philadelphia, free or former enslaved person, there is a school sponsored by the anti-slavery society and help with finding work and housing. Much of this work is funded by the fair.

Harriet finally sees us in the back of the hall and claps her hands. "I have a special treat for everyone today," she says. "I know that some of you are not too keen on us using these events for the pursuit or furtherance of the arts."

There are a few murmurs in the room but not many. The Friends who are against the performance of instrumental music are also at odds with all things Lucretia Mott. The Motts' ministry is aligned with the more liberal side of the Society of Friends, who had broken from the traditional Quakers some years ago. But the Black co-laborers in this vineyard are Methodist, Baptist, and every Black denomination in between, and we love instrumental music, singing, and praise.

"But, please, humor me on this one occasion," Harriet continues, "because this artist's gift is surely bestowed upon her from God. We have had the pianoforte tuned especially for her visit today. Please, come forward, Miss Elizabeth Taylor Greenfield, and bless us with a selection. She will also be performing at the fair."

All eyes are on me as I make my way to the front of the room. I smile at the familiar and unfamiliar faces until I have reached the pianoforte. Now I don't need anyone to tell me what to do next. My fingers are touching the keys, and music is flowing forth, and then I am singing.

First, I sing "No Place Like Home," and then I follow with my favorite, "When Stars Are in the Quiet Skies." Both songs are crowd-pleasers, and even the staunchest Friends in the room seem to be enjoying themselves.

The ladies applaud at the end of each song, and I take a small bow. If this was a true concert, I would perform an encore, but since it isn't, I return to my seat, with Mrs. Brown's eyes trained on me the entire time.

"Do you approve?" I ask her when I'm seated, since she's still looking at me.

A tight nod is the only affirmation I receive. I wink at Caroline, and she winks back. I know that Mrs. Brown is more than pleased, whether or not she admits it or showers me with praise. I do not care if she's proud of me or not, but it does tickle me seeing her at odds with herself.

After the meeting is adjourned, the men join the women inside where it's cooler for more conversation and refreshments before we begin the late-afternoon trek back home. We will aim to make it home right before dark, because it is much safer to travel during the daylight hours.

Caroline, Beatrice, and I bring plates of mincemeat pie, apple pie, and cups of lemonade to our table, although I am not very hungry. A few ladies have approached me to tell me that they'd love to have me come sing at their church services, and of course I graciously accept those engagements, but I cannot make a vocation of those. The pay from those events is usually in the form of a love offering, and that could be a dollar or two depending on the congregation. And sometimes there is no pay at all, because some believe, if my gift is from God, then why should God's people pay for it?

While Lucien and the rest of the family eat, I scan the room to see if there is anyone I should try to greet or have a conversation with before we leave today. I am feeling anxious, impatient, and desperate for things to happen.

Robert and Hattie Purvis approach our table as they make their rounds saying hello to everyone. Mrs. Brown perks right up, while Lucien and Silas rise.

Seeing the Purvises standing next to each other, looking like the miscegenation nightmare of many white men in this country, reminds me of the reason they live here in Byberry. Miss Lizbeth told me of a time when Robert was seen helping Hattie out of a carriage at an anti-slavery convention, and a mob of angry white men burned down the hall where the convention was being held, thinking that Robert was a white man married to a Black woman. They might be heroes in our community, but not everyone views them that way.

"Please sit," Hattie says. "Enjoy that mincemeat pie. You know Mrs. Mott still bakes them all by hand for every meeting and for the fair?"

"It's amazing how you both manage to find time for your work here with the abolition movement and your families," Mrs. Brown says to Hattie. "My future daughter-in-law here also seeks to have a vocation, you see. And my son is hoping for a family. Perhaps you can share your secret."

Lucien's eyes widen with embarrassment, but for once, I appreciate

Mrs. Brown's candor and shamelessness. I would like to hear the answer to this question and then see Lucien's reaction to it.

Robert gazes down at Hattie with affection and kisses her forehead. "Hattie's passion for the abolitionist work is what drew me to her. There was no way I was going to ask her to stop doing what she loved in order to raise a family."

"It also helps that we have the resources for maids and nannies," Hattie says. "I say this not to brag upon wealth. I say that because I do not diminish the contributions that women can make to this movement even if they cannot travel to a conference. Even if they cannot abandon all to run a fair. We can all support in some way. Every bit helps."

"Well, Eliza fancies herself onstage and touring the country singing," Lucien says to Robert. I hear an undercurrent of derision in his tone, and it irritates me immensely. "Perhaps if we were talking about abolitionist work it would be a different conversation."

For a moment, there is an awkward silence. Lucien locks eyes with me briefly and then looks away, withering under the heat of my glare.

"Is that so?" Hattie asks. "Well, perhaps you should get more involved in PFASS, dear. It sounds like your husband approves. Then we'll engage you in suffragist work as well. We also believe a woman should be able to do exactly what she fancies."

Mrs. Brown's jaw drops, while Caroline and Beatrice gasp. My fury dissipates, and I must quickly hide my grin.

"Eliza, thank you for that outstanding performance today, and I look forward to hearing more from you," Hattie says. "And thank you all for coming."

Robert and Hattie move on to the next group of guests, leaving Mrs. Brown fuming. She snatches the fork from Silas's hand as he eats another bite of mincemeat pie and rises from her seat.

"I am ready to leave now," Mrs. Brown says. "My son was just humiliated, and we're supposed to keep eating their food? I think not."

"If he hadn't been trying to humiliate Eliza, it wouldn't have happened that way," Beatrice says, "so allow my husband to finish his meal."

It shocks me to hear Beatrice defend me, though I am grateful to have her as an ally. Especially since Mrs. Brown's scowl in my direction is sharp enough to slice me in two.

"He's had enough pie for five men," Mrs. Brown barks. "Let's be on our way."

Mrs. Brown does not wait for anyone's retort. She storms right out of Byberry Hall, her daughters at her heels, and so that is the end of that. We are on our way back to the heart of Philadelphia.

"Eliza," Lucien calls out as I follow his family. I turn to face him. "That was not my intention," he says.

"To humiliate me?" I ask quietly, not wanting anyone to hear our conversation.

He nods.

I step closer to him, so that we can speak plainly without being overheard. "Then what was it? I heard the tone of your question. You were all but laughing at me. I *fancy* myself onstage?"

"I—I wanted you to hear . . . I wanted Hattie to extol the virtues of marriage and family. Because you do not seem to place any value on them."

"What do you mean, Lucien? I said yes. I accepted your proposal."

"You did so under duress, Eliza. I know that if you had your inheritance, you would have rebuffed me."

I swallow hard. "Then why do you want to marry me?"

Lucien tilts my chin upward until he is looking directly into my eyes. "Because I love you, Eliza Greenfield. I do not care whether you have an inheritance or not. And I am hoping that if I love you hard enough, you'll start to love me back."

"You are one of my dearest friends, Lucien." The tenderness in my voice and in my touch as I stroke his cheek are not a result of mutual passion. They are derived from pity, and from the look of disappointment on Lucien's face, I think he knows it.

"That is not the same thing, Eliza," he says, removing my hand and placing it at my side. "Come, before Mother does something to embarrass us all."

Here I thought the ruse was one-sided, but this entire time, Lucien's known. He's waiting for love to grow in my heart, but for that to occur, there needed to be a seed planted long ago. If he tried to plant it, it has long since withered and died.

I must find a way to extricate myself from this madness and secure my future. It is selfish to do otherwise, even if Lucien thinks that he wants me. He will not be happy with the version of me that settles for him.

And I would like to be a woman who does exactly whatever it is she fancies.

# CHAPTER EIGHT

*October 1851*

*S*ince our trip last month to Byberry, everything—and I do mean *everything*—has been weighing heavily on my mind. My finances, my plans, this sham of an engagement. I cannot find a way to escape, and I've not made peace with the way things are quickly progressing to this spring wedding. We're set to be married the first Saturday in April, but it feels more like my execution date.

I pace my bedroom, looking at the dresses I've selected to wear to a concert tonight with Lucien. I should be excited to see the Philadelphia Orchestra, but all I can think about is that I'm attending with Lucien as his fiancée and that people will want to hear about our wedding plans when they see us, and I will not want to talk about that.

Miss Ophelia stops in the hall outside my room. She tilts her head to one side as she peers at me. "Should I come in? Is it safe?"

I release the tension in my shoulders and sigh. "It's safe."

She walks in and perches on the settee at the end of my bed. "What's been bothering you, Eliza? You've been out of sorts for a few weeks now."

"I don't want to marry Lucien."

This is the first time I've declared this out loud to anyone other than Mary, and I'm shocked to hear myself say the words. But I do not want this, no matter how much I keep trying to convince myself that I can live with this choice.

What's even more shocking is Miss Ophelia's reaction. She isn't the least bit fazed. She lifts one eyebrow and shakes her head.

"Well, that's obvious," she says to my consternation and chagrin. "But you are not the first woman who has found herself in this predicament. You do have options."

"Do I truly have options? The women telling me to pursue my gift at singing have options. They're either wealthy white women or supported by their husbands."

Miss Ophelia bites her bottom lip, considering this. "And who are the ones telling you to marry Lucien?" she asks.

"Black women who know what it's like to try to scrape by without a man. But even my lawyer told me to marry him. And everyone says he's a good man."

I can hear Mrs. Brown's words echo in my head: *a bird in the hand*.

"Well. He *is* a good man."

"See! That's exactly what I mean. And I feel like a dolt not wanting this." My voice rises, turning frantic, and my arms flail as my pacing continues, but who cares? I feel panicked at my life. "Fat, homely Eliza. Never-had-a-suitor Eliza, turning down a proposal from a *good* man. One with *money*. What could I possibly be thinking?"

Miss Ophelia stands and embraces me. "All right, all right. Calm down." I break down in an avalanche of tears. "Eliza, do you really think you can't sustain yourself at all? You're a smart woman. You can read and write. You are a gifted musician. You can bake better than many a skilled bakery owner. You will not have a problem earning wages. And if I have a home, you will have a room."

"But that's the thing, Ophelia. I don't want my life to be limited to Philadelphia. I want to go to Buffalo. To Europe. I want to bring my mother back home from Liberia."

"And marriage is going to give you this?"

"No, not without my inheritance, and maybe not even then, since Lucien gets to control it."

"So, either way you don't have what you want, but if you choose to stay unmarried, at least you have your freedom."

"Unless I am kidnapped and forced to work on a plantation in the South."

Miss Ophelia rolls her eyes and swats at the air. "And are you going to come up with every possibility of every horrible thing that might happen to you? Eliza, you might have to do something without knowing what the end looks like."

"But these kidnappings are happening, Ophelia. Every day another Black person turns up missing. These are not just possibilities. They are realities."

"I am aware of that. But you can't live your life in fear. Now, do you have any money saved?"

I nod. "Yes. Almost fifty dollars."

"A fortune."

"It's not a fortune."

"It is enough to carry you comfortably to Buffalo, to lodge you, to feed you, and to pay for your lessons with Bella."

"But . . ."

"No buts," Miss Ophelia snaps. "I know people who have started empires on less."

"Were they white people?" I must ask the question, though I am quite sure of the answer already.

Miss Ophelia inhales deeply and then slowly exhales. I see compassion in her eyes but not understanding. "If that is how you're going to win every argument, marry Lucien and get it over with."

"You can't act as if things aren't different for me because of that."

"I'm not. Things are different for you. And if you're going to accept those limitations, go ahead and marry Lucien and sing at church." Her words are clipped, and her tone exasperated. She has become impatient with my indecisiveness, it seems. "But the only way to have what *you* say you want is to challenge everything people believe. And you can't do that afraid."

"You say I should not be fearful, but I am terrified of the South."

Perhaps if Miss Ophelia had helped tend to the fugitives on the Underground Railroad, like I have, instead of only sending blankets, food, and money, she would know what causes the chill in my bones when I picture myself being kidnapped. To see women and children with lost limbs, broken and twisted bones, burned and bruised skin, and all manner of injury—internal and external, seen and unseen— then she would understand my terror.

Ophelia sighs wearily and then points to the burgundy dress. "Wear that dress. It's the less flattering of the two."

"Why would I pick the less flattering dress?" I ask, not understanding the change in conversation.

"Well, you aren't trying to get any fresh compliments from Lucien, are you?"

I quickly gather the burgundy dress into my arms. "No, I'm not. I think I'll try this one."

"I'll be out in the parlor in case Lucien arrives before you're fully dressed. I'll keep him company while you're getting ready," Miss Ophelia offers. "No need to thank me, it's no trouble at all."

"Well, thank you anyway."

"Hurry now. Get dressed. Don't keep Lucien waiting. You have a concert to attend."

She backs out of the room and eases the door closed. I regret causing Ophelia grief and concern, because I know that she wants for me the same thing that Miss Lizbeth wanted for me. But very much like Miss Lizbeth, she simply cannot bestow upon me the one token that could make this journey a simple one.

\* \* \*

"Eliza, I love your dress," Lucien gushes as I emerge from my bedroom and into the sitting room where he awaits. "The color is perfect for this autumn evening. You'll match the leaves falling all over the streets."

My eyes shift quickly over to Miss Ophelia, who sits silently grinning in her corner, before settling back on Lucien's eager smile. So much for escaping his compliments. I've spent less than one minute in the same room with him, and I've already been showered with praises.

"Thank you, although I didn't think this dress was very beautiful. I was just trying to wear something warm and decent." Once I say these words, I realize how foolish I sound. Who wouldn't want to look beautiful for a night out with her fiancé? "Will anyone be joining us for the concert tonight?"

"This concert is special, so I am afraid I was only able to procure tickets for the two of us," Lucien says with a wry smirk. "I hope I am company enough."

"Of course, you are, but what is so special about the Philadelphia Orchestra? We've heard them many times before."

Lucien's grin spreads. He seems to be excited about something, and I don't know why, but this worries me. "I have not been completely honest, Eliza."

"And you're smiling about it?"

"Yes, because I have the best surprise. I've got tickets to the Jenny Lind concert."

My eyes stretch wide with elation and shock. I think this may be the first time I have been truly pleased since Miss Lizbeth passed. Finally, Lucien has done something to bring a smile to my face.

Jenny Lind is only the most celebrated soprano of the day. She's known as the Swedish Nightingale and has toured all over Europe and is now launching a tour here in America.

She and I are nearly the same age, if the biographies in the newspapers are to be believed, but she has had everything that I've always dreamed of having. Training in Paris, a debut at the age of eighteen, and an opera written especially for her by an Italian composer.

"I had forgotten that was tonight. How did you come across tickets to the Jenny Lind concert?" I squeal. "I heard they sold them at an auction because of the demand."

"It's been in all the newspapers," Miss Ophelia says from her corner. "I assumed you two were going to see her."

"I guess I haven't been paying much attention," I say to Lucien. "Good thing for you, because your surprise wasn't ruined."

When the concert was first announced, I had been tempted to use some of the money I had saved to purchase my own ticket, but I had convinced myself not to. But since Lucien came through with tickets instead, God must have wanted me to hear her.

"Well . . . a friend of mine works for the promoter and he was able to get me two," he explains, with sheer delight punctuating every word. "They have a section for Black folk at the Musical Fund Hall, and we have the best seats in the section."

"My brother heard her in Europe," Miss Ophelia says. "He says he has never heard anyone quite like her before. It should be some concert."

I look down at my dress, wondering if I should change but quickly deciding not to. I don't want to risk missing a single moment. Not one note.

"Well, this is the best surprise. Thank you, Lucien."

I throw my arms around Lucien's neck and hug him tightly to show my thanks, and almost immediately regret doing so. There is too much affection and hope in his eyes, and too much longing in the squeeze he gives me in return. No matter. We are going to see Jenny Lind tonight.

*The* Jenny Lind!

* * *

THE CONCERT HALL is packed to capacity, and I can feel the anticipation in the crowd. My own heart races with excitement as sounds come from the orchestra pit. Our seats might be the best in the section for Black folk, but they are so far from the stage that the piano in the center looks like a toy, and the orchestra members seem like ants moving in unison. Still, as the lights go down, I feel more thrilled than I've ever been.

Lucien touches my hand as if he's trying to soak up some of my joy. Any other time I would be bothered by this uninvited intimacy, but tonight I do not mind sharing my enthusiasm. He should enjoy this moment with me, since he is the one who coordinated it.

"You have not stopped smiling since we left the house," he whispers. "Perhaps I should see if Miss Lind will perform a concert every week."

"You would be a powerful man if you could do such a thing."

He lifts his eyebrows as if he's putting thought to how he can make it happen, and I can't help but burst into laughter. These hilarious moments with Lucien are the ones that are etched in my memories. This is what I enjoy of him. Not the attempts at romance, which I cannot and do not receive.

"I see that you do not believe in my powers," he says, his voice trembling on the verge of laughter as well. "Have you no faith?"

"Oh, me of little faith!" I touch the back of my hand to my forehead in a dramatic and comedic flourish.

Lucien shakes his head and chuckles, then points to the stage. "Look, it's about to begin."

When the lights come back up, Jenny Lind is center stage. And now I clutch Lucien's hand as I gasp for breath, overwhelmed with emotion. For a moment, time seems to have stopped. Lucien has disappeared and so has the orchestra and the crowd. The only two people in the concert hall are me and Miss Lind.

Like the concert piano, she appears small and delicate as she stares into the distance, directly at me. She sees me—Elizabeth Taylor Greenfield—in the section reserved for Black people, in my unremarkable burgundy gown. She, a contrast in her shimmering pink dress and hair adorned with a crown of roses and baby's breath, seems angelic.

This ethereal quality fits perfectly, because when she opens her mouth to sing the first notes of "Casta Diva" I am transported—if not to heaven, then somewhere other than this concert hall. The first phrase of the aria, in Italian, is a feat of perfected breathing exercises with its long and drawn-out opening trills.

Then Miss Lind's voice grows stronger as the notes start to climb. Her high notes are perfection, and tears spring to my eyes as she does run after run, and trill after trill. Next, she pulls back and goes into her lower octave again, with a rich and robust sound. There is so much emotion in this part of the aria. The sadness of it hovers over me until a sob comes from my throat, which I quickly quiet, not wanting to detract from the sound of Miss Lind's voice.

I wonder if she is singing for a lost lover, and how such a beautiful and delicate woman could conceive of such a loss. She must have men clamoring for her at every show and throwing roses at her feet. Miss Bella always tells me that I must feel what I am singing, so that I may evoke the same emotions in my audience.

Now she's climbing again. This time right up a scale and down again. I have no idea what the words mean, but when she sings the last notes, Miss Lind conveys pure melancholy. I do find it peculiar that at the very end, Miss Lind, instead of singing full voice, gives us a falsetto. She had sung higher notes in the middle of the song, so it has nothing to do with her range. It was probably a choice she made during her practices, but I believe the ending would have been better if that last note had been in her robust full voice.

"That was incredible," Lucien whispers to me while the crowd applauds, bringing everyone and everything back to my awareness.

It is more than incredible. It's as if I can feel Miss Lizbeth's spirit in the room, reminding me of my promise and of the expansiveness of my own gift.

From hearing this first selection, I can tell that Jenny Lind's range is fantastic, at least two and a half octaves. Her high notes are the strongest, while her lower register is not as impressive. My ear isn't as learned as some others, but there was a phrase or two where Miss Lind struggled to maintain enough breath to make it to the final notes.

And yet, no one in this crowd notices those imperfections. To the untrained ear, there was only the beautiful sound. I imagine that a heavenly chorus of angels singing on roads paved with gold would not have sounded better than Miss Jenny Lind.

But my range is better. I have three full octaves, and where Miss Lind needs a baritone to sing a duet with her on this next song, I can sing those low notes as well as a man. Miss Bella says my lungs must be twice the size of any other woman's, and that my rib cage must be made of bamboo the way I can bend my voice around notes.

With every song Miss Lind sings, the applause gets louder and louder, and the crowd gets more emotional. I have never seen so many men moved to tears outside a church service where the Black preacher has worked everyone into a shouting frenzy. But this phenomenal singing feels like religion.

What if I could move a crowd to worship? I know I am not ready, because my studies are incomplete, and if I want to stand on a stage like this one, with an orchestra in the wings and the crowd throwing roses at my feet, I must be trained in Europe. And to go to Europe, I must be unencumbered by finances or by a husband and children. I must be free.

As we give Miss Lind a standing ovation and demand encore after encore, I now know that the promise I made to Miss Lizbeth is a wish I'd already had for myself. With every syllable of Italian I agonize over, with every aria Miss Bella taught me, and with every chord I play on the pianoforte, my heart chooses this destiny more than anything. It chooses this more than it fears enslavement or death. My heart chooses this destiny over Lucien.

My heart never chose Lucien.

I look down at his hand still clutching mine, still grasping on to hope, and I snatch my hand away. The gold band glistens on my finger, as much a shackle as any other. This must end. I will finish this tonight.

I join the crowd in their applause, relieved that the tears that streak my face will be mistaken for awe at the Swedish Nightingale. But I weep instead for the inevitability of Lucien's broken heart.

# CHAPTER NINE

*I* am glad we chose to walk home from the concert instead of taking a carriage. The air is balmy and warm, and the stars dazzling above in the night sky remind me that there is a world outside of Philadelphia that I am destined to see.

I have been quiet with my thoughts since we left the concert hall, trying to think of a way to begin this conversation with Lucien. My silence must be foreboding, because Lucien seems nervous and fretful. He walks close to me but cannot quite seem to decide what to do with his hands, since I don't take hold of his arm.

"That concert was something else, wasn't it?" Lucien asks in a tentative voice, perhaps testing the waters for my mood.

"It was everything I thought it would be, and more." My melancholy tone doesn't match my sentiments, and Lucien certainly seems to notice this, as he takes my hand and squeezes.

"Then why do you not sound joyful?"

"I almost don't know how to describe it, but I'll try. On the first song, I was simply mesmerized. Taken away by her gift, almost to another place."

"I felt that way too," Lucien says.

"But then, on the second song, and on the next," I explain, shaking my hand loose from Lucien's, "something changed. I started to think of how I would sing the songs differently."

"How *you* would sing them? But, Eliza, the woman is a world-famous prima donna."

My feet stop moving, and my arms drop to my sides as my breathing slows. The time to end this is now. I know that Lucien loves me, but he can never see me the way I see myself. He cannot envision me on that stage, and that is why I cannot be his wife.

When I have breathed long enough, I look down at my hand. Slowly, I remove the gold band from my finger.

"What are you doing?" Lucien asks, as I take one step toward him to place the offensive yet glimmering thing in the palm of his hand. He stares down at it as if it's a foreign object.

"You are a dear friend, Lucien, and I appreciate you rescuing me from my unfortunate situation with a marriage proposal. But I cannot marry you."

Lucien's gaze now finds me. "You know full well that my proposal was not only to rescue you from your situation. You'll make a fool of me in front of my entire family and all our friends."

"I understand if you're angry with me. If it makes things easier to accept, I struggled with this decision. I didn't truly know I'd call it off until tonight. But I know that I cannot make you happy."

"Did you ever want to marry me? The night of the proposal . . . did you want to say yes then?"

I think back to the night of my birthday. I had intended to stop things before they'd gone this far, but I hadn't stopped them. I wept and brooded and waited for providence to give me a way out. I should've created my own escape then. I know that now.

"I did not want to say yes, but, Lucien, what other choice is there for a woman, really? What I'm going to do is foolish. Anyone that hears my plans will tell me I should marry you and abandon them. Mary already has."

"I have wasted too much time on this," Lucien says angrily, as he grips the ring now in a tightly closed fist. "I could've already been married and started a family with someone else."

This stings. The words and the pain in his voice as he says it. I have not asked for his time, but I have entertained the ruse. There has never been passion between us, at least not from my perspective, but if nothing else, Lucien has been a trusted friend.

"It was not a waste, Lucien. Our friendship is dear to me."

"Is there another man?"

There is an accusatory bite in Lucien's tone as he asks this that I do not appreciate. It is one thing to be shocked, saddened, and upset. I understand these feelings. But to start accusing me of things contrary to my character is quite another thing. I recoil from him and stumble backward on the cobbled sidewalk.

"No, Lucien, there isn't anyone else. I want to pursue my gift."

He charges in my direction, eyebrows furrowed, fists balled at his sides. Infuriated. "*That's* the only reason why you're calling this off?"

I glance around the mostly abandoned street, feeling dread in the pit of my stomach at not knowing what Lucien is going to do next. Although I'm mostly certain this man who has declared his love for me countless times would not do me harm, I cannot be sure. Not with the fury in his eyes. And so I'm shaking as he advances, but I stand in place. I cannot run from him or this anymore.

"Yes. I am going to sing, Lucien."

Finally, the anger seeps out of him like steam from a tea kettle. He drops his head and sighs. "You are foolish, then, but you are not to blame. It is Miss Lizbeth who's to blame. She has you believing that you can succeed as a singer. You want to be Jenny Lind, and your voice may be better than hers, but no one will allow a Black woman to be a success at singing."

"That's what Mary said to me on the night of your proposal," I respond. "That was the reason I said yes to you."

"What if I said I would wait for you to play out this fool's mission?" Lucien's voice is now full of desperation.

Now that I'm sure his anger has dissipated, I move closer to my friend and take his hand in mine. I squeeze it tightly, but he does not squeeze back.

"We are still young, Lucien. You have plenty of time to have your dream and I have plenty of time to have mine."

"Do you remember when we were very young, and all of the girls teased me?" Lucien asked.

"They all thought you were nice, Lucien, but too serious."

Back then he didn't just act older, he looked older. Wiser. It was the mothers who always gazed upon Lucien with approval. He's like me . . . capable and reliable. I suppose that is why our friendship blossomed when nothing else did. We were always kindred spirits.

"I was single-minded. I've always known that I wanted to be like my father and have a wife like my mother who would provide a loving home. When we were very young, I knew."

It is true. Lucien has never wavered in his desires, hopes, and dreams even during his youth when maybe he should have been enjoying a life free from cares and responsibilities.

"I am sorry, Lucien. It was not my intention to hurt you, but if we don't stop this farce now, we'll never have happiness."

"My love for you is no farce. You tell me to go and find my dream somewhere else when my dreams have only included you."

He untangles his hand from mine. Tears rim his eyes, but he is too stoic to let them fall.

"I will not beg. Pursue your vocation with my blessing," Lucien says. "Come, let me walk you home."

"Do you mean that, Lucien?"

He takes a long pause before responding. I would pay to know his true thoughts. The ones that he is too proper to say aloud.

"I am a godly man. I would never send you away with curses. But you don't need my blessing if this is the will of God."

"Thank you."

"I will keep you in my prayers."

We walk side by side in silence. Lucien has left me in God's hands, and that is the most I can probably hope for from him. I hazard one sidelong glance, and when I catch a glimpse of the tears that dampen his face, I turn my gaze to the sidewalk ahead of me. Better he shed them now and forget about this while he is still young and robust enough to recover.

Now there is one more goodbye to make before I use my savings to purchase a ticket to Buffalo to resume my lessons.

* * *

I MUSTN'T LEAVE Philadelphia without telling Mary. She'd never forgive me, and even though she won't agree with my plan, she loves me and I her.

But first, I'm up, before dawn, baking pies for my loved ones and packing my meager belongings. I can hear Miss Ophelia's steps in the hall outside my bedroom although I'd hoped not to wake her. She is not an early riser, and most days neither am I.

"Eliza?" she calls out sleepily. "The house smells like a bakery. Are you having guests over this morning?"

I open my bedroom door and step into the hall. She's still wearing her sleeping robe and bonnet. "No, Miss Ophelia. Something more exciting. I'm packing for Buffalo. Hoping to get a ticket on Tuesday or Wednesday morning's packet boat."

First, she chuckles. Then she claps her hands and shouts with glee. "I knew you had it in you, Eliza. I knew you'd make the right choice. Wait. I have something for you."

I shake my head as Miss Ophelia sashays back down the hallway. Inside my bedroom, I take inventory of the dresses on my bed. Although it is still rather warm, winter is quickly approaching, and Buffalo's winters are unrelenting and cruel. I should take more warm frocks than summer ones. By summer I should have earned enough to replace what I've left behind or at least be able to have Mary send me the dresses I have in storage here in Philadelphia.

"Eliza."

Miss Ophelia has returned, and in her hands she's holding a small velvet pouch. She extends her hands toward me, and I take the pouch from her.

"What's this?"

"Your words pricked my heart last night when we spoke, dear. I cannot imagine what it must be like for you. To have such a gift and to only see limitations. It isn't much, but I want to help."

I open the pouch, and inside is a pile of coins. Tears fill my eyes, but these are the joyful kind, so I let them flow.

"It's a little over twenty dollars," Miss Ophelia says. "Hopefully, enough to help tide you over until your inheritance finally becomes available or until you're commanding the stage."

"I welcome either."

"You'll have both," Miss Ophelia declares as she sits on the edge of my settee maybe for the last of our chats. "I have a way of knowing things."

"Well, I love hearing that."

"You have so little time to finalize your plans. When will you visit Mr. Howell?"

"Tomorrow. I need a letter from him indicating where I will live in Buffalo and where I'll be employed."

Miss Ophelia nods. "Yes, yes, of course. You have your certificate of freedom, correct? I don't want anyone to call anything into question."

I close my eyes and deeply inhale. I do not travel anywhere without it. I have never been asked to prove my status, but with the waterways being used more and more to move fugitives to Canada, I know that it is only a matter of time.

"If you're planning to leave in a few days, who are you baking for?

As much as I love your pies, I certainly don't need to have them all to myself."

"Oh, well, I need to go and say goodbye to Mary and Isaiah."

She nods slowly. "And a pie will soften the blow?"

"Nothing will soften it, but apple pie may sweeten it, I hope."

"And what about Lucien? Will he have a pie as well?"

I lift the burgundy gown from last night and carefully fold it, since I will bring it with me to Buffalo. There isn't enough pie in all the bakeries in all of Philadelphia to take away the tartness of last night's words, but he's swallowed them and now it's over.

"No, I won't be baking for Lucien or the Brown family. Best save that for his future bride."

"I see. Well, he may not understand it now, but it is for his good."

"It is. I hope Mary sees it the same way. She was as big a supporter of the marriage as anyone else."

"Even though she knows you don't love him?" Miss Ophelia asks, but before I can respond she sighs. "Ah, but you have reminded me of the truth when it comes to these things. We do not always have the luxury of love."

"I just hope she supports me pursuing my gift. Jenny Lind was amazing, Miss Ophelia. I must try. I can't live with myself if I don't."

"And no one else will want to live with you either," she says. "You'll be a grumpy, unfulfilled, bitter mess of a woman. Even failure is better than never trying. I'll let you finish packing, and if there's anything you'd like to leave behind for me to sample—a cookie, a muffin, or what have you—I'd be happy to oblige you one last time."

I give my dear friend a hug and hope it conveys all the thanks I feel in my heart. Nothing can prepare me for what's ahead, but I appreciate the extra finances and knowing that I have a place to come back to if I ever need shelter.

After I finish packing my belongings, I gather two cooled apple pies and place them in a basket. Even if Mary is cross with me after I leave, Isaiah and the girls will be happy until the last crumb is consumed.

The walk over to their home is a pleasant one with this streak of warm weather we're enjoying. I pray it holds for my trip to Buffalo.

When I approach their tiny bungalow, the ever-industrious Isaiah is outside sweeping dust from their front steps. He looks up at me with a combination of surprise and delight. At least I know this is one other place where I'm always welcome.

"Good morning, Isaiah. I thought I might join Mary for breakfast."

"Did you bring me anything?" he asks with a twinkle in his eye. "There may be a price of admission."

Knowing exactly Isaiah's price, I smile as I lift a small towel from the top of my basket to allow the wonderful smell to waft to his nose. He closes his eyes, inhales, and grins. My dear brother who takes such great care of my sister and provides a soft life for her and my nieces deserves all the pie he can eat.

"Breakfast?" Mary asks as she peeks out the door. "You're not usually out and about so early. Come on inside."

We leave Isaiah outside and head into the kitchen. Mary gives a curious glance at my hair. It's tucked into my neat and tidy travel bun.

"Where are you off to?" she asks. "Does Hattie have you attending to PFASS business? I heard there was a new group of fugitives over at the Mulberry Street Friends Meeting House."

"There is. Miss Ophelia sent food last night while Lucien and I were out at a concert, but I'm not out on PFASS business this morning."

"A concert? I must hear about this."

"Are the girls going to be awake soon?" I ask as we sit at the kitchen table, the aroma from the freshly baked pie filling the small space with its sweet spicy scent.

"Yes, but Isaiah will take care of them while we chat. Tell me about the concert. Do you want coffee?"

I nod. "Lucien surprised me with tickets to see Jenny Lind!"

"Ooh, the prima donna." Mary places a tin cup filled with coffee in front of me, and she sits across from me with her own cup. "I bet you enjoyed that."

"Mary. *Enjoy* isn't the word. It felt like church. I was saved, sanctified, and washed in the blood of the lamb last night."

"All that?"

"More." I take a swallow of coffee and let the sweetness linger in my mouth before I drop the bomb. "And then I called off my engagement with Lucien."

"You did what?" Mary's eyes dart to my now-naked ring finger, I suppose for affirmation.

"I can't marry him. It would be a mistake for both of us. I should've never said yes."

Mary takes a long sip from her coffee tin. Her furrowed brow and flaring nostrils give her the look of a mother thinking of a way to scold her unruly child.

"Did your inheritance come through?" she asks, and I steel myself against the argument that I know is coming.

"I am going to Buffalo to continue to work for the Howards. And during my spare time I will resume my lessons. When I save enough money, I will go to Europe. If I can make it to Paris for instruction, I know I will make it to the stage."

"So, we're here again. The stage. I thought you had decided that marrying Lucien was the better option."

"No, everyone else decided that for me. I don't want the same things you want, Mary. I don't feel for Lucien the way you feel about Isaiah."

"You and Lucien have always been close. Since we were very young."

"Friends, yes, but there is no spark."

"That's what you think love is about? A spark? You need more than a spark when things get hard. When the business you started together is barely making enough money to put food on the table."

"I know that."

"I don't think you do. You're looking for something that may not even exist."

I know the words she's not speaking. The things that went unsaid before. She doesn't think that spark exists for *me*. Because I'm dark, my bosom is heavy, and my waist is thick. She may be correct, but if so, I will let my spark be my music.

"Maybe when I earn the money to go to Paris, I will find a swashbuckling Parisian man who loves exotic Negresses." My words drip with sarcasm, and Mary's eye roll tells me that she feels all my mockery.

"You think earning the money to go to Paris will be easy?"

"I don't think any of this will be easy." But it will be easier than bearing Lucien's children.

"But how will you even get started?"

"I start by leaving Philadelphia, Mary."

Her sigh is defeated, but it needn't be. "Well, you do know that you can always come back home. Lucien may not have you back, but Isaiah and I will always help you."

"I was hoping you would want to sew my performance dresses."

Mary's eyes light up, and she hugs me so tightly that I can feel all the love our sisterhood provides. Even if she doesn't agree with this choice, she can't help but get excited at creating a fancy gown.

"Eliza, you will have the best gowns. After every one of your shows, people won't be able to stop talking about your dresses."

"I hope they won't be able to stop talking about my voice."

Mary laughs and hugs me again. I didn't know how much I needed this acceptance from her. Perhaps because Lucien will never release me to do this with his blessing. It helps to have someone I love and cherish wish me well, even if she doesn't believe in the dream.

"Lucien will be inconsolable," Mary says, her mirth turning somber, "but I am sure his mother will help him find many ways to forget about you."

"Mrs. Brown undoubtedly already has a list of better candidates in mind."

Mary covers her mouth to stifle a giggle. I am making light of it, but even though I don't want to marry Lucien, it still angers me that Mrs. Brown never thought I was good enough for their family.

"Okay, maybe . . . maybe I'm starting to see this thing. You onstage. But I can't help also wanting the other life for you as well. An easier life."

Choosing this life for myself, onstage and subject to the praises or critiques of others, will not be easy. But the alternative is unfathomable.

"Thank you for trying to understand. That's all I ask. Oh, and for beautiful gowns, of course."

"Oh, you have them all. And my love. If you ever need anything, you'd better not hesitate to write. You *must* write."

"I should carry a trunk of paper, ink, and pens for the writing I will do. Thank you for wishing me well, Mary."

"Always."

Now that I have talked to the closest people in my life, I must go home and finish packing for this adventure. I hold back a new flood of tears until all the hugs and goodbyes are complete.

Whatever comes of this journey, I must press forward toward this destiny. I believe in my gift, and I pray that I will never look back and wish I had chosen the path of childbirth and domestication. With ancestry on this soil and across the ocean, I feel a wildness at heart that cannot be tamed by Lucien and his overwhelming love.

My pursuit of freedom will serve another purpose besides ensuring my future. It will free Lucien from this one-sided love story, where he pines away for me and I continue to delay the things he dreams about. He should have a home with a fireplace, rocking chair, and wife. He should have his progeny.

And I shall have my applause.

# CHAPTER TEN

*T*hree days on the Erie Canal Extension in the tight confines of a packet boat have made me restless, so I am ecstatic to board the steamer to Buffalo for the last part of my trip. The last time I took this journey, life was so different. Miss Lizbeth had sent me with an escort, although I had insisted that I hadn't needed one, and a glowing recommendation to Miss Bella. I had been full of wonder but not particularly determined to do anything. A bit spoiled, perhaps, and maybe convinced that Miss Lizbeth was going to live forever. And now everything has changed.

After securing my meager belongings inside my tiny sleeping cabin, I venture to find a seat on the deck to catch a glimpse of the activity on the dock. Since it is only a twelve-hour ride from here to Buffalo, and the warm weather has held, I may sit here the entire time.

I place my guitar case under the bench and nestle in comfortably with my tote full of snacks. I brought freshly baked cookies, and bits of cheese and crackers, things that would keep for my entire trip to Buffalo.

Although I had planned to observe the dockside goings-on, there are interesting sights right here on the ship with me. I watch a man who seems very much past his youth try to wrangle an energetic young woman—maybe his daughter—as she storms across the steamship deck. Her golden curls fly loose from the pins that hold her hat onto her head, and the warm lakefront wind is so brisk that the young woman clamps her hand down on top of the hat to keep from losing it.

The man, who probably isn't as spry as he once was, goes sprawling onto his face after tripping. At this, the woman stops and shakes her head. She seems exasperated as she helps the man to his feet, and he moves considerably slower than he did before the fall.

Once the young woman and her father disappear from my sight, I take the guitar from its case and lightly strum the chords for "When Stars Are in the Quiet Skies." The melody of that song always soothes me even if the lyrics do not.

The young woman from before must've helped her father get situated in his sleeping quarters, because she is back on the deck and unattended. Her eyes dart from one corner of the deck to the other as if she's searching for something to grab her attention. There are an elderly couple, a family with several small children, and a group of older, wealthy-looking women who have managed to have a service set up for their early morning tea. The last group looks very classy in their expensive dresses and hats, making me assume they have traveled from Chicago, the beginning of this steamship's route.

A loud whistle blows, signaling to the passengers that it is time to go. It is nine o'clock in the morning, so barring any emergencies or delays, we should be in Buffalo between seven and nine o'clock in the evening. I sent him a telegram, so Mr. Howard knows to collect me from the dock, and I will finally get to see the home in Buffalo that the girls raved about during their lessons.

The frustrated young woman sits next to me on my bench as I pop a cookie into my mouth. I chew it quickly in case the girl wants to make introductions, although there is no need for her to do that. I am content with sharing only the bench and not my thoughts.

The woman, on closer inspection, is not as young as I thought she was when I saw her storming across the ship with her father. I estimate she is close to my age, about mid-twenties. At once I notice that her dress is of very high-quality silk, and her shawl is cashmere. This is a woman of means. And yet, while dressed quite properly, she's acting quite improperly in plopping down next to a stranger.

"I am so tired of being on this steamship," she says in my general direction.

I am not sure if I am supposed to respond, so I sit quietly and wait.

"Is it safe for you to be here unattended?" she asks somewhat rudely. "Somebody might think you're a slave. Wait, do you belong to someone on this ship? Is that why you feel so comfortable sitting out here playing a guitar?"

Well, now, this is direct enough, especially as I'm the only one on this steamship deck that anyone might mistake for a slave.

"I am not enslaved." I try not to sound offended, but I am not sure that I am successful.

But if I do sound offended, she doesn't seem to notice as she leans in close to me. "Oh . . . are you a fugitive?" she whispers. "Are you on the railroad?"

I close my eyes and press my lips tightly together. I know my irritation is evident. How could it not be? If I was a fugitive, it wouldn't be wise or safe for me to share this information with the first white person who asked me.

"I am not a fugitive," I say in an even and measured tone, trying to add a bit of pleasantness to my voice, remembering that she is a white woman, and I am alone. It is not safe for me to anger her even if she angers me. "I can produce my certificate of freedom for whoever would like to see it."

"Well, that was a stupid question anyhow." She sounds apologetic. "I have forgotten my manners. I'm Electra Potter."

Electra enthusiastically shoves her hand toward me. She's smiling now, so I suppose she might be friendly, even if she is very strange. And rude. I take her hand and shake it gingerly.

"Elizabeth Taylor Greenfield. Is your father well? That was a nice spill he took earlier." I'd very much like to change the subject from fugitives and freedom papers.

She looks confused for a moment, and then she nods. "You're speaking about my husband, John. My father has gone to heaven."

It is now my turn to be amazed. I remember when the church ladies were trying to marry me off to Deacon Odom. I wonder if someone married Electra off to a man old enough to be her father.

"Electra. That is a unique name."

"My given name is Phoebe. It was too drab for my tastes."

*Drab* is not a word that can be used to describe Electra. Her features, taken separately, are unremarkable. Her hair, though styled in very fetching pin curls, cannot seem to decide if it wants to be brown or golden and so it has settled somewhere in between. Her eyes are the same shade of indecisive—a muddy brown. Her nose is a bit too round on the tip and bulbous, and her lips without the angelic pout that many men seem to find attractive.

But there is something about the spark of curiosity in her eyes and the way her lips settle into a tiny smile when not speaking that makes her pleasant to behold. I am also sure that most men would not be able to look away from the creamy skin of her bosom that she has expertly allowed to puff out of the bodice of her bright purple gown.

"What song were you strumming earlier?" Electra asks. "It sounded familiar."

"The song is popular, I believe." I strum the opening bars again and start singing. Electra's eyes brighten with recognition. She sings along with me, slightly off-key, but she does, at least, know the words.

"I should stop!" Electra says. "Your voice is so heavenly that my croaking has no place next to it."

"Oh, don't stop. This is the kind of song that makes everyone sing along."

"Why do you think that happens?" Electra asks.

"People like to sing about love. It warms their hearts."

Electra considers this. "I don't think it's the talk of love that made me want to join in. It was the beauty of your voice. Sing something else."

Electra clearly is used to people moving and doing things at her command. I am singing today at my leisure, so I will decide if I should continue.

"First, tell me how you came to be married to such an—"

"Old bugger?"

I gasp at Electra's crude speech. She laughs, loud and strong, not caring about the fancy lady tea party within earshot of us. They are giving us decidedly harsh and judgmental glances. It makes me a bit uncomfortable, because while I do not hide myself from the world, I do not go out of my way to make a spectacle of myself.

"Admit it," Electra says while laughing. "That is exactly what you were thinking."

"The sentiment perhaps, but not in those words."

"It's all right. People always have that question, but very few are bold enough to ask."

"Are you going to answer?"

"I suppose I must since you are withholding the next song until I do." She says this with a smile, and so I respond in kind.

"I wouldn't say withholding. Simply delaying."

We both laugh, again drawing the ire of the tea party ladies. Electra notices the scowling women and waves over at them. I cover my mouth to stifle my giggle at their expense.

"They should pay more attention to one another. At least one of them is going to faint in this heat with those big hats and tight corsets." I can tell from the scorn in her tone that she has bad blood with some if not all of the women.

"Are you acquainted with them?"

"Oh yes. Society ladies from Chicago. One of them is a friend to my husband's first wife."

"I'm sure she's happy to see the widower being well taken care of."

"Oh, now that is very funny, Miss Greenfield."

We have strayed away from the question, but I appreciate the laughter. It seems I have found a travel companion for the ride.

"This is an aria I learned recently. It's called 'Casta Diva.'"

I lift my left hand to the guitar and lightly strum the strings. Just a few chords for this one. The tea party ladies glance over briefly while I sing, but not long enough to make me think they took notice. When I finish the song, Electra's face is wet with tears. The sad choice of music was on purpose, since I imagine it wasn't a happy love story that has Electra married to a man old enough to be her father.

"You asked how I ended up married to John. His wife died a few weeks after my father died. He needed comfort. My mother and I were penniless and needed resources."

I don't need to ask if she loves him. The defeat in her tone tells an entire story.

"The first song you sang," Electra says, "reminds me of my love. It made me sad, but only for a moment."

"Not John?"

"No. Not him."

Electra stares out at Lake Seneca as if she's lost in thought. Perhaps she's thinking about her choices or the love she left behind.

"Why are you headed to Buffalo? Is it home for you?" Electra asks, snapping out of her briefly pensive mood.

"No, Philadelphia is home."

"Well, why on earth are you going to Buffalo? Philadelphia is a much better place to live. So is Chicago. I'd much rather live anywhere other than boring old Buffalo."

"My employer is there," I say.

I hold back the rest of my reason for going to Buffalo. I know better than to share my dreams with a stranger, especially a white stranger.

"What kind of work do you do?"

"Nothing exciting. I take care of their children."

"You are telling me that you are taking care of someone's snotty-faced crumb snatchers when you have a voice like that?"

"Well, yes. And—"

Before I can piece together an explanation that would make sense, Electra has hopped up from her seat and is marching over to the tea party ladies.

I cannot determine whether I should follow. Did one of the women make a gesture of some sort? Was there another insult that I failed to notice?

Electra's arms flail about as she speaks, but she is too far away for me to see the expression on her face. The other women don't appear to be threatened by whatever she is saying; they seem to be paying rapt attention.

Now Electra is striding right back over to me with a triumphant look on her face. Whatever she said to those women, she must be proud of it.

"Are you ready for a concert, Miss Greenfield?"

"A concert?"

"Yes, an impromptu one."

"For the tea party ladies?"

"And their husbands. They overheard you singing, and they were intrigued. If you will agree to it, for dinner tonight, you will be the entertainment."

My first instinct is to politely decline their invitation. I could feign exhaustion, like a true prima donna might do. I am unprepared. I have only traveling clothes with me. The request is ridiculous, really. Only a Black person would be expected to perform on demand at the whim of a group of privileged white women.

But perhaps this meeting with Electra on a steamship deck was not a chance encounter. It could be divine providence launching me forward to the end I seek. Because aren't these the exact kind of white women whom I need to sing my praises among their peers?

I must keep reminding myself that I am not yet Jenny Lind, and if I want to get anywhere near that stage, my pride needs to be packed far away, into the bottom of a chest along with any doubt or fear.

"A dinner concert?" I ask with a bright and accommodating smile. "How lovely. I would be happy to accept."

I suppose this will be my professional debut.

* * *

WITH ONLY MY guitar and the night air to accompany me, I stand before a group of about fifteen. They have eaten and are ready, but I am a ball of nerves. I try to push the butterflies in my stomach away by imagining myself on a stage with an orchestra accompanying me. The tea party ladies stare at me in anticipation, and Electra, of course, beams with pride.

The first song is something simple. A popular song called "The Cradle Song." The choice is more for me than for the listeners. It helps me warm up my voice, from the lower register all the way to a high soprano. I enjoy the shock on their faces when I open my mouth and those baritone notes come forth. And then their surprise to hear, from the same vessel, notes high enough to shatter their wineglasses.

"Bravo," cries one of the tea party ladies as she comes to her feet with tears in her eyes.

Electra winks at me and stands as well. "Encore," she shouts with glee. "We need more."

And so I sing more. Every song in my repertoire. And when I run out of those, I give them a cappella versions of arias they have never heard. It is a true concert, and the more they applaud and sing my praises, the more I give them.

Electra brings me a glass of water when it seems as if I am running out of steam. The cool drink gives me energy afresh, and I sing yet another aria. I am sure that I pronounce half the words wrong because I am still learning this one, but no one seems to notice.

The crowd grows as I continue, until even the steamship's crew watches and listens. All of them in awe of me out-singing their beloved Jenny Lind. But their awe doesn't come close to matching mine. To plan a thing and want a thing is much easier than seeing the thing through to completion. Providence decided not to give me the chance to get to Buffalo and change my mind.

"You must sing for my friends when we get to Buffalo," one of the tea party ladies says. "This voice must be heard by all."

"Her name is Miss Elizabeth Taylor Greenfield," Electra says. "Remember her name, for when she appears in concert on stages far and wide, we can say we heard her first concert aboard the steamer to Buffalo."

My first concert and an invitation to sing more once I get to Buffalo. It matters not if this is the work of providence or Electra Potter. I will receive blessings from wherever and whomever they come.

# CHAPTER ELEVEN

*A*fter getting to Buffalo and settling in at the Howards' home, I set out for Sunday morning worship at the Michigan Street Baptist Church. Of course, Mrs. Howard invited me to meeting with the Society of Friends, and she didn't seem happy that I declined her invite. But I had fellowshipped at Michigan Street Baptist when I was in Buffalo previously for my music studies. There's something about the singing and preaching in a Black church that is good for my soul, and I am ready to be reunited with my friends.

When I walk through the doors of the church, the mood is somber and a far cry from the joyful atmosphere that I remembered. In the time since I was here last, the membership has grown from a few dozen to nearly one hundred people, and the church is in their new building. There are many new and unfamiliar faces, and they're all Negroes.

Service hasn't started yet, but there are no groups of ladies laughing and gossiping and no children running up and down the pews trying to escape their mothers. The few conversations taking place are in hushed whispers, but most everyone is seated and quiet.

I slide into a pew next to my friend Ruby. Her eyes become saucers, and she squeezes me with her plump, strong arms. There is love in this hug, and I hope she can feel the same from me. I met her on my very first visit to Michigan Street Baptist, and once she invited me to Sunday dinner, we've been like family ever since.

Things happened so quickly with breaking the engagement from Lucien that I hadn't had time to let her know that I was coming back to Buffalo, so my being here this Sunday is a surprise, but her grin, which stretches from ear to ear, tells me it's a pleasant one. She leans back to take a look at me and hugs me again for good measure.

"Eliza," Ruby whispers, "it's been too long. I suppose I will let you sit on my pew, seeing that you've been away for a month of Sundays. You're almost like a new visitor."

"Your pew?" I look all around the freshly shined wood for Ruby Pennyman's name, and sure enough, it says *Dedicated to the Pennyman Family* right on the outside edge.

"Mmm-hmm. That's how we built our new church. The members pledged ten dollars a year for a pew."

"Well, this sure is nice. And not a hand-me-down building either. Built just for a Black church. That's something."

Ruby hugs me once more, but her smile fades and is replaced by a look of concern.

"It's so good to see you," Ruby says. "We were all praying for you after the loss of your dear benefactor. We didn't know what to expect when you left town so abruptly."

"Thank you so much for the prayers. I'm sure I could feel them all the way in Philadelphia."

"Are you here visiting? How long are you here?"

"Girl, that's a long story. I'm going to have to tell it to you over some pie."

"Ooo-wee. Does it have anything to do with that man of yours? Willie Boyd mentioned that he'd shipped some lumber through Lucien Brown's company and that Lucien said you all were getting married."

"Well . . . we were."

Ruby's jaw drops, and she swats at me with her handkerchief.

"Sound like we need more than pie for this catching-up meeting," she says before leaning in close. "Sounds like we need some good ol' hooch."

We can't help but let out a few giggles, but sharp looks from a few of the church mothers quickly hush our mouths.

"What's going on?" I whisper to Ruby. "Why is everyone so glum?"

"Oh, something terrible has happened. A washerwoman by the name of Pearl was arrested by slave catchers and taken south before anyone could step in and speak on her behalf."

"This has happened in Philadelphia too. It's scary for the ones who have finally made it to freedom."

"Well, Pearl wasn't a fugitive. She was a freeborn woman who ain't never seen a plantation."

"Oh my."

"Yes, and everyone's nervous and worried about who could be next."

Hearing this news chills me to the bone. It's a helpless feeling to know that at any moment I could have my freedom snatched away by a greedy plantation owner. Especially now that Miss Lizbeth is gone, and I am making my way in this world without her protection. It makes me think of Armand and Charlotte and their unspoken threats, and the fact that I know very few people here who can vouch for me other than the Howards, and my Black friends. And everyone knows that with this Fugitive Slave Law in place, a whole town of Black people don't hold sway over one white plantation owner claiming to own a person.

Before Reverend Brown gets up to give the sermon, the congregation sings from the hymnal. This is easily my favorite part of the service. Without any direction at all, rich vocal tones rise all through the sanctuary, with harmonies and counter notes as if they had been instructed by Miss Bella. Oh, there are a few sour notes here and there, but instead of detracting from the glory, they blend in with the beauty. This is a time when I join in, and although I could, I never try to out-sing or outshine anyone. I believe the goal is for God to hear us all. A collective prayer. And today's outcry is a troubled one.

A man whom I've never seen before plays chords on the pipe organ as we sing. His skin, a dark, smooth ebony, glistens with perspiration as his fingers expertly navigate the keys. Although he plays as if he was born to it, I can't help but notice that his muscled arms and back suggest that he's no stranger to manual labor. I try not to gaze at him too long, because he is quite handsome (especially how he keeps biting his bottom lip as he changes octaves), and my mind wanders to things that shouldn't be thought of in a church.

After the melancholy singing, Reverend Brown trudges to the pulpit as if he's going to his execution. An eerie quiet descends upon the congregation as he takes his time getting to the podium. A few of the sisters dab at their eyes with handkerchiefs and silently weep. The sadness is almost overwhelming, but it's a shared emotion. Even the children, who are usually oblivious to these things, aren't jostling about in their seats and whining. Everyone seems to be waiting for words of encouragement from Reverend Brown.

"My brothers and sisters in Christ," Reverend Brown says in a low and even tone, "I do not know where to begin or how to help lift our heavy hearts. Ten years ago, we were celebrating the emancipation of our countrymen who arrived on our shores on the *Amistad*, and now our spirits are grieved."

I remember also celebrating the *Amistad* in Philadelphia. It felt like a victory not only for the people who were kidnapped from their homeland, but also for the abolitionist movement.

"These monsters in the South are, more and more, encroaching upon our freedom. And now, with their Fugitive Slave Law, they are marching into our communities and kidnapping our brothers and sisters from their homes and off the streets. To whom can we plead our cause?"

One thing Reverend Brown will never say in the pulpit, because this detail is spoken only in whispers lest someone overhear, is that this very church is a stop on the Underground Railroad. I came to know of Michigan Street Baptist only because of PFASS and our abolitionist work. The fear of discovery is real, especially since many sitting in these pews once fled southern plantations and made Buffalo their home instead of going on across the Niagara River to Canada.

"Many of our members have gone west, in recent years, looking for their fortunes in gold, and we have sent them with prayers on their way. And now we must lift supplication for those who came here not seeking fortune or riches, but freedom from enslavement and the ability to command their own movements."

"Yes Lords" and amens rise from the audience, which is usually quiet when the good reverend speaks. But these words are soul stirring. I find myself moved to also make sounds of agreement.

"Brothers and sisters in Christ, we step through the church doors and prepare ourselves to hear a word from our Lord over this sacred edifice. We search for salvation for our sin-sick souls. This salvation comes only from the blood of Jesus. But today, we speak of a different salvation, one we must rise and take for ourselves. We must rise up, church."

"Rise up!" This shout comes from one of the deacons on the front pew.

"As the abolitionist movement grows in this country, we must be aware that our white brothers and sisters who are in support of our cause do so from a place of comfort. Their wives don't shudder in fear when their husbands leave the house. Their mothers do not have to be concerned about children being sold to the highest bidder. We appreciate and need the support and resources of these very important allies. But our freedom—our salvation—from these demonic oppressors is a thing that we must rise up and demand for ourselves."

The congregation, now sufficiently roused, erupts in a cacophony of applause and shouts. I am on my feet with tears streaming down my face. Despite having never truly known the bonds of slavery, this terror of capture is visceral and real. And I weep for poor Pearl the washerwoman, whom I've never met. She could be me. But for the grace of God, her story could be my story.

* * *

AFTER SERVICE, THE mood is still heavy, but everyone seems to have been at least encouraged by Reverend Brown's words. Little groups converse and hug, perhaps reflecting on the fact that this could be the last time seeing a friend or family member.

Ruby is having a lively conversation with the handsome organ player, and I am hoping for an introduction. I'm standing right next to her and have cleared my throat multiple times, but Ruby doesn't seem to be getting the hint. It wouldn't be proper for me to be forward or obvious, but I'm almost to the point of abandoning all things proper.

Since they aren't talking to me, I take this moment to behold this man in his full splendor. The first thing that strikes me is his height. He does not stoop to make himself appear smaller. He seems quite comfortable in his stature and confident in the amount of space he consumes. That confidence is attractive even without looking at his face.

And his face is God's artwork.

His broad nose is fully African, but his eyes are what really draw my attention. Thick, shapely brows and dark lashes that make his gaze intense and intentional.

Perhaps I should be ashamed for being this moved by the organ player's beauty, since it hasn't even been two weeks since I left Lucien with his engagement ring in the palm of his hand. Alas, I am not ashamed. Not one bit.

"I truly enjoyed your playing this morning," I say, interrupting their conversation, since it seems as if they're going to continue ignoring me. "Did you study abroad, or did you learn to play right here in Buffalo?"

Now Ruby seems to remember that I'm standing next to her. She gives me a sidelong glance and a knowing smile.

"Oh, I am so sorry. Charles Monroe, meet my friend Miss Elizabeth Taylor Greenfield. She is a musician like yourself."

Charles finally turns that gaze upon me, and I feel my breath hitch, but his smile is everything. It is easy, confident, and sincere.

"Hello, Miss Elizabeth Taylor Greenfield," he says with that rich, smooth voice I already admire. Is there anything wrong with him? If there is any defect, I cannot find it.

"Oh, everyone calls me Eliza."

"Well, Eliza, I am very happy that you enjoyed my playing, as rusty and rough as it was this morning. I did some studying abroad, but I did most of my learning right here in America. Do you play as well?"

"Nowhere as expertly as you, I'm afraid," I respond. "I am functional on the pianoforte and maybe even less so on the guitar. But this morning, I heard nothing rusty or rough. You, sir, are downplaying your ability."

Ruby bursts into laughter. "And you are downplaying yours, Eliza. I am sure the good Lord is pleased with all the humility this morning. Charles, Eliza's voice is truly special. I've never heard anything like her singing."

"I would love to hear it," Charles says with what sounds like hope and anticipation in his voice. Or that could be wishful thinking and imagination on my part. Maybe he's simply being polite.

But I do hope he doesn't ask me to sing right now, because I can barely think of two notes to string together with him gazing at me this way, much less a song.

"Perhaps you could accompany me," I say, echoing his friendliness. "I have an engagement very soon where your musical talent would be appreciated."

"An engagement here in Buffalo?" he asks, now with furrowed eyebrows and genuine interest, not just good manners. Maybe he's impressed by this. Or maybe not . . . What if he doesn't care for a woman who has a vocation? Perhaps I should have kept this to myself.

"Yes. At the home of a white society lady I met on the steamer here from Philadelphia."

"You met her on the steamer and left with an invitation to her home?" Charles chuckles. "This must be some voice. I can't wait to hear it."

"Why wait?" Ruby asks. "Come to my home for dinner this evening. William and I would be honored to have you both, and then you can continue this conversation."

Charles leans back on his heels and gives Ruby a playful grin. "I would never turn down a meal at your table, Sister Ruby. Count me in."

"You know I'll be there, Ruby," I say as I loop my arm through hers. I wish I had time to go and bake a pie for dessert.

Charles makes a little bow to both of us. "Ladies, please excuse me while I go greet Reverend and Mrs. Brown. I look forward to the evening."

As he walks away, I get to behold his beauty from another angle, and I am not disappointed. His legs are slightly bowed, his back broad and muscled. I want to bake pies for him. And cake. And cookies, muffins, bread, and biscuits.

"Whew, my Lord," I say.

Again, Ruby laughs at my expense. "I'll make sure I have my smelling salts at the dinner table."

"I highly recommend that you do."

It must have been providence and a move of God that had me attend Michigan Street Baptist this morning. *This* surely would not have happened at a meeting of the Society of Friends. Hopefully, nothing sinful transpires this evening that causes me to repent.

## CHAPTER TWELVE

*A*fter dinner, Ruby and William, our gracious hosts, make excuses to disappear into their bedroom, leaving Charles and me alone to sip our coffee and converse across their dining table. The proper thing probably would have been for Charles to escort me home, but I am enjoying his company too much to make this suggestion.

Unlike the formal dining rooms I'm used to in Philadelphia, with tables meant for entertaining, Ruby and William's home is cozy and mostly used only for their small family. I am most certain that William built all the sturdy, well-used furniture himself, and the room is lit only by a few candles in the center of the table. I appreciate the soft lighting not only for providing an intimate setting, but hopefully hiding some of my flaws.

"I thought they would never retire," Charles says.

My eyes widen at his boldness, but we both erupt into laughter. I have never felt this disarmed by a man and beside myself, but it is a good feeling.

"So, tell me more about where you learned to play like that. Do you read music?"

Charles nods. "Oh yes, I did study abroad. You asked me that earlier. I once had a wealthy patron who took me to Paris with his family."

"It is nice to have those kinds of patrons." I wonder if the patron is white, but I am not bold enough to ask.

"Well, it turned out to be quite disastrous, I'm afraid. I did leave with a great musical education, though."

"Oh no! *Disastrous* is a very strong word."

"And one that describes the situation completely. The patron was a man with a stubborn daughter whom he wanted to marry off. His patronage came with matchmaking."

"Ah, and you were not interested?"

Charles shrugs as he sips his coffee. "I was a penniless urchin after my father's blacksmithing business was run out of town by his white competitor. I was in no position to be against marriage to a young woman from a wealthy family."

"*She* wasn't interested?"

I hope my tone doesn't sound too incredulous, but I cannot imagine any woman anywhere who could be impervious to Charles's charms. Aside from his good looks, his wit and humor has me already smitten.

"She was not interested in the attentions of any man, which is why her father was so desperate in his matchmaking that he would pay for my musical education."

Confused, I ponder this for a moment, and then it becomes clear. I have heard whispers of women who prefer another woman in their bed instead of a man. Once, I heard that rumor about Miss Lizbeth, because she had no interest in remarrying after her second husband died, even though she was already an old woman when he passed.

"Well, at least you escaped the ordeal with your talent."

Charles laughs. "Still penniless, but talented."

We laugh again, even though there is nothing funny about being poor. Although, if I didn't have one foot planted in the poorhouse myself, I wouldn't even be here talking to this man. I would be in Paris studying with some famous vocal coach.

Charles sets his cup of coffee on the table, which draws my attention to his hands. I remember how swiftly his fingers danced across the organ's keys, and now I long for those same fingers to be entwined with mine. Suddenly, the room feels warm.

"Ruby raved about your amazing voice all evening," Charles says. "Let me hear it now. I've grown impatient."

"How demanding you are."

"Are you going to continue to tease me, fellow minstrel?"

"No, I won't, but Ruby and William's children are asleep. I don't want to make too much noise."

Charles stands. "Then join me outside in their garden. There we can make as much noise as we want."

This man's flirtations have my insides feeling sweet and gooey like strawberry jam. But I find myself rising from my seat as well. I never felt this way with Lucien; nothing about Lucien ever left me yearning for him or wanting more. But here tonight, proper or improper, I cannot resist an invitation to spend more time with Charles.

Charles gives me his arm to grab hold of as he guides me to the garden. It's twilight, and the evening's breeze has cooled things from the warmth of the late-autumn day.

"Now we're outside, away from the children," Charles says as he sits on a nearby bench. "Will you bless me with a song?"

Charles asks this as if I would ever be able to resist a request from him. Even if I wanted to, I believe my vocal cords would open on their own and grant his every wish.

"Let me think . . ."

I purposely choose a light and feminine aria that shows off my soprano range. It's fun and upbeat and in French. I think I'll perform it during my concert at Electra Potter's home, so this is good practice. It was one of my favorites to sing with Miss Bella, and I am sure when I resume my lessons next week, she will start with this one, among others. But let's see if I can get over my nerves to sing it tonight.

At the very beginning of "Salut a la France" are four ear-shattering high notes that transition into a waterfall of descending notes. It certainly grabs the attention, and Charles's reaction is appropriate.

"Encore! Encore!" Charles shouts when I am finished.

I give a huge, exaggerated curtsy before falling onto the bench beside him. "I have eaten too much of Ruby's pot roast for an encore."

"That was amazing, Eliza. I don't know what I was expecting, but it wasn't that."

"Thank you."

"I know the song was in French because I could pick out a few words, but what was it about?" Charles asks. "Was it about a lost lover or a newly found romance? It seems like most of the arias I've heard are about one of those."

"You are correct about most arias. This one, however, is all about the lady's love of France."

Charles chuckles. "That is a safe choice for an evening with a new friend."

Charles extends his arm across the back of the bench, and I can't help but notice the closeness of his touch. I am also keenly aware of his masculine scent, which reminds me of pipe smoke and shoe leather.

"You asked me this, and now I'll ask you," Charles says. "Were you trained abroad? I have heard opera singers, and I have never heard a more impressive soprano."

"Not yet, but that is my plan. I'm saving money to go to Paris, because it is very hard for me to find a teacher in America. My only instruction has been right here in Buffalo, and Miss Bella tells me there are limitations to what she can teach me."

"You will get to Paris, then," Charles says without hesitation.

This is so different than Lucien's and Mary's reactions, and they are the ones who love me most. How can he be so confident about this when he's only just met me?

"How can you be so sure?" I ask him. "Are you a fortune teller?"

"Anyone who gets on a steamer to Buffalo from Philadelphia and sings her way into an engagement at a rich white woman's home must be pretty tenacious," Charles says.

I laugh out loud, remembering I'd invited him to play for me. "So, will you accompany me at my engagement, then?"

"I didn't think you were asking in earnest."

"I was. Mrs. Electra Potter tells me that she has a beautiful pianoforte. I know it's different from an organ . . ."

"I play pianoforte as well."

"Splendid. I think we will make quite a formidable pair. Your gifted playing and my singing."

Charles scoffs. "My playing pales in comparison to your singing."

"Well . . . they are coming to see me, so I think that will be fine."

Charles laughs and laughs until there are tears in his eyes. I am trying not to compare him to Lucien, but I can't stop myself from thinking of the ways in which they are different. Lucien never gave himself over to mirth this way. I have seen him amused, but his seriousness keeps him from enjoying moments like this.

"I love hearing you laugh," I blurt before I can stop myself. If I wasn't too forward before, this most certainly is. "I'm sorry. You must think I am most unladylike."

"There is nothing unladylike about a compliment. I haven't laughed like this in months."

I wonder what could've stolen his joy. A part of me marvels at this the same way I was always surprised when Mary was sad or heartbroken. Clearly beauty does not shield a person from life's harsh realities.

"I am happy to bring you joy, then."

"Thank you for this evening, Eliza. And yes, I will accompany you anytime you ask."

My insides warm at the thought of spending more time with Charles.

But just as quickly, I chide myself for feeling this way. Lucien has already floated to the back of my memory, but I carry guilt from the pain I must have caused him.

Perhaps I should quiet my thoughts and continue down this serendipitous path. And if there is a reckoning that comes from what happened with Lucien, then I will look to providence to guide me through it.

# Chapter Thirteen

With the date of my engagement approaching, the giddy excitement of my eventful steamship ride and budding friendship with Charles gives way to something different: a sense of sheer terror at what is to follow.

So in preparation for not just the concert, but for Europe, I have returned to my teacher, Miss Bella. I'd like her to hear the selections I've chosen. Standing before her, with the straight posture she taught me, best for pulling air into my diaphragm, I admit feeling nervous. Her assessments always come with a bite. Her words are most times sprinkled with vinegar. Compliments are rare, and even then, they are intertwined with admonishments.

Yet, Miss Lizbeth believed she was the best who would teach me on this side of the Atlantic. I can hardly afford to pay her without my inheritance, but if I truly wish for these small, in-home concerts to be my launching pad, people must leave the evening feeling as if they just left the concert hall.

Even though I impressed my fellow steamship passengers with my current level of singing, this will never do for Miss Bella. She will uncover and lay bare every flaw until perfection emerges. And then we will do this again and again, for song after song and aria after aria, until I have a flawless repertoire.

Modest is perhaps an understatement in describing Miss Bella's studio. It is pristine and white, with unblemished and undecorated walls. The only furniture is the necessary—Miss Bella's pianoforte, also white and pristine.

The diminutive yet still intimidating Miss Bella struts around me, silver tresses pulled into a bun so tight that it slants her eyes. Her heavy heels click in time with her cane as she looks me up and down, silently taking note of every little detail. As her eyes linger on my midsection, it makes me wish that I had not eaten the second biscuit with my breakfast.

"You're looking well, Eliza. It is good to see you in my studio again."

"It is good to be back, Miss Bella."

"Let's get straight to it, then. For your warm-up, an *accentus acutus* of your choosing. Legato."

Of course Miss Bella would go for one of the most difficult warm-ups. An *accentus acutus* is simply an ascending string of six notes in which I modulate on each one. Each note has several modulations, and the entire string is done in one breath. Since she specified legato, there is no rushing through, quickly hitting each note. Every note must be drawn out. The exercise shows the strength of my diaphragm and breathing. Before I left Buffalo to be at Miss Lizbeth's deathbed, I was performing this task easily.

I wet my lips, inhale deeply, and then hold for a moment before exhaling. When I draw in a second breath, Miss Bella taps her heavy cane on the floor.

"You're stalling. One and two, and one, two, three."

On my cue, the notes come forth, but the delivery is sloppy and ragged. Halfway through, I know I'm not going to complete the *accentus* in one breath.

"Again." With the flare of her nostrils and the irritation in her tone, Miss Bella shows her displeasure.

I attempt the phrase a second time, and the result is the same. I am unable to finish in one breath. It is the progression of notes that is giving me trouble. One note or even a trill with two notes would be effortless, but this is beyond difficult. It feels impossible and yet I know it isn't.

"Singing is thinking, Eliza. Before you open your mouth, before you release a sound, you must analyze the work set before you. An almost instantaneous calculation must happen. As you learn to command your voice, you will know exactly how much breath to expend on each syllable."

"I understand."

"You should. I have already taught you this. Now execute. Again."

I do a little better this time. I have to shorten the very last note, but at least I make it to the end. I smile, triumphant, but Bella shakes her head and frowns. She is not satisfied.

"You write to me ahead of your arrival claiming you are ready to be a prima donna. You say you take inspiration from the Swedish Nightingale. She was here in concert in July. Her performance was nearly flawless."

Of course Jenny Lind has been to Buffalo by now, but I didn't realize it was such a short time ago. People will compare us, and I am bound to be the one spoken of in unfavorable terms. Even if I am better than she is. Especially if I am better.

"I have heard Miss Lind in concert myself. My range is better than hers. She must duet with a man for bass or baritone notes."

"Better range or not, you stand before me with half-baked cookies. What is a half-baked cookie but mush? I would rather have them burned to a crisp. You are supposed to bring me bel canto. Beautiful singing."

If she had not chastised me for my less-than-perfect singing, I would be entertained by Bella's rant. This is how she prunes every one of her students, but with me, she cuts harder and deeper.

"You have taken too much time away from daily practicing. It will be difficult for you to reach your maximum potential. You waste my time, Eliza. Go back to Philadelphia and marry that nice young man."

My nostrils flare with frustration and perhaps a little arrogance.

"I have booked engagements here with this less-than-perfect voice. Electra Potter has invited me to sing for some of Buffalo's elite."

Bella kisses the back of her teeth with her tongue. A sound that I am used to hearing from Black women.

"Electra Potter wouldn't know good singing if it came up and wailed in her ear. She lacks culture, and you have not practiced since you left Buffalo."

"I have done more than practice. I have taught myself guitar and pianoforte."

"These are props. Accoutrements. These are not your gifts."

"Well, it was enough to hold the attentions of the passengers of an entire steamship." I sound arrogant and overconfident in my self-defense, but I do not care.

"Listen to yourself. I do not recall you being so puffed up." Miss Bella cackles. "There is no greater instrument than the human voice, and yours is ragged and undisciplined. Perhaps in six months, with a grueling daily practice schedule, I can get you almost ready to be heard by an audience."

"That is too long."

Bella shrugs. "Well, you are the one who has neglected your gift. Change my mind. Sing it again!"

Determined now to prove her wrong, I narrow my eyes and concentrate. For the last time, I take in a massive breath, filling my lungs with air. Fully focused on the exact number of notes and the full amount of breath I need to execute, the notes, this time, flow smoothly. The task is complete. Every note sung with a puff of breath to spare.

Miss Bella lifts an eyebrow. "Perhaps it won't take months, then. Should I pepper you with insults at the beginning of each practice, so we can get right to the part where you sing it correctly?"

"No, Miss Bella. That will not be necessary."

"All right, then. Now give me an aria."

My entire body relaxes, and the frustration dissipates. It is time to work, and Miss Bella will ensure that I do.

* * *

IT HAS BEEN three weeks since I got to Buffalo, and the practices with Miss Bella have progressed well. Tonight is the concert at Electra's home, and while I know I am ready, there is still a nervous anxiety in my spirit.

I pace my bedroom humming an aria in a light vocal warm-up. The space is much larger than the room in Philadelphia at Ophelia's, but it still pales in comparison to my suite in Miss Lizbeth's home. Electra has sent over multiple bouquets of flowers to congratulate me for the night's concert, giving my bedroom the fresh fragrance of a spring meadow.

Perhaps this is not just preperformance nervousness. This could have something to do with the letter I received from Mr. Howell. There has been another hearing on the matter of the will, and still there is no solution. The cousins have presented so-called witnesses from the South, whom we do not know, who suggested that Miss Lizbeth was coerced into abolitionist activities by her Northern friends.

Of course, Mr. Howell has had several members of the Society of Friends testify about Miss Lizbeth's being a pillar in our Philadelphia community and that her abolitionist activities were not coerced but the result of crises of conscience.

I am infuriated by this foolishness, although Mr. Howell begs me to be patient and insists that I shouldn't take things personally. He says that whenever there is a fortune left behind, there is often this amount of litigation before things are settled. But I cannot help but take things personally when that Southern scoundrel and his wife showed up at Miss Lizbeth's funeral, salivating over me like chattel to be bought and sold. I believe if they could have done so, they would have put me in shackles then and carried me back south with them.

Mr. Howell and other Northern whites, in my opinion, don't always treat these slavers with the disdain that they should receive. These people are the worst kind of monsters. I have seen the massive tangles of scars on the bodies of men and women. I've tended to open wounds. And I know that when they look at me, they do not see an equal or even a person. So, no matter what Mr. Howell says, it is a personal matter.

There is a tiny knock on my bedroom door, so light that I nearly miss it. It must be one of the girls. They are so worried about beginning school this term. It is an elite school for girls as wealthy as they are. I have no idea what terrible things they are imagining will happen, but I know that things will go fine for them. Maybe always. Their beauty, status, and whiteness will have them never want for any need or pleasure.

The freedoms they possess are things I can't convince them of, because they are liberties that I do not have myself. The only lessons I can teach these girls are the ones found in their schoolbooks.

When I open the door, I am surprised that the almost inaudible knock came from Mrs. Howard. Annabelle, as she wishes to be called. Although she doesn't have a vocation outside of rearing her children, and rarely entertains visitors, she rises every day and dresses herself as if she expects to receive formal guests. Her simple brown hair is parted in the middle, the style of the day, and she is wearing a corseted gown. Perhaps choosing her dress, jewelry, and hairpin are the highlight of her day, or maybe she does these things to please Mr. Howard.

"Oh, do come in," I say. "I took my time responding because I thought you were one of your daughters."

"Do they worry you? They have been insufferable with all this school talk." Annabelle invites herself to the velvet armchair in the corner of my room, so I suppose this will be a social visit.

"They don't bother me at all. I am tickled by their excitement."

"And once they find their friends and start sharing notes about who they fancy at meeting, they'll forget they ever fretted about it in the first place."

"So very true. May I help you with something?"

When we were in Philadelphia, Annabelle made several overtures of friendship, but we never got to know each other very well with my living under Miss Ophelia's roof. Now that we're here in Buffalo, in her home, I expect we'll have more opportunities to get better acquainted.

"I was hoping I could help you."

Annabelle places a beautiful blue-stone brooch in my hands. I turn it over and examine its golden metalwork in the shape of a rose. The blue stones have been ground and shaved to fit into small openings in the metal.

"It's for your concert at Electra's estate. Not that your voice alone won't command the crowd. It will," Annabelle says, her voice full of kindness. "Besides, the late Mrs. Greenfield would have wanted you to go out into society looking like a proper lady."

I am so overwhelmed by Annabelle's consideration that I almost don't know how to respond. It is something that Miss Lizbeth would have done. She would not have wanted me to look or seem like someone who was just hired to perform. She would want everyone to know that I had been groomed for this. Educated for this purpose. Miss Lizbeth would want the crowd assembled in Electra Potter's home to feel privileged to behold my gift in such an intimate setting.

"This is so thoughtful of you." I struggle to hold back my tears, thinking of dear Miss Lizbeth. "Thank you so much, Annabelle."

She clasps her hand over mine. "You are so welcome, dear. It sounds strange saying 'Electra's estate.' John is an associate of Hiram's, and I was cordial with his late wife, although we weren't friends. She was much older than I am, but she was a lovely woman."

"And Electra?"

"Oh, I am sure she is delightful." Annabelle looks down at her dress and smooths out wrinkles that aren't there, avoiding eye contact. "I didn't mean to imply otherwise."

I think she absolutely *did* mean to imply something other than delightful. But I think she wants me to draw my own conclusion. Annabelle is much too polite to overtly besmirch Electra's character—not when Electra has been so kind to me.

"She has been a dear," I say. "I am very grateful she was on that steamship with me."

"I can only imagine such a meeting being ordained by heavenly hosts."

"I hope those same angels are with me tonight. My debut comes on the heels of Jenny Lind's concert here in July."

"Hiram's friends in the Buffalo Musical Association are still talking about that. I hate that we missed it while we were summering in Philadelphia. They had gone through such lengths to convince her to come here, and she did not disappoint."

"That's exactly what I am worried about. She didn't disappoint. What if I do?"

"Eliza, your voice is amazing, and you will do a great job. I'm sure of it. I will stay up late, and you can tell me all about it over a cup of tea."

"A midnight tea party?"

"Those are where the juiciest stories are told, and more often than not the tea is whiskey."

I lift my eyebrows in surprise, and Annabelle laughs. I thought her too proper and too Quaker to sneak whiskey into her teacup.

"Don't tell Hiram. He'd be very disappointed in me being such a pitiful influence on you."

"Except that I am a fully grown woman not too easily influenced."

"Of course, Eliza. You look so young sometimes. I forget that I am only a few years your senior."

It is true. Annabelle is only thirty years old, and though I trail her by only three years, she looks at least a decade older than me.

"Maybe it is I who is the poor influence."

Annabelle cackles. "Hardly. You're such a virtuous woman."

I think of all the time I have been spending with Charles and feel a twinge of guilt. We have been virtuous enough—in our actions—but I can't control the things I think when we're rehearsing together.

"I haven't been feeling very virtuous lately."

"I have noticed your new friend," Annabelle says with a knowing glance. "I didn't want to pry into your personal business."

"He's a musician from Michigan Street Baptist. He's going to accompany me at my concert tonight."

"Oh, I see. Well, you couldn't find a more handsome accompanist."

"I didn't choose him for his looks. He is very gifted."

"I'm sure he is."

"Mrs. Howard!"

"Forgive me," she says with a laugh. "Hiram would wonder what has gotten into me today."

Not only Hiram. I wonder if she's already snuck a little whiskey into her teacup. She is quite free with her words.

"I wish I had gotten an invitation to the Potters' house," Annabelle says. "I suppose I have not entered that society circle as of yet."

Ah, now I understand why Annabelle is acting strangely. Perhaps this is why Angelica and Diana are so apprehensive about their new school. Affluent and white though they are, they are still outsiders here, not yet part of society.

"How does one find herself in those circles?" I ask, knowing for certain that this circle is not for me.

"I am not entirely sure, but I do know one must be invited."

I remember what Electra had said about the ladies on the steamer. They hadn't seemed very welcoming to her. If they had been, she wouldn't have been conversing with me on the deck. She would've been sipping tea and cackling with them.

Perhaps it is possible for a lady on the outskirts to create her own circle. And then make that circle so deliciously attractive that others will find it impossible to resist. I believe I find myself the attraction for Electra's new circle. But I do not mind it if it results in patronage and concerts here and abroad. In fact, I welcome it.

# CHAPTER FOURTEEN

$C$harles and I arrive at the Potters' mansion at precisely the requested time. My official invitation states six o'clock in the evening, with dinner to be served first and then a performance of four songs. Charles and I will not dine with the guests, however, even if that was implied with the invitation (and I believe it was), because I cannot eat a large meal and then sing.

From the outside, the mansion is enormous yet understated, which makes me think it was built while the first Mrs. Potter was still alive. Electra strikes me as someone who would want her home to be unique and eye-catching. The large, ornate door knocker with its elaborate scrolling and craftmanship around an oversize letter $P$ does, however, seem worthy of Electra's tastes.

"I wish I had something more elegant to wear," I whisper to Charles as we wait for our knock to be answered.

"You look very nice, Eliza. It is I who am dressed like a simpleton."

My dress is a plain pale-blue brocade with a slightly plunging lace-trimmed bodice. The empire waist flares out, removing the need for a tight corset. I would probably perish in this heat trying to sing in a corset, although I have done it on occasion. I avoid heavy meals in the days before I perform so my midsection does not appear bloated in any way. Countering the plainness of the gown are Annabelle's pin and the jeweled earrings gifted to me by Miss Lizbeth. Since she cannot be here to see how her charge has fared in the world, I will wear something to remind me of Miss Lizbeth every time I am before an audience.

Even with these adornments, I am sure my attire will not be up to par with that worn by Buffalo's elites. Hopefully, they will be distracted by Charles, who can wear a burlap sack and still be stunning.

The door is opened by a young Black man, who looks surprised to see us standing there.

"Brother Charles!" the young man says gleefully as he invites us inside.

Charles and the young man embrace, and then I remember where I know him from. He and his wife attend Michigan Street Baptist, and I think they have a little one. I can't recall his name, though, so I hope Charles knows it.

"You look lovely, Miss Greenfield," the young man says.

I give a sidelong glance to the ballroom to the left of the entrance. It's illuminated with gas lamps along the walls and an intricate chandelier. There is no dancing, but the room is buzzing with conversation while a harpist plays softly. The men are dressed sharply in suits, and the women in long, bustled, and ruffled gowns. They all look as if they're going to the opera. I am indeed underdressed, and this young man is being kind with his compliment.

"Thank you."

"You see the young lady in the pink gown?" the young man whispers. "That's Mary Fillmore."

"Brother Patrick, do you mean President Millard Fillmore's daughter?" Charles asks.

Patrick! That's his name. It sure took Charles long enough to say it. I've had half a conversation with him while desperately searching my mind for a clue.

"Yes. She's usually with her father in Washington, D.C., on account of his wife being so sickly, but she and Mrs. Potter are quite friendly," Patrick says. "She comes here for tea. Well, I think they're drinking tea, but I can't be entirely sure."

A chuckle nearly escapes as I think of Annabelle and our midnight tea party. I didn't know that so many proper ladies snuck whiskey and other spirits behind their stuffy husbands' backs.

I guess I shouldn't be surprised that Electra is friends with someone as important as the president's daughter. She seems to situate herself however she pleases.

"They are in for some good music tonight, I see," Patrick says. "I knew Miss Greenfield was going to sing, but I didn't know you were playing."

I feel myself relax as we follow Patrick away from the ballroom down another hall. Luckily no one sees me in my less-than-spectacular attire.

"I am here to do Miss Greenfield's bidding, Brother Patrick," Charles says. "Are the Potters your regular employers or you only here for the evening?"

"Oh, yes, sir. I'm usually a butler of sorts to General Potter, but Mrs. Potter paid me extra to help this evening."

"They pay well?" Charles asks.

"Yes, they do. I heard the general talking about needing someone to accompany him on his longer trips. Want me to put a word in for you?"

"Yes, sir. I sure appreciate it."

I admire how Charles gets right down to business with just about everything he wants. I could learn a few things from him.

"Here's your dressing room, Miss Eliza. Charles, do you want to stay with her, or would you like me to introduce you to General Potter?"

"I don't want to talk business to the man while he's trying to enjoy his evening," Charles says. "It can wait."

"He hates these parties and would welcome a conversation where he feels in command," Patrick says. "He won't be angry at all, and it will give him an excuse to escape the political conversation he has no doubt been dragged into by his friends."

Charles takes my hand, and I feel a tingle. He pauses as if he feels it too, but perhaps I'm being silly. I may be interpreting his good manners and kindness for another type of interest.

"Will it bother you if I go meet Mr. Potter?" Charles asks. "If he has work, I need it, and this may be my only chance."

I shoo Charles and Patrick out of the dressing room. "Go, go. I'll be fine. I need to warm up anyway, and that doesn't require assistance."

Once they've gone, I avail myself of the fresh tea that's been set out. While it is the perfect temperature and quite tasty, it does nothing for my nerves. The president's daughter and probably many of Electra's guests were at Jenny Lind's concert in July, and now they're waiting to hear me sing.

The tea has done its work on my throat, so now it's time for scales and vocal warm-ups. Quietly at first and then increasing the volume as I feel my vocal cords come alive. Even with my nervousness, the notes flow easily and smoothly. I think Miss Bella would be pleased.

There's a knock on the door. But, before I can open it, the door cracks open and Electra pokes her head into the room.

"Eliza! I didn't know you were here. Why didn't Patrick bring you to the party? We're assembling for dinner."

Electra strides into the room with outstretched arms as if this is a reunion of old friends. She hugs me lightly and makes kissing sounds near my ears, but her lips do not touch my face. Although it feels strange, I do the same.

"I'd much rather enter after dinner when it is time for me to sing."

"A grand entrance." Electra does a twirl around the room. I wonder if that's supposed to be an imitation of my entrance. If it is, that is hilarious, because I would never twirl like that. "This is perfection. I left you tea—did you have some?"

I nod and motion to the half-full cup on the small table. "It was delicious. Thank you."

"Everyone is excited to hear you sing. We've been talking about your impromptu steamship concert all evening."

"Make sure you serve them strong wine with dinner," I say, only half joking. "That way they'll be in a generous mood with their applause."

"You don't need their generosity," Electra says in a serious tone. "You will have patrons after this, I promise you. Or I should say additional patrons, because you already have me and General Potter."

"Thank you for your support. This feels like a dream."

Electra squeals. "This is not a dream. Tonight is your debut. You have a crowd of all of Buffalo's elite to impress."

"Enjoy your dinner and spare a prayer or two extra for my nerves."

"I will, even though you don't need them!"

I can hear Electra's shrill laughter as she moves away from the door. Her confidence in me puffs a bit more air into my sails. It is funny the things that go through my mind in the moments before I perform. I know the range of my skill, and what I've practiced, but there's an insanity that happens right before my name is called. Sometimes I think I'll forget all the words. Other times, I feel my throat will close and no sound will come forth. All irrational, and foolish, but no less terrifying. Miss Bella says these frights are common to performers and that I should work hard to overcome them with practice and peaceful time to relax before I begin. For now, it helps to have someone like Electra come and tell me wonderful things about myself, but hopefully, one day soon, I'll be able to encourage myself.

\* \* \*

SILENCE ENGULFS THE ballroom where I am set to perform, and the only sound I hear as I enter is the clicking of my boots on the marble floor. Several rows of chairs have been set just a few feet away from the pianoforte, where Charles sits beaming at me. I focus on his smile and not the curious glances from the audience, who don't seem to know what to expect.

I nod in greeting to the audience and then to Charles. Charles lifts his hands to the pianoforte to play the opening of our first song, when Electra Potter hops up from her seat. My eyes widen and my concentration is shaken, but I motion for Charles to wait.

"Forgive me, Miss Greenfield," Electra says, "but I cannot let you begin without a proper introduction. I came upon Miss Elizabeth Taylor Greenfield on the deck of a steamer on my way here to Buffalo. Her vocal gift is so amazing that she entertained the guests on the vessel for the entire journey. Tonight, you are about to bear witness to one of God's natural wonders. I have been to opera houses from New York City to Paris and have not heard a greater talent. She is a rare gem. Now please prepare yourselves to be amazed."

Electra eases back down into her seat while giving me the most gracious smile. I am sure it was not her intent to add pressure when I am already nervous enough, so I will not charge that to her heart. But I am sure the spectators in the front row can see the butterflies flitting in my stomach through the material of my gown.

Again, on my signal, Charles lifts his hands and plays the introduction to my favorite song to perform, "When Stars Are in the Quiet Skies." I sing the verses as I normally do, showing my full range as the song progresses. I see more than a few shocked faces at my baritone and then the typical pleased smiles at the soprano.

The ones who seemed unmoved by the first song seem to change their opinion with "Salut a la France." I don't know if it is the upbeat and fun tempo or my singing the lyrics in French that cause a few to stand and applaud, but their enthusiasm lifts my spirits further.

Next is the most challenging piece tonight, "Casta Diva," an aria peppered with notes at the top of my range but easily reached. In Italian, the aria is not a love song but a prayer. When Miss Bella first sang it for me, even with her long-ago-diminished high notes, it brought tears to my eyes, like it had when I heard Jenny Lind perform it in Philadelphia. Tonight, it does the same for several ladies in this crowd. I do mispronounce a few words throughout the complex lyrics, but I doubt there is anyone in this room with keen enough ears to notice my mistakes.

My final song is "Home Sweet Home," the same rousing popular piece I did for the PFASS meeting. Now there are some singing along with me, or at least moving their lips as I move mine. It is an easy song to sing, with a simple melody, but I love it because I can belt out the notes and sing with my full power throughout.

I hold the last note for what seems like an impossible amount of time, then dip into a low bow amid cries of "Encore!" Electra has risen from her seat again, along with several others, but not enough to constitute a standing ovation.

Charles and I had prepared for an encore, so he immediately starts to play. I repeat the last verse and hold the note again, but this time I wait for the applause to erupt before I bow. Very few have decided to remain in their seats during this round of clapping.

Spent and parched, I close my eyes for a moment to concentrate on breathing. Then I feel arms around me, moving me from my spot, guiding me. I open my eyes to Charles's handsome face.

"Come sit, Eliza. You need to have water and maybe something to eat."

"Only water," I say. "I can eat later. I need to talk to people tonight."

Charles leaves me seated at a dinner table as the partygoers' chatter begins. As the hostess of the party, Electra strides up to me with a familiar face in tow. It's one of the ladies from the steamer. She's much older than Electra but has attempted to cover that gap with a very elaborately curled red wig. I forgive her hideous hairstyle, because her golden silk gown is becoming, and on her bodice, she wears an eye-catching sparkling peacock pin.

I try to rise, but it is a struggle. "Eliza, you look completely exhausted," Electra says. "We will sit."

Both Electra and the tea party lady sit across from me beaming. I feel anxious and surrounded and tired. I know I must talk to them, and be wonderful and cordial, but oh, how I hate this part. Undaunted, I force a smile onto my face.

"I am spent, but I am enjoying myself," I say to Electra. "I hope you both liked the songs tonight. Some of them you heard on the steamer, but not with the pianoforte."

"Yes, of course we liked your singing. We loved it," Electra says. "This is my friend Catherine, Mrs. Richard Martin. She and her husband were quite pleased and want to have you sing at their holiday party. I didn't know if you would be here over the holidays."

"I plan to be." Unless a huge promoter discovers me and takes me on a European tour, but I don't need to discuss that with them yet.

Someone calls Electra, so she excuses herself. I expect Mrs. Martin to walk away with her, but instead she switches seats and takes the chair next to me. I glance around the room, looking for Charles to rescue me, because I am not in the mood to converse.

"You know my holiday party is the toast of Buffalo," Mrs. Martin explains in a hushed tone, as if she doesn't want to be heard bragging, but I doubt there's anyone in this room who isn't aware of her thoughts on the matter. "Nothing like this."

My jaw drops at her candor. I glance around quickly to see who might have heard, but Mrs. Martin chuckles.

"Don't worry, dear. Most of us are here because we heard your voice on that steamer and wanted more. That is all."

I glance across the room at poor Electra, trying her best to impress the women of this tightly woven social circle while one of its queens is telling me it's all for naught. But maybe I shouldn't pity her too much. She didn't invite Annabelle this evening, so she's also intent on leaving someone out. A social circle wouldn't be exclusive if they let everyone in. There must always be someone on the outside of things.

"For my holiday affair, we will have many things to discuss," Mrs. Martin says. "Everything must be planned. From your musical selections right down to your clothing."

The way she says clothing—with a bit of disdain as she wrinkles her nose—worries me.

"I do hope I'll be able to live up to your standards," I say nervously, scanning the room for Charles, desperate for an escape.

"If I may, I do have one bit of advice on the subject of your appearance," Mrs. Martin says.

*No, Mrs. Martin. You may not.* Where is Charles?

"Your gown is beautiful, and the color is suitable," she continues, without being given permission, "but, because there are those in America who will be offended by someone of the Black race baring so much flesh—"

My eyebrows shoot up in surprise. What flesh? There is hardly any bosom showing. There's nothing heaving. I find this gown modest and tasteful, but I'm too shocked to even respond. And even if I could respond, what would I say when this woman is offering me another opportunity?

"—you may want to try something more genteel," she continues. "A gown with a high neck and a dark color, preferably black. And always, always wear gloves, dear. No one will be able to speak on your virtue if you adhere to these things."

"Th-thank you." I manage to stammer.

"I only mean to assist you. If you'd like to succeed, and I do believe there is much opportunity for you in this vocation."

So many other things occur to me to say, but I cannot make the words cross my lips. I'd like to tell her that clothing does not determine virtue. And that I never asked for her advice. But nothing comes out. I can hardly inhale.

The worst part is the look of satisfaction on Mrs. Martin's face. I am sure she thinks she has accomplished a good deed this evening.

Finally, thankfully, Charles approaches. But he's accompanied by an older, bespectacled, gray-haired white man, with a look on his face like he also wants to converse. Also, Mrs. Martin does not leave my side, although I am sure I do not want to speak with her any more tonight. God forbid, she may have more advice.

"Miss Greenfield," the white man says, "my name is Gerald Reed, and I would like to personally congratulate you on your debut. I would also like to arrange a meeting with you and the president of the Buffalo Musical Association, Hiram Howard, so that everyone in Buffalo might have the opportunity to hear you sing."

My eyes stretch wide as I burst into laughter, now cured of my inability to breathe. Charles joins me as well, but poor Mr. Reed looks both confused and slightly offended by our sudden lack of decorum.

"I am sorry, Mr. Reed," I say once my laughter fades a bit. "I am staying with the Howards. I met them in Philadelphia and teach their daughters music and other lessons. I would appreciate your discussing me with Mr. Howard. He has not yet heard me in concert, only singing in the house, and has not witnessed a true showcase of my vocal abilities."

Now understanding, Mr. Reed gives a tiny smile. "I presumptuously thought you were here in Buffalo with no contacts at all other than Mrs. Potter. I will speak to Hiram myself about more performances."

I notice that Mr. Reed addresses this last sentence to Charles, as if he is the one in charge of my comings and goings. Charles is here in my employ and will be given a portion of whatever wages Electra deems fit to give me. No one ever assumes a woman is making her own choices, not even a talented one.

"Thank you. I look forward to hearing more about this, of course," I say, drawing Mr. Reed's gaze away from Charles and back to me.

"Perfect. I'll say good night, then. I am sure you are quite tired after gracing us with such a powerful voice," Mr. Reed gushes. "I must say, I thought there was some sleight of hand or ventriloquism act when you sang those deep notes as well as any man."

"I understand. God bless you, and good night."

As Mr. Reed goes off to speak with other guests, Charles extends his hand and helps me to my feet. He offers to assist Mrs. Martin as well, but she waves him away and stands on her own.

"Eliza, do not forget what I said. We will be in contact about the holiday affair."

After she walks away, Charles leans in and whispers, "What is it that you have to remember?"

"Oh, it was nothing."

Because that's exactly how I feel about her advice. It's a nugget of nothingness that I wish I didn't have to adhere to or follow, but I know that rebellion against women like Mrs. Martin may hinder the glorious career I seek.

I recall how enraptured the audience had been with Jenny Lind at her concert. How angelic and pure she'd looked in her shoulder-baring shimmering ivory-silk gown. She was the epitome of virtue, and she had shown more flesh than I am displaying tonight. I'm sure no one gave her a lecture about gentility.

What is it about my dark skin that equates with vulgarity in Mrs. Martin's mind? I have never been touched intimately by a man. Not even kissed. Lucien was careful never to insult me in that way, and I've had the extreme good fortune of protection and shelter from any untoward advances from strangers or familiar villains.

But even with all this sanctity, piety, and purity, Mrs. Martin still imagines me as an erotic temptress. Is it the darkness of my flesh alone that causes her to think this? Am I like a wild berry picked from the vine? Inherently sweeter and more tempting as it ripens and darkens? If the latter is the case, then it is not my virtue that is the concern. The one who snatches and devours the fruit from the vine without permission is the villain, not the fruit itself.

But it is always the Mrs. Martins of the world who are sent to ensure gentility is upheld. To make sure their villainous men do not embarrass them. Somehow, their spouses and sons can be trusted to look upon the creamy flesh of Jenny Lind, but my darker skin is too tantalizing a treat.

"But she did give me an idea," I say to Charles as he escorts me out of the Potters' mansion. "I must write to my seamstress friend in Philadelphia to fit me for a few concert gowns. It seems like I am going to need them."

And none of them will be black. Or have a high neck.

## CHAPTER FIFTEEN

To Annabelle's dismay, the Sunday after the concert, I choose to attend Michigan Street Baptist again and not go to meeting with the Society of Friends. I suspect she wanted to show me off a bit to her friends, especially since she wasn't high society enough to make Electra's guest list. But, even though I cherish the friendship of many Quakers, I do not prefer being the only Black person in their spaces. I want the solace of my friend Ruby, to hear good preaching, and to lay eyes on that fine man again.

Besides, I am not Annabelle's prize Negro. It feels too much like what happens on plantations when Master and Missy strut their best slaves out for their company. I take care of their children for wages, and I hope a friendship naturally progresses from that arrangement. Until then, I will worship with my own community.

Now Charles and I are having Sunday dinner at Ruby and William's house again. And Patrick has joined us with his plump but pretty wife Darla. I couldn't come empty-handed this time, so I rose very early to bake a butter cake for dessert. It pleases me to see Charles greedily cut his second slice. There's something about a man gobbling up something I prepared that makes me feel warm inside.

"Eliza, Patrick can't stop talking about your concert at the Potters' house," Darla says as she also enjoys a second slice of cake. "I sure wish I had been there to see it. Sometimes I cook for them or take in their wash, but I'm usually not there for their parties."

"It went much better than I thought it would. Mostly because I was able to look at Charles the whole time, and he kept on smiling and encouraging me the whole way," I say in earnest.

Charles waves his hands in the air and shakes his head. "Don't be modest, Eliza. Your voice was the star of the evening. There were a few times when I almost stopped playing, because I was in awe of you. It was really something to behold."

"We been listening to Eliza in church for years," Ruby says. "These white folk been missing out. We already knew about her."

"That's right," I say, with just the right amount of pride and a wink at Ruby for good measure.

"Someone wrote something about you in the newspaper, Eliza," William says as he passes a folded newspaper page to Charles. "Look here, Charles. Read it out loud, so I don't have to grab my spectacles."

"A newspaper article? About Friday night?" I ask. I want to grab the newspaper myself, but I wait patiently for Charles to unfold the pages.

"'A few months ago, there was a clamor for the Swedish Nightingale,'" Charles reads. "'Instead, give us the Black Swan!'"

"The what?" Ruby shrieks. "How in the world did they come up with that?"

"Hush, Ruby, let him read it," Patrick says. "I want to hear what else they say."

Charles continues. "'In the home of General J. Potter, at the invitation of his lovely wife, Electra, I heard one of the most powerful voices to ever give a concert in this city. Mrs. Potter discovered the vocalist, a Miss Elizabeth Taylor Greenfield, on a steamer to Buffalo and convinced the unpolished talent to abandon her teaching career for one on the stage. A free Black woman, of medium size and distinctly African features, she did not have the look of a typical prima donna, but once she opened her mouth to sing, any doubt was sufficiently cast aside. She graced us with four selections, with the highlight of the show being the aria "Casta Diva" (Bellini). Her range is at least three octaves, from the strong baritone to the soprano. If I was not watching closely, I would not have believed that the low notes emanated from Miss Greenfield. The talent is indeed a credit to the fine Philadelphia education and upbringing that Miss Greenfield received from her recently deceased former mistress. I expect that we will hear and see more of the Black Swan in coming months, here in Buffalo and abroad. Where is Barnum?'"

My jaw is slack with surprise. I suppose I should be ecstatic that someone has written an article about me singing at a private party. But there are so many objectionable things in the piece that I can't quite muster the appropriate amount of joy.

"First of all, swans aren't black. They're white," I grumble. "And do they sing?"

"It seems to be a poor take on Jenny Lind's nickname," Charles carefully explains, as if I didn't already figure that out. "But I suppose since us Black folk don't have a country, they just said black?"

"Am I not American?" I ask. "Yes, my father was born in Africa and moved back there when I was little, but I was born right on a plantation in Mississippi. 'American Swan' would be better."

"But are you offended at being called Black?" Charles asks. "Are you *not* proud of being Black?"

The question is infuriating and annoying, and I am offended by it, even coming from Charles. But there is something about the reviewer making note of my race that does bother me. I simply don't know how to make these feelings plain.

"I am proud of being me. And I am Black. But why was it necessary for him to say that? No one ever marvels when white people do anything."

"Yes, but when they say, look at this amazing *Black* woman," Charles says with such passion that I'm captivated by his words, "they are reminding the ones who think we are not humans that we are."

Immediately, the insult I felt dissipates.

"And what does he mean 'medium size'?" Ruby asks with a chuckle. "Are you supposed to be a petite thing like that white woman they're comparing you to?"

"Not eating cake like this," William says as he chomps another bite of the butter cake. "But we like you the way you are."

"Only a dog wants a bone," Charles says. Then he, Patrick, and William have a good, bawdy laugh about that.

"Awww, don't look at the negatives, Eliza," Patrick says. "This is a good thing. Your name is in the newspaper, and even though the article is a bit strange, he raves about your talent."

"What does 'Where is Barnum?' mean at the end?" Ruby asks.

"That's what I mean," Patrick says. "They said 'Where is Barnum?' 'cause that white fellow P. T. Barnum is the one who's touring Jenny Lind all over the country. I hear he's become a rich man behind her sold-out shows."

"So they think Barnum should come take Eliza on a tour?" Charles asks. "Shoot, Patrick and I can set up concerts and transportation, and I bet she'd get a bigger share of the profits too. What do you think, Eliza? Do you want me and Patrick to manage you?"

"We can have a discussion about that when I'm ready," I say, not prepared to commit to anything yet.

I still have an entire repertoire of music to learn from Miss Bella and performance costumes to have created by Mary, and things are not safe for three Black people launching a tour around the country. But I am not going to dim anyone's enthusiasm tonight, especially not Charles's. Not when he's gazing across the table at me like I'm the treasure he's searched all over the world for and finally found.

* * *

THERE IS A frigid chill in the night air as Charles walks me home after our dinner. Fall weather in Buffalo is so unpredictable. I was worried that it would snow and that we'd have to trudge home through the slush, but it is dry, and the sky is clear.

A white man I don't recognize has crossed the street and is now walking behind me and Charles. His steps are more rapid than ours, and I feel my heartbeat quicken. If we don't know him, then it means he doesn't know us, or the fact that we are free. Charles pulls me in closer and loops my arm in his. He then guides me closer to the buildings and slows his steps to allow the man to pass. I don't think I breathe until he does.

"How does it feel, Eliza, to make money from your craft?" Charles asks when the man has moved out of earshot.

I was pleasantly surprised at the envelope Electra pressed into my hand at the end of the evening, which contained fifteen dollars. I gave five dollars to Charles (and I do think that was more than generous) and kept the rest. More than a month's wages to sing for two hours.

"It feels amazing. I have managed to save quite a bit by living with the Howards and spending frugally, but the payment for the concert felt like a windfall."

"You may be able to afford to rent your own room or maybe an apartment if you continue this path. And then I won't have to bring you home to the Howards."

The smile that teases my lips is a sad one. Charles sounds like Lucien in this moment, but I understood Lucien's concerns. As of today, Charles and I are only friends. After those first moments of flirtation, I haven't felt anything that I could interpret with certainty as a romantic overture.

"Well, I don't mind living with the Howards. I don't want anyone questioning my virtue as a single woman living alone. I wouldn't want to give them anything salacious to talk about."

As we pass a shop window, I glance at our reflection. My arm hooked in Charles's arm—we appear to be a couple. Then I examine Charles's face. The stubble on his chin, the heavy lashes that frame his eyes. If the passersby could know my thoughts, they would find plenty salacious things, and they would indeed question my virtue.

I want to ask Charles what he's thinking, but I am afraid to know. What if I misread his signals? I would rather imagine that he finds me attractive than know for sure that he doesn't. But what if I haven't misread the signals, and he is interested in more than friendship?

As much as I enjoy the warmth of Charles's touch, gazing at his face, and inhaling his scent, I don't know if it is wise to begin anything that looks like a courtship. Would it lead to the same crossroad I just fled? Choosing between a family and singing? The strong attraction I have to Charles will serve only to make the decision more difficult.

I will not pelt Charles with questions when the answers may remove this wonderful feeling I have. The answers can come later, and the decisions as well. Tonight, I will enjoy simply being a woman and walking arm in arm with this mouthwatering, lust-inducing man.

# CHAPTER SIXTEEN

$\mathcal{S}$everal times today my mind has revisited the idea that Charles placed there about having my own apartment or room. Especially now, as I am trying to commit this new aria to memory and Angelica and Diana are making a ruckus. It's not their fault that the piano is in the dining room, right in the running path to their bedroom. But, Lord, I wish they would find something quiet to do.

Charles squints at the sheet music and plays the introduction for the fourth time. Twice he's missed a few notes, and once, Diana shrieked at Angelica about a book they're sharing. Perhaps we should try practicing another day when the girls are at school. Maybe we should use Bella's studio.

Hiram walks into the dining room holding a stack of envelopes. He's a man of short stature, so when he enters a room, he does so with loud and heavy steps. I think he wants people to feel he's much more intimidating than he is, and that may be why he wears a full beard as well. But Hiram is so friendly that his ready smile cancels out any fright he may have caused with his entrance.

He flips through the mail and smokes his pipe as if Charles and I aren't trying to rehearse. With his cherry-scented smoke filling the room, we will certainly have to do this in another location. I cannot sing with smoke coating my vocal cords.

"There's something here for you, Eliza," Hiram says with a mischievous grin on his face, but I am nervous to receive any mail at all.

I always dread receiving a letter from Lucien, or worse a letter from Mary with bad news about Lucien.

I turn the smooth, ivory-colored envelope over in my hands. My name is drawn in magnificent golden calligraphy, and there is no return address. It almost looks too beautiful to open.

"I wonder what that could be," Hiram says, still grinning.

Charles and I both eye him suspiciously, but since it doesn't seem like he's leaving the room anytime soon, I go ahead and rip the red wax seal on the back of the envelope. Inside is a folded sheet of paper. I narrow my eyes to read the elegantly written words.

*Dear Miss Greenfield,*

*Having witnessed your vocal abilities and giftedness at the residence of Mr. and Mrs. Potter, several members of the Buffalo Musical Association have entreated our president, Mr. Hiram Howard (of whom you are well acquainted), to extend an invitation for you to perform at Townsend Hall for the general public on the twenty-second of January. Upon acceptance of this invitation, and confirmation with Mr. Howard, we will discuss compensation and all particulars pertaining to the concert. We truly hope that you will accept and bless the rest of Buffalo with your exceptional talent.*

*Regards,*
*Benjamin Mills, Buffalo Musical*
*Association Treasurer*

After reading the note over twice, I look up at Mr. Howard while blinking back tears of joy. An invitation from the Buffalo Musical Association. In a *real* concert hall. Not a church and not someone's ballroom.

"What does it say, Eliza? Is everything all right?" Charles asks.

Unable to form words yet, I hand the note to Charles so that he can read the good news. I think he reads it more than once too, because for a good long moment, Charles is silent. Then he slowly stands from the piano bench, rushes over to me, and hugs me so tightly that he lifts my feet right off the floor.

"Eliza, this is . . . I don't even know how to describe this," Charles says.

"Me either," I respond, because to me it does feel as if this can't be happening in real life.

"I do have to say I was at a loss for words," Hiram says, "because I had no idea how talented you are, Eliza. I've heard you sing in the house, but nothing like what my colleagues reported."

Charles goes back to the pianoforte and plays the opening for my aria, this time getting all the notes correct. I give Hiram a little thirty-second show with the first verse. The look on his face is pure wonderment and amazement.

"Well, good heavens, Eliza," Hiram says. "No wonder they insisted on giving you an invitation."

"Townsend Hall is a large venue," Charles says. "How many people does it seat?"

Hiram sticks his chest out proudly. "Nearly one thousand guests can see a show at the same time at Townsend Hall."

"Will Black people be able to attend?" Charles asks.

Hiram seems shocked by the question, but Charles does not allow Hiram's discomfort to make him take the question back. With all the Black friends I have in Buffalo, it makes sense to ask.

"They are not expressly disallowed," Hiram says truthfully. "Usually, the Black people have their own shows at different venues."

"It would be nice if they were allowed at this concert. With everything going on in the country, it might do our spirits well to hear Eliza sing," Charles says.

"Eliza, do you have an opinion about this?" Hiram asks, turning his attention away from Charles.

"I agree with Charles. I would enjoy seeing my friends in the audience. Most of them have heard me sing in church, but this is entirely different."

The look of discomfort has left Hiram's face, but he still appears to be undecided. He and Annabelle are both strong abolitionists, and I live quite freely and comfortably under their roof.

"Will the great men and women of the Buffalo Musical Association be unable to enjoy Eliza's voice with Black and brown faces in the room?" Charles asks.

"That is a peculiar question seeing that Eliza is a Black woman, and it is she who has received the invitation," Hiram says, sounding offended. The look of defiance on Charles's face tells me that he cares very little about Hiram's feelings.

"So, it's settled then?" Charles presses. "You'll see to it that Eliza's friends may attend the concert?"

"I will take your request up with the Buffalo Musical Association," Hiram says.

"Over whom you hold great sway, since you are their president," Charles says. "I believe, Eliza, that we can tell Ruby and William to procure their finest concert attire for the evening."

"Please excuse me, I have some urgent business to attend to." Hiram rushes from the room looking quite cross and perplexed.

Charles's eyes follow Hiram as he leaves the room. When we hear the door to Hiram's study close, Charles gives me a knowing glance, and I shake my head. Another moment of Charles's directness that I envy and admire. Of course, I want my friends at the concert, but I would have never pressed the issue with Hiram and perhaps ruined the opportunity set before me.

When a few moments ago the house seemed full of noise and activity, now it is eerily quiet. Charles sits back down at the piano and plays a few chords. Then he stops.

"Eliza, you should stand up for the things that are important," Charles says. "Especially now, when you are coming into a time when your gifts are in demand."

Like most men, Charles seems not to be content to let his example teach me a lesson. He also must follow up with a lecture. For as wonderful as they can be, they can also be insufferable in the next breath.

"I will remember that," I say.

"It will be critical that you keep these things, your demands, at the forefront of your mind as these opportunities come your way," Charles says. "Because when you become famous, you will be able to open doors not only for yourself, but for Black people everywhere."

"I will see what unfolds after this concert, Charles. Nothing may come of it. I still would like to pursue more education in Europe, and perhaps I need that before I am to have any true fame. The whole reason I'm here in Buffalo is because Miss Bella is the only vocal teacher in America who will train me."

"More education? Eliza, you may require a tutor here and there on how to pronounce words that aren't your native tongue, like any other singer would. But your gift is from God, and it needs very little grooming. What will these Europeans be able to teach you that you have not already mastered?"

"I don't know, but I will not allow my lack of training to be the straw that people grasp on to when they want to compare me to the likes of Jenny Lind."

"Don't allow those comparisons to make you doubt yourself. Today, they have invited you; tomorrow, they will be clamoring for you. If we do this properly, you will not have to worry about that inheritance you might never claim."

He says *we*, as if these are decisions and choices he must also make. He's reminding me of Lucien with all his plans and his advice.

"I will have my inheritance," I say with conviction, even if I am unsure. It bothers me that he doubts it, because he is not here to rescue me. I don't want or need him for that.

"If those white people allow it. This is something you can control on your own. I bet P. T. Barnum is a rich man now, all because of Jenny Lind's American tour."

"Is that what you envision? Is that why you said *we*?"

Now Charles looks as offended as Hiram had a few minutes ago. He stands and crosses the small space between us. Taking both my hands in his, he looks deeply into my eyes, his hurt feelings apparent. I see nothing nefarious in that gaze, but I realize I cannot be trusted regarding Charles. I can hardly breathe with him looking at me this way, much less make rational business decisions.

"What I envision is everyone in the country knowing your name. I envision you singing before the president. If I am by your side, and I hope to be, then I will bask in your glory and cheer you on from the shadows."

If he is by my side how? As my manager or as my husband? I have not agreed to him managing my career and he has not suggested anything other than friendship.

"Then, please, let me take this one moment at a time," I say. "This is everything I hoped for when I left Philadelphia and got on the steamer."

"When you broke your engagement with your fiancé in Philadelphia," Charles says in a way that is almost an accusation but not quite.

I take two steps away from Charles and puff out my chest defiantly. I don't regret that decision, and how dare Charles accost me over it? He hardly knows me, and he certainly doesn't know Lucien or the circumstances of the engagement or what led me to break it.

"We should never have been betrothed. The entire affair was a mistake. How did you come to hear about it?"

"It doesn't matter," Charles says, softer now, with less bite, but I haven't forgotten the previous sting.

It does matter, because whoever shared the information did so for a reason. Was it a man who shared it as a warning about my character? Or was it perhaps a woman who may be interested in having Charles for herself? Has my sudden appearance derailed someone's plans? I hate that I even care enough to wonder. If someone had conveyed similar news to Lucien, I would not have been concerned at all.

I am both overly smitten with Charles and insecure about whether I should allow myself to be smitten at all. It is an uncomfortable situation, one that I can barely manage with the anxiety of my newfound fame.

"Let us perfect this aria," I say to Charles wearily. "I intend to sing it at my concert."

I do not turn around to see if Charles complies with my request. I simply wait for the music to begin. When I hear the opening bars, I can exhale and begin.

One thousand and one thoughts rush through my mind about Charles. I wish I knew if he had any romantic intentions toward me, but I am too frightened to ask him. And must a woman ask at all? Lucien, at least, was clear with his attraction. He found me pleasant to the eyes, when most men find me homely, because of our close bond of friendship and the kindness I'd shown toward him when no one else would. But what about Charles? Is he drawn only to my gift and the potential fame? What if Charles is simply tolerating the stars in my eyes so that he may bask in my glory? I am not a simple woman. Charles isn't like Lucien, and I am certainly not his only option.

Perhaps I am being foolish even allowing myself to have these feelings at all. My devotion should be firstly to my music and to this gift. If there is any left over for love, it will come later. Because I am starting to have doubts about whether these two masters—the gift and love—can coexist.

# CHAPTER SEVENTEEN

*Buffalo, New York*
*January 1852*

A week before the concert at Townsend Hall, Hiram arranges a dress rehearsal with the Buffalo Musical Association orchestra. Miss Bella, here to supervise me and give pointers after the rehearsal, walks across the stage tapping her cane. I cannot guess what is bothering her, but I'm trying to enjoy my first moments standing on this stage. Hopefully the first of many large stages.

While the orchestra warms up, and a disgruntled Charles gets settled in at the pianoforte, Bella approaches me with a furrowed brow. Honestly, I don't wish to hear any complaints, but I know Bella does not care about my wishes. She is the teacher, and I am her student.

"What is the matter?" I ask, not waiting for her to divulge.

"Your friend, the accompanist, is asking the wrong question of Hiram Howard. He is worried about other Black people attending the show, but he should've been concerned about the quality of this orchestra. It's sparse. Hardly an orchestra at all."

I feel myself relax. This is nothing to fret about, in my opinion. "No one will blame me for the quality of the orchestra."

"The critics will blame you for everything that happens during your concert."

Bella struts over to Charles, the cane marking her steps with a dramatic flourish that gives a glimpse of how she might have behaved if she'd gotten the chance to be a prima donna herself. I scan the faces in the audience for their reactions. I would have preferred a closed rehearsal, but Hiram had insisted that members of the press and the Buffalo Musical Association be allowed a preview to help with ticket sales. But if they had agreed to open it up to Black concertgoers, all of the tickets would already be sold. Perhaps it was a hasty decision to tell Ruby and William to prepare their concert attire, because Hiram has still not told us if Black people will be allowed to attend.

Finally, Bella nods to me that we are ready to begin the rehearsal, and not a moment too soon. The observers seemed to be tiring of the wait, and the longer it takes to get started, the more time there is for my stomach butterflies to flutter.

My voice is in excellent form as I easily perform the three rehearsal songs, one popular and two arias. Even the orchestra that Bella maligned did well. The observers give me a standing ovation, and I can see Hiram's toothy smile all the way from his seat. He is well pleased.

A rare smile graces Miss Bella's lips at the conclusion of the rehearsal, and it is with outstretched arms that she congratulates me. I have never seen her in such high spirits.

"It was almost perfection, my dear. Ask for whatever you like, because you will have them in the palm of your hand after this. The articles written about this rehearsal will be complimentary. I suspect every promoter from here to Philadelphia will want to take you on tour after this show."

I say nothing about Charles and Patrick's plans to manage a tour, but I agree with Bella that they won't be the only ones to make the offer if all goes well.

Charles joins me and Bella on the stage. "You did well, Eliza, but I think the last time you sang 'Salut a la France' you held that last note and did a little flourish. It was like a waterfall of notes. You started high and then tumbled down the scale to a big finish. I think you should go back to that ending."

Bella gives Charles a slow blink, and my hand flies up to cover my mouth.

"Are you her vocal coach? Her lover?" Bella asks, and now my hand drops to my side, revealing my shocked expression.

"I am neither," Charles says.

"Correct. You are the accompanist with aspirations of being the lover. I am her vocal coach, and I say she sang 'Salut a la France' to perfection."

"Is there no room for any other opinion?" Charles asks. I can tell he is offended, but I am not getting in the middle of this. Besides, Bella is right. The flourish he's referring to was quite accidental, and I am not even sure I can accomplish it again. Certainly not in concert while singing a very demanding list of songs for the evening. Charles, in his overzealous desire for me to do well, may be overreaching.

"No," Bella replies firmly.

She doesn't give Charles time to respond. Instead, she strides over to Hiram and one of his fellow Buffalo Musical Association members as they step onto the stage.

I am glad that Hiram approaches us before Charles gets to continue his conversation with me, because I also do not want to hear his objections regarding Miss Bella.

"Good evening, Charles," Hiram says, giving Charles the acknowledgment Charles seems to think he deserves. "Eliza, every time you open your mouth to sing, I am amazed that I didn't know."

"Don't worry about that now, Mr. Howard. You paid me to teach your daughters, not to sing."

"Indeed, but your voice is so unique that I'm still embarrassed to have had it brought to my attention by my colleagues. I'd like to introduce you to Sherman Chambers. He was one of the men who signed your letter of invitation. He also writes for the *Buffalo Daily Herald*."

"It is a pleasure to meet you, Miss Greenfield. I intend to give your rehearsal a spectacular review. It is well deserved."

"Are you going to mention in the article that Black people will not be allowed at the concert?" Charles asks, speaking out of turn.

"That point is still an ongoing discussion, and not appropriate for Mr. Chambers's column," Hiram says, clearly incensed that Charles has brought this up.

"I disagree," Charles says. "Many of the Buffalo Musical Association, including yourself, profess to believe in the equality of Black people. So, if you need to garner support for the decision, public discourse is a good way to do that."

"I would like the public discourse to be about Eliza's singing, but I understand your point. I'm sure Mr. Chambers will consider it." Hiram gives his associate an apologetic nod, probably hoping to cover for Charles's lack of decorum even if he doesn't need to apologize for Charles's actions.

I want my friends to see me in concert, but I know that this will not be the only chance for them to see me sing. If I am successful with this, there will be many, many concerts and countless occasions for my friends—even my loved ones in Philadelphia—to see me sing. And they already have, even if it's been in church. But if I fight too hard on this one point right now, I may not have another opportunity to sing in a concert hall like this one.

For so many reasons, more than Charles understands, it is important for me to achieve prima donna status. It's more than money. To bring my mother home I require power and influence. And to move about the country without someone being able to kidnap me and take me to a plantation in the South, I need people to know who I am. I can only do that by singing before large audiences like this one, and once I am able, once I have fame, I can open doors for others to walk through.

"Thank you, Mr. Chambers," I say. "I am glad you enjoyed my rehearsal. I hope you will attend the concert."

Mr. Chambers's eyes gleam as he takes my hand and squeezes it. "I wouldn't miss it, young lady. Take care not to debate too much with these fine gentlemen. Save your voice for the stage."

We laugh—well, Hiram and I laugh; Charles glowers—as Mr. Chambers tips his hat to us and leaves with the other journalists who came to see my rehearsal. I hope that they were all as impressed with me as Mr. Chambers, and that they tell their friends.

"You both do understand that it is a wonderful victory to have Eliza headlining a concert at Townsend Hall. The invitation is a milestone," Hiram says.

"They compare Eliza to Jenny Lind and then throw her crumbs," Charles replies sourly.

"Not crumbs. Five percent of the ticket sales, a private dressing room, and the full Buffalo Musical Association orchestra to accompany her," Hiram says firmly, letting Charles know that he is done arguing. "This is good for Eliza's first public concert. I must go and speak with my colleagues. Please, enjoy your evening."

"Thank you, Mr. Howard." I am sincere in this sentiment even if Charles is silent. "I appreciate everything you've done."

Hiram's warm smile lets me know that he does not blame me for Charles's impatience. I feel fortunate for that, at least.

"You're letting him off too easily," Charles says when Hiram is out of earshot. "You could've had exactly what we're asking for if you had spoken up with me."

I turn to face Charles, and even though it might cause tongues to wag, I take one of his hands. I want him to leave his anger and activism for a moment and join me in my reverie.

"Can we celebrate that this is happening? I'd like to do that now. Look around. This stage. That orchestra. Soon, all these seats will be filled with folk who paid to see me perform."

Softening, Charles gazes out at the seats with a mournful expression. Then he looks at me.

"I want to be as joyful as you are about this, Eliza, but how can I be when they are content to toss crumbs to only a few of us? They say they are abolitionists, but our brethren are still in chains. Meanwhile, they live, gather wealth, and consume art. I cannot rest while only a few of us are free, and even the free are not equal to whites."

I squeeze tight the hand that holds on to mine. Again, I admire his passion for freedom and equality, even if we believe in different methods. So if I can admire in the midst of understanding his frustration, can't he try to feel even a small part of my joy?

* * *

EVEN THOUGH I didn't exactly ask for their help, Ruby and Annabelle have joined forces and descended upon my bedroom to choose a dress for my concert. But neither of them is a substitute for Mary. I wish she was here to help me decide or, even better, to create something new for me to wear.

I have taken the two choices out of my closet and spread them across my bed. One is an emerald-green damask with a high neckline and puffy sleeves. The other is a heavier golden brocade material, with burgundy embroidery. What I love about the second gown is the bare shoulders and neckline.

"These are the only ones I have that are appropriate for the occasion," I say. "I am leaning toward the golden one. Remember, I can't be heavily corseted with either. I must be able to breathe."

Annabelle walks over to the bed and examines them both, while Ruby sits in my reading chair. I suppose she needed only a quick look before making up her mind.

"What do you think, Ruby?" I ask, while Annabelle continues to deliberate.

"Neither of them. What else do you have in that wardrobe?" Ruby says. "Both of them are boring and not befitting a prima donna."

"I have not reached that status yet, I don't believe."

"You sing as well as Jenny Lind, or at least that's what the newspaper said," Ruby says. "So, if she's a prima donna, then so are you."

"The green one is a bit too virtuous, and the golden one is too bold," Annabelle says. "We need something that falls somewhere in between."

"I don't see anything wrong with bold," I say, remembering Mrs. Martin and wanting to rebel against her not-so-well-meaning advice. "Besides, I don't have time or money to buy anything else, so I have to choose one."

"If you wear a petticoat with that green one, you might very well suffocate right on the stage," Ruby says.

"Indeed—"

"Electra Potter should have purchased a performance gown for you, or had one commissioned, since she is going around town telling everyone she's your patron," Annabelle says with a bit of ire, as if she's been holding this information for a while and it's been bothering her.

"A patron would purchase a dress?" Ruby asks the question I'm thinking, as I don't exactly know what all a patron would do.

"Perhaps. I think she feels responsible for Eliza in a way."

"Responsible." The word crosses my lips but doesn't sit right with me for some reason. Perhaps because it implies that I am a child who requires a keeper.

"Well, in that she presented you to Buffalo society," Annabelle explains. "There was, of course, more than one reason for her to do this. It wasn't only out of the kindness of her heart."

"I thought it was because she enjoyed my singing on the steamer."

"Of course she did. But it was a chance for her as well. To make a name among the women who haven't really embraced her," Annabelle says.

I haven't heard very much from my patron, though, since I sang at her home. She hasn't called on me or sent a note. Perhaps she's gotten what she needed from that one interaction, and additional mingling is not required.

"You must understand, Eliza, that as you rise in fame and notoriety—and you will rise—there will be many who want to hitch their wagon to your success. It will soon be very hard to tell the difference between friend and opportunist," Annabelle says.

"Which do you believe Electra is?" I ask.

"I believe she's a little bit of both, but you will have to decide that for yourself."

"So, what does this have to do with the dress tonight?" Ruby asks. "I'm enjoying your thoughts about Electra, but we don't have much time, and these options are . . . abysmal."

"Abysmal? They aren't so bad," I say. "You sound like Charles."

"Tuh," Ruby says. "You ought to listen to a man when it comes to what is pleasing to the eye."

There is a loud and angry knock on my bedroom door. We all exchange glances, knowing there could be only one person who'd dare to make that level of ruckus in this home.

"The girls said you were all in here," Hiram says from the other side of the door. "If everyone is decently dressed, I'd like a word."

I nod to Annabelle to open the door, because I don't know why he sounds so cross. She can deal with her angry husband.

Slowly, Annabelle eases the door open. Hiram's cheeks blaze red with either anger or frustration, and his usually calm demeanor is absent.

"What is the matter, Hiram?" Annabelle asks, taking her husband's hand, administering a calming touch.

Hiram trains his infuriated gaze in my direction. "Eliza, Charles is downstairs in my living room with a Mr. William F. Johnson. Please come down and speak sense into them before they ruin the entire concert."

"Isn't William F. Johnson that blind lecturer?" I ask Ruby. "How does he know Charles?"

Ruby shrugs. "Who knows how men know each other? There's no telling."

Worried more by Hiram's fury than Charles and his guest, I rush downstairs, with Hiram on my heels. Both Annabelle and Ruby step out into the hall and watch over the staircase railing. I don't blame either of them for not coming down; their perch is a safer one.

"Eliza," Charles says, "I've brought someone for you to meet. This is William F. Johnson, and he is here on a lecture tour. He read about your concert in the newspaper and wanted to meet you."

Although Charles has an angry scowl on his face, Mr. Johnson is the picture of calm. He's a slim and neat man. His hair and mustache are groomed to perfection, and he's wearing a crisp pressed suit and dress shirt. His hands rest atop his walking stick, and his lips are turned up into the tiniest of smiles. I don't understand why Hiram seems so out of sorts, unless he assumes the worst because of his previous dialogue with Charles.

"Hello, Mr. Johnson," I say. "It is an honor to meet you. I've heard great things about your lectures."

"The pleasure is mine, Miss Greenfield. I did come here to meet you, but I also was hoping to speak with Hiram Howard for a few more moments," Mr. Johnson says. "He cut our conversation short to find you, but my dialogue with him is much more urgent. I seek a favorable decision for Buffalo's free Black community regarding attendance at your concert, Miss Greenfield."

"And I have told him," Hiram says, frustration punctuating his words, "that the most we can do is allow Blacks into the gallery area for the show. I have at least convinced the rest of the board of this much."

The corners of Mr. Johnson's mouth twitch, the only sign of his irritation. Every other action is calm and measured. "A segregated concert with only the inferior seating for Black people is not the concession we are hoping for," he says. "You see, until we are treated as equals in this country, our kin will remain in chains."

"I do not believe Black people to be inferior to whites," Hiram says. I can tell he's choosing his words carefully, because now his tone matches Mr. Johnson's. I wonder if he's using caution because Mr. Johnson is blind, or because Charles looks ready to burst with fury.

"But you'd rather not sit next to a Black person while enjoying Eliza's singing?" Charles asks.

"This is foolish talk," Hiram says. "Of course I would sit next to a Black person! Eliza lives in my home and is treated well. I will not let you treat me like one of those monsters in the South."

It is true that Hiram should never be put in the same category as a Southern enslaver. He is like the Quakers I've known my entire life. He's an abolitionist who is against slavery and for equality. Not only in his words but in his actions. It's not fair to make him responsible for the viewpoints of every white person, but our desire for equality is not foolish talk just because he is frustrated. I don't think he gets to be frustrated when we are the ones oppressed. No matter how well he treats me.

"You're nothing like the Southerners," Charles says. "They are quite forthcoming with their feelings."

This volley of words between Charles and Hiram is making me very nervous, yet I feel powerless to stop these men from bickering. Charles is pushing this too far and seems to have forgotten that Hiram is still a white man, and *this* is dangerous. Hiram looks about ready to abandon the conversation altogether and with it my concert invitation. And that I cannot allow to happen. My heart is pounding in my chest as I try to think of something—anything—to offer that can break through this impasse.

"Miss Greenfield," Mr. Johnson says, causing both Hiram and Charles to break their glares and look in his direction. "If I may,

I'd like to encourage you not to perform in venues that do not allow equal access to Black citizens. Those of us who can carry the burden for the ones left in chains should do so, without hesitation."

All eyes are on me. Somehow this battle of wills between men has suddenly been left for me to decide. I am pleased with the abolitionist work I did in Philadelphia with PFASS and moving fugitives on the Underground Railroad. I will continue to do those same activities here in Buffalo. I don't know, however, if I want my burgeoning career to be at the center of a protest or rebellion. That could end my dream before it is born. I must achieve fame first, before I can carry the burden for anyone else.

Although my words are directed at Hiram, I lock eyes with Charles. "Maybe this one time, seating in the gallery is an acceptable compromise."

Charles sighs, and the peaceful-looking Mr. Johnson's calm façade cracks a little as his smile fades.

"Well, I have done what I set out to do, and that was to make a request of Mr. Hiram Howard," Mr. Johnson says. "I have an engagement, and I do not wish to be late. Thank you for accompanying me here, Charles, but I must bid you all a good evening."

"I appreciate your visit and your candor, Mr. Johnson," Hiram says. "I consider this matter closed. I am open to revisiting it if and when Eliza is invited to perform future concerts for the Buffalo Musical Association."

"Good evening," Charles says as he leads Mr. Johnson out of the house.

Unable to take the look of disappointment on Charles's face, I follow them out and close the door behind me. When Charles glances over his shoulder and sees me, he shakes his head and frowns.

"Don't be cross with me, Charles," I plead.

I hate how desperate my voice sounds, but it accurately reflects my feelings. Even though I disagree with the stand Charles is taking,

I do not wish to lose his friendship. My feet rush to catch up to them, so that Charles can see the sincerity in my eyes.

"I am not cross, Eliza," he says in a voice barely above a whisper, as if Hiram is still listening. "But Hiram was going to do what you told him to do. And you let him wriggle away with half a solution."

"I let the man who is helping me launch my career escape with his dignity. Nothing more. He would have never been able to convince his colleagues even if I had insisted that Black people attend."

Mr. Johnson pats Charles on the back and surprisingly Charles relaxes. I wish my words had that same effect on him.

"Rome was not built in one day," Mr. Johnson says by way of comfort. "I believe we can continue to work on Hiram Howard. He is not the enemy."

"But he does the work of the enemy," Charles says angrily. "Do not worry, Eliza, your next concert, and the ones after that, will be open to all Black people. Together, we'll fight for it."

I don't know that we're going to fight for that, and if I refuse to fight for that specific thing, will Charles and I be on opposite sides of a battle I don't want to wage? My career, and becoming a prima donna, is a separate thing from the abolitionist views that we both share.

"Charles, I don't want you to fret over this anymore. We have a concert to prepare for, and you are my accompanist."

Charles pats my back, but it feels polite and perfunctory. Again, the two masters are at odds—my career ambitions and my friendship with Charles. Every time the two sides come into conflict, I am worried that I will never have them both.

# CHAPTER EIGHTEEN

*T*onight, the night of my concert, my nerves are in shambles. I have prepared as much as I can prepare. Every song has been practiced more times than I can count. Even Charles, who acts as if he has more on the line than I do, is weary of preparation.

I do not know how she managed to do so, but Annabelle did procure a dress from Electra. Pink lace with a modestly plunged bodice. I am not sure if the dress suits me. Perhaps if we'd had more time, and if it had been designed especially for me, the results would be different. It is better, however, than either choice I had at home.

Ruby insisted on lip stain, even though on my dark skin I find it both unnecessary and gaudy. My lips feel as if they're being smothered, and upon inspection in a mirror, I cannot tell how this potion gives a better result than my plain face. But since I am no expert on things pertaining to beauty, I will trust Ruby.

The dressing room feels too small, but I am grateful for this space, filled with the aroma from flowers from my well-wishing friends. Some of them have bought tickets, and they've promised that I will hear their cheers from the gallery to which they've been relegated. I am sure that more than a handful would've made the ticket purchase, but by the time Hiram and the Buffalo Musical Association finally announced that Black people would be admitted, not many had time to gather the fifty-cent ticket price.

I imagine Jenny Lind sitting in the same dressing room before her Buffalo concert. I wonder if she was as nervous as I am now, or if she simply looked forward to the worship from the crowd. Unlike me, she was probably well assured of the crowd's affection before setting foot onto the stage.

When I hear the knock on my dressing room door, I feel my midsection seize. Is it already time to go onstage? Even with all my preparation, I still don't feel ready.

"Come in," I say quietly, reserving my voice for the show.

Ruby steps through the door and gasps. This is the first time she's seeing me in the lace gown, and I can tell that at least she approves.

"How did you get back here? Aren't you supposed to be in the gallery?" I ask.

"I have found if you look like you're supposed to be a place, people rarely ask you why you're there."

"Be careful with that," I warn. "I don't want William to have to worry about you disappearing."

Ruby squeezes into the tiny chair in the corner of my dressing room. I'm not entirely sure that chair was meant for sitting. Ruby is not a very large woman, but she still seems to ooze over the sides.

"You look gorgeous, Eliza," Ruby says. "I'm glad you listened to us, because you were going to look like a church mother with those dresses you picked."

"Well, everyone keeps reminding me about virtue and looking genteel."

"Everyone who? Those white women?" Ruby rolls her eyes. "They think their husbands lust after us even when we're wearing burlap sacks. There's almost nothing we can do to be virtuous in their eyes."

I can't do anything about this fear of our high round behinds, heavy breasts, and wide hips. It is no fault of mine that slave owners secretly sire dusky children with the women they enslave on their tobacco and cotton plantations. It is no fault of the enslaved women either—they are not allowed to remain virginal. Their bodies are not their own.

"I suppose I shouldn't care about those reminders and admonishments."

"Tuh. I think not. I bet they don't whisper a word about these things to Jenny Lind."

"Well, they want to *be* her. They aren't concerned about her wanting their old, crotchety husbands."

We both find this funny, and the laughter feels good. It helps to calm my nerves some, but not enough.

"How are you feeling? Ready?" Ruby asks.

I hesitate to share my inner turmoil and fears. Do they come true if you say them out loud?

"I have practiced. So has Charles. So has the orchestra."

"You didn't answer the question."

"I had a bad dream last night. That I got on the stage and forgot all the words to the songs. And then when I opened my mouth to sing, a croaking sound came forth like a frog."

And now that I've given voice to the dream, I feel paralyzed with fear of it coming true. I close my eyes as my hands begin to tremble. I feel Ruby's arms encircle me and squeeze tightly as a single tear steals its way down my face.

"Sister," Ruby says. "I have never been disappointed by that voice of yours, and I don't intend to be tonight. Go out there and use the gift God gave you."

"What if the gift doesn't show up?" Images from my nightmare pepper my imagination even now.

"God will make up the difference. You must trust Him."

All I have done on this entire journey, since I left Philadelphia and stepped onto that steamer, is trust God. He hasn't failed me yet. Still, I can't seem to shake these fears.

I take my handkerchief from a secret pocket sewn into the lace and dab my eyes before any more tears fall.

"I'm ready," I say as I untangle myself from Ruby. "Now go get to the gallery before Hiram sees you and his head explodes."

Ruby kisses the top of my head and smooths down a few flyaway hairs from my braided bun.

"Listen for me and William. We will be cheering for you."

With the same amount of stealth as when she slipped into my room, Ruby scurries out the door and hopefully to her seat.

Now, whether or not I am ready, and whether or not I feel afraid, it is time to get this concert under way. I whisper a prayer and hope that God meets me on the stage.

* * *

ALTHOUGH I AM unable to make out any faces in the crowd, I can tell that most if not all the seats are filled. A packed house. For me.

Terror settles into the pit of my stomach, and a taste like copper pennies fills my mouth. I swallow several times, willing the nauseous sensation away, but perspiration gathers under my arms and my breasts. Although outside it is quite a chilly evening, in Townsend Hall the air is warm and dense with expectation.

After the applause dies down, the hall descends into silence. It seems an impossible feat for nearly one thousand people to become silent all at once, but it happens. The only thing I can hear is the thumping sound of my own heart and my even breathing. Slowly dragging air into my lungs, allowing them to expand, and then emptying them once again. Stretching them to capacity and readying them.

Then, finally, after staring into the crowd and allowing their anticipation to excite me, I look over at Charles and give him the cue that I'm ready. Charles plays the opening to my first song, and the orchestra joins in after his introduction. He gazes at me with what I hope is pride and admiration.

As my voice rings out loud and strong, it is as if the crowd is in a trance. The silence continues until I hit the last note of the first aria.

It is a nature-defying run from baritone to soprano, all in one breath, with the last note held for an impossible amount of time.

A part of me expected the applause that erupts. But there is another part of me that doubted everything. The second side is the one that gets butterflies. The fierce side of me revels in the applause, craves it even. So much so that I launch right into the next song and let Charles catch up to me in the accompaniment. I am lucky he is used to following my vocal notes wherever they may lead.

Nonstop, song after song, there is the cycle of singing, applause, encore, and then even more singing. This goes until the intermission, when I escape to my dressing room for a much-needed break and cup of tea.

Charles bursts into my dressing room and closes the door behind him. Before I get a moment to complain about his intrusion, I notice that he seems out of sorts. I hope that nothing has gone wrong between him and Hiram. I don't want anything to ruin this night.

"Charles, is everything all right?"

"Eliza, there is something that I must share with you. And now is most likely not the appropriate time, but I feel I will explode if I do not."

He stands with his back pressed against the wall, with sweat on his brow and a look of sheer agony on his face. I have never seen him like this, and we have a concert to finish.

"Tell me, whether it's appropriate or not. I don't want you feeling upset."

Charles sighs with relief and drops to one knee in front of me. "Do you know how much I enjoy our friendship?"

"Yes, of course."

"Well, I have not expressed what it does to me to hear you sing."

I look down at my hand that Charles has gripped between his, and at the intensity of his gaze. This is making me nervous yet intrigued. I want to hear more.

"What does it do?"

His hand strokes my face with a touch that is so intimate, I suddenly recoil. I am shocked and overwhelmed by his affection, yet simultaneously hungry for it.

"I'm sorry, Eliza. I know it's improper. But when you sing, there is an attraction I feel that is both spiritual and carnal in nature."

"I've never . . ."

This has been one of my greatest fears in pursuing this friendship with Charles. Men are never required to remain virtuous, and they do not. He, I'm sure, has seen and done all manner of things. There are whores and widows both who are willing to teach young men anything and everything they need to know about things of a carnal nature. But I have no knowledge of these things.

Miss Lizbeth always said that there would be a discussion before I was wed, but that I was to always remain above reproach. In fact, being alone with Charles in these close confines is beyond improper. It is scandalous. This is enough to cause people to question my virtue.

"I know that you are innocent, Eliza," Charles says as the hand that touched my face now trails my arm back down to my hand. "And that is what makes this impossible."

Charles's hand has lit a fire on the skin he's touched. Miss Lizbeth impressed upon me the need to remain virtuous but did not prepare me for these feelings. Things I never felt in the company of Lucien.

"May I kiss your hand?" He is lifting my hand toward his lips, but he hovers there, waiting for me to consent.

I nod, but when he turns my hand over and opens it, then places the softest kiss at the center of my palm, I am confused and disarmed. It is not what I expected. I thought he was going to give me a gentleman's kiss. This was not that. My entire body tingles from this.

"If we weren't only friends, I'd place a kiss like that on your lips," Charles says lustily. "And I do not wish us to be only friends any longer."

"Because of my singing?"

"Not only the singing. But there are things women do that can bring a man to his knees. Every woman has her charms, and every man has a different charm that's the key to his . . . carnality."

"For you and me, it is my voice?"

He nods while lifting my hand to kiss it again, but I gently pull it away.

"I'm sorry," he says. "Have I offended you? Are you worried someone will see? There was no one backstage."

"No. I think I'd like to feel the kiss . . . on my lips. I've never—"

His lips crash into mine with a sense of urgency, the flavors of mint and honey from my tea commingling with Charles's natural taste. I savor every sensation, including the heat that rises between my thighs as Charles kisses me deeply.

As we separate, I feel as if I might explode from longing, and Charles does not look anywhere close to being satiated. This must be the feeling that causes people to abandon all reason, because for a moment I forgot about the stage, bringing my mother home, and my inheritance. I wasn't thinking about anything other than what Charles's skin might feel like touching mine.

"Charles," I gasp. "The concert. We must . . . we must stop."

"Yes, I am aware. I wanted to ravish you right there on the stage in front of the world, or at least Buffalo. You are spectacular. It's your voice, and the way you have this crowd in complete awe of you. I had to taste and touch you."

"Ravish me?" Taste me?

"I would never, but I wanted to."

Three sharp knocks on my dressing room door cause Charles to quickly scramble to his feet. I motion for him to open it quickly before anyone believes anything untoward has transpired. It is bad enough we are behind closed doors alone, but at least it can be explained as me giving my accompanist instructions for the remainder of the concert.

We are both fully dressed, and neither of us is disheveled. Hopefully, it is no one who would create a rumor.

I exhale a sigh of relief when I see it is Miss Bella, but she gives Charles a disapproving scowl.

"What are you doing in Eliza's personal dressing room, accompanist?" Miss Bella rants, her Italian accent thicker than I've ever heard it.

"Miss Bella, I am giving him instructions on things I'd like changed," I say. "I'm sorry, Charles."

Charles shakes his head. "No, she's right. I should go."

He rushes out of my dressing room under Miss Bella's fiery glare. She looks like she wants to swing her cane at him on his way out. And she certainly doesn't look like she believes my ruse. She slams the door behind him and then turns her anger upon me.

"Eliza, what are you thinking? Are you trying to ruin everything we've worked for?" she fumes. "If I had been one of the Buffalo Musical Association, this could've been the end of your career as a prima donna. Over before it began!"

"But nothing happened."

"Nothing needs to happen for someone to create a tale. You are not dumb, Eliza. You know this!"

Chided like an unruly child, I stare at the floor. Tears sting my eyes. But I quickly gather myself. This is *my* concert. Not hers. They are here to see me. Miss Bella is not my mother. She is not Miss Lizbeth, and she is not my guardian. I am a grown woman.

I lift my chin and stare directly into her eyes. "Was there a message you came to deliver?"

Miss Bella is shocked into silence for a moment. And then she chuckles. She sighs and hobbles over to the seat in the corner of the room and uses her cane to ease into a seated position.

"You have learned well, haven't you?" Miss Bella says with a hint of sadness in her voice. "I came back here to congratulate you for singing perfectly for the first half of your concert, and to tell you that I do not know if there is much left for me to teach you."

I regret my harsh tone now and want to take it back. "Thank you, Miss Bella. For everything."

"But I regret not sharing with you my heartache and my shame." She sighs heavily. "Did Miss Lizbeth ever tell you how we came to be acquainted?"

"She said that you'd come over from Italy, and that you were going to be a prima donna yourself."

"I was. But I was ruined by a man who I thought loved me. A priest."

"A priest?"

"Yes, and I brought shame to my entire family." Tears leak from her eyes with this sorrowful memory. "That's why I had to come here. To America. This gift that we possess attracts men and even women. Charles won't be the last."

My eyes widen. "But Charles . . . I can see myself with him in a way I couldn't with Lucien."

"Do you want marriage and family or the stage?" she asks with what sounds like annoyance. "I thought you had already made that choice."

"I did, until he kissed me. Isn't there . . . isn't there tea a woman can take to keep her from becoming pregnant?"

Miss Bella pounds her cane into the floor, and I jump from the sound. "The teas do not always work! Eliza, you must be sure. When you choose this path, be committed."

"Must I remain untouched and unloved my entire life?" This comes out sounding like a whine, but I feel desperate for a middle ground. Why can I not have them both?

"Your voice will not last. A prima donna has ten, maybe fifteen years of youth and vigor, and you have started late. Lovers can come later . . . when you can no longer bear their children."

What man will want me then? Will Charles?

Miss Bella rises slowly, using her cane for leverage. She smiles at me though I am now a tear-streaked mess in pink lace.

"Pull yourself together for the remainder of your concert. When the crowd demands encore after encore, then you tell me you would trade that for the interest of a man. And I assure you, Eliza, there will *always* be a man. They are not hard to come by. You will be a wealthy woman very soon. You will have whatever you want. Finish your show. Take your bow and sing your encores. Then talk to me again about a man."

Miss Bella leaves my dressing room with confidence, as if she knows for certain what my choice will be. But as I lick my lips to taste Charles's lingering flavor, I don't know if I share her assurance.

\* \* \*

DURING THE SECOND half of the concert, the audience is just as gracious with their applause and praise. I save one of my most stunning pieces for the end. And like Miss Bella told me, they are captivated by the very first note of "Where Are Now the Hopes I Cherished," another selection from the same Bellini opera as the aria "Casta Diva." But this song is translated into English, and is a duet, and I effortlessly sing both the male and female parts.

When I reach the final note and hold it for as long as I can, with my arms thrust triumphantly toward heaven, the applause that breaks lasts for an impossible length of time. Right before I bow, I catch a glimpse of Charles smiling brightly in my direction and realize that Miss Bella was right about something else. I am less besotted with Charles's attention while this crowd is calling for encore after encore.

We have planned for this, so I motion to Charles to play my encore song, "When Stars Are in the Quiet Skies." I take my time singing all four verses, lingering in my lower register, and then taking them to the top of my impressive range once more. I want the audience to remember and the reviewers to take note.

I try not to weep when I look up and see that almost every concert attendee is on his or her feet. A standing ovation at my first concert. The same worship that the crowd gave Jenny Lind. But to me, a Black woman.

That doubting part of me, even with the invitation from the Buffalo Musical Association, and reassurances from Hiram and Miss Bella, and adoration from Charles, still believed that this show was not going to go well. That people would merely clap and say, *That was nice*, and go home like they'd seen nothing special.

But now that it's happening, now that I can hear people calling for the Black Swan, I don't know how I can choose a life where this isn't taking place. I cannot go from this to anything ordinary. After a night like tonight, there can be only nights like this.

Miss Bella was trying to tell me that I wouldn't want to trade this adoration for anything, not even a man. And, of course, I'd already suspected this to be true. It's why I walked away from my engagement with Lucien. The kiss had momentarily clouded my thoughts, but the applause quickly caused it to fade from my memory.

I take one final bow as the curtain closes, and then I am ushered directly to a reception where I will greet any important people in attendance. There is no time for me to deal with Charles and any implied promises that he may have taken from that kiss in my dressing room. I will have to tell him later that I've chosen to delay debauchery and carnality in exchange for the thrill of the stage.

The first thing I notice about the reception area is how small and intimate the space is. It is truly for a select few—the elite.

The second thing I take note of is that I am the only Black person in the room, although I am sure I requested that Ruby, William, and Charles join me for refreshments post-concert. I can't say I'm surprised that they neglected to find their way here. Surely men and women who don't wish to enjoy the concert sitting next to Black people don't want to share their bourbon with Black people either. As their entertainment for the evening, I appear to be the sole exception. The scent of strong whiskey and tobacco smoke hangs in the air as I plaster a smile onto my face. This is my moment. Even if I am the sole raisin in this bowl of rice, I will smile and enjoy myself.

"Eliza, my star pupil!" Miss Bella. A familiar voice to ground me, at least.

Now I see why she is so elaborately dressed this evening, and why I didn't hear her approach with the familiar tapping of her cane. She holds the arm of a gentleman who looks at least twenty years younger than her actual age, though Miss Bella in this pale-blue lace gown, with strategically placed facial powders, does not seem out of place beside the handsome man. I always say it is very difficult to discern Miss Bella's age. People believe she is in her sixties when she is in her eighties, and in the right lighting, like this dimly lit room, she could pass for late fifties.

"Your star pupil? You must be proud of me tonight for me to receive such an accolade," I say, accepting the hug from her outstretched arms.

She beams at me. "I have never been prouder, my dear. Meet my friend Silvio Luna."

"Miss Greenfield, your singing brought tears to my eyes," Silvio says, with such passion in his voice, I think he may burst into tears. "Bella has raved about you, and now I understand why. Please, when you come to Venice, you must allow my family to host you. We would love for you to stay at our villa."

Bella lifts her eyebrows playfully. "Silvio is very kind, and he has such a love of the arts, but his family grows weary of his American projects," she says to me. She turns to Silvio. "We will, however, keep your generosity in mind when we are creating Eliza's list of European benefactors."

"You must. I want to be a part of the rise of the Black Swan," Silvio says.

Bella's shrill laughter makes her sound like a much younger woman than her eighty-plus years. "Leave us for a moment, Silvio, and find Bella a glass of wine or something stronger. We'd like to talk."

Silvio scampers off, and Bella takes my arm to steady herself. She motions with her head for me to move to a less populated side of the room. I do and notice that many pairs of eyes follow us. Some of them members of the Buffalo Musical Association.

"Do you see that, Eliza?" Bella whispers. "You are the center of attention. They all want your time."

"I should see what they want. Perhaps to book my next concert."

"Make them wait, dear. They will." Bella smiles at someone in the room as she guides me away from their watchful eyes. "You mustn't be so accommodating."

I look at Miss Bella as if she's lost her mind. Because I think she has.

"You took their souls from their bodies with your voice, Eliza. That is the power of a prima donna," Bella explains. "I know what you are thinking. But this power transcends your skin color."

Even though I have evidence that what she says is true, every fiber of my being wants to defy Miss Bella. But I force myself to stay put. To make them wait. Miss Bella said she had nothing left to teach me, but this is as important a lesson as any.

"Is Silvio your lover?" I ask Miss Bella.

She laughs. "A lady would never admit to such debauchery. Besides, I am an old woman."

"You did not say no."

"I did not say no."

Silvio joins us again, this time with a glass of wine in each hand,

and a glance for Miss Bella that lingers longer than it would if it were only for a friend. It is an intimate gaze. One that has seen its subject in several stages of undress. And this makes me think about Charles and the promises made with that kiss.

Miss Bella's advice is sage. I don't have to remain untouched my entire life, just until after—as Silvio says—the rise of the Black Swan. I wonder if Charles will wait. If he will not, perhaps I should trust another piece of Miss Bella's advice and believe her when she says there will be others.

# CHAPTER NINETEEN

Things have been tense between Charles and I since the night of the concert. I have not revisited the topic of the kiss, and neither has he. I am half glad that he hasn't brought it up because I do not wish this to be a matter of consternation between us, but I also do not want matters left unsettled either. I do know, in situations like these, where a man's pride is on the line, it is best to let him save face, so I am attempting to let him do exactly that.

If nothing else, I want to retain him as my accompanist for the time being, and since I have no one else to assist with my business affairs, I've agreed to let Charles manage my next concert engagement. I've been invited to sing in Rochester, New York, at Corinthian Hall. It's a venue even larger than Townsend Hall, but I have not yet responded to the invitation.

We sit at Ruby and William's table, our official meeting place it seems, to discuss the upcoming concert. Except the only ones talking are Charles and Patrick.

"What I take issue with is that the invitation was sent to Hiram, as if she needs his permission to perform or go anywhere," Charles says.

"They think he's her massa of sorts," Patrick says.

"No one thinks that," I snap, finally jumping in. "He is my employer, and I live in his home. Perhaps they assumed he is my manager as well, since he's the president of the Buffalo Musical Association."

"Well, if I had managed the first show, you would have walked away with more than twenty-five dollars in payment," Charles says.

I agree that the first deal wasn't necessarily in my favor, but it was my first concert, and I felt compelled to sign, regardless of the terms. My only goal was to make it onto the stage. But Hiram had shown me everything. All the receipts and who had been paid. The contract stated that I was to have one fifth of the proceeds. The ticket price was fifty cents, and after the theater, orchestra, ticket takers, and everyone else had been paid, there was only $125 remaining. Hiram had paid me according to the contract which stipulated that I was to receive twenty percent of the proceeds.

"I was paid what the contract said I was supposed to be paid," I say.

"After everyone else was paid," Charles says. "On this invitation, you will get your fee up front. Fifty dollars or you don't perform. If they cancel the invitation, there will be other venues."

"Fifty dollars? Will they pay that much? It seems like too much," Patrick says. I share his concerns, but I remember what Miss Bella said: I must start believing that I am worth more.

"Jenny Lind is paid more than one thousand dollars a concert," Charles declares firmly as he pounds his fist on the table. "If the reviewers compare Eliza to Miss Lind, then they can pay her more money. If they really want you, they can charge more for tickets. And trust me, they really want you."

Ruby emerges with a tray of cake slices, mugs of warm tea, and William at her heels. She sets the tray down, and William takes a seat at the head of the table.

"I brought y'all some of my spice cake and apple cider. Eat and drink, so that you all can calm down all this fussing," Ruby says.

"No one's fussing," Charles says. "I simply want to feel like we're on the same side. I'm inclined to think Corinthian Hall will meet our requests, since they have agreed, unlike the Buffalo Musical Association, to allow Black people to sit anywhere in the theater."

"We've already started making requests?" I ask, irritation starting to rise. "Why didn't you tell me?"

"I spoke on your behalf as a manager," Charles says with a shrug, which irritates me further. "Are we not in agreement on that issue?"

The forkful of cake cannot make it into my mouth quickly enough. Charles has an agenda that includes me but that also goes above and beyond me. And it is the above-and-beyond-me part where we may have conflict.

"My wife must be wondering what's keeping me," Patrick says as he stands and takes his hat from atop Ruby's bookshelf, trying to escape the heat of this brewing conflict between me and Charles. "I best be getting home."

"I will speak with you later this week," Charles says. "We'll need to make sure every Black congregation in Rochester knows about Eliza's concert, so you and I may have to take a trip."

"I cannot go on any additional trips," I say to Charles, although he was not speaking directly to me. "I take care of the Howards' children after school and teach them music lessons. I do this in exchange for my living arrangements."

Charles cocks his head to one side and thinks about this. "I think Patrick and I can promote the concert without you being with us."

"Perhaps you won't need to ride back and forth to Rochester on a carriage at all," I offer. "When the reviews of my Buffalo concert appear in the newspapers, there may be enough interest to sell out the Rochester show."

"That is true," Charles says, finally considering something that I am saying useful information. "But we cannot leave anything to chance. Let's promote from every angle to ensure our success."

There may not be a concert if Charles goes asking for fifty dollars, but I keep this to myself because everyone is already frazzled enough, although I do plan to revisit the topic later. Ruby sips her apple cider and so does William. Their eyes shift back and forth from me to Charles and back to me again.

I wonder if Charles and I need also to start our stroll to the Howards' home so that we can get there before darkness falls. I do not want to be out too late with slave catchers afoot.

"What are you planning to wear this time?" Ruby asks. "The dress you wore here caused quite a stir."

"That's an exaggeration," Charles says. "Only one reviewer made mention of her dress, and I'm almost convinced that reviewer did not attend the concert, because all his comments had something to do with her appearance. If he had heard her sing, he would've had something more to talk about."

That reviewer had been especially worrisome in his description of my clothing, but even more offensive was his commentary about what my low-cut dress meant. Charles unfolds a small piece of paper from his pocket.

"I saved his article," Charles says. "He may not have been moved by your singing, but he's curious about your parentage, and so are others."

"He doesn't care to know my parents," I scoff. "He's only asserting that there must be the blood of Europeans coursing through my veins because of my talent."

"He mentioned your Seminole heritage," Charles says.

"Yes. Anything other than African blood." I take the article from Charles's hand. "Look, here he says I'm not much darker than a mulatto."

"He mustn't know any mulattoes. As far as I'm concerned, Eliza is good and African," William says.

We all stare at William for a moment while he shovels cake into his mouth. Then he realizes we're staring at him.

"What?" William asks.

Charles stands and walks Patrick to the door. They mumble things between them that the rest of us can't hear. More strategizing and planning about things that concern me without asking my opinion.

"I didn't mean nothing by what I said," William says, still chewing and swallowing cake. "Hope I didn't offend you."

"By saying I look African?" I ask. "If I can be offended with the truth, then I ought not bring myself into the company of other people. You didn't offend me at all."

Truth is, I'm not convinced he didn't mean anything by his statement. I believe he thought he was being funny. Ruby might not be the prettiest woman, but she's the color of a cinnamon stick. And William had chosen her. I'd bet my inheritance that he'd passed over many darker girls for Ruby and not because of her wit and temerity. Black folk can be just as bad as that white reviewer when judging someone as beautiful because of their skin color.

"Let me wrap up some of this cake for you to take back to Annabelle and the girls," Ruby says.

"Not Hiram?" I have no idea why Ruby excluding Hiram is so funny to me, but I start laughing and can't seem to stop.

"Naw, not him," Ruby says. "He made me sit up in the rafters for your concert. I could barely make out your face from where I was sitting."

"I'm sure you could see my African features from your seat," I say with a chuckle. "Isn't that right, William?"

"I'm gone keep quiet on that one," William says, sufficiently chastened for the evening.

"You think they know what they're doing?" Ruby says, motioning to Charles and Patrick.

"I don't know. They look like they do."

"Well, they could be looking wise and acting otherwise. I don't know if I like them taking a gamble haggling with white men," Ruby says.

"Somebody might get hurt."

"Or worse," William says.

William's somber tone conveys all our feelings. While I know many good and decent white men, I am not foolish enough to trust them all. The men who sent the invitation are friends of Hiram's, so I feel some comfort, but I am not sure, and Charles cannot be either.

After whispering and plotting and seeing Patrick off, Charles heads back to our trio with a wry smile on his face.

"Patrick says there is a woman at church who has a gown for you. It will be modest and genteel. Everything they want. I'll not have another review written about what you're wearing."

*He'll* not have another review written about what I'm wearing? Did he purchase the dress? There is something about Charles in this moment that feels too overbearing. Perhaps it is because of the newness of our friendship. It is only a few months old. I met him when I stepped off the steamer. He is in league with Electra Potter and Hiram Howard. It is as if they are all angling to be the ones responsible for a plan that had already been set into motion before their interference. The only thing that holds back my ire at Charles is my attraction to him and the lingering feelings from that kiss. I need to address those feelings, because although I want his help, I won't have him derail my career just because his lips touched mine.

"So that's settled, then," Ruby says. "Will you let me do something with your hair? I can put soft curls in and pin it up so nice, it'll look like one of those powdered wigs, except shiny and black."

I open my mouth to agree with Ruby's idea, but Charles holds up one hand while shaking his head.

"No. Let her continue to wear this style . . . What is it called?"

"A church bun," Ruby says. "Is she going to church or to the stage?"

"If modesty is what they want, we'll give it to them."

"We will give them what I want them to have, but, Ruby, this shiny powdered wig is not what I envision."

Charles raises a curious eyebrow. "What is it that you envision, Eliza?"

"I am currently undecided on my hairstyle, Charles. When I have decided, I will let you know."

He stares at me, perhaps waiting for something more, but he can continue to wait. Ruby looks uneasy , but she needn't be worried. I am not angry. I would like to make things clear with Charles. It is my fault that I haven't. I made that mistake once with Lucien, and I won't do that again.

"Charles, will you walk me home?" I say. "I don't want to be out too late, and it's already getting dark."

He takes both of our coats from the coatrack by the door and helps me into mine.

"Thank you, Ruby, for your hospitality," Charles says, "and your cooking."

"And your patience," I say as I hug her.

"Be kind," she whispers in my ear as she embraces me. "That man is in some kind of way over you."

I kiss Ruby's cheek and give her a wink. I do intend to be kind to Charles, because the attraction certainly goes both ways.

The winter air is bitter cold as we step outside the warmth of Ruby and William's house, but it only makes us walk quickly, which we should do in these perilous times. Charles offers his arm, which I take. His offer is a chivalrous one, with there being patches of ice on the cobbled street, but it could also be interpreted by onlookers that we are courting, and that is not an accurate portrayal.

"Charles, we should really discuss what happened during the intermission of my concert," I say in a tone that I hope is much warmer than the weather.

"I kissed you. You kissed me back. Men and women have been doing this for ages," Charles says in an aloof manner. "What would you like to talk about?"

This is not the response I was expecting. He seemed so vulnerable and open at the concert, and it was somewhat refreshing. This is a stark change.

"Well, I have had time to think about it, and I do not think it's wise for me to embark on a romance right now. Not on the precipice of my career. It would only make things complicated, I believe."

Charles does not say anything, but I feel his body slightly shift away from mine. Perhaps I should have expected this, but I did not prepare myself for it.

"I hope it does not affect our friendship, because I am already starting to cherish it."

Charles shakes his head. "It should not. Above all, I am dedicated to assisting you in reaching the pinnacle of success for the advancement of the Black race."

"My success is part of your abolitionist movement."

I state this as fact, because I know it is so, and I understand it, even if I don't completely agree.

"But it is not part of yours?" Charles asks. "I do not see how you can separate the two."

"I know you cannot. But we must agree to disagree on that."

Charles sighs, but I feel his body relax and once again draw close to mine, although not as close as before. I hope this means we are at least friends again. I will let the matter rest for now to allow Charles to have some dignity. However, if his interests continue to differ from mine, we may have to separate. This friendship with Charles cannot be the thing that hinders my journey from ever taking flight.

\* \* \*

TONIGHT, THE NIGHT of my concert at Corinthian Hall, I have an even greater case of nerves than I did in Buffalo, but for a different reason. This is not performance anxiety but concern about the crowd.

When it was announced in the Rochester newspaper that Black people would be allowed into the concert hall and that the seating would not be segregated, the uproar began. There are, of course, the whites who don't believe the free Black population in Rochester should sit alongside them. Also incensed are the Black folk themselves because of the steep price of tickets—one dollar to see me perform when it had been fifty cents in Buffalo.

Charles has chosen a rooming house somewhat far from the concert hall in case any overzealous protesters seek to do me harm. And because the room rate was lower. Lodging is covered by the concert host but will be deducted from my final earnings, so Charles and Patrick share one room, while I have one to myself.

I hardly got any rest in this room alone, though, because I don't know anyone in Rochester, and all I could imagine was someone breaking down my door and loading me onto a carriage and kidnapping me.

"Come, Eliza, the carriage is here."

Charles's tone is businesslike and gruff, and he doesn't even tap on the door. He just stands outside barking orders. Gone are the sweet, gentle encouragements. My success is all he seems to care about since I have made it clear that friendship is the only thing I desire.

I wish Ruby was here to help calm my nerves, but when I mentioned bringing her along, Charles said there wasn't enough money to pay for a room and meals for her, not if we want to have something to show for after the concert. She probably could not have come anyway on account of the children, but I did not much care for Charles's attitude about it.

I take my time emerging from my room. It is my concert, and they cannot start without me. It gives me a bit of satisfaction to see Charles be annoyed by my tardiness. He shakes his head and storms out to the carriage while Patrick stays behind.

Patrick holds out his arm for me to clutch. The ground is slick with ice, so I am happy for the assistance. But I wish it was Charles helping me to the carriage.

"He takes all the fun out of things lately," I whisper to Patrick, who responds with a chuckle.

"He's worried that's all. If it doesn't go well, then other halls won't want to book concerts. Especially not through us. And he wants everyone to know that we manage you and that they cannot get to you without going through us first."

So many disrespectful thoughts bubble up at Patrick's definition of a manager. No one must go through Charles to get to me. I suppose this is what it means to have managers, but it feels like I am not in charge of my own destiny with these decisions.

Charles scrambles up into the carriage right before we arrive, so Patrick helps me into the tight and confined space. Already, Charles is deep in thought.

"You two go ahead, and I will meet you at the concert hall," Patrick says. "There are a few things I need to handle here before the show."

I feel my nostrils flare a bit as I shift on the hard wooden bench, as I am suspicious of the *things* Patrick needs to handle. Women, specifically women who are not his wife, Darla, buzz around the rooming house. At first, I thought they were there for Charles.

"You look too wound up to accompany me on the pianoforte," I say, feeling a bit uncomfortable being in the carriage alone with him, as he seems very agitated. "Are you going to be all right?"

"We really need this concert to be a success. There is a lot at stake."

"I know. People have invested funds, and the concert hall manager has trusted you to bring a crowd, so your reputation as a manager is at stake . . ."

Charles leans forward and fumes, "It's not just the business of things, Eliza."

"Oh, well, yes, I know. There's a cause as well."

"It's not *a* cause, it's *our* cause," Charles raves. "You sound as if you don't care about it, even though either one of us can be kidnapped and sent to a plantation at any time. If that doesn't make you want to change things, I don't know what will, but you've never known life in chains."

"I was born enslaved," I say, feeling offense that he continues to ignore my own work with PFASS.

"And your parents probably never imagined this life for you."

I've always wondered if this talent is something that runs in my family or if I'm some anomaly, with a gift imparted from the heavens. When my father opens his mouth to sing, I wonder if the angels rejoice. Or perhaps it is my mother's Seminole ancestors who hear her melodious chants on the wind.

"They imagined freedom for me, so I suppose that would include the ability to do anything I set my mind to do."

"Do you know how much others would be inspired by your testimony?" Charles asks, his voice full of righteous indignation. "Your success would give hope to those still in chains, and your gift will give abolitionists ammunition in proving that all of us are worthy of freedom, not just a few."

The carriage slows as we approach the concert hall. Charles looks out at the street and frowns.

"I was worried about this when they said Black people would be allowed in your concert."

"Worried about what?"

Charles points at the crowded streets. "Protesters. Poor whites who can't afford to buy a ticket to hear a Black lady sing opera music."

"If they can't afford a ticket, then why do they care if Black people come?" I ask, not quite understanding the issue.

Charles gives me a glare that goes straight to my core. He looks at me as if I'm a dullard. I wish I hadn't asked the question.

"If they can't buy tickets, because they can barely afford bread, why would they be happy about Black people being prosperous enough to purchase a ticket when they cannot?"

Charles leans forward to the carriage driver. "Take us to the rear entrance of the concert hall. I do not want them to see Eliza go inside."

"Do you think they wish to harm me?"

"They wish to stop anything that makes them feel inferior to Blacks. You performing here is a reminder of how flimsy their claims of superiority are. You are never safe around poor whites, especially the angry ones."

The chanting and ruckus being made by the crowd of people in the streets make me uneasy. Charles is right. These poor and furious whites are as dangerous as slave owners, if not more so.

The carriage driver gets us very close to the concert hall back door, and Charles whisks me inside. My feet barely touch the ground as he lifts me with his strong arms. Being this close to him, if only for a few moments, reminds me of everything I'm giving up for this dream of the stage. Though, ironically, Charles would not even be interested in me unless I was on the stage.

Inside the concert hall, the manager, Mr. Phipps, waits for us outside my dressing room. He appears to be skittish and anxious—two very wrong ways to look before my concert.

"Charles, I am happy you were able to get Miss Greenfield here," Mr. Phipps says. "That mob in the street is concerning."

"And what about the Black concertgoers? Have they been accosted when attempting to get to the concert hall? We can't have anyone hurt," Charles says.

Mr. Phipps seems very worried. "I am not sure that we will have any Black guests for our concert tonight."

Charles narrows his eyes and clenches his fists. I have never seen him this furious, and the tiny Mr. Phipps trembles under the weight of Charles's rage.

"You promised Black people would be able to attend," Charles says through clenched teeth, trying, it seems, not to raise his voice. "That was our agreement when we signed this contract."

"Yes, but there was an advertisement in the local paper . . ."

"An advertisement?" Charles's voice rises with this question.

"Y-yes, warning Black people that there would be slave catchers posted outside the concert hall."

As Charles frowns and balls his fists, it does not help that his height and musculature make Mr. Phipps seem even smaller. "And you didn't think to inform me of this?" Charles asks.

Mr. Phipps shrugs helplessly, backing away from Charles, who is steadily advancing toward him. "I didn't want to worry you or deter Miss Greenfield from performing here. Most of our city is excited to have you perform. The detractors are fewer than your supporters."

"And has the law been contacted about the mob outside?" Charles asks. "How can you ensure our safety?"

"We have contacted the sheriff about help dissipating this crowd, but he's Irish and is not much help." Poor Mr. Phipps is shaking so badly now that I think he's going to fall over. "We do have adequate security for the concert hall, though, so do not worry."

Disgusted, Charles shakes his head at Mr. Phipps and turns his attention to me. He ushers me into my dressing room.

"The sheriff is Irish," Charles says. "Don't worry. Drink your tea, do your warm-ups, and say your preperformance prayers. I will handle the rest."

Before closing my dressing room door, Charles turns to Mr. Phipps. "If there are no Black concertgoers, she will not perform here tonight."

"Then she will be in breach of contract! We upheld our end of the contract. We made tickets available to all. Many Black residents have purchased tickets. We cannot control who comes to the concert."

"No matter," Charles says. "She will—"

"I will perform, regardless of who is in the crowd," I say to Mr. Phipps. "Anyone who bought a ticket and arrives will hear me sing tonight."

Charles swivels to face me. The fire is gone from his eyes, and his shoulders droop. I know what I've done, but I don't care. This is my dream, not his. I will not allow him to destroy it for his cause, even if I share his views. If I am not successful, there will be no way for me to contribute to the cause, and no way for me to bring my mother home.

Mr. Phipps, now emboldened, steps around Charles and takes both my hands in his. "Thank you, Miss Greenfield. I can assure no harm will come to you tonight. You will be safe."

"Thank you."

Mr. Phipps gives Charles a nervous glance as he scurries off to handle whatever needs handling before the start of the concert. I stand face-to-face with Charles, knowing that his fury is now directed at me. He steps into my dressing room and closes the door behind him.

"I never intended to go through with the threat," Charles says in a low voice. "You gave away our power just then."

I sit at the vanity and examine my hair while trying not to get angrier at Charles. "Your threat was baseless. What can Mr. Phipps do if none of the Black ticket holders arrive? Do you think he can produce Black people at will?"

"I do not think that they won't come."

"Well, they should stay away from an angry mob of white men. I would. I don't want them risking their lives and freedom to hear me sing, Charles." I hate that my voice sounds so exasperated and tired, but I am both.

"I believe he intends to turn them away at the door to stave off any violence, and you empowered him to do so," Charles counters, equally frustrated.

I did not consider that Mr. Phipps might be lying to us, not with Charles hovering over him. Not while Mr. Phipps stood quaking with fear.

"I do not see it that way."

"Eliza, you missed an opportunity to stand up for Black people, your people. Again."

"How does it help anyone for me to breach my contract? That is my signature on the papers, not yours."

"You clearly do not recognize the power you have."

"The power afforded by my gift. A power I will not have if no one is willing to hire me."

"But you are a gifted *Black* woman. People know you're Black before they know about your gift. And you can be damn sure those slave catchers outside don't care about your singing. They only care how strong your back is and if you can bear them mulatto children."

"I cannot live my life in a constant uproar. I don't want my days filled with controversy."

"But you must. If one of us is in chains, then none of us are free."

Why does Charles think he needs to keep reminding me about the horrors of slavery? Like every other free Black person in this country, I am fully aware of the very real threat that lies in the South.

"And I will support these causes in the way I see fit."

"You can make more of a difference than the average person, Eliza." Charles softens his tone, now almost pleading. "That is all I would like you to understand. You must not shirk this rare opportunity."

"This is what troubles me, Charles. You keep telling me what I must and mustn't do. What I can and cannot do. I believe I preferred when you played the pianoforte for the love of it and when we were friends."

"Are you saying you don't want me to manage you?"

"I am saying it seems we have two different goals. And I do not know how a manager can have a separate goal from the artist."

Charles gives a solemn and resolute nod.

"After tonight you will need a new accompanist as well as a new manager."

"This is your choice. Not mine. I am asking that we find a way to be of one accord."

"It is your choice, Eliza. All of this. You're choosing to exist exactly how these white men tell you to exist. Within their boundaries and rules."

But Charles prefers I exist within the boundaries and rules that he sets for me. There is no compromise or meeting in the middle. The only things that matter to him are what he thinks, feels, and believes.

"I am weary of this dialogue, Charles. Please leave me, so that I may warm my voice and try to calm down before going out before an audience."

"You think God gave you this gift for you to be able to live like the white woman who raised you," Charles says in a surprisingly cold tone. "With no need for a man and no family ties. But you are not that woman."

"I know who I am."

"And I hope that you aren't soon reminded of what you are. Good-bye, Eliza."

Another goodbye from another man wanting to control my fate. Well, perhaps as Miss Bella has warned me, I may not find love and companionship until old age. And I may have to be content with that.

It seems as if only a few moments pass before I am collected to go to the stage. Not nearly enough time to settle my spirit and calm my fears. Barely enough time to run my warm-ups and prepare my voice. But it is time, and the audience awaits.

The first person I see when I step onto the stage is Charles. I was planning not to make eye contact with him, not wanting to add any butterflies to the ones already flitting around my stomach. But I feel none of the earlier fury in his gaze. In fact, he sports a slight, satisfied smile. When I give him a look of confusion because I am perplexed by his change of mood, he nods toward the audience.

I turn to face the crowd, who has already erupted in applause. While it is hard to see individual faces with the lanterns not providing much in the way of illumination, the reason for Charles's smile is readily apparent.

Of the faces that look up at me from the tightly packed concert hall, many of them are as brown as my own. My brothers and sisters, some born free and some manumitted, have used their resources to come hear me sing. They have navigated through an angry white mob and perhaps slave catchers to bear witness to my gift. They do not think of me as a spectacle, like some of the wealthy whites in attendance.

I will give this crowd the show they came to behold, but especially my kinsmen who have risked life, limb, and freedom. To them, I will give much more than a spectacle. I will give them excellence. I will give them a story to tell their children.

# CHAPTER TWENTY

Even though the Rochester show did end up doing well despite the protests and angry mob, Charles stayed true to his promise to leave my company, and I did nothing to try to convince him to return. Just like the concert in Buffalo, the Rochester engagement was favorably reviewed in local newspapers and resulted in another letter to Hiram, this one from a concert promoter.

Hiram is over the moon about this meeting and is driving poor Annabelle crazy with his demands that everything be perfect in time for the promoter's arrival.

"Annabelle, we mustn't bring out the tea until Colonel Wood arrives," Hiram says as Annabelle stands in the living room's entryway holding a tray laden with a full tea service and tiny delectables.

"Why not? The water is in the teapot. It will stay quite warm until his arrival," Annabelle replies. She blows away a soft tendril of hair that has broken free from her top bun and fallen into her face. Her arms look wobbly as she tries to manage the heavy tray, so I rush to help her.

"No, Eliza, you mustn't be flustered when he arrives," Hiram says. "And we certainly don't want you to appear as a servant, but as a treasured member of our household."

"But, Hiram . . . I work here," I say, very confused about all this hullaballoo.

"Yes, Eliza, but we also treasure you very much."

"But what about me?" Annabelle asks. "Am I also a treasured member of the household?"

Poor Hiram shakes his head as Annabelle bursts into a flurry of giggles. I wish I could share her mirth, but the best I can do is smile.

"You would think the president is coming here to visit, right, Eliza? It's just another concert promoter."

"Who has the connections and credentials to take Eliza all over the country and even to Europe. Did I tell you he has a recommendation letter from P. T. Barnum himself?"

"No, you didn't," Annabelle says. "Then I suppose you're right. His tea should be piping hot. Back to the kitchen I go."

Annabelle spins with a dramatic flourish and marches back toward the kitchen, holding the tray high in the air. We can hear her laughter even after the kitchen door has swung shut behind her.

"Even though Annabelle finds much humor in my anxiety, I am nervous for a good reason," Hiram says as I take my seat again on the love seat. "This could be huge for you. I have heard of the chicanery associated with your inheritance, and it is a travesty. A tour could get you on good financial footing."

"I appreciate your fervor, Mr. Howard. I am not making light of this meeting, but I must also say I am not yet convinced as you are that this is the right idea or that this Colonel Wood is the one who should be leading the charge."

"Eliza, I know you were somewhat dedicated to having Charles's guidance for your career, but unfortunately, he was not learned enough in business to open many doors for you. Perhaps he did you a favor by quitting."

Even though Hiram is right, I feel myself bristle at this comment. Mostly because Charles is not here to defend himself, but also because I know Hiram doesn't like Charles simply because he defied him.

Hiram jumps at the knock on the door. I fold my hands neatly across my lap and let Hiram rush over to the door to answer. He seems as nervous as a young groom about to see his virgin bride disrobe for the first time, and just as clumsy.

When Hiram opens the door, I am completely underwhelmed by the appearance of Colonel J. H. Wood. Everything about him seems average. His medium height, medium build, and even the mousy and thinning brown hair atop his head would make him quite forgettable and easy to pass over in a room full of other, more interesting male specimens. The only curiosity is his elegantly waxed handlebar mustache.

Colonel Wood gives Hiram a hearty slap on the back as if they are old army buddies, a gesture that Hiram seems to enjoy. Then Colonel Wood makes a beeline toward me with outstretched arms, as if we're old friends.

"Is this the Black Swan? Lovelier in person than I had imagined." He bends at his waist, takes one of my hands, and plants a kiss on the back. He smells of pipe smoke and something else. Liniment, perhaps?

What he lacks in dashing good looks, he makes up for in flourish, I suppose.

"Please have a seat here," Hiram says, directing Colonel Wood to the armchair typically used only by Hiram. The seat of honor.

As if on cue, Annabelle reappears with the tray of tea. There is a slight smirk teasing her lips, probably left over from her laughing fit from earlier. Colonel Wood scrambles to his feet, but Annabelle waves him back down. She sets the tray on the coffee table and then sits next to me on the love seat.

"This is my beautiful wife, Annabelle," Hiram says as he sits in the armchair across from Colonel Wood.

"It is a pleasure to meet you all. Miss Greenfield, also known as Black Swan, Mrs. Howard, and Hiram. I feel as if I am among friends, so you may call me Colonel Wood. Unless any of you are in the United States Army, and then Colonel Wood will suffice," he jokes.

"I'm afraid I haven't had the privilege of serving," Hiram says.

"Consider yourself luckier for it," Colonel Wood says. "There is nothing to brag upon in living the military life."

"Indeed," Hiram says.

"But we are not here to talk about depressing topics. I am here to offer you, Miss Greenfield, the opportunity of a lifetime. What would you say to a twenty-city tour starting in February and going through the end of May?"

"Is this a serious question?" I ask, because how in the world would I ever say no to this? "Are there even twenty cities interested in having me do a concert?"

Colonel Wood nods and smiles, the sides of his mustache twitching as he moves. "There are indeed twenty cities interested. As soon as we execute our contract, they are willing to allow us to book concert halls with no deposits, based on my relationships and recommendation from P. T. Barnum."

"You're willing to put your relationships on the line for a concert tour with me?" I ask, not believing this mustachioed stranger. "We've just made each other's acquaintance."

"I do understand Eliza's apprehension," Hiram says. "This is a bit sudden, and she is at the beginning of her career. Perhaps if you could explain how you came to learn about her and make the decision to inquire about touring with her."

As much as it bothers me when men take it upon themselves to interfere in my business dealings, in this moment I am thankful for Hiram speaking up on my behalf.

"Yes, that would be helpful," I say.

"Some friends of mine in Philadelphia shared a newspaper article about this amazing mulatto woman who is America's answer to the European Jenny Lind. And then, after attending your concert in Rochester, I immediately sent telegrams to my connections in ten cities."

"Even though we hadn't spoken?" I ask. "That seems a bit presumptuous of you."

Colonel Wood chuckles, but his eyes are serious. When I give Hiram a sidelong glance and note that he seems anxious, I wonder if I am speaking out of turn. Even though Colonel Wood is here trying to woo me into a contract with him, I mustn't confuse him with Charles. Colonel Wood is still a white man, after all.

"You are correct, Miss Greenfield. I am a risk taker and a presumptuous man. A man cannot expect to be extremely successful without taking such risks."

"I see."

"Please hear the rest of the offer, and I guarantee you will see that I am above reproach and that this is the chance you've hoped for since you got on that steamer from Philadelphia."

"How did you know about that?" I ask.

"I have done my research. I also know that your expected inheritance has been delayed and is currently in litigation."

My eyebrows raise in surprise. "I didn't know it was possible to find these kinds of details out about a person."

"You only have to know the right people and be equipped with the right questions."

"Apparently."

"Miss Greenfield, I must say that it is quite unexpectedly refreshing to learn that you are so well spoken," Colonel Wood remarks, in what I'm sure he believes is a compliment but, of course, is not.

"I attended the Clarkson Hall School for Girls in Philadelphia, sir. My guardian, the late Mrs. Greenfield, insisted that I be educated, and she spent a considerable expense seeing to it that I was."

"Sounds like she was a remarkable woman."

"She was. If I may, I'd like to ask your experience in managing a concert tour." Since he wants to remark on my intelligence, let me give him a taste of what's really going on inside my head. "I know that you have a recommendation letter from P. T. Barnum, and that is quite impressive, but I am interested in what motivated you to pursue this undertaking."

Colonel Wood seems shocked at my line of questioning and looks to Hiram, perhaps for a lifeline. But Hiram does not contradict me and allows my inquiry to stand uncontested.

"I wish I could say that I am an afficionado of the arts, and that the mere mention of your three-octave voice made me shudder with glee," Colonel Wood says.

"It didn't?"

"Oh, I shuddered indeed. Over the possibility of making a great profit at providing audiences with something new. I am a business-man, my dear. I wish nothing more than to make us both wealthy with this undertaking."

"In the footsteps of Barnum?" Hiram asks.

"I will not lie and say that I don't have sincere admiration for the man. But again, I have strayed from the point of my visit," Colonel Wood says. "Currently, I have twenty cities ready to host the Black Swan in concert. In those twenty cities, you will receive payment of fifty dollars per concert and have all meals and lodging covered by the host committee in the city."

I try not to let Colonel Wood see any glimmer of excitement. I am not convinced yet, but one thousand dollars in four months is more than I imagined I would accomplish this soon. This is almost as much as I would have had of my inheritance after ten years. With this tour, Europe is within my reach, and so is bringing my mother home.

"That seems to be a small fraction of what Jenny Lind is being paid for her shows," Hiram says.

"It is indeed. But Miss Greenfield cannot command ticket prices of two hundred dollars."

"Two hundred dollars!" Hiram exclaims. "That is sheer insanity."

"And that is exactly what Jenny Lind's tickets fetched at auction. The typical ticket price for her concerts is six dollars."

"How much will people spend to see Eliza?" Annabelle asks.

"This is Miss Greenfield's first tour, so in most of our venues we should be able to draw fifty cents to a dollar, but there are some things we can do to make the Black Swan more appealing for concertgoers."

"What kinds of things?" I ask.

"Do you play any instruments?" Colonel Wood asks.

"I play guitar, harp, and am able to accompany myself on the piano-forte on the simpler selections."

Colonel Wood clasps both hands and wiggles his shoulders with excitement. "Oh yes, absolutely. That is splendid."

"Will she not have an accompanist?" Hiram asks. "A twenty-city tour can be quite taxing. It will take a toll on her voice, no doubt. She mustn't have the added stress of playing instruments as well."

"She will indeed have an accompanist, but should we not display the full breadth of her talents? Miss Greenfield, you were born here in America, correct?"

I am sure that this bit of information emerged during his research, but I will humor him.

"Yes, I was born on a plantation in Natchez, Mississippi."

Hands still clasped, Colonel Wood rises to his feet. "Oh yes . . . yes. I can imagine it right now in the concert program: a young child, born to a life in the cotton fields, freed by an enterprising mistress and then molded . . . no, groomed to greatness."

That is not exactly what happened, but I suppose I will credit this to Colonel Wood's penchant for the dramatic.

"After we do this first tour and introduce you to the world, you will draw larger crowds and command a larger ticket price," Colonel Wood explains. "It will take time for us to build to this, but I believe you will be the most sought-after prima donna in the nation."

"If I decide to go on this tour—and I haven't yet decided—what will happen next?"

It seems my voice pulls Colonel Wood out of the fantasy he created, and he looks me squarely in the face. He smiles and eases back down into the armchair.

"The next thing would be to, of course, sign the contract. I'm sure you'd like to have Hiram look that over."

"I would."

"And then I would advance monies to procure everything you need for a tour. Silk performance gowns, sheet music, and any other requirements. We must move quickly, however, because your presence has been requested in Lockport, New York, on February fifteenth."

"That's merely two weeks away," Annabelle says. "That's hardly enough time to prepare performance gowns and the like."

"Perhaps it is," I muse. "But I know a dressmaker here in Buffalo who might be able to handle the task."

"It sounds like we are closer to a yes than a no on signing the contract, then?" Colonel Wood asks, sounding a tad more desperate than I'd like for him to.

"We will review the contract you've provided," Hiram says. "And I will send word if and when Eliza is ready to sign."

Everyone stands, so this dialogue has come to an end. Colonel Wood seems hopeful, as do Hiram and Annabelle.

"I am sure you will make the prudent choice, Miss Greenfield. The Black Swan deserves to go on the road. Accolades await you, my dear." For the second time, Colonel Wood reaches out for my hands and kisses them.

Hiram ushers him to the door, and I ease back down onto the love seat. Colonel Wood's words begin to sink in and resonate with me. *Accolades. The nation's most sought-after prima donna. Wealth.*

Above all, having wealth is more important than anything else

Colonel Wood promised. Accolades are based on the opinion of the person giving them, and being sought after does not last forever. I cannot remember who the most famous prima donna was before Jenny Lind, even though there were many who came before her.

Wealth is the thing I need. It has been denied me in my inheritance, but now it seems I can attain it on my own terms. Wealth allowed Miss Lizbeth to move through this world even though she was a woman without a man to open doors for her. Charles wants me to use these opportunities to help those in chains, but how can I be of help when, even though I'm not trapped on a plantation, at any moment I could be kidnapped and forced onto one? Wealth and fame could keep me from that fate.

With Colonel Wood there will be no worries about love or passion, only performances, concerts, and the amassing of a modest reward. Enough to carry me across the ocean to Europe, where I will mark the completion of my music education. After which no one will be able to comment upon my mispronunciation of French and Italian words or be able to write reviews about what I will accomplish with the proper instruction.

And though it appears that Colonel Wood wants to embrace the comparisons to Jenny Lind, perhaps after my studies in Paris, the Black Swan will stand on her own. Separate and apart from the Swedish Nightingale. Separate and apart from this Colonel Wood as well.

## CHAPTER TWENTY-ONE

*G*etting fitted for a gown is tiresome work, particularly when Mary is doing the fitting. She is a perfectionist and must measure, then remeasure the same areas multiple times to ensure accuracy. My arms burn from being held above my head while Mary pulls her tape around my waist for a third time, but I will not complain. Nothing I've purchased from any boutique has fit better than the frocks Mary has designed for me over the years.

"You've lost three inches from around your waist since I last measured you," Mary says. "Are you trying to lose weight on purpose or are you troubled to the point of not eating?"

"I am not troubled at all, sister. In fact, I have never felt so free."

Mary moves about my bedroom with ease, as if she were in her own dress shop. She holds up the measuring tape and shakes her head as if she doesn't believe her own eyes.

"Does this have anything to do with that handsome beau you bragged about in your last letter? Charles?"

I had not given Mary the entire story about Charles in my letters. Only that I had experienced things I never felt for Lucien and that I understood why women ended up abandoning every dream they ever had for the love of a man.

"Charles is a dear friend, but he has moved on, I'm afraid. I have not talked to him since my concert in Rochester," I explain. "I have a new manager now who arranged for this tour and the advance to pay you for these gowns."

"Oh, I see. Well, maybe that explains the smaller waist. A broken heart might have that effect."

I refuse to tell Mary that she's correct with her suspicions. I am not refusing meals, but I no longer get excited about Sunday dinners with Ruby and William. Dining in their living room reminds me that Charles won't be dining with us. It may sound a bit foolish, but food seemed to taste better when I shared meals with Charles.

"I think I've been practicing so much with Bella that I've been skipping meals," I lie. "I am in no way lovesick, Mary. Of that I assure you."

"Lovesick or not, with a proper whalebone, you are going to look absolutely ravishing."

Mary rolls her measuring tape and places it in her basket, so I think I'm free to lower my arms. They were going to come down on their own if she had gone on a few moments longer. But I cannot sit yet. I'm covered in fabric and pins.

"Perhaps I should not wear the whalebone," I say as I regard myself in the mirror. "It pushes my bosom up so."

"That is the entire point of a whalebone, I believe. That's where the ravishing comes in."

"Exactly. I don't know if my goal is to have men salivating over me and my mounds and soft places."

Mary titters with glee even though I am not joking. "Eliza, you are so silly. You don't think men go to concerts for the singing, do you?"

"They go with their wives."

"Yes, and they lust over the prima donna. Haven't you heard the rumors about Jenny Lind?"

"The only rumor I have heard about Miss Lind is that she is not the friend abolitionists thought she might be."

I heard that a writer from the *Frederick Douglass' Paper* had asked Miss Lind for a quote that showed her to be in favor of abolition. She never gave the quote, nor has she said anything about the struggles of Black people.

"Why would she align herself with abolitionists? She's European. It is not her battle or concern," Mary says. "She is selling tickets at ungodly high amounts to the elite. She doesn't care about Black people; she cares about the people who pay to see her."

"Indeed. I hear she contributes most of her earnings to charity but not to any abolitionist causes. Not yet anyway."

Mary shrugs as she adds more pins to my bodice, exposing more flesh. "Well, if abolition becomes fashionable, I am sure she will become a part of the cause."

"Maybe she gives in secret," I say. "She is a singer, not a politician."

"That's fair," Mary says while moving to pin the waistline. She sticks me by accident. I yelp. "Forgive me, Eliza. At any rate, I was not speaking about Miss Lind's politics. I've heard other rumors."

"Salacious ones?"

"Yes, that she is quite the temptress and maybe even has P. T. Barnum in her crosshairs."

"I don't believe that. Do you?"

Mary laughs. "I don't know if I believe it or not. But the rumors, in my opinion, make her more desirable to the men."

"And what does that have to do with me and this low-cut gown?"

Mary straightens from her pinning and smiles. "Two things you need as a prima donna: One, the men should want to bed you. Two, the women should want to be you."

"This is ridiculous advice, Mary. Best suited for Jenny Lind, but not the likes of me."

"Why is it not for you?"

"Because the white men who buy my tickets for their wives would never admit that they find me alluring."

"But they do."

"Correct, to the horror and chagrin of their wives. They call it an abomination to lie with a Black woman."

"And regardless of that, they do lie with us. In many places in Europe they do so openly, and even here in the United States. In New Orleans."

I kiss the back of my teeth with my tongue in irritation. "Yes. This is true. At least in Europe and New Orleans, the free Black women have a choice in this. On the plantations, those disgusting brutes take what they want from the women they enslave."

Mary knows this much better than I do, having experienced it herself. She presses her lips together and smooths the fabric of the gown, shaking her head, maybe at the memory of harsher times.

"Even if the husbands and white men in the audience turn their lustful eyes upon me," I say in a more exasperated tone than I intend, "there is no white woman who would want to be me. Why would a white woman wish to be a Black woman?"

"They wish to be everything about you except Black."

"What do you mean?"

"You are talented, free, and moving about your life without the ownership of a man. You have a sense of agency that many of them cannot imagine in those mansions that are like gilded cages."

"But to be me, they would have to adorn themselves in this Black flesh and risk slave catchers and a life in bondage."

"A thing they would never do, but they can admire all else about you. And, believe me, while your luscious bosom will bother some of them, others will emulate your style of dress."

"Colonel Wood wants me to embody the comparisons to Jenny Lind. Sing music she sings, and even dress like her."

"Dress like her? It sounds like he has a secret desire for the Swedish Nightingale himself."

"I think it's a good way to make people pay attention to the tour."

"Well, these two gowns will be done in the spring, so I suggest that we go with spring colors. Pale blue and perhaps ivory?"

"Ivory, like wedding-gown ivory?" I ask. "I don't know about that. What about black?"

"Prima donnas stand out."

"You don't think I should try to be . . . genteel?"

"Only in actions, my dear. Let them have rumors and never facts."

"I do think I need at least one black gown. With a high neckline. I must be prepared to perform to the most conservative audiences, correct? Shouldn't I have a range of gowns?"

Mary rolls her eyes and kisses the back of her teeth with her tongue. So exasperated, I'm sure, but this is my career and not hers.

"I will make one boring black silk gown. You will look like a schoolteacher, but I will acquiesce."

"I am a schoolteacher, though," I say with a laugh. "So that is not insulting."

"When you are on that stage, you are a prima donna. And you will not be a teacher for long."

"I wish you could see me perform before you go back to Philadelphia. It is such a thrill to stand in front of hundreds, sometimes more than a thousand concertgoers."

"I must get back to the children, but does your new promoter not have plans to bring you to Philadelphia?" Mary asks.

"I am not sure. But if we receive an invitation, I have no doubt that he will accept."

Mary inhales and does a little happy twirl. "Can you imagine Sadie choking on her words when you take the stage in Philadelphia?"

"Has she disparaged me a great deal?"

I ask this with good humor, because I know that Sadie has probably dragged my name through the muck of a Philadelphia street after a rainstorm. She probably takes great joy in it, and I do not care.

"Well, she did for a while. Right after you broke the engagement. Mostly because Lucien seemed so out of sorts."

"That makes me sad."

"Does it? I thought you had put Lucien out of your mind. That's why I haven't written about him."

"I wish him joy and nothing less than that."

"He married quickly. A young girl, barely eighteen years old."

I am not surprised that this doesn't affect me at all. I don't even feel an inkling of sadness. No urge to cry or weep.

"Old enough."

I wish we had not started discussing Lucien. But it's now too late, because we have already traipsed down this road.

"The girl will soon be with child if she isn't already," Mary says. "And the girl is so light, she could pass."

Of course she is. Everything Sadie wants all wrapped up in one young woman, who deserves and has my pity.

"I pray that her childbearing hips remain strong and that all of Sadie's grandchildren have hair that blows in the wind," I say.

Mary tosses her head back and cackles, though I am only partially joking. I am disappointed that what I predicted for Lucien came to pass. The head part of me knew exactly what Sadie would do if I broke things off with her son. The heart part of me hoped that Lucien would follow his own path and not fall prey to his mother's plans.

I suppose that is why we were not destined to be together. We would've both needed bravery to live our lives apart from Sadie's meddling, and Lucien was never courageous where his mother was concerned.

"I cannot wait for you to see the ivory gown I am going to create for you. You'll want to be photographed in it. So that one day your nieces and nephews can brag that their aunt is the famous Black Swan."

My nieces and nephews, and not my children. Finally, Mary understands me. My life. My choices. Or maybe she doesn't, but at least she cares enough to make me think that she does.

"When I wear your dresses, I will make sure to have your name and the name of your shop in the program. If the women want to be me, maybe they'll want to wear dresses like mine."

"Of course. How will you be styling your hair?"

"Why do you and Ruby always ask me that? My poor hair can have no peace with the two of you constantly making plans for it."

"I must meet this Ruby. She sounds like a lovely woman," Mary says with a laugh. "We ask because your hair is beautiful, and you waste it in that coil on your neck."

"I think the coil is regal."

Mary helps me out of the pinned fabric pieces, and she carefully places them each in her basket. Those pieces will be the pattern for my spring performance gowns.

"Hmmmm," Mary says as she closes the top of her basket. "I sure hope you don't gain these inches back in your waist, but I will leave enough in the seam in case we need to let them out."

"Since I didn't lose the pounds on purpose, I cannot promise that they will stay off."

"Choose meat and vegetables instead of pastries, and you should be fine. Come, sit. I want to try something."

"What?"

"Do you not trust me?" Mary says with a chuckle. "Wait. I am not sure I want to know if you don't."

I settle into the chair and wait. Mary grins and pulls a large-toothed comb and a small tin box containing hairpins out of her basket. I have seen this tin box on several occasions, and every time I see it, no good comes of it.

"Mary, we have tried these things before, and they have not been successful."

"Hush, Eliza. I've got an idea that I think you'll love. Just relax until I am finished. Then, if you don't like it, feel free to go back to your church bun."

"That's what Ruby calls it."

"I am liking this Ruby more and more."

I close my eyes while I feel Mary's expert fingers untwist my recently washed and tamed hair. I feel it tumble down over the chair, the weight of it pulling my head back a bit. She gently detangles the curls and then takes her comb and makes one part from the center of my hairline to the nape of my neck. Then she makes another part from ear to ear, dividing my hair into four sections.

Next, I feel the comb pulling through each section, smoothing and lengthening. After she combs each section once, Mary takes the back two sections and combines them into one huge braid that falls to the middle of my back. Then I feel her twisting and pinning the front two sections. I can't tell what she's doing, but I resist the urge to reach my hand up to touch. After a few more pins, she pulls loose tendrils out over my ears, looping the ends around her finger so they curl.

"All right. It's finished. Open your eyes and look in the mirror," Mary says.

When I see what Mary has done—the sheer genius of it—I cannot believe I didn't trust her skill in the first place. The reflection that stares back at me has the same hairstyle as Jenny Lind. The side coils that cover her ears and the long braid in the back.

"We can either pin the braid up in back or let it hang down. What is your preference?"

"I think pinning it up will be best."

"Your new promoter will love this," Mary says, "since he wants you to copy Jenny Lind. If you put some flowers in each of these side coils, no one should be able to tell the two of you apart."

I laugh out loud at that. "Twins, indeed."

It is bold and daring. The embodiment of the nickname we have embraced, although it was in some cases meant to disparage. A version of their heroine, the Swedish Nightingale, wrapped in ebony flesh.

"I wouldn't say twins," Mary says. "You are simply more beautiful and alluring. Also, I heard she doesn't have your range."

We laugh together as we both marvel at the creation who stares back at us from the mirror. Introducing Miss Elizabeth Taylor Greenfield.

The Black Swan.

# Chapter Twenty-Two

*Springfield, Massachusetts*
*March 1852*

With neither friend nor lover to accompany me to serve as a distraction from the drudgery, this tour feels more like work than reverie. Performing three or four concerts a week, sometimes in more than one city, is a demanding schedule. We have been to Lockport, Utica, Albany, and Troy. Each city colder and grayer than the last. Although the Howards' home is not my true home, I miss it just the same, and look forward to breaks when I will get time to spend with them.

Perched atop a hard wooden bench in a rickety carriage, I pull my scarf tightly around my throat and face to protect my voice from the bitter, freezing air. Through a slit in my scarf, I read sheet music I purchased so that I may better accompany myself on pianoforte. Before I strike one note on the instrument, I work out the rhythm and cadence of the music by sight. Soon, I will be able to pick up any piece of music and play it without practicing beforehand, but I have not arrived at that level of expertise yet.

"Am I mistaken or is this winter the coldest you've ever experienced?" Colonel Wood asks. "I am a bit older than you are, and I cannot recall a cold that chills me this way."

I look up from the music and at Colonel Wood. I am a bit perturbed that he has distracted me from my task, but perhaps he is feeling lonely on this tour as well. The least I can do is be pleasant.

"Winter is my least favorite time of the year. The air is horrible for my voice, and I can never seem to get warm enough. My fingers are so cold I can hardly grip these sheets of music."

"Eliza, you don't need to learn to play new music. The songs you already know will suffice. You should focus on your singing. I promise I will find an accompanist who will go on the rest of the tour with us," Colonel Wood says. "Relying on the venue or local orchestra to provide musicians has not served us well."

I know that I don't have to memorize or practice the music. In Colonel Wood's eyes, my playing is simply novelty and spectacle, and certainly not the reason people are buying tickets to the concerts.

"What is the issue with the Springfield orchestra? Shall I take a guess? They've all caught their death of cold."

Colonel Wood gives a dry chuckle. "The orchestra conductor would not agree to lead his musicians to accompany a Negress."

I hate that word. *Negress.* It sounds like white men have created a separate category for Black people. Not men and women, but Negroes and Negresses. Not human, but like a species of birds who fly south for the winter, except we fly north for our lives. Especially the ones kept in cages and chains.

"None of the musicians were willing to perform? Perhaps we can cobble together a small group to accompany me."

"Unfortunately, it does not work in quite that way," Colonel Wood says. "The orchestra members would lose their jobs for such an infraction, and none of them are willing to risk their pay for one concert."

"So, am I to play the entire concert?"

"No, I have procured an accompanist for this concert. And I have meetings to procure another soon."

His words give me no comfort. How am I to become a world-famous prima donna if I cannot even maintain an accompanist or orchestra. I cannot perform without those.

And the musicians are terrified only because of the protesting mobs that have shown their faces in every city we have visited. None of the crowds have been as large as the one in Rochester, but then none of these other cities have allowed Black concertgoers to attend.

So, if they are not protesting Black and white people mixing while being entertained, what are they protesting? My very existence? The audacity of a Black woman to fancy herself as good as a white woman? How can I feel safe when my very existence offends?

"Eliza, I can see the concern on your face, but you have entrusted this to me, and I need you to do exactly that. Trust me. Your singing is going to take us both to the pinnacle of success," Colonel Wood says. "You are going to have wealth beyond your wildest imagination. There is no one more precious to me than you are."

"Not even your wife and son?"

Colonel Wood draws in a long breath as if he is deliberating. Then he exhales and grins. "Not more precious than my son. He is my progeny. My wife, on the other hand . . ."

"Stop." I almost can't contain my laughter at this. Colonel Wood certainly makes no secret about his romps with whores on these tour stops. I look the other way, because it is not my place to say anything about his activities and proclivities.

"Wealth is a lot harder to come by than a good woman. But a wealthy man never has to sleep alone," Colonel Wood says lightheartedly.

Sometimes it almost feels as if he is trying to be my friend, which makes me respond in kind. "I hope to meet your wife one day, so that I may enlighten her."

Colonel Wood narrows his eyes and shakes his head at my joke like I've said the most ludicrous thing he could ever imagine. But then he smiles.

"There are times when you're speaking that . . . Eliza, if I wasn't looking at you, I'd swear I was talking to a white woman."

I believe he means this as a compliment, so I force the sides of my mouth upward in what is supposed to be a smile. But I am sure it doesn't look the way I imagine it in my head.

"What does that mean, Colonel Wood?"

He looks flustered now and red about the cheeks. I suppose his entire face is flushed, but I cannot tell because he's let his beard grow in for the winter. It looks odd with the handlebar mustache. Makes the mustache look glued on like something a child would do playing make-believe.

"Look there, up ahead on the left. Hampden House Hotel," Colonel Wood says, abruptly changing the subject. "It's where we are lodging. Guess who else laid her head in this very same hotel?"

"I could hazard a guess, but I am sure you're going to tell me."

"Miss Jenny Lind herself. When she was here on her tour stop."

I am starting to believe that Colonel Wood may be more obsessed with surpassing Jenny Lind's popularity than I am. He is certainly more concerned with making more money.

Hampden House Hotel is indeed as grand as Colonel Wood's exclamation suggests. Three stories tall, with a two-story verandah, its grandness looks amiss alongside the other buildings and businesses. It would be much better to behold if the sun were shining brightly, but the clouds and gray skies take something away from the hotel's beauty.

"That is special, I suppose. Is this establishment open to lodging a Black woman, or shall I be embarrassed at the door?" I ask, also wondering if I should have my freedom papers ready too.

"Have you no faith in me, Eliza? The hotel's management is fully aware that you are of African origin."

"Splendid."

The carriage pulls in front of the hotel and makes an almost complete stop. The ice-encrusted street makes it slide forward a bit before finally remaining motionless enough to exit. To my surprise, Colonel Wood jumps down and rushes into the building, leaving me in the carriage.

I peer outside at the cobbled street, wondering if I can manage the two steps without slipping on the ice below. The carriage driver climbs down from his seat and walks across the street to a tavern, also not offering any assistance.

The only thing gluing my rear end to this hard wooden plank is my dignity, but even that is fading with the way the wind whips through this wobbly carriage. Colonel Wood will have to come back to gather his belongings, though, and then hopefully he will handle me with the same care he would Miss Jenny Lind.

Since my fingers can barely hold on to the sheet music because of the cold, I slide the pages back into their folder to protect them from the elements. The music cost me nearly one hundred dollars, but it is an investment I do not mind. This is all preparation for what I will learn in Paris when I earn the funds to sponsor myself on that voyage across the Atlantic Ocean.

Just when I have decided to give up and carry myself inside the hotel, a young Black man emerges from the building. He's wearing a nice suit coat and a sturdy hat. The coat can't be doing much for him in this cold, not if my own bundles and layers have started to fail.

Smiling through chattering teeth, he approaches the carriage with an outstretched hand. Even though he's shivering, he's still very handsome. I can't help but return his friendly expression with one of my own.

"Miss Greenfield," he says. "Welcome to Hampden House. We are honored to host the Black Swan."

I beam at the young man, take his hand, and glide down the two carriage steps that I most certainly could have managed without help now that I see the ice isn't as slippery as I thought. The young man's grip is strong and sure, and I am grateful for his chivalry, kind words, and pleasant face.

What I am not excited about is the group of angry-looking Irishmen standing near the hotel's entrance. They do not seem to be paying me any mind, but the mobs and protesters that we have met in every city have me on edge. Perhaps they are, like me, simply disgruntled because of the bitter cold.

"We've set aside one of the best suites in the house for you, Miss Greenfield," the young man says. "I know you'll be right cozy in there."

"What is your name, so that I might thank you properly?"

"It's Michael, Miss Greenfield, and it's really no trouble at all," he says with a friendly and eager tone as he swings the heavy door open. "I sure wish I could hear your singing."

"You should come to the concert as my guest."

"Oh, no, ma'am," Michael says as he glances warily at the group of angry men. "Not this time. They aren't allowing Black folk to attend, but I'm sure I will have another chance. They say you're going to be famous."

I quickly move into the building so that Michael can close the door on the glaring spectators.

"Who are they?" I ask. "The ones saying all these things."

"The writers of the newspapers."

"I hope they know what they're talking about."

Michael leans in close. "Is it true what they say about your manager?" he whispers.

"I don't know. What is being said?"

"That he supports the Fugitive Slave Act," Michael says in a clandestine whisper, "and he's been asking the concert halls to make sure they don't allow Black folk to attend."

My eyes stretch wide before narrowing in Colonel Wood's direction. His neck must burn from the fire in my gaze, because he looks up from his transaction with the hotel clerk at the desk.

"Eliza, I was going to send someone to fetch you from the carriage."

"Luckily, Michael here took it upon himself to collect me. I might have been frozen solid before you remembered I was outside."

Colonel Wood laughs heartily as if he cannot hear the bite in my tone. "Don't be silly. You are my most precious cargo, my dear. Your safety is of my utmost concern."

My safety perhaps, but certainly not my comfort. And even that is in question, because never has a Black woman been safe with a group of angry white men.

"I'm Mr. Barclay, Miss Greenfield," the friendly hotel clerk says. "Your room is ready. If you'd like, Michael can escort you up and then bring your bags."

I nod warmly at the clerk, who should feel none of my ire. "I would like that, thank you."

"You're welcome. We will take great care of you here."

Mr. Barclay's smile is gracious and sincere, so I truly believe him when he says that I am welcome. He's a small man, but well groomed, in a perfectly tailored suit. He motions to Michael to escort me to my room while he attends to more business with Colonel Wood.

The heat from a beautifully decorated fireplace feels exquisite as I follow Michael past a pristine white pianoforte and up a winding wooden staircase. The banisters and floors have been polished until they gleam, and there is a scent of something in the air that reminds me of spring.

At the top of the stairs, I follow Michael to the end of a long narrow hallway. There do not seem to be many guests lodging here in the dead of winter, which is probably for the best. The only ones who might brave this cold to travel are slave catchers up to no good deed.

"I hope this is satisfactory," Michael says as he opens the suite's door.

The gasp escapes my throat before I have time to catch myself.

This is the most luxurious room I've ever slept in. The huge four-post bed covered with a burgundy velvet bedspread looks like it would be reserved for a dignitary.

"Are you sure this is supposed to be my room and not Colonel Wood's?"

"Your manager?" Michael says. "The manager isn't supposed to have a better room than his prima donna."

"He's supposed to if he's white." I laugh out loud. "But I will not quarrel about it, on account of how warm the room is and how tired I am."

Michael laughs with me and helps me remove my layers of over-coats and bundling. Once free of the heavy coverings, I stretch my arms above my head, causing my neatly tucked bun to come untucked. My heavy hair spills loose down my back and seems to be of interest to Michael. He helps me onto a plush sofa, where I take a moment to sloppily pin the wayward hair back into place.

"You got hair like an Indian woman," Michael says, his voice now sounding deep and mannish, as if seeing the hair has stirred something in him.

The warm air in the room feels thick as Michael stares longingly at my locks as I pin the last wayward piece into place.

"Not quite," I explain in what I hope is a calming, matriarchal tone. "My hair is much curlier and harder to tame than theirs, but my mother was Seminole."

Michael marvels at my words for a moment, as he allows his eyes to linger upon me, now that I am without the coats that covered up my form. He can't be more than nineteen or twenty, but that gaze belongs to an older man.

"Are you comfortable, Miss Greenfield?" he asks, seeming to snap out of his trance. "Is everything to your liking?"

"The only thing I might need now is a tray with tea and cookies. Oh, and maybe a book. Then I can settle in for the evening."

"I can see to that for you. Anything else for your comfort?"

"Do you think you might take a stick to those menacing-looking characters outside the hotel?" I say this as a joke, but it really isn't one.

Michael chuckles. "You don't have to worry about them. They heard that there was a runaway hidden here, but Mr. Barclay sent them outdoors."

"But they stayed nearby?"

Michael shrugs, then sighs. "I suppose they need that ten-dollar reward they get for turning a slave over to the law."

"Ten dollars?" I knew there was a reward, but I wasn't aware it was that much.

"Mmm-hmm. They get five dollars if they can't prove the person is a runaway."

"They get paid even if they didn't have cause to snatch someone. Well, it's no wonder, then, that folk are scared to venture out of their homes for anything other than work and church."

"You don't have to worry, though, Miss Greenfield. Mr. Barclay will keep them at bay."

"Mr. Barclay doesn't look too dangerous, Michael."

"Not dangerous at all."

I am surprised as Michael closes the space between us and kneels next to the sofa. He leans in close as if he wants to tell me a secret.

"Mr. Barclay is a conductor," Michael whispers.

I close my eyes and nod as Michael stands. Now it all makes sense. The warm welcome, the beautiful room. Mr. Barclay helps freedom seekers to escape. I wonder if the very hotel is a stop on the Underground Railroad, but I dare not utter the question.

The only reason the system works is that no one has knowledge of the entire network of conductors and stops along the way. In Philadelphia, we knew only the stop we receive freedom seekers from and the stop we're sending them to next.

If Mr. Barclay has taken on the heavy responsibility of leading folks to freedom, then he understands the danger that comes with it. He probably has a pistol on his person and a shotgun under the desk where he checks people into the hotel. He looks so peaceful, like a loving grandfather who gives candies and orange slices to his grandchildren. But I do not doubt that he will use the appropriate level of violence if called upon.

"I will make sure they bring your refreshments, Miss Greenfield. You ring that bell outside your door if you need something else, and I will send someone straightaway."

I almost respond flirtatiously that I'd prefer if Michael brought the things I need instead of sending someone. But even if Michael was older, he is not the sort of man who makes my heart flutter. He's too soft-spoken for my tastes. It's just that he seemed so intrigued by my hair, I like the idea of letting him touch it.

"Thank you again, Michael."

When Michael leaves, I walk over to the window to look out at the gray street below. I can see the men huddling in the cold. Lingering. Waiting to catch a glimpse of whoever might be hiding on their way to freedom.

My thoughts drift back to the questions Michael asked me about Colonel Wood. I would not be surprised if the rumors Michael heard were true. There's no reason to believe Colonel Wood cares about the causes of Black people. Not unless they can help him turn a profit.

And that is why it gives me great satisfaction to know that he's laying his head at a stop on the Underground Railroad. He and his money are supporting that cause, whether he knows it or not.

\* \* \*

THE CONCERT WENT as well as could be expected with an unrehearsed accompanist and a heavy snowfall leading up to the concert time. I was afraid everyone would stay in their homes where they would be warm. But the crowd did show up, ready to applaud, cry, and beg for encores. Of course, I obliged them.

Although it's late, and mostly everyone has retired for the evening, I step outside my suite to ring the small bell for service. I am restless and cannot sleep, and perhaps a cup of tea or warm milk will help me get some rest. I am ready to leave here and go to Boston, where I perform next. I heard Colonel Wood express frustration at the ticket sales there, but I am not worried about that.

The knock on my door startles me even though I had rung the bell.

"Miss Greenfield! Miss Greenfield!" Michael's voice sounds frantic.

"It's only a cup of tea I desire," I say as I swing the door open. "It's nothing to be upset about. If it's too late—"

"Miss Greenfield, you must come quickly. There is a fire in the basement. The furnace."

Before I can even react, black smoke billows up the staircase, causing my eyes to water and my throat to burn. Michael dashes into my room and takes my coat from the hanger on the door.

"Put this on, so you'll be warm," Michael says between coughs. "We must get outside now, before we are unable to escape."

"But what about Colonel Wood?"

"Someone will see about him."

In my reach is my small purse with my money and certificate of freedom. That is all I manage to grab before Michael pulls me out of the room and down the staircase.

"Try not to breathe the smoke in," Michael says in a surprisingly calm voice, since this entire ordeal is terrifying, "and crouch low like I am doing. There is less smoke closer to the ground."

I follow Michael's instructions without questioning, especially since I spot flames coming from the kitchen area of the hotel. We join with other hotel guests on the first floor, and the scene is utter pandemonium. Mr. Barclay and other staff usher the frightened, shrieking, disoriented, and half-dressed guests outside.

The wind whips icy shards of frozen snow in our faces, but thanks to Michael I am at least covered, unlike some of the other guests, who have their sleeping clothes on or thin bedsheets. I scan the crowd frantically looking for Colonel Wood, but I don't see him.

I grab the hand of a Black woman who has on hotel staff attire. "Excuse me. Did you see the man I came to the hotel with? Colonel Wood? He has the waxed mustache. He's very loud and boisterous."

"Sorry, Miss Greenfield. I didn't see him. I'm sure someone got him out. We went to all the rooms."

The woman rushes off before I can pepper her with more questions. I feel myself starting to panic, even though I am trying very hard not to. What if they didn't get Colonel Wood out? What will happen to my tour? My life?

And then guilt consumes me for feeling this way when Colonel Wood has a wife and child. If he is inside a burning building and doesn't survive, their lives will be changed in a way that I cannot imagine.

People wander out into the streets from the surrounding homes to assist the hotel guests, though some just gawk at the flames as they envelop the building. My eyes dart from side to side trying to catch a glimpse of Colonel Wood or Michael or any other familiar face. Finally, I see Colonel Wood stumbling toward me, coughing and wearing only his suit coat, slacks, and a scarf.

He grabs me in what I think is going to be an embrace, but it is more like an inspection. He feels like a mother duck checking to see if her duckling is in one piece. Or something else more sinister, but I push the image out of my mind as soon as it forms.

"Eliza, I'm so glad you made it out of there. The fire is going to consume the whole building," Colonel Wood struggles to say between dry coughs. "I was assured this hotel was the best in town and here we are with the furnace exploding. I cannot have you in danger. I simply cannot!"

"Did you see what became of Michael?" I ask, now feeling a nervous sense of dread that I may never see him again. I send a prayer up for his safety.

"Who is that?" Colonel Wood asks, attempting without much success to brush the dust and soot from his suit coat.

"Michael. The young bellman." I am bothered that Colonel Wood does not remember him. How could he not? "He's the one who helped me out of the hotel."

"Oh, that young man. As I was running out of the hotel, he ran back inside. He was going back to help Mr. Barclay."

Mr. Barclay. The conductor. Slowly, I turn to look past the huddled crowd of hotel guests for the group of angry slave catchers. It cannot be a coincidence that they are missing from their post outside the hotel. This fire is probably their doing, and if there are fugitives hidden at the hotel, Mr. Barclay may be trying to move them to safety.

"Wait here, Eliza. I will be right back," Colonel Wood says. Then he takes the scarf from around his neck and hands it to me. "Cover your face with this. And stop fretting."

As Colonel Wood rushes off to God knows where, I stare nervously at the hotel entrance, waiting for either Michael or Mr. Barclay to emerge. Then an explosion pushes flames out the front door, and I know there is no way for them to exit unscathed.

After the explosion, the hotel guests scatter about yelling and screaming, the tiny bit of order that was in place now completely gone. The more I stare and wait for movement to come from the flames, the more I see nothing.

"Someone has to help them!" I yell, but no one is listening to me. Everyone is trying to assure their own salvation.

A carriage stops in front of the hotel, and the hotel guests start to move toward it. I don't know how they will decide who to shuttle to safety first, but the slave catchers have started to emerge from the shadows, and I now fear more for myself than I do for Michael and Mr. Barclay. With the number of older white people standing outside, they will be sure to take precedence over me.

But then Colonel Wood is rushing toward me with outstretched hands. He not-so-gently pushes through the people moving toward the carriage.

"Come, Eliza. Our carriage is here," Colonel Wood says. "We must get you out of this smoke. It will be terrible for your voice."

"Where are we going?"

"To another hotel, and then onward to Boston in the morning."

All my things have been lost. My dresses, my sheet music. Everything. But I am a professional and we have an engagement in Boston. We must continue.

Colonel Wood helps me into the carriage and then climbs up behind me. I know my possessions can be replaced, but I still weep over losing them. But my tears fall harder at not knowing the fates of Michael or Mr. Barclay.

"Before we leave for Boston, I will send a telegram ahead of our arrival," Colonel Wood says. "Try to rest tonight and put all this out of your mind. There are many anticipating your concert, and you must be in great form."

I pull my coat tightly around my body and wrap my scarf around my face to warm the air I draw with each breath. As much as I would like to heed Colonel Wood's advice, I cannot push Michael's face out of my mind, nor can I stop thinking about his kindness, or that he may have perished in the fire along with Mr. Barclay.

I whisper prayers into the cold wind for his safety and for the safety of the freedom seekers in Mr. Barclay's care. It would be a tragedy to make it so far north and then die before truly being free.

And then I thank God for sparing me from the flames. Perhaps it was He who sent Michael to me, as an angel. When I was left uncherished and uncared for in the harsh and angry cold. And then again when Colonel Wood had ensured his own safety before inquiring after mine.

I thank God for angels and men. And for angels of men.

# CHAPTER TWENTY-THREE

*Boston, Massachusetts*
*March 1852*

$C$olonel Wood and I arrive in Boston on Friday afternoon to very little fanfare. Not that I expect any. Perhaps one day there will be parades announcing my arrival or auctions of my tickets to the highest bidder. Today, it is only me and my grumpy and grumbling manager. But we are here and unharmed.

I am still reeling from the events of yesterday evening. The weather is still frigid, so being indoors is one thing to be happy about. Being alive is another.

Boston looks very much like every other city we've visited on this tour. The same streets, assorted buildings, and people bundled in layers to keep out the invasive cold. One thing that is different here is the number of people milling about outdoors in this weather. It reminds me of Philadelphia, where the winter does little to impede commerce and moneymaking ventures.

Revere House, where we are lodging, is a lovely hotel that I'm sure is intended for the upper crust of society, several stories high with a grand entrance in an area called Bowdoin Square. There is no one loitering who looks like a slave catcher, so that is a comfort.

"We will be staying here until Wednesday morning," Colonel Wood explains to the hotel clerk.

Colonel Wood mentioned in passing that it will cost us one dollar a night to stay here. I am glad that dollar does not come out of my wages, because I would have no problem finding more reasonably priced accommodations.

"Please ensure Miss Greenfield's room is well dusted and not drafty. We must protect her voice for her concert on Tuesday at the Melodeon."

I want to ask Colonel Wood to lower his voice, because he's drawing attention to us. The thought that people might believe I am his property rankles me, so I stand as tall and as regal as possible, so that I am not mistaken for an enslaved person. Which I know is probably a ridiculous thought, because why would an enslaved person be staying in this hotel? But I cannot shake the thought, because I am standing here mute, not conducting any business myself. I hate it. I'd like to sign into the hotels on my own accord and move through the world as a woman on my own terms. Will fame and wealth grant me that freedom as well? If so, that is another reason to work hard and attain it.

As Colonel Wood continues to blather on, it occurs to me that the attention is his expected result. He receives our room keys and turns to me just as a well-coiffed older couple approaches.

"Miss Elizabeth Taylor Greenfield," the woman says in a friendly and disarming voice. "I look forward to hearing you sing in concert. You may not remember me, but when you were a little girl, I spent a great deal of time in Philadelphia with your guardian, Mrs. Greenfield. We fellowshipped at Mulberry Street Meeting. My name is Penelope Platt, and this is my husband, Roman."

My smile is genuine when I shake Mrs. Platt's extended hand. She's dressed in the very plain and understated style of most Quaker women, with a simple black dress and gauzy white shawl. I don't remember the round elderly woman, but if she was a friend of Miss Lizbeth's, I welcome her greeting.

"I am thrilled to make your acquaintance, Mrs. Platt. I only wish

Miss Lizbeth could have heard me sing in a concert hall. It was her encouragement that started me on this path."

"She was a wonderful woman. I greatly admired her," Mrs. Platt says. "My husband is writing a piece about your concert in the *Boston Herald*. I am sure it will be favorable."

"Thank you very much for your kind words. I hope you both enjoy the concert."

"Perhaps we can find time for tea before you leave town," Mrs. Platt says.

"I would enjoy that."

Colonel Wood grins as he watches the Platts cross the room to meet their friends at the hotel's restaurant. I wonder what amuses him so, but I have learned not to ask this man's thoughts.

"It is truly a marvel that you were raised the way you were, in the presence of wealth and privilege," Colonel Wood muses. "Your ability to hold discourse with those in higher stations is surprising. I am certain your gifts would have been wasted if these other characteristics were not at your disposal."

"My guardian told me that my gift would make room for me. I'd like to believe the gift would have flourished no matter the nurturing."

I wonder if he can even hear the irritation in my tone. Or if he even cares that his words are offensive. Probably not. Because these are the little things that roll off his tongue with ease, these things he marvels over.

Colonel Wood lifts an eyebrow and points toward the staircase. "Well, my dear, we will never know the answer to that. It's best not to even speculate."

"Agreed."

Without question, I have no desire to imagine the way my life would've unfolded had I been born to a different mother on a different plantation and raised by a different guardian.

"I have some contacts to visit today and tomorrow, because I need to procure an accompanist for the remainder of the tour," Colonel Wood explains. "I have requested the delivery of a fine dinner frock and performance gown to your room. Of course, all the appropriate undergarments and accoutrements will be delivered as well."

"Such a pity my other dresses are not yet ready. I would love to debut them here in Boston."

"Ah, yes, your friend, the costly Black dressmaker out of Philadelphia."

"She is worth every penny."

"I pray so."

I wonder if he would doubt Mary's skill if she wasn't a Black woman? I hate that in recent weeks, everything, it seems, has become about Black and white. My entire life I have been Black and never have I been more aware of this fact. I know that it is the privilege of my upbringing that has allowed me these decades of respite without having to ask myself these inner questions about every interaction.

Either someone wants me to carry on a protest, or someone else wants to protest that I exist. There has been no peace since the Black Swan was born. And yet I must persist. I have no privilege to return to, only the fruits of my own labor.

* * *

TODAY, WHILE COLONEL Wood continues his search for an accompanist, I have been left to my own devices. There has not been any communication from him, but this does not surprise me. Once he gets off to doing his business, he has little need for my input or participation.

Two things prevent me from leaving the hotel. One, the coldest winter ever. And the fact that I have no friend or loved one here to vouch for me in case I am kidnapped. It troubles me that the latter reason is more pressing than the first.

The farthest I wander from my room is to the hotel's restaurant downstairs. I will make one visit and purchase enough provisions to last me the entire day. I have books to keep me company while I rest my voice, and then perhaps tomorrow I will try to find a church to attend.

At my request, I am seated far from the restaurant's entrance, to avoid drawing any attention to myself. It was printed in Roman Platt's newspaper article where we are lodging, so perhaps a nefarious character might come looking for me. Especially since there aren't very many women staying here who look like me.

I peruse the restaurant's bill of fare as I sip tea from a dainty cup, but nothing strikes me as especially appetizing. There are all kinds of fancy foods, like leg of mutton with caper sauce, when I would give anything for some of Ruby's fried chicken or a bowl of pepper pot soup. Perhaps I'll try the curried lobster. I am told Boston is known for this dish.

"Eliza!"

This voice must be in my imagination, created by the drudgery of this tour and the longing for companionship. But I allow myself to look up. It is not my imagination at all.

"Eliza."

Charles's smile matches the pleasantness in his voice, and involuntarily I smile back, because he is beautiful. Also, I am shocked that he is here. It's been two months since I've laid eyes on him, but it feels like longer.

He lunges in my direction as if he intends to walk over but is stopped by one of the waiters. The grip of the much smaller man's hand on Charles's arm worries me. It looks threatening. Charles could be one moment from trouble.

I scramble to my feet. "Sir, he's meeting me here. I'm sorry."

The waiter looks Charles up and down with disbelief, and then he glares in my direction. I whisper a silent prayer that he knows who I am, and that I am here to perform a concert, and that he remembers what he saw in the newspapers about me.

Slowly, the waiter's grip loosens, and he gives Charles a silent nod. Not an apology, but an acknowledgment that Charles will not be thrown out. At least not yet.

Charles rushes over to my table and takes a small bow. It is very . . . genteel.

"Miss Greenfield," he says. "It is so good to see you."

"Charles—"

He closes his eyes, gives a tiny shake of his head, and then motions for me to sit. So I do, and Charles pulls out the chair across from mine and does the same. Our feet touch beneath the long tablecloth. I snatch them away. No touch from Charles feels safe.

"You're performing here this week," Charles says. "It's in all the newspapers."

"Yes, that is correct. Tuesday evening."

"Perhaps I will be in attendance."

There is a wistfulness in his voice. Is he hoping for an invitation? He would not get that from me.

"I believe there are tickets still available," I say.

I wonder if Charles read in those newspapers that the Black citizens of Boston are not going to be admitted to the concert. If he does know, it would be just like him to toy with me. I can no longer hold his intense gaze, so I look back down at the bill of fare in front of me.

"I thought I might never see you again," Charles says with a deep and heavy sigh.

"That seemed to be your choice. You did not call on me, nor did you write." I try not to sound like a jilted lover, because I am not, but he did hurt me by disappearing.

"There needed to be space between us."

I didn't need space. *He* needed space. I thought I had found a friend with whom I shared a common love of music, and of course a shared attraction. And I hoped we'd share the understanding that the flames of that attraction wouldn't be stoked until much later. But we never got to have that conversation. We never explored our friendship further. It was his way or nothing. His management ideas or none. Everything on his terms.

"But I did visit the Howards and they told me about the tour," he adds. "Congratulations, Eliza."

I wonder why Annabelle did not mention his visit in her letters to me. Did she think I'd lose focus on my tour by being lovesick? Or maybe she thought I didn't want to hear anything about him.

"Why would you visit the Howards? You aren't their friend."

Charles narrows his eyes and shakes his head. "Eliza. Of course, I went there looking for you. We are friends, aren't we? Even if we don't agree?"

"You and I have a different definition of friendship, Charles. Let us leave it there for now."

He takes a huge inhale and sighs. I do not think he hoped for this kind of reunion, and neither did I. I never thought we'd have a reunion at all.

"How has the tour been so far?" he asks, changing the direction of the conversation, and I am grateful for that.

But now my thoughts go to the fire, and I am overwhelmed for a moment before gathering myself.

"It has been . . . lucrative."

"Well, that is good. Isn't that the reason for all this hard work?"

"Yes. I have decided to go to Paris as soon as I'm able to save enough money for passage and lodging."

I know Charles does not agree with my plans to go to Paris for education. But he does not understand how it feels when every accolade I read is wrapped in admonishment. How every review outlines how much better I will be once I've had tutelage from European teachers.

"Still seeking validation from those less gifted than you are," Charles says. "But I know you will save the money and reach your goal."

"It is not validation I seek. It's freedom."

Charles closes his eyes and nods. Perhaps he does not wish to argue with me about choices for my life. Especially as he believes there should be space between us.

"What have you been doing for work?" I ask, not wanting him to leave in frustration. Not sure if I want him to leave at all and hating that I feel this way.

"Hauling loads from Buffalo to Canada. I have been on steamers and carriages for weeks. And this winter is the worst I've seen since I came up north."

"I don't care how cold it gets up here, you will never find me wintering in Mississippi."

Charles laughs at this. "Never."

The waiter walks up to our table accompanied by Colonel Wood. He does not look pleased, and the waiter wears a smug look on his face. I wonder what falsehood he shared with Colonel Wood that has him looking sour.

"Eliza, you did not tell me you were entertaining gentlemen callers."

Entertaining gentlemen callers! My nostrils flare with anger at Colonel Wood's implication that anything improper is taking place.

Before I can lash out in anger, Charles scrambles to his feet. "No, sir, I am no such thing. I was only saying hello to Miss Greenfield. I accompanied her a few times on the pianoforte in concert. She's blessed with one of the most amazing voices I've ever heard."

Colonel Wood squints at Charles. Assessing. "Indeed."

"Charles Monroe, sir." Charles extends a friendly hand. Colonel Wood looks at it a long time before shaking it but finally does.

"Colonel Wood. I am Miss Greenfield's manager."

"Pleased to make your acquaintance, Colonel Wood. Good afternoon, Miss Greenfield. It was lovely seeing you again. I will send your regards to Ruby and William."

"Hold there one moment," Colonel Wood says. "You say you accompanied Miss Greenfield in concert?"

"Yes. In Buffalo and Rochester."

"Are you going to be here in Boston long?" Colonel Wood asks. "We may have need of an accompanist."

Charles looks at me, and I nod in agreement. I'd much rather Charles play for me than some untested stranger Colonel Wood might find in a church or parlor.

"What is the pay?" Charles asks. "If I stay too long, I may have to find a replacement to finish my haul."

"Ten dollars for the concert," Colonel Wood says. "And find the replacement to finish your haul. If you're any good, I'll invite you on the rest of the tour. It runs through the spring."

"Lodging and meals covered on the tour in addition to the pay?"

Colonel Wood nods. "Don't expect to stay in hotels like Revere House, but you will have somewhere clean, dry, and warm to lay your head."

As much as I want Charles to come on this tour with me, it pains me to see him take crumbs from Colonel Wood when he'd wanted so badly to be my manager. It makes me wish that he had been more skilled at managing, because the dedication had been there from the beginning.

Colonel Wood turns to walk away, with the waiter at his heels, but then he stops and turns back to Charles.

"Are you available this evening?" he asks.

"I can make myself available."

"Miss Greenfield is invited to rehearse several selections from her concert in Jonas Chickering's music room."

Charles's eyebrows lift in excitement. He must know who Jonas Chickering is, but I do not. I am somewhat annoyed that an invitation has been accepted on my behalf without speaking to me first. But I cannot say I'm surprised.

"The piano manufacturer?" Charles asks.

Colonel Wood seems pleased at Charles's response. "Yes, one and the same. Please join us this evening at six o'clock. A carriage will be sent for us here."

Charles turns to face me just in time to see I'm fuming. "Miss Greenfield, Jonas Chickering gifted Jenny Lind a grand piano that is being used during every concert on her tour."

"So, they would like to see the Black Swan and compare me to their fair Jenny?" I quip saucily. "Why can they not make their comparisons at my concert?"

Colonel Wood glances around the sparsely filled restaurant, perhaps to see who may be listening. No one except the nosy waiter seems to be privy to our discussion.

"Will you excuse us, please?" Colonel Wood asks Charles and the waiter, who gives me a nasty look before he scurries off.

Colonel Wood sits in the seat previously occupied by Charles. I can tell he's annoyed, because his skin has reddened a bit, but I am tired of being ordered here and there without being consulted.

"Eliza, this invitation is an honor," Colonel Wood says. "Only Boston's elite will be in that room, and they will surely sing your praises. Their accolades will help sell tickets to your concert."

"The tickets will sell as the rest of them have."

"Jenny Lind was here performing in December. We will have to whet their appetites for this concert, and we need all the goodwill we can muster," Colonel Wood argues, struggling to keep his voice from rising. "Not everyone wants to see a Black version of their favorite prima donna."

He's stopped short of using the actual language from one of my worst reviews. A reviewer in Lockport, New York, had written that I was nothing but Jenny Lind "all blacked up." A trick. As if someone had greased Jenny Lind's face with black polish, put her on the stage, and called her Elizabeth Taylor Greenfield. As ridiculous as it was, it cut to my core, because who could hear us both and mistake my voice for hers? My baritone alone separates me from Miss Lind, and while she might be pretty and have the skin of a porcelain doll, her slim form is no match for my curves.

"And the tickets are not moving as quickly as your other venues," Colonel Wood adds for good measure. "They have sold less than five hundred. If you want to continue to receive invitations, and make your fifty dollars per show, there must be profits, Eliza."

I finally acquiesce. "I will attend this rehearsal, but my voice needs resting. The smoke from the fire is bothering my throat."

"Choose your easiest songs, and then after tomorrow you can rest until Tuesday night," Colonel Wood says.

He stands from his seat and nods at Charles, bidding him a good day. The waiter is here again lingering next to the table with his arms crossed. Waiting. If he were Black, I'd tell him to scoot along until I need him, but his whiteness makes his word superior even if he's in a servant's role.

"Miss Greenfield," Charles says, "I must go and attend to some details before this evening if I am to make it back on time. I am looking forward to this engagement."

"Thank you for accepting."

Charles turns and leaves, and I sit with this for a moment, trying to figure out how to feel about it all. I do not believe Charles's visit is an accident at all. He found out where I'd be from the Howards and took a job to put himself nearby. That was simple enough. It *was* a coincidence that we desperately needed an accompanist, though, and that he's available. So perhaps this bit is providence, and our connection, at least in friendship, is ordained for now.

But the formality of it all was infuriating. If he called me Miss Greenfield one more time, I was going to hurl this elegant teacup across the room.

"Would you like anything to eat?" the annoying waiter asks me.

I am too nervous to eat now. A rehearsal in front of Boston's elite with a scratchy throat and very little rest? This feels like a disaster in the making. But men must be impressed, and tickets must be sold. All else be damned.

It is something of a miracle that Charles showed up now, at a time when Colonel Wood's demands are becoming more and more self-serving. My full trust in him is starting to wane, and I could use an ally and a friend. Hopefully, this time, Charles will be that for me. If he can bridle his emotions and stay through the end of the tour.

# CHAPTER TWENTY-FOUR

*U*nder the guise of practice, I am having breakfast at Charles's place of lodging. He's rented a room from a friend of Patrick's, a Quaker abolitionist who lives alone in a large three-story home. Charles has an entire suite to himself, and, quite frankly, it is much nicer than my room at the Revere House.

Charles prepared the breakfast himself: eggs, toast, and thick sausages, along with strong coffee. It is a rare thing for me to have a meal prepared by a man, so I try not to allow my sour mood to spoil this simple luxury.

"Did you try the marmalade?" Charles asks. "Apparently, Mr. Banks makes it himself. When his wife was alive, it was an activity they did together."

"And he keeps the tradition? How nice."

"I thought so," Charles says as he spreads marmalade on a slice of toast and places it on the edge of my plate. The sweet orange scent pleases me, but not enough to lift my mood.

Charles sighs. "Eliza, it was not that bad."

"Wasn't it?"

I pick up the newspaper page from the table and clear my throat. Charles sighs even louder.

"Don't read it again," Charles says. "You're making it worse."

"How could it be any worse than this?" I ask.

"Eliza . . ."

I snap the paper in the air with a dramatic flourish. "'Miss Green-field performed to a half-filled house, though it was to be expected with the tickets priced at one dollar,'" I read. "'Her program contains many of the same songs delivered previously by Miss Jenny Lind. It cannot be denied that Miss Greenfield is blessed with a natural gift and was encored several times. Under European tutelage, she will, without question, become one of the greatest prima donnas of our time. Though not a criticism, because to the untrained ear it would have been unnoticeable, I would be remiss if I did not remark on the fact that Miss Greenfield was not in top form yesterday evening. I am told by her manager that she is recovering from severe indisposition, which came upon her after the fire at Hampden House in Springfield, where Miss Greenfield barely escaped with her life. It will be interest-ing to see if she has recovered in time for Thursday night's perfor-mance. The Thursday showing should be better attended with ticket prices more aptly set at fifty cents.'"

"There are many complimentary things said in that review," Charles says. "You are only focusing on the negative parts."

"'Not in top form'? 'Severe indisposition'?" I rage. "My singing was without flaw. You know it. You were there."

"And many other reviews said exactly that. Why do you choose to talk only about this one?"

"Because the bad reviews are the ones people read. They're the ones people believe."

"I think critics and admirers alike will flock to the Melodeon on Thursday to see for themselves."

"And who told Colonel Wood to speak on my behalf? I do not need him making excuses for me."

Charles licks a bit of marmalade from his top lip, and I am suddenly mesmerized by something else. His tongue, and his lips, probably still sweet from the marmalade. I am irritated that I could be distracted by a small thing like that when I have more important things to fume about.

"He probably wishes he hadn't. I am sure he's read this same review."

The air in the room has become thick, at least to me, and even though it's freezing outside, I'd love to throw open the windows so that I can breathe.

"Well, no matter what he says, I am on vocal rest until Thursday. No more exhibitions for any potential benefactors."

"Mr. Chickering seemed very impressed with you, Eliza. I wouldn't say it was a wasted effort."

"Colonel Wood spent the whole evening talking about the museum he plans to build in Ohio. He really wants to be another Barnum, doesn't he?"

"He did talk a great deal about that," Charles says, "which was confusing, because I thought he'd entreat those rich men to invest in your tour. But they *were* in awe of you. I watched their faces as you sang."

"Well, then where is my grand piano, Charles? Has it been commissioned? Is it on the way?"

Charles opens his mouth to respond but instead he erupts into a flurry of laughter. I stare at him until he manages to calm himself.

"I am so sorry, Eliza. That was funny."

"Happy to entertain you, Charles. Hopefully we won't both be without income after all this."

"I missed your humor."

And now I think Charles is feeling the closeness of the room as I am, and the heaviness of the air. His breathing slows, and his mirth fades. We have not spoken again about how we left things, but just because we left things, it doesn't mean the feelings dissipated. Mine did not.

"What else do you love, Charles? In case you disappear from me again, I would like to call your admiration to mind in my memories."

"Are such theatrics necessary? I did not disappear from you. I could not bear to be near you. And we couldn't seem to agree on the management of your engagements."

"And what about now?"

"Seeing you again felt like a second chance in some way. And now I cannot bear to be apart from you."

"But things have not changed for me. We are not speaking directly about what caused the separation."

"I know. Nothing has changed for me either."

"So what do we do? I do not like this awkwardness between us. I want nothing more than for you to be with me on this tour through the spring. But if we are going to start having disagreements again, then I would rather you disappear now before I become accustomed to your presence."

I am trying not to appear frantic and emotional and all the things that men complain about. The theatrics. But my breathing has become ragged, and my eyes are rimmed with tears. The thought of Charles leaving again while I am already feeling so much pressure from Colonel Wood and this tour is terrifying.

Charles stops eating. He takes the cloth napkin from the table and wipes his face slowly and deliberately as if stalling. Charles never has a problem finding words. He has all the words in his possession and uses them without hesitation, even when they sting.

"Will you allow me to answer your first question?" Charles says in a calming voice.

I nod, because unlike Charles, I have no words to give.

"I love your humor, your self-confidence, and your ability to overcome things that would destroy most people."

While I appreciate these compliments, and I also admire Charles for similar qualities, these are not the kinds of things making it difficult for me to breathe. I love the way he smells like a clean shave and the mint in his tea, the way his shoulders fill out his suit coat, the way he shifts his weight to one side when he's thinking, and the bow in his long legs when he strides.

"Those are admirable qualities for you to love, I suppose," I say.

"But is this the reason you can't bear to be apart from me? I do not mean to spurn your compliments, but you could very well say these things about Patrick."

Charles leans forward and rests his chin atop one closed fist and grins at me. I lift an eyebrow but do not grin back. I am aware that my words are bold and the opposite of genteel. I also know that this is stoking a fire that we may not be able to quench.

"Do you trust me, Eliza?"

"I do."

Charles rises from his seat. He slowly walks over to my side of the table and squats next to my chair. My body trembles at his closeness. I may trust him, but I do not trust myself.

"Now, I am going to tell you the other things I love about you, Eliza. The things I have not said aloud because, while I am a man of honor, I am still a man. Shall I continue?"

"Yes."

"I love the way this one piece of hair always escapes your bun and curls down onto your cheek."

Charles reaches out, takes the unruly tendril, and tucks it behind my ear. Then the tip of his index finger makes a trail down the outline of my chin and caresses my throat.

"I love how when I lean in close to you, I can smell the soap you wash yourself with every day, vanilla and something else I can't identify—"

Charles brings his nostrils to my throat and inhales, then groans on exhaling. The warm rush of his sweet breath across my neck makes me shudder, and I struggle to keep both hands on the table. I want to reach up and dig my fingertips into his hair and pull his face to mine. Every part of me is aflame.

"P-patchouli. That is the scent," I whisper. "My friend Ophelia introduced it to me after traveling to India."

"I will have to thank your friend," Charles whispers in response.

I cannot stop myself from bringing my hand to his face. He closes his eyes as I rake my fingernails lightly through his dense beard. When he opens them again, the intensity of his gaze nearly stops my heart from beating.

He catches my hand in his and kisses my palm and each finger. "This is another thing that I love. How soft your hands are. I dreamt about your hands after we separated."

And I dreamt about him kissing my hand.

"I love every curve of your body, even what you seek to conceal with corsets and stays. The way your lips slightly part when I am near. An invitation?"

I nod.

"I accept."

Charles pulls my bottom lip into his mouth with a sucking motion. It feels so good, a tear escapes my eye, and Charles wipes it away.

"Save those tears," Charles says. "There is more."

"But, Charles. I cannot."

"Trust me. I will not ruin what you have worked so hard for, and we will both have our finale."

I close my eyes and nod in consent. I do trust him, and my body longs for his touch.

Charles pulls me to my feet, guides me to his bed. He unhooks the buttons on the back of my dress and slowly slides it down over my shoulders while kissing me and trailing circles in my mouth with his tongue. I feel the dress fall around my ankles, but I do not care.

With one gentle touch on my shoulder Charles urges me to sit. I do, and instantly he is at my feet, unlacing my boots while kissing the stockinged flesh behind my knee.

I almost cry out, but Charles puts a finger to my lips.

"We don't want anyone to hear," he whispers, "so we must be quiet."

What if I cannot comply?

I do not have time to answer this question, because now Charles is removing my stockings one by one. His fingers move deftly, as if he's disrobed many women. But I do not want to think of any others. In this moment there is only us.

After my stockings have been discarded, Charles reaches into a slit in my petticoat and his fingers help themselves to my moist folds. I cannot stop my hips from rocking back and forth, but Charles does.

"Not yet. I want to show you something new," Charles whispers. Then he retracts his fingers from my nether regions and sucks the juices from them one by one.

"Lie back," Charles whispers, and I obey. I am nervous and excited about what else I could possibly learn outside of the actual coupling, but I am still trusting.

Charles pulls my petticoat free, leaving my sex barely covered by a thin bit of fabric. I am so far gone now that if he unsheathes his member and mounts me, I do not think I will stop him.

But Charles is much more trustworthy than I have given him credit for. He does not disrobe, but he uses his mouth to probe and caress the same places his fingers just traveled, and the pleasure is so extreme that I must force my fist into my mouth to keep from screaming out.

And then, when I think I cannot take any more, there is something greater building. Instinct tells me to pull away from this, that nothing will be the same after.

"Don't run from it." I hear Charles's voice, but it feels far away. "Trust me."

I relax and allow Charles to continue. His tongue moves rhythmically over my folds, and they throb and pulse as if my heart has shifted downward. And as the building continues, tears leak from both eyes. Charles doesn't stop me from crying now, so I suppose it is time for my tears to flow.

When I feel I might perish, Charles, while still caressing and sucking, makes use of his fingers once more. Now I cannot hold back my cries. Now I cannot stop the thrusting of my hips until the building culminates in an explosion. A tiny death.

I tremble and shake, but I cannot cry out anymore. The sound is caught in my throat.

Finally, my breathing returns to normal and I relax the grip I didn't know I had in Charles's hair. He rises from his handiwork and gives me a salty, patchouli-scented kiss.

"We can please each other this way during the entire tour, and there will be no threat of a child growing in your womb."

"I don't know how. I'm afraid it won't bring you pleasure."

"I will guide you."

And in this I also trust him.

# CHAPTER TWENTY-FIVE

*Cleveland, Ohio*
*April 1852*

The weather has broken, and there is finally a hint of spring in the air, as we find ourselves in Ohio on the final leg of this tour. Even with Charles here to break the monotony and to provide the pleasure of his company, I am weary and ready for home. But where would home be? At the present, my inheritance is still in dispute, and I have nowhere to call my own.

Since the rivers and lakes have thawed after the tempestuous winter, Mary has traveled by packet boat to deliver the two performance gowns she crafted for me. So that she wouldn't have to travel alone, she'd waited until Mr. Howell had business that corresponded with one of my tour dates. Fortunately, this Cleveland date was available when Mr. Howell had a meeting with a client; otherwise, the dresses would've had to be shipped if I was to have them in time for the remainder of my spring concerts.

I nervously await her arrival right outside Weddell House, while Charles runs errands for the concert with Colonel Wood.

Charles has become an assistant to Colonel Wood in all matters of concert business. I do not object to this, because I know Charles is collecting information to become more adept at managing concerts himself. As our friendship deepens and blossoms into something more, I hope that we will be able to revisit his management of my career.

Surprisingly, I am overcome with emotion when the carriage pulls in front of the hotel. Too many months have gone by since I have spoken to my sister, and I am bursting with things to tell her.

As soon as the carriage stops, the driver scrambles from his seat to assist Mary with her trunk. He's nearly tripping over himself to make sure she doesn't trouble herself walking down the steps without his help. She, as usual, seems completely oblivious to the attention.

"Mary, I'm here!"

She squeals and rushes over to me with outstretched arms. Our greeting never changes, no matter how many months have passed since we've seen each other.

"Eliza, it is so good to see you, my dear," Mary says. "And look at this hotel where you're staying. What does it feel like to be a famous prima donna?"

I laugh as I direct the hotel's Black bellman over to the carriage to collect Mary's things.

"I do not know if I am famous yet," I say. "But it has been nice hearing applause every other night, dining on roasted leg of mutton, and having tea in the homes of some of America's most elite citizens. So, if you consider that famous . . ."

Mary roars with laughter as she links her arm in mine, and we stride into the hotel lobby. "Oh, you are in great spirits, my sister. I almost expected you to be forlorn and homesick."

"Oh no. I am in great spirits indeed."

My giggle tells Mary everything she needs to know about my mirth. She stops walking, takes both of my hands, and stares directly into my eyes.

"Do tell."

"Let's wait until we're behind a door."

"Ooh, now I am really excited."

I feel many pairs of eyes on me and Mary, laughing like schoolgirls as we walk arm in arm through the lobby to the staircase leading to my room. Since we have been lodging here several days, most of the hotel staff knows who I am, but some of their guests do not. To them, I suppose we might look out of place.

"This hotel is bustling with activity," Mary says. "Is there some sort of meeting going on?"

"Perhaps they have come from far and wide to behold the Black Swan."

She laughs as she gazes at a group of men as they walk by. "Would anyone travel far and wide for that?"

"They would," I say as I pull Mary closer to me as the men look back at her with interest.

As we approach my room, I feel apprehension at the two young white men who wait outside my door. I look for the bellman to see if he is close with Mary's trunk, but I see over the staircase that he has enlisted another bellman's help and they are moving slowly up the stairs.

"Excuse me, gentlemen, I'd like to get into my room," I say, making sure to keep my eyes averted and looking at the ground.

"Are we blocking your entry?"

I shudder at the sound of his voice. He has a distinctly southern drawl.

"I didn't know they allowed Blacks to stay at this hotel," the other young man says. "Didn't know it was Blacks that could afford a room. You see all kinds of things up north."

"This one's right pretty," the first man says as he steps a little too close to Mary. I push her behind me, as if I can block anyone who may want to molest her.

"I appreciate the compliment, sir, but I am married," Mary says in a sweet voice. It's sweet, but it also trembles. She's as nervous as I am.

"I don't believe I asked you a thing," the young man says. "But your husband is a lucky man. He gets to bed you every night without you putting up a fuss with that sassy tongue of yours."

Mary hadn't said anything sassy, but any conversation could be a trigger for that accusation. My heart is pounding so loudly in my chest that I'm sure these two can hear it and sense my fear. It is best to avoid the southern variety of white men at all costs, especially when, like these two, they have had too many cups of whiskey.

Thankfully, the bellmen arrive with Mary's trunks. The two lascivious men step to the side so that we may enter. Once we're inside, I lock the door behind us. Then I breathe.

"Do you think they've gone?" Mary whispers.

"I pray so. Charles and Colonel Wood should be back soon from their errands."

Mary tilts her head to one side and smiles. "Charles? He has returned to you? And you did not write me about it?"

"I told you there was a surprise. That was it. Charles is my accompanist on the tour."

"What serendipity," Mary says as she eases down onto a cushioned chaise. "Have you two reconciled? If I recall correctly, there was trouble between you."

I sit next to Mary. "We have indeed reconciled."

"Have you allowed him to—"

"No, but, Mary, he has shown me other things. I don't dare to even whisper them, they're so scandalous."

Mary laughs. "I am sure there is nothing you have discovered that I don't already know."

"Oh, I don't know. Some of these things, I get the feeling, are distinctly European. Charles must have learned them on his travels."

"Good heavens, what things?"

"Things with his mouth."

Mary's eyes stretch, and her jaw drops. "And do you—"

"Yes."

My hands fly up to my face to hide my embarrassment, even though I have no need to be bashful with Mary. We have spoken about all manner of sexual things. Perhaps it is the fact that we're usually discussing someone else's exploits.

"Well. I think Sadie was right to marry her pure son off to someone else. You've become quite the whore since this whole prima donna business."

We laugh until we are both in tears, until we can hardly breathe, and until we feel safe again. Behind the locked door of this room, I do not allow myself to worry about those young men who might intend to do us harm.

"Speaking of Sadie," Mary says, "I heard her at church talking quite gleefully about some article in the *Frederick Douglass' Paper* that painted you in a disparaging light. Did you know about this?"

I roll my eyes at Sadie and her gossip. "Unfortunately, yes, that is true. Almost every concert hall where I have performed has refused to allow Black people to attend, and if they do, it is in inferior and undesirable seating."

"That is infuriating. Our money purchases tickets just as well as theirs."

"Yes, and the ones writing letters to that newspaper want me to cancel concerts where Black people aren't allowed. Charles wanted that as well."

"I understand their impatience, Eliza. We are ready for real freedom. Not this flimsy thing we have that can be snatched away at any moment. If canceling concerts will help the concert promoters understand the power of our money, then so be it."

"Shouldn't I secure my own freedom before trying to help anyone else? What other work is there for me to do outside of singing? To take care of someone's children? To clean their home?"

Mary takes my frantically waving hands and places them by my sides. "There, there, Eliza. I did not mean to upset you."

She never means to upset me, but her viewpoints on how I choose to live my life are always upsetting. Mary may not say these things directly like Charles or the editors in the *Frederick Douglass' Paper*, but her opinions carry a more painful sting.

"I just remembered, I have a package for you," Mary says. "It was sent in Mr. Howell's care, and he thought you might like it while you're out touring."

Mary rises from the chaise and pulls a carefully wrapped package out of her travel bag. She hands it to me as she returns to her seat. "Open it, so I can know what it is," Mary says. "I was curious when he brought it in."

"What if it's from a handsome admirer and I don't want you to see it?"

"The return address says it's from Harriet Beecher Stowe. She is a handsome woman, but I don't think that's what you mean."

I'm curious as well, so I rip open the paper like a small child on Christmas morning. Inside the wrapping is a book and a card.

"*Uncle Tom's Cabin*, by Harriet Beecher Stowe," I say. "She's written a book."

"Did she sign it? What did she say?"

Inside the front cover of the book is a note. I quickly read it to myself to make sure there's nothing objectionable or private before I read it aloud.

"Well?" Mary asks. "What does it say?"

"It says, 'For Elizabeth. The tenacity you have displayed in the pursuit of your gift is inspiring. You are proof that the enslavement of Black people is a sin against God. I hope that this book will help convince those in power to repent and abolish this great crime. I named a very powerful character in this narrative after you. I hope you enjoy the narrative of your namesake and all the other characters in this novel. It is fiction that I pray soon comes to fruition. Sincerely, Harriet.'"

"She named a character after you?" Mary says. "Do you find that strange?"

"No, I think she has very good intentions."

"Your life is full of well-intentioned white people. Most of us have not been so lucky."

"I have been blessed with some, yes. And those few I do cherish."

Mary's long and pregnant pause cannot begin to articulate the terror she faced in her early years at the hands of a different kind of white person.

"Why don't you try on your gowns?" Mary asks, forcing her face into a smile. "Let us decide if they are wholesome enough."

Mary again leaves her seat on the chaise and pulls the first gown from her trunk. Before it is even unfolded, I am pleased by the color and the fabric. Ivory silk.

"Step out of your dress, so that we can put this one on."

Mary holds the gown up for me to see, and it is stunning. It has a low-neck bodice and bell sleeves. There's a bertha attached for modesty's sake, but I hope I can detach it on the occasion I decide not to care about modesty. Both the edges of the sleeves and the entirety of the bertha are covered in hand-stitched lace roses. The ivory reminds me of a wedding dress.

"My goodness, Mary," I say. "You have outdone yourself with this one."

"Let's see if I need to make any adjustments."

Mary helps me slip out of my everyday dress and into this masterpiece. As I had hoped, the bertha is detachable, but Mary snaps me into every piece. The fabric balloons around my body and onto the floor. I am terrified that we are going to somehow soil it.

"I will have this transported to the concert hall. If I wear it through these filthy streets, the hemline will be ruined."

"It will lift a bit with your cage and petticoats, but I agree with you. It must be purity on the stage. When those lights come up, I want the audience to think you're an angel."

"I feel like one."

Mary and I both look at the door when we hear a light knock.

"It's probably Charles," I say. "He and Colonel Wood's errands took longer than I thought they would."

"Well, you stand here. I don't want you to snag the dress on a nail."

"Eliza, it's Charles," we hear from the other side of the door. "Are you here?"

I never thought I would be this relieved to hear Charles's voice. Hopefully that means our earlier harassers have found something or someone else worthy of their attention.

Mary opens the door, and she's greeted with one of Charles's most disarming smiles. She looks at me and fans herself.

"This is Charles?" she asks.

"Yes, I am Charles the accompanist." He steps into the room and closes the door behind him.

"You are doing more than accompanying," Mary says. "I'm Eliza's sister, Mary."

"The Black Swan's seamstress," Charles says as he takes his hat off and bows his head in greeting. "This dress is spectacular."

"It truly is," Mary says. "And even more so now that Eliza is wearing it."

Charles moves closer to inspect the dress further. He holds both my arms out so that the bell sleeves fan out at my sides. It is always unnerving the way Charles seems to consume me with his eyes. I am glad for the modesty piece over my bodice. If it was not there, Charles might have misconstrued my heaving bosom as an invitation.

"We must have you photographed in this dress," Charles says. "Then that image can be placed on the front of your concert programs."

"Colonel Wood isn't going to pay for a photographer," I say. "He's been complaining about the cost of this and the cost of that. He was murmuring about paying for Mary's packet boat ride."

"He's desperate to turn a profit," Charles says. "I think he oversold these concerts to the concert hall managers."

"Well, he couldn't have known that Black people would be chased away from the concert venues."

"At any rate, it sounds like he's not getting as wealthy as he thought he'd get from this tour." Charles says.

I look at myself in the mirror in this splendid gown, and though I want to feel pleased at the beauty of it, in the back of my mind I feel trepidation. The only way I can continue this journey is for my concerts to be profitable for Colonel Wood and all others involved.

In every city I've performed there have been letters of recommendation sent ahead of me, with the signatures of all the important white men who have heard me sing and been impressed by my talent. I am aware that the loyalty of those supporters is predicated on success. If they remove their support, not even Colonel Wood with all his grandstanding and showmanship will be able to book concert engagements for me.

As always, I feel at the mercy of the whims of men. Pursuit of this dream has always been subject to their support and approval. And while I understand the chains of slavery weigh heavier than these, how can Charles and the men sending letters to the *Frederick Douglass' Paper* not understand that women are in bondage whether on plantations or in lovely Philadelphia brownstones?

No. I cannot fight the battles of men, until I am victorious over my own.

# CHAPTER TWENTY-SIX

*Toronto, Ontario*
*May 1852*

We have reached the final city on the tour, but not for lack of invitations. Colonel Wood has received requests from at least ten other cities for a visit from the Black Swan, but I am at the point of sheer exhaustion. I fear that if we continue at this pace, I will cause irreparable damage to my voice.

Of course, Colonel Wood is not happy about this, but unfortunately for him, I have agency over my own body, and it is not his to command. Not only do I need to rest, but I have business to attend to in Philadelphia. Mr. Howell has given me an update on my inheritance, and there is a hearing next month. After many of Miss Lizbeth's friends and my mentors wrote letters to the court, the judge would like to hear arguments from me, the Briggs, and other members of the community. Mr. Howell believes that after the hearing, the judge will rule favorably, and then no one will be able to stand in the way of my funds being released.

I will be overjoyed to have all that unpleasantness behind me. Once my inheritance is released, I can be rid of Colonel Wood and go directly to Europe to continue my music education and gain more notoriety on the stage. The savings I have made from the tour will be an extra cushion and will assist with locating my mother and bringing her home, if that is a possibility.

But for now I will focus on giving a concert here in Toronto that is a fitting finale to my debut tour.

At the invitation of a wealthy Black Toronto citizen named James Mink, Charles and I will be lodging at his hotel, the Mansion House on Adelaide Street. Although Colonel Wood does not like to lodge at a different location than I, so that he can keep me under his watchful eye, this time he chooses separate accommodations, because he does not prefer to stay at a Black-owned hotel, much to Charles's delight.

Charles has escorted me downstairs to the hotel's restaurant and tavern, and it is bustling with activity. The tables are full of Black couples, families, and groups of friends. The aromas coming from the kitchen are tantalizing, and there is a harpist playing lovely chords. But what is most evident to me is that these Black people are living without fear or care about being seen.

"I love your face clean-shaven," I say to Charles. "You look like a very young man, ready to make his way in the world."

"What do I look like with my beard?" Charles asks with a wicked grin on his face. "Do I look like an old man ready to retire for the evening with my cup of whiskey and a blanket?"

"Without it, you have the look of a schoolboy."

"Well, this schoolboy is sweet on Eliza."

As always, his intense gaze communicates more than his words. It makes me curious if Charles has anything else to teach me before the end of the tour. His lessons have been enlightening and amazing. I do not wish to be apart from him in Philadelphia. Not even for a short amount of time.

A short, plump waiter appears at our table, and we order bread, soup, roasted chicken, and vegetables. Charles requests whiskey for himself and brandy for me. We both chuckle as the waiter's round belly scoots the table a bit as he leaves.

"We should have asked him what his favorite thing on the bill of fare is," Charles says, "because he seems to enjoy it. Immensely."

"Nothing wrong with enjoying good food and drink. The fact that we can taste things is a gift from God."

Charles laughs. "Is that so? Well, what happens when one must waddle from the consumption of all these delicious things?"

"Moderation is the key to virtue."

"I prefer to overindulge in many delicious things," Charles says.

Since we've arrived in Toronto, Charles has been very randy and flirtatious. Not that we haven't been enjoying each other to the extent that I've allowed. In every city, we find a secret place to hide away, where we throw away all manners and modesty. I fear our time together will soon expire, because it seems to be the nature of a man to always press for the full ecstasy that results in children. The one thing I am not ready to oblige.

"What are your plans after we go back to America?" I ask, attempting to steer the conversation away from our carnal pursuits. "Will you go back to Buffalo?"

"I do intend to, yes. I enjoy playing in church, and my friends in Buffalo are more like family. What about you? I know you have your hearing in Philadelphia, but where will you settle when you finally collect your inheritance?"

"We have talked about this. I am going to Paris or Venice for musical instruction. Miss Bella has recommended several teachers. There is a young woman in Paris whom she has sent a letter of recommendation to on my behalf."

"Have you made enough money on the tour?" Charles asks hesitantly, perhaps not wanting to cross the line into my business affairs, because I have made it a point not to share those with him since he's returned.

"Not enough yet. My goal was to save nine hundred dollars, so that I may be able to move about Europe as a woman of means, and pay for my lodging, lessons, and meals without having to work," I explain. "It seems, around the elites and aristocrats, that they can sense desperation, and I do not want to be treated as a beggar."

Charles grins. "You are a very proud woman."

"Shouldn't I be? I want to be respected. It is bad enough they will already judge me as less than because I am Black. I cannot go to Europe seeking charity and goodwill."

If I learned anything from Miss Lizbeth, it is that money is the greatest of equalizers. They may not respect my person or my gift, but at least I will have my own resources and be able to hold my head up with dignity.

"How short are you of your goal?" he asks.

"About five concerts short if I count the money I have to spend to take care of my everyday needs," I say with a frustrated sigh. "And that's if I can continue to command fifty dollars an engagement."

A young white woman timidly approaches our table. Although I have no idea what she wants, I am quite happy to have the distraction from Charles's line of questioning. I don't want to think about the money that I have yet to earn, and the inheritance that may never materialize.

"Hello, please forgive my interruption of your dinner," the young woman says, "but are you Miss Elizabeth Taylor Greenfield?"

"I am."

"Oh, my father told me you were staying at the hotel, and I could not believe someone like you would be staying here of all places."

"Your father?" Charles asks. "Who might he be?"

I glance over at Charles, and he has a look of concern on his face. I suppose he is right to question the intentions of any white person, but I find myself sometimes giving them the benefit of the doubt because of the well-intentioned ones I've had in my life. Although, sometimes this has not been wise, because my instincts have not always been correct.

"My father is James Mink, the owner of the hotel. I am Mary Mink, soon to be Mary Williams. I am to be wed this coming Friday."

Now, this is shocking. I can usually tell when a person is Black, no matter what their parentage might be. There's usually a telltale sign—a little extra thickness around the nose, an extra curl to the hair, a fullness in the lips. Most Black people can tell even if white people cannot. But this young woman would fool even me.

"Congratulations! You must be excited," I say. "I hope you get to come to my concert the next evening. Or will you already be on your honeymoon?"

"Yes, I will be on my honeymoon, but I wanted to ask if you might sing at our wedding?" Her voice is timid, hopeful. "My father will pay whatever fee you request."

Would I like to sing for the daughter of a Black millionaire? Of course. And I hope that they always remember my kindness. Who knows when I might need the help of a millionaire?

"I'd love to. Are you getting married here at the hotel or at a church?"

Mary Mink soon-to-be Williams squeals with delight and claps her hands while jumping up and down. It tickles me to see her so excited and makes me even happier to sing for her.

"We're getting married at Good Hope Baptist Church on Friday. Following the wedding will be a reception here. If you wouldn't mind singing at the church. A nice wedding hymn."

"I think I know a few."

"And, of course, your gentleman friend is invited."

Charles lifts his eyebrows at me, probably waiting for me to correct her and say that he is my accompanist. For some reason, in this space, I do not want to deny Charles, and I don't see a reason to. The need for perfect decorum is reserved for those who might judge me, and I don't think she will.

"We accept your invitation, and if there is an organ at the church, my gentleman friend, Charles, will accompany me."

"Splendid. There is an organ. I will have our bellman leave a note with all the information on your door."

Then Mary surprises me by hugging me. The gesture is so sincere that I can't help but hug her back. She stops short of hugging Charles but does give him an enthusiastic wave before rushing off through the restaurant.

"Your gentleman friend?" Charles asks.

The laughter I had been holding in comes bubbling out. Charles grins as though he is enjoying every bit of my discomfort.

"How should I refer to you? Are you not a gentleman who is my friend?"

"Hmmm, I suppose. But I find myself to be less gentlemanly than most gentlemen."

"Oh, you are not. Charles, you know how I feel about you. Why do you tease me?"

Charles draws in a deep breath and slowly exhales. I cannot tell if that sigh is resignation or acceptance.

"I do know how you feel about me. And about your music."

He doesn't need to say more. His message has been communicated many times and received.

"So, what should I sing at this wedding?"

"'Ave Maria.' With your soprano, it will be exquisite."

"Oh, yes, that is a wonderful idea. Do you think I should mention this to Colonel Wood?"

Another long inhale and exhale from Charles, but this one ends with a furrowed brow and a frown.

"The man manages your tour. He is not the manager of your social engagements. Even if pay is involved, he is not entitled to a share."

"I agree. Your thoughts are confirmation of my own. Now we must practice for a concert and a wedding."

"The wedding of a millionaire's daughter. A millionaire who was previously enslaved and now has made his fortune in Canada."

I shake my head in disbelief. "How do you know these things, Charles?"

"In every city we visit, I connect with those who are with the cause of freedom. We have supporters here as well as in America."

"James Mink is a supporter?"

"Why would someone who escaped to freedom himself not want to support others? And a man with his resources can be a great ally."

"And I thought I was just granting a favor to a young bride. Who knew it was a call to action?"

"Your very existence is a call to action, Eliza. One day you will understand this."

Perhaps Charles speaks the truth, but that day is not today.

* * *

THE CHURCH IS packed with well-wishers, but they are not all Black citizens of Toronto. Many of them are white as well. It reminds me of many celebrations back home in Philadelphia. Wealthy, upper-class white people frequently break bread with their wealthy Black counterparts, especially when there are things to celebrate, like weddings, or on occasions to grieve.

Charles and I are seated with the family even though it is my preference to not have to interact with people before singing. It was impossible for me to have a private space, though, because the bride and her maids are using the rooms that would be set aside for that purpose.

"There are a lot of people here," Charles whispers. "They must be well loved."

Or people are here because they want to be seen as being connected to a wealthy family. Either way, the family seems pleased at the turnout.

I chose to wear a dress that I would don for any church service. Black with a high neck and bell sleeves. Today, I appear as Eliza, not the Black Swan, so my hair is in my signature church bun.

Charles and I are led to the front of the church, and he sits at the massive pipe organ. It is not time for me to sing yet—they will give a signal for that—but Charles begins to play chords so that the attendees will know it is time for the wedding to begin.

When the usher nods at me, I start the hymn. Quiet and sweet at first, as the bridesmaids make their way to the front of the church where the groom and groomsmen are waiting. The groom is young, eager, and stunningly handsome. He's the kind of man most young girls dream of having. Tall, with broad, strong shoulders, and smooth dark skin. His smile is warm and inviting and seems to beckon Mary forward.

As the bride walks down the aisle on her father's arm, I take the singing up an octave and give them all the appropriate trills and runs—the kind Black people expect in church—but of course, the attention is on the breathtaking beauty in her white lace gown.

After the last note, there are no encores and no standing ovations. The bride has tears streaming down her face, but perhaps not because she was moved by my singing. What if she doesn't want this but feels she has no other choices? If I had married Lucien, I would've had tears coursing down my cheeks, and everyone would have misconstrued them as tears of joy, because that is what everyone assumes on a wedding day. I pray she has chosen for love and that she is overjoyed.

My job is done, and Charles and I promptly return to our seats. It feels refreshing to sing simply for the joy and ministry in it.

The ceremony is a short one, and it seems that almost as soon as it starts, the minister is saying the groom may kiss the bride. They share a chaste kiss, and then it is all done.

I have no intention of mingling, but Charles has other ideas. He's shaking hands and making greetings almost as soon as the ceremony finishes. I suppose I shouldn't expect to go back to the hotel until Charles has had his fill of the upper-class citizens of Toronto.

The father, Mr. Mink, walks toward me. I look left and right to see if I can save myself from the interaction, but there will be no salvation. I will have to give him an audience even though I do not feel much like talking.

Like his daughter, James Mink is very light, but his features are distinctly African. Since they say he escaped to freedom, I would not be surprised if he was one of his enslaver's children.

"Miss Greenfield, your singing was outstanding," Mr. Mink says as he takes both my hands in his in a greeting. "I regret that I have not heard of you before my daughter asked about having you sing at the wedding."

"Thank you for your kind words."

"I believe you have many new admirers who will be attending your concert tomorrow evening. Are there still tickets available?"

"I am not sure. Tell them to make haste, because my manager expects for this concert to sell out."

"Eliza!"

The angry, booming voice yelling my name catches my attention and Mr. Mink's as well. I spin on one heel to see who it is and feel my heart rate quicken at the sight of Colonel Wood storming toward me.

"Is everything all right?" Mr. Mink asks. "Do you know that man?"

"That is my manager. I'm sure there's nothing to worry about," I say softly.

But I am worried, because he looks furious, and I can't seem to locate Charles in the crowd of wedding guests. Mr. Mink must not believe me, because he remains at my side. I am grateful for his presence even though he is a stranger.

"Excuse me," Colonel Wood says to Mr. Mink. "I do not mean to interrupt your conversation, but I require a word with Eliza."

I do not like how he is using my first name, my nickname at that, in the company of all these strangers. It is condescending and demeaning as we are in mixed company.

"Well, this is a wedding gathering," Mr. Mink says in a tone that is quite authoritarian and unwelcoming. "Might I offer you a private room to converse with Miss Greenfield?"

"I can speak to Eliza right here. Thank you."

"Miss Greenfield, please let me know if you need anything," Mr. Mink says. "I shall not be far away."

Colonel Wood gives Mr. Mink a sweeping glare from head to toe but does not say anything further. And it dawns on me that he believes Mr. Mink to be a white man, an equal. Clearly, he doesn't view me in the same manner.

"Eliza, I have been looking all over for you," Colonel Wood says, his voice still booming. "Why did you not tell me where you would be? Why did I have to pry the information out of the bellman?"

"I'm sorry, did we have an engagement planned? You have not informed me of any scheduled events." I purposely speak in hushed tones as Colonel Wood is drawing unwanted attention to us.

"You are not free to move about the city as you please. We have been invited to perform a rehearsal at a wealthy gentleman's banquet this evening, an event that will assure we sell more tickets to your concert."

I am not going to respond to the first part of Colonel Wood's tirade. I am indeed free to move about wherever I please, but if I give the reply that is on my heart, this working relationship will be finished.

"We are currently at the wedding of a wealthy gentleman's daughter. This event will also yield more concert attendees."

"The guests are a hodgepodge, and only a fraction of them seem to be able to purchase a ticket. You should have checked in with me prior to accepting this engagement. Did you sing here? Were you paid?" His voice is still too loud, and now many of the guests are staring at us. A few of the men have moved closer.

"I am done with these questions in this very public space."

"You are done when I say you're done."

I turn to walk away from Colonel Wood, and he grabs my arm tightly and squeezes, turning my body back to face him. I will the tears not to fall as his nails dig into my forearm. This is unthinkable.

"*Remove your hand from my arm*," I hiss. "I do not belong to you. I am not your slave."

Now I see Charles pushing past guests, hurrying over to me and Colonel Wood. I plaster a fake smile on my face to disarm Charles and to keep him from making a mistake that may cost his life. My wounded pride can be repaired, but I may not be able to help if he lays a hand on Colonel Wood. The scowl on his face and the curl of his upper lip both tell me he intends to do exactly that.

Colonel Wood looks around the room, his eyes taking inventory of the situation. I suppose he decides that he doesn't like his odds, because he removes his hand, and my arm drops limply to my side. His lips then curl into a wicked smile. It's as fake as the one I have on my face, because his eyes are as evil as they were when he was digging his nails into my arm.

"We will continue this conversation at your hotel," Colonel Wood says, now speaking in a voice barely above a whisper. "I will be waiting for you. You have one hour."

"Please send my regrets to the gentlemen," I whisper back. "I am committed to attending the wedding reception."

"I already promised them—"

"That is unfortunate."

Colonel Wood is unable to maintain his smile; it melts right off his face at my obstinance. Again, he scans the room, then storms off the way he came without apologizing for his disruption.

I take a deep breath and then beam a smile at the wedding guests. "Please forgive my manager. He is quite concerned about ticket sales for tomorrow's concert since it is our first time here in Toronto. I assured him that many of you have expressed your desire to attend. I appreciate your support and look forward to giving my full performance tomorrow evening. Will there be cake at the reception?"

There is a short moment of nervous laughter, and then the guests go back to their previous conversations. I nod a thank-you to Mr. Mink, and he acknowledges me with a curt smile in return.

I beckon now for Charles, and he quickly closes the space between us. Not a moment too soon either, because my entire body begins to tremble from anxiety at what could have happened. And what may still happen if Colonel Wood finds his offense to be greater than my value to him.

Not caring about any tongues that might wag, I collapse into Charles's arms. I feel safety and comfort in his embrace. He swiftly ushers me out of the sanctuary and into a quiet room.

"What happened? What did he say?" Charles asks as he closes the door.

"He wanted me to perform somewhere else tonight. I refused," I say breathlessly as tears start to fall. I can't stop them or my body from shaking.

Charles's nostrils flare, and he embraces me again. This time planting kisses on the top of my head and on my face.

"H-he grabbed me. Like he was an overseer yanking a field slave to the whipping post. I don't know what he might do, Charles. I'm frightened. There are slave catchers here too, even if there is no law that says we must be turned over to them."

"Do not fret," Charles says. "There are very powerful abolitionists here, and they will see to your safety. He will not harm you prior to the concert. His greed will not allow him to do that."

"What about after?"

"I will arrange for you to be transported back to Buffalo after the second encore. We'll get you out of here. When you are back in Buffalo, all will be well."

"Are you going to be with me?"

He shakes his head. "Don't worry about me. We will meet in Buffalo."

I weep into Charles's chest as he holds me tightly against his body. After singing before a crowd of admirers, I am going to be secreted away like a runaway on the Underground Railroad. There is one thing Colonel Wood was correct about. I have indeed forgotten my station. While I am still Elizabeth Taylor Greenfield, also known as the Black Swan by my admirers, I am also someone else first.

A Black woman in a world where white men determine the value of lives.

# CHAPTER TWENTY-SEVEN

$\mathcal{N}$ever have I felt so uneasy before the start of a concert. My breathing exercises haven't helped. Neither has my usual cup of warm tea and honey. All I keep thinking about is the plan we've hatched to ferry me back to Buffalo and far away from Colonel Wood immediately after the final encore.

Several times I've thought that maybe Charles and I overreacted, and perhaps I shouldn't conclude the tour here. That maybe I should continue with whatever additional dates Colonel Wood can conjure to keep the peace. But then I remember the pure rage in his eyes when I defied him, and the way his nails dug into my arms deep enough to draw blood. He had finally shown his hand. He thought he owned me, and one day he might push that past the bounds of a contract.

I hate the idea of sneaking out of town under the cover of night like a fugitive, but what else can be done? If Colonel Wood decides to suggest that I am in some way defrauding him by parting ways with him, or if he even hints to a slave catcher across the border in Michigan that I am a fugitive, I may find myself kidnapped before I am able to get word to someone who can save me. And even if it is less likely to happen to me, being well known as the Black Swan, what about Charles? I am afraid I've endangered us both by standing up to Colonel Wood, and now we must both flee.

Colonel Wood seems to think something is afoot, because he keeps hovering near my dressing room. I hear the clicking of his boots right outside the door, pacing back and forth, making what is supposed to be my preperformance sanctuary a locked cage.

And then a sharp, rude knock. Too loud to be for something considerate. This knock is demanding.

But I take my time responding, because the knocking annoys me. I've already told him I am free to do what I please. Now, for my final act, he will get the prima donna treatment.

The door creaks as I slowly guide it open. Colonel Wood rudely pushes it open the rest of the way. I have to step aside to keep from being hit by the door as it swings.

"Eliza, are you not preparing to go onstage?" Colonel Wood barks his question as he marches inside the dressing room, not waiting to be invited. I feel even more apprehension when he closes the door behind him. "I do not hear any warm-ups."

"I am on vocal rest due to a little soreness, but I'll be fine," I say quietly as I ease down into the chair in front of my vanity. "I will run scales in a moment."

"Why is your throat sore? Because of that unauthorized performance you did yesterday?" Colonel Wood asks brusquely. "We still need to settle the books on my portion of whatever payment was received, since that engagement was procured during the tour."

"There was no payment," I lie. "It was a favor for a friend."

Colonel Wood stares down at me, probably trying to discern if I am telling the truth. But my face is a stone, and he will not be able to detect any falsehood. The way he's glowering makes me wish I had stayed on my feet instead of placing myself in this vulnerable position.

"I did not think we had come to this, Eliza," Colonel Wood says now in a more benevolent tone. "Have I not always treated you well?"

I have no desire for this conversation to turn into an argument, particularly since it is only me and Colonel Wood in the room, and whatever transpires will be his word against mine. A white man's word against mine will never turn out in my favor.

"I do not think you want me to answer that question."

"Because I interrupted you at a wedding?" Colonel Wood asks. "I'm going to be honest here. I was worried about you being with Charles alone. He's a bit of a rake, isn't he?"

So this is how he's going to paint the picture? He was being paternalistic and caring. Simply worried about the image of the Black Swan, seen out carousing with her dashing accompanist at a wedding the night before her big concert.

Except there had been no carousing, and Charles and I hadn't been alone at the wedding once. We had been seen only within a group of people.

"I don't know what Charles does in his private time," I respond. "But I am above reproach, and I do not appreciate you insinuating otherwise."

Colonel Wood cackles, and I give a worried glance at the closed door. "Above reproach. I have the hotel staff keep track of your comings and goings, and I know that you visit Charles wherever he lodges, in every city."

"To practice our concert list, nothing more."

Colonel Wood throws up a halting hand. "Eliza, I am not here to accuse you of indecency."

"Then why are you here? And right before a concert?"

"I am here to inform you that how you behaved last night, in front of that Black man who looked white, was unacceptable. It cannot happen again. Do you understand?"

I stare unblinking at Colonel Wood, knowing what I must say but unable to form the words. Not even when I see the redness blotching his cheeks.

He slams his fist onto the vanity, knocking over some of the expensive bottles, one of them crashing to the floor and shattering. I sit frozen in place. "Eliza, you have forgotten your station. You are a Negress, and *this* is as good as it gets for you."

I blink back tears as Colonel Wood motions to the dressing room around him. He purposely knocks a few more of my bottles of lotion onto the floor. Determined not to panic, I keep my breathing steady. I know he doesn't want to lose the money this venue has promised for tonight, so at least I will have the opportunity to get onstage. Then I can run.

"You keep talking about Europe and getting training in Paris. You are dreaming a young white woman's dream. You are almost thirty years old, Eliza. And you are a Negress. No one in Paris is going to educate you."

Colonel Wood seems to have run out of steam. Apparently, he has gotten off his chest everything he wished to share. His load has been lightened.

"Is there anything else you want me to know or remember?" I ask in a calm and even tone, only wanting him to leave, because I won't feel safe until he is on the other side of the door.

"That if you forget yourself again, there will be no more engagements, or concerts. I will see to that." Angry droplets of saliva fly from the sides of Colonel Wood's mouth. I close my eyes to keep from being disgusted. "You will be back in Buffalo or Philadelphia, wiping the snot from white children's noses. That is all you are suited for outside of singing."

This is not too far from the truth. I don't have many skills outside of singing and teaching children. So I do not take offense to Colonel Wood's words like I think he wants me to. But there were requests for concerts outside of him, and prior to him. Providence has opened doors before, and it will continue to make a way.

A calm descends over me that I cannot describe. For one moment of precious clarity, I am not anxious about slave catchers or Europe or where the next concert will be. I am not vexed about my inheritance, or about my mother. In that instant, my spirit confirms I will bring her home.

"If that be God's will, then so be it." My voice even seems to float out on a cloud of tranquility.

Colonel Wood laughs in my face and spins one end of his greasy mustache. It's funny, I didn't want to judge him on the mustache when I first laid eyes on him. I told myself it wasn't his fault that most men who wear that style of mustache are sketchy characters. But then he molded himself to that exact description.

I am so relieved when he walks out of the room and closes the door that my body almost goes limp in my chair. But this is not a time for relaxation. It is a time for action, and for executing the plan that will take me far away from this evil man.

* * *

THE PLAN IS quite simple, really, but requires the cooperation of an entire team of Black stagehands and the goodwill of friends we made outside the concert hall. After my first encore of "When Stars Are in the Quiet Skies," the stage curtains are going to close during my bow. I will be quickly secreted away to a waiting carriage. The driver will, along with the escorts, take me farther into Canada for a couple of weeks, and then I will travel back to Buffalo.

As I stand center stage, all I can see are ominous halos around the attendees, caused by the glow cast from the gas lamps illuminating the space. But I sing from my heart to the ghostly figures. All my favorite arias and popular ballads. If there is a flaw or imperfection in my singing, I cannot detect it, although I am sure that the critics will find some imperceptible failing to pounce upon. Some shortcoming to magnify.

I cannot be concerned with any of that now. My only thought is making it to the curtain call and ensuring that both Charles and I make it away from here without any incident.

My gaze falls on Charles as he accompanies me. His playing is as fervent as my singing, as if he feels the same foreboding that I do. The same heaviness and need to hasten this concert program to completion.

With every run, every trill, turn, and embellishment, I take the lessons from Miss Bella and use them to stun and enchant this audience in Toronto. And, of course, they give me the thing I desire and usually enjoy. The applause, the praise, and the ovations.

But I did not listen to all of Miss Bella's lessons.

She warned me not to allow my heart to be captured the way Charles has captured mine. I am more terrified of what Colonel Wood may do to him than what he may do to me. He wants to keep me under his control and grasp. Clearly, he is not done making money on the Black Swan, but he does not need Charles. And for him to highlight my visits to Charles's lodging in my dressing room tonight. *That* was intentional. That was meant to rattle me, and to make me fall in line.

Similar tactics are used by plantation owners on enslaved women every day. They use their hearts against them. The love for their men and their children and their families against them. They are kept docile because of their tender hearts.

But I will not be kept docile.

Finally, we are at my encore song, and the emotion pours from my soul into the lyrics. I am singing this love song to my love. We will separate after this, and if anything goes wrong and Charles is kidnapped, or I am captured, either of us may end up in the Deep South, trapped on a plantation.

The last verse is where I always bring my powerhouse soprano, and I swear there has never been a time when I've sung it better. I can hear Miss Bella's voice in my head cheering, *Bel canto! Bel canto!*

"'I can but know thee as my star.'" I hold this note for as long as I can, trilling until the crowd is on their feet and applauding. "'My guiding star, my angel and my dream.'"

On my final and dramatic flourish, I take a deep bow, and the curtain abruptly falls. Immediately, a stagehand runs from backstage and rushes me past the orchestra and Charles. He moves from the pianoforte in the opposite direction. We briefly touch our fingertips as we pass. A lover's farewell and a promise to meet again.

The plan is to leave the auditorium, go down the back hallway and past the dressing rooms to the rear exit and the waiting carriage outside. All before the curtain is raised again and before anyone realizes I am gone.

But either a little birdie or the devil must've whispered something in Colonel Wood's ear.

And my spirit must've known this would happen, because I'm not even startled when he steps out of the shadows in the back hallway. The dim light from the lamps casts a long shadow across his body, making him appear an even larger demon than he is in real life.

"Eliza, that was an exceptional concert. Bravo! I must say, it was one of your best," Colonel Wood says, in extremely high spirits compared to our earlier dialogue.

"Thank you."

"I came to escort you to the reception," Colonel Wood says as he approaches and steps between me and the stagehand. "There is an investor I'd like you to meet."

I take a deep breath and close my eyes. How do I get out of this? "I am feeling very tired," I say, "and a bit weak. I believe it is the whalebone under the dress. Either way, I need to lie down."

"Oh, but, Eliza dear, this is part of the show. And you are a professional." My entire body cringes as Colonel Wood slides his arm in mine and locks it tight. There is no getting away for now. "The show must go on. This gentleman is very wealthy, and weren't you talking about Europe?"

I give him a suspicious sidelong glance. "You said no one would train me in Europe."

"Well, that is true, but I did not say there wasn't an audience for you there. And I did not say there wasn't money to be made."

The stagehand has gone, and I am left alone with Colonel Wood, who leads me to the St. Lawrence Hall reception room. As we enter, I plaster a fake smile on my face as my mind scrambles for a way to salvage our plan. I do not want to go to Europe or anywhere with Colonel Wood. I want to be done with him tonight.

A wave of relief washes over me when I see Charles in the reception space. Someone had gotten word to him that things had gone awry, and he has also stayed behind. Thank goodness for that. Perhaps Colonel Wood is none the wiser.

"There is my investor friend," Colonel Wood says. "Let's meet him, before you get too tired to socialize further."

I nod in agreement but keep my eyes on Charles. Charles lifts an eyebrow at me and nods. This lets me know that something is coming, but I cannot be sure of what. With Colonel Wood's arm locked in mine, I don't know how I will manage to untangle myself from his grasp, but I will trust that Charles and the others have thought of my options.

"Mr. Lance Edgewater, meet Eliza," Colonel Wood says with a grand gesture of showmanship as he spreads his arms wide before linking back with me again. "The Black Swan."

Immediately, I am annoyed at this introduction. It is too informal. Why should this stranger call me by my nickname and not Miss Greenfield?

I am riled even further by Mr. Edgewater's response. He lets out a big, throaty, gut-busting laugh. Like he and Colonel Wood are old drinking buddies, and they've just shared a randy and indecent joke.

"I've seen lots of swans in my day, but this is the first black one I've met," Mr. Edgewater says while cackling and half choking on his pipe smoke. "She does sing real pretty, though."

"She does indeed," Colonel Wood says.

A young Black woman approaches our party with a tray heavy with glasses of white wine. Both Colonel Wood and Mr. Edgewater greedily reach for glasses. When I reach for a glass, the young woman gives me a glance that clearly communicates *no*.

"Miss Greenfield, after your taxing concert, would you prefer a hot toddy for your throat?" she asks. "They have prepared one for you with bourbon, honey, and lemon. It is said that you prefer this."

I nod and smile. "Yes, thank you so much. I have had some soreness since yesterday. I overextended myself."

"Eliza sang at someone's wedding when she should've been resting for her concert tonight," Colonel Wood says as he finishes one glass of wine and takes another. "Naughty, naughty girl."

The young woman nods and smiles as she quietly backs away to serve other guests. Inside, I silently fume at being called a girl, but I keep calm, because things are in motion, and I do not want to miss another signal.

"My theater will be complete late this summer, and I think it would be nice to have her come around for a concert or two," Mr. Edgewater says. "To test the waters before we discuss anything in Europe."

I notice that Mr. Edgewater has not addressed me once. Another annoyance. Wherever his theater is, and I can guess from his deep southern drawl that it is somewhere I'd rather not be, I won't be gracing its stage.

"Mr. Edgewater is building a theater and concert hall right in Natchez, Mississippi," Colonel Wood explains. "You are familiar with Natchez, aren't you, Eliza? Isn't that where you were born?"

"I don't remember it."

A slow and diabolical smile pulls at the sides of Colonel Wood's mouth. "Well, then we must see about getting you back there."

Beneath my gown, my knees knock, and I feel myself swooning, but I must stay alert and not let Colonel Wood know that this has unnerved me so. I force myself to smile even at Mr. Edgewater, who clearly is a Southerner, because of his mannerisms and speech. I wonder if he is a plantation owner as well.

A young man starts playing the harp on the other side of the room, and a few of the people in attendance take this as a cue to take to the small dance floor. This seems to amuse Colonel Wood. He shakes his head and laughs.

"It seems everywhere I go here in Toronto, there's dancing," Colonel Wood says. "I can hardly conduct any business, it seems, for the dancing."

Mr. Edgewater grins across the room at a pretty mulatto woman. "I make deals between the songs. That way I get in all my dancin' and all my dealin'."

Colonel Wood closes his eyes and scratches his head before stumbling to the left. I look over to where Charles was standing, and he has already exited the room.

"That wine a little strong for you, Colonel Wood?"

He shakes his head and stumbles again. "Perhaps I drank it too quickly. I th-think I need to sit down."

Mr. Edgewater flags down one of the servants. "Boy! See about getting Colonel Wood a chair. He's not feeling well."

Then Colonel Wood stumbles again and grabs on to my arm to hold himself up. I laugh nervously, because he's making a scene, and everyone is looking in our direction. Several Black servants come to my rescue by bringing Colonel Wood a chair, but when he passes out cold, they kindly remove him from the reception.

Because no one has given me the signal to leave, I continue to work the room, greeting the concertgoers and thanking them for coming. Then the young lady from before brings me a steaming mug.

"Here is your hot toddy, Miss Greenfield," she says.

"Thank you."

Then she leans in close. "The time is now," she whispers. "The stagehand is waiting for you right outside the door. Charles is already gone—do not worry about him."

Without a slip in my demeanor or expression, I sip my hot toddy and continue to smile and greet people as I work my way around the room and toward the exit. There is nothing between me and freedom now.

"Eliza."

I look down at my arm. Mr. Edgewater's hand is pressing my skin. He hasn't grabbed me, but he is touching me and smiling. Both the touch and the smile are unwanted. I look up at him.

"I will make sure to finalize things with Colonel Wood regarding your visit."

"My name is Miss Greenfield, and I'm afraid my contract with Colonel Wood expires at the end of spring," I say, with what I hope is the aloof arrogance of a proper prima donna. "Perhaps you will be able to send correspondence to whoever replaces him."

"Well, all right, Black Swan. I will do that." He then bends over into an exaggerated gentleman's bow.

I turn on one heel and walk away, feeling frightened and empowered all at once. Outside the reception hall door, the stagehand is waiting, and I nearly collapse into his arms.

"Please," I beg. "Get me out of here."

This time, we are not stopped by anyone on the way to the waiting carriage, but my heart does not stop racing until I see St. Lawrence Hall become a tiny dot in the distance. I know that my heart won't stop aching until I see Charles again. Until I know he's safe.

# CHAPTER TWENTY-EIGHT

*Buffalo, New York*
*July 1852*

𝓘t is rare for me to receive visitors at the Howards' home, but Miss Bella has recently returned to Buffalo from a trip abroad and hasn't seen me since my tour. Naturally, she would like to hear all the intimate details. So I bake an apple pie and invite her over for tea. I also ask Annabelle to join us, because Hiram's work has kept him here in Buffalo this summer instead of traveling to Philadelphia where her usual social circle resides. Somehow, Annabelle still hasn't managed to make inroads with the elite ladies of Buffalo.

"I must be special indeed to dine with the Black Swan and have her serve me freshly baked apple pie," Miss Bella says as she rests her cane on the side of the sofa in Annabelle's parlor. "Isn't this something, Mrs. Howard?"

Annabelle laughs out loud. "You're special? Then what about me? I get to have the Black Swan living in my house and practicing her arias right in my kitchen. And please call me Annabelle."

"You are both very funny with this Black Swan business. At home I am Eliza, and I still love baking pies for my friends."

"Well, I am proud of you, Eliza," Miss Bella says with a sparkle in her dazzling blue eyes that lets me know she really means it. "And I know Lizbeth is smiling from heaven. Tell me. What became of that insufferable Charles?"

Annabelle and I exchange glances and burst into laughter. Miss Bella pounds her cane into the floor and shakes her head.

"I knew she wouldn't get rid of that handsome devil. Annabelle, if you could only see the way she looked in that dressing room."

"Miss Bella!" I gasp while Annabelle keeps cackling.

"What? It seems like she already knows. Her pantaloons were ready to melt right off her body. If I hadn't interrupted, her feet would've been pointing straight to the heavens."

Now all three of us are choking with laughter. I don't think I've ever laughed this hard. Annabelle doubles over, holding her midsection, and tears are pouring down my cheeks.

"Well, have you seen Charles?" Annabelle asks.

Miss Bella shrugs. "I suppose he is handsome."

"He's more than handsome," I say. "He cares about my career as much as I do, Miss Bella. He's done nothing to put it in peril."

Miss Bella sighs. "Every time he touches you, he puts it at risk."

"But he does not, Miss Bella. Trust me. He does not."

Miss Bella tilts her head to one side and stares at me. Then she purses her lips. Perhaps understanding, perhaps not. I cannot tell without divulging further, but she seems to be satisfied.

"And where is Mr. Charles now?" Miss Bella asks. "I'd like to interrogate him further."

"He is out on a hauling job with his friend Patrick." I don't add that Charles is not the kind of man who appreciates interrogation, because I believe she'll find that out on her own if she tries it with him.

"Tell me, why are you no longer performing? You must still be in demand," Miss Bella says. "Outside of the typical foolishness one expects to see in reviews, I have not seen anything that would keep you from the stage."

My mood turns somber as I think on the events that ended the tour. I believe that Colonel Wood has somehow soured concert hall managers on booking concerts with me. I have not received any invi-

THE UNEXPECTED DIVA 291

tations through Hiram, but that can change at any moment, so I have not given up hope.

To protect myself, I wrote to Mr. Howell after I made my escape. He was shocked and assured me that Colonel Wood's threats in Toronto, which were made in front of witnesses, would be enough for me to legally part ways with him without injury. That's if he should want to pursue damages for the few remaining concerts—but so far he has not been heard from.

"I will be back onstage soon, and Mr. Howell tells me that my inheritance is very close to being settled. Then, with what I've saved from this tour and those funds, I will go see about that teacher in Paris."

Miss Bella nods. "Splendid. You are at the point in your career where small refinements can help you, but you are already a better singer than most singers in the world. There are few that have the vocal gifts you possess."

"I don't think she needs to go to Europe," Annabelle says. "You've done a splendid job, Miss Bella."

"But I did not complete my own education before I was run out of Italy. There are things that even I don't know how to impart. But I have given Eliza everything I have to give, and she has multiplied it beyond measure."

"That is the best compliment you've ever paid me. Thank you," I say, trying to hold back tears.

"Don't cry," Miss Bella says. "Get to Paris. There is more for you to do, my dear."

Yes, the work is unfinished, and I have only scratched the surface. But lack of finances loom large. I must find a way to add to my savings before people forget that they became enamored with the Black Swan.

* * *

TODAY, ON THE Independence Day holiday, we are all together at Ruby and William's house after church. Ruby has fried a huge batch of chicken, and the table groans with plates of potato salad, fresh bread, and pound cake. All the adults sit in our normal places at their dining table, while the children try to catch a glimpse of fireworks outside.

As much as I enjoy this feeling of togetherness with my friends, and I especially revel in the comfort of having Charles nearby, this is starting to feel too comfortable. And too much like the life I rejected when I turned down marriage and children with Lucien. I yearn for the excitement of the stage, and the more time I spend away from it, the more I itch to be back in front of an audience.

"I was thinking about having a benefit concert right here in Buffalo," I say. "I've got all these beautiful performance dresses, and so many Black folk haven't had the opportunity to hear me sing in concert."

"If you have it at our church, Pastor Wilcox won't make you pay anything specific. But you will have to leave an offering," Ruby says.

"I'd like to have it at Townsend Hall."

I wait to see everyone's reaction, especially Charles's, before I continue. He has a mouthful of chicken, but his chewing slows, and he puts down his fork. He looks over at me, but his expression is stoic.

"It is an excellent venue, and now that I've been on tour, I believe we are in a much better position to demand everything that we want," I say confidently. "Including seating for Black people."

"There was seating before. In the gallery," Charles reminds me, his voice dry and emotionless. "And it was segregated."

"Yes. That is not what I want, and I will not agree to those terms this time. I will take the concert to a different venue if they do not accommodate my wishes."

Charles picks up a napkin from the table and wipes his face. He says nothing, but I do not think he believes me. This stings after what we've been through with Colonel Wood. Ruby and William seem to sense the tension between us, so their eyes stay trained on their food.

"Tell me what you're thinking, Charles," I say. "Do you think it's a good idea?"

He doesn't respond to my question with words. He gives me a look. And the look says a plethora of things he probably doesn't want to say in front of Ruby and William.

"William, I need to show you something outside by the well," Ruby says, having caught the look passing between me and Charles.

"Probably take a good minute to show me, huh?" William asks, catching the hint.

"Mmm-hmm."

They scurry away from the table so fast that it would be funny if things weren't so heavy between Charles and me. But this conversation has been building since we got back from Toronto. Things would've never soured with Charles managing me the way they had with Colonel Wood, but there were other reasons why it didn't work for us, and I don't think he ever accepted that.

"Now that they're gone," I say to Charles, "please tell me why you looked at me that way when I asked your opinion."

Across the table, Charles sits with shoulders squared and eyebrows furrowed. Ready for battle. I don't want him to feel this way. Or to have this wall between us. Our friendship should not be wrapped around the business of the Black Swan. I want us to exist outside of this, and after this.

"I looked that way because I do not believe you value my opinion when it comes to your singing career."

I allow his words to sit with me for a moment, because I need to think about how I want to reply. There are things I do value, and spaces where I believe his opinion is worth noting. But there are other areas where I would like for him to listen more and ask what I would like to do.

"First of all, and above all, Charles, I value you. And I thank God that you were with me on that tour. Especially in Toronto."

His wall seems to crumble a bit, and his shoulders soften. "But?"

"And . . . I want to hear what you think about my ideas. All of them. Even the ones about my career."

"But you don't want me to manage your career."

"I do not want you to manage my career."

He scoffs. "Because you think white men are better at that?"

"No. Because I do not want to have arguments with you that will ruin our friendship or our bond. I am happy to hire a Black manager who has the connections to book a multicity tour. Preferably a European one. But I reserve the right to fire at will. And on any disagreements, I will assert my will, because this is *my* career."

"And you do not want to assert your will with me?" Charles asks.

"I prefer being a softer version of myself with you. And I love that I can do that. I don't want to be the Black Swan with you. I want to be Eliza."

His defenses now completely overtaken, Charles reaches both hands across the table and grabs mine. "All right. I understand. And I will not be offended any longer that you don't wish for me to manage things."

"Thank you. You don't know how much I appreciate you saying this."

"You're welcome. And I agree with you about your benefit concert. I think it is an excellent idea. Why should you wait for someone to make an opportunity for you? You are the Black Swan. I'm sure Mr. Howell will be happy to review the contract from the concert hall."

"That's exactly what I was thinking. And I won't have to share the proceeds with any manager. Only the orchestra, my accompanist, and the concert hall. It will greatly help my savings and put me much closer to my goal."

"Well, you have my support. Should I go outside and let Ruby and William know it's safe to come back?"

I can't help but laugh thinking about them pacing back and forth outside, wondering if Charles and I are inside their home screaming our heads off. They're such good friends, allowing us the space to figure these things out.

"Please do."

Charles kisses both my hands and leaps up from the table. I will never get enough of looking at his manly and muscular physique. Part of me feels a bit melancholy knowing that this fragile arrangement we have could be over at any time if Charles decides he wants or needs more than I am willing to give.

Ruby comes back inside the house without Charles or William, meaning the men have probably decided to have whatever discussions they have about their man things. Leaving us to have woman talk. Ruby starts clearing dishes from the table, and without a word I help her. This is the usual order of things at our gatherings.

"What's ailing you, sister? You haven't said much all day," Ruby says as she piles the dirty dishes into her washing tub.

"I think I've made a terrible mistake."

"What have you done?"

"I didn't listen to Miss Bella's advice about Charles. She told me not to let myself get too attached to a man, but I let myself do it anyway."

Ruby presses her lips into a thin line and furrows her brow, considering my words. I join her at the washing tub and scrape the leftover food into the trash pile for the dog.

"Well, if you don't make it to Europe, you can always marry Charles and have abolitionist babies." Ruby finds this so funny that she doesn't mind laughing all by herself, because I don't join her.

"It wouldn't be the worst thing in the world, Eliza," Ruby says when she notices my lack of laughter. "He's a good man, and he's obviously smitten with you."

"What if one day Charles wakes up and decides I'm not all that interesting?" I ask, being very serious. "Then he'll find another woman to have his babies."

"Maybe he doesn't want a family either. He doesn't seem like a very traditional man."

I let out a deep sigh. "Men are simply resigned to the fact that copulation brings about children. They may not want the child, but they certainly want the copulation."

"Has he been pressuring you?" Ruby asks, peeking out the window to see if Charles or William is coming.

I haven't told Ruby about the things Charles and I do to fulfill both our desires. She is a churchgoing woman, and as openly as we talk about these things, I do not think she would approve. She believes only a husband and a wife should share in these pleasures. She accepts that men sometimes go astray, but when it comes to women, she turns a judgmental eye, like many church women seem to do. It is one of the many reasons Miss Lizbeth steered clear of church women. But I love Ruby so much that I don't hold it against her.

"No, but he doesn't have to. I am not foolish enough to think his abstinence is permanent."

"Or maybe he isn't abstinent at all. There are . . . brothels for the very purpose of ensuring the purity of young virgins."

This is something I do not want to think about. Any carnal affairs that Charles may have when he's not with me are not my concern. I do not believe Charles would consort with whores, but there are a few widows at Michigan Street Baptist who would not mind keeping him warm on cold nights.

"Forget I put that terrible thought in your mind," Ruby says. "Charles is an upstanding gentleman. And you have his sole attention."

I may have his sole attention for now. But I must be ready for a time when that may change. Like the approval of the critics after a series of concerts, the attentions of a man are oft temporary.

# CHAPTER TWENTY-NINE

*Philadelphia, Pennsylvania*
*December 1852*

𝒠ven though I am home and will spend the holiday with Mary and her family, my mood is melancholy. Charles has taken a shipping job that will have him away for months, and although he promises to write, again I feel distance creeping in between us.

Before he left, we shared a lovely late-autumn night at a concert, and I prepared him dinner at Ruby and William's home. We sang and read poetry in their garden until late in the evening and shared mostly chaste kisses when the children and homeowners retired. I will miss him immensely.

Nothing has changed about our one and only disagreement. My desire is to travel and live for a time in Europe, while his interests are affixed on the freedom movement. I do now see ways to use my platform to advance the cause, but to do this I must have a platform, and it appears that the novelty of the Black Swan may be waning.

The planning of my benefit concert has so far been nothing short of disastrous. The only thing that has gone well is that the manager of the concert hall has agreed to my request for desegregated seating. It's everything else that has gone wrong.

Mostly, everyone wants money in advance for everything. I find myself going into my savings for things I had no idea were even an expense. For example, to have a concert program, first there is the sitting fee for the daguerreotypist for the image and another fee to have the daguerreotype engraved. Then I must pay for the paper to make copies. And let us not forget the typesetter fee.

And that is only for the concert program. I have already spent more than one hundred dollars, and we don't have a date for the concert yet, nor have we started to promote it. Because I've already spent from my savings, I feel dedicated to the cause, but I don't want to spend more than I am projected to make in proceeds. This is more complicated than I want to admit, and I am ready to hand it all over to a capable manager should one come along.

On top of these anxieties, I have arrived at Mr. Howell's office for an update on my inheritance. Nothing in his letters has indicated anything good, so I am not optimistic.

"Do not spare me any bad news or cover it with pleasantries," I say as I ease into the same leather chair I always sit in when I come here.

"Eliza, you have always been direct with me, so I will do the same." Mr. Howell's countenance tells me everything I need to know.

"Thank you."

"I apologize for promising a quick resolution to these matters. The hearing had a positive outcome. The judge reviewed all the statements from Mrs. Greenfield's friends and associates, and seemed to agree that your inheritance is warranted."

"This is good news. When will the funds be released?"

Mr. Howell sighs. "Three days after our hearing . . . But before rendering a final judgment, the judge fell ill with cholera."

I squeeze my eyes shut and inhale a weary breath. The exhale is even wearier. If I wasn't in such dire straits with achieving my goals, I would laugh at the irony of this.

"Is he dead?"

"Unfortunately, he did not recover from the illness."

I slump in my chair and shake my head. "Send my condolences to the family."

"I'm so sorry, Eliza. I know this is exasperating, but we are closer now than ever," Mr. Howell says with more cheer in his voice than I am willing to accept. There is nothing to be cheerful about. "Hopefully, you have been able to sustain yourself with touring. I heard many great things about your concerts."

"I am sustained at present," I grumble.

"Oh, that reminds me, you have received several letters here at my office, in my care. Perhaps one of them will contain better news than what I have delivered."

"Have you ever encountered an inheritance dispute that has taken as long as this one?"

"Unfortunately, yes, I have," Mr. Howell says as he hands me several envelopes from his drawer. "But in our favor is that Mrs. Greenfield was very explicit in how she wanted her wishes executed. The disputes that never seem to end are the ones where there was no will left behind."

Clutching the letters to my bosom, I stand, no more dissatisfied than when I arrived here. I believe I already knew in my spirit that I was not going to receive good news.

"Any additional correspondence may be forwarded to Hiram Howard in Buffalo, New York. When I am not touring, I reside with the Howard family still."

"I will do that. I hope you have a Merry Christmas."

Merry. *Merry?*

"You do the same, Mr. Howell." I hope he cannot tell the smile on my face is forced, and the tone of my voice is more wretched than joyous. "Send my love to your family."

"I will."

I leave Mr. Howell's office and go back out into the bitter cold. I contemplate stopping to buy sweets for Isaiah and Mary's little girls before heading back. Mary is very strict about what they consume, but perhaps she will be more lenient since it is Christmas.

Even though the cold is relentless, the sun has come out, and that is something good. The snow that was fresh this morning is now gray and slushy from being trampled by hooves and booted feet, but the familiarity of it all gives me comfort and reminds me of Miss Lizbeth.

As I turn the corner of Seventeenth and Mulberry Street, I hear a sound I will never forget. Lucien's laugh, full and robust, near enough that I look around to see where it's coming from. Right on the same sidewalk, he walks arm in arm with a petite beauty. Her midsection is heavy and round with a child.

While I wanted Lucien to find love and joy again after me, I never imagined having to witness it. And certainly not at my lowest point when, after chasing a dream, I find myself not much further along than when I left him.

I nearly turn to go in the opposite direction, but Lucien catches sight of me and surprises me by smiling as if his love hasn't wavered. It's been only a little over a year since I broke our engagement, but it feels like a whole lifetime has passed.

And now he's pulling his pregnant wife in my direction, so there is no chance of escaping. But instead of walking forward to meet them, my feet are stuck in place. Maybe I want them to change their minds and go the other way.

"Eliza!" Lucien hugs me warmly but not intimately. Although I understand, it feels strange. "I'd like you to meet my wife, Gertrude. Gertrude, this is—"

"Miss Greenfield. The Black Swan. Yes, honey, I know." Her tone is clipped and as cold as the winter weather. That's understandable. What wife wants to meet her husband's first love?

"Pleased to meet you, Gertrude. It looks like congratulations are in order. When is your baby due?"

"In March," Gertrude replies, thawing a bit. "I'm hoping it's a boy."

"And I'm hoping for a little girl," Lucien says as he puts an arm around Gertrude and pulls her close.

Gertrude beams up at Lucien. "Yes, of course. We want a houseful. As many as the good Lord blesses us with."

"Have you moved back here to Philadelphia?" Lucien asks.

"No, I am here visiting Mary and Isaiah for the holiday. Then I will be back in Buffalo."

"I hope to see you in concert someday," Lucien says. "I have read so many things about you in the newspapers."

This is getting uncomfortable. If I do not put an end to the chitchat, I fear Lucien will have us standing on this street corner for hours.

"I am sure you will get the opportunity soon. Have a Merry Christmas and give my very best to your family. Blessings for the safe birth of your child."

Lucien hugs me again. This time it feels like a goodbye hug, and I don't mind this goodbye. I welcome it.

I had been afraid that I would see Lucien again and feel a longing for the life I rejected. But as I watch Lucien and his waddling wife go on their way, I feel a peace that cannot be described.

If I never grace another stage or sing another note, I know that at least one decision I made was the right one. That life was not mine. If I had not walked away from that, I would have never experienced the sheer joy I have with Charles. Even if that proves to be temporary, I will take that over the nothingness I felt for Lucien.

The bliss from Charles and the ecstasy of the stage are indeed worth everything to me. So, Godspeed to Lucien, his wife, and their future brood.

* * *

As soon as I told Mary I had seen Lucien, she went to prepare an entire tea service before hearing the rest of the story. It is our custom to share tea and sandwiches as we spill gossip. Tasty morsels for tasty tidbits.

"You saw Lucien and his wife? How did she look?" Mary asks as she pours my cup of tea. "I bet she was so pale you could see her veins."

I love telling Mary a story. She gives the appropriate reactions every time. If I had been crying and distraught after seeing Lucien and Gertrude, she would've been consoling and comforting. But since I am neither sad nor bothered, she gleefully wants details—especially disparaging ones.

"She could pass if she wanted to," I say with distasteful abandon, "and I suppose she's cute. I'll tell you one thing, the only curve was the one carrying the baby."

"What a shame that poor Lucien let his mother choose his wife. He would have waited forever for you to change your mind."

"That's exactly how long it would've taken."

"Indeed. Tell me good news. What did Mr. Howell have to say?"

That disappointing conversation had been eclipsed by the Lucien sighting. Her question reminds me of the letters tucked into the folds of my dress.

"He gave me my mail and sent me on my merry way. Without my inheritance."

"That's hardly merry," Mary says. "Are you sure he knows what he's doing? Should we enlist someone else? A Black lawyer, perhaps?"

"Now you sound like Charles. Mr. Howell is doing the best he can. This situation is a delicate one. I believe he just wants me to be able to win once and for all. I do not want to constantly live in fear of another challenge from Miss Lizbeth's estranged family."

"I suppose."

I examine the first letter. It is from a friend of Miss Lizbeth congratulating me on my success as the Black Swan but admonishing me for not giving all my income to charity like Jenny Lind had done on her tour. A waste of paper, ink, and the postage it took to mail it.

The second is from a Mr. Edward T. Norris, an unfamiliar name. The handwriting is quite elegant and has many flourishes, as if the sender is trying to make a good impression.

"What does that one say?" Mary asks. "It's so pretty."

"'Dear Madame . . .'"

"'Madame'? This one doesn't know French very well does he, mademoiselle?"

"Do you want to hear it or not?" I ask.

"I do. I'm sorry, keep going."

"'Dear Madame, I am writing to inquire about your desire to engage new management for a series of concerts in England, Scotland, and Ireland, and in some states where you have yet to perform. I am very experienced in this business and am related to Mr. P. T. Barnum. I am also associated with Colonel J. H. Wood, with whom you are well acquainted. Since Barnum is my relation, I am able to host a concert in New York City in his name. I can provide letters of recommendation if you so desire them. Please let me know by return of this letter if you are interested in proceeding. Yours, Edward T. Norris.'"

I fold the letter neatly and attempt to put it back in the envelope, but my hands are shaking too fiercely to complete the task. Mary reaches over and takes both letter and envelope from me, and she finishes what I could not.

"Are you going to write him back?" Mary asks.

"Yes, as soon as I can pull myself together to put pen to paper."

"All you've talked about for years is going to Europe to perform and study. This might be a chance to do that."

It might be my only chance seeing how this benefit concert is going. But the mention of Barnum's and Colonel Wood's names gives me pause, although I'm sure Mr. Norris intended to cause the opposite effect. Still, I do not have any other opportunities or invitations, so can I afford to say no to someone, even if he might be trying to advance his own career while advancing mine?

"Why don't you look happy?" Mary asks.

"Because what if this goes horribly wrong as things did with Colonel Wood? If Mr. Norris knows of Colonel Wood, perhaps they are cut from the same cloth."

"Maybe he mentioned Colonel Wood's name to make you more comfortable with accepting his invitation. He is poaching Colonel Wood's client without apology. I presume he has heard of your separation and wishes to capitalize on it. Surely, they aren't friends."

"Perhaps you're right. I will reply to this Mr. Norris and speak to him soon."

"What about the last letter? It looks ragged, like it has been to hell and back," Mary says.

I take a moment to examine the envelope more closely. It does look like it's been through a great ordeal to get to me. The paper is yellowed, and the ink is starting to bleed and fade. I have to squint to read the script on the return address. It is small, and some of it has washed away, perhaps from rain or some other contact with moisture.

"Can you read that, Mary?" I hand the envelope to my sister, because I want to make sure I see what I think I'm seeing.

"Ummm . . . I think it says Mon-Monrovia. Is that Monrovia, Liberia? Is that right? I can't read the rest of it."

I cover my hand with my mouth and try to keep from trembling. A letter addressed to me from Liberia. This must be from my family. The sender's name on the envelope has been washed away, but what if it is from my mother?

"Well, are you going to see who it's from, silly? This might be from your mother."

Now trembling, because I can't help it, I let my hand fall from my mouth. "Or it could be from someone telling me my mother is no longer living. I don't know. It could be bad news, Mary. I don't want to open it. Not right before Christmas."

"But aren't you going to drive yourself mad wanting to know what's inside now?"

I nod.

"Do you want me to read it?"

"No. No, I'll do it." The words come out breathlessly, as if I don't even believe it myself. But if it is from my mother, I can't let her first message to me be read by Mary. I just can't.

Slowly and carefully, so as not to rip the already weather-beaten and delicate pages, I open the envelope. My lips move in silent prayer that all is well, although I know that the prayer is foolish. The words have already been written, and whatever is enclosed in the letter has already been set. So I change the prayer to ask God to prepare my heart for whatever I am about to read, good or bad.

I can hardly stop my hands from shaking as I unfold the pages, and Mary places a calming hand on my knocking knees.

"It's okay, Eliza. Take your time," Mary says.

At the first three words, I have to set the pages down, because I burst into tears. I don't know how I am going to do this without being a weepy mess.

"What?" Mary asks, concern in her voice. "What's wrong?"

"N-nothing. Nothing."

I take a deep breath and exhale. Then I pick up the pages again. I can do this. I can read this letter. I must.

*My dearest Eliza,*

*I have wanted to write to you since Mr. Howell informed me about the passing of Mrs. Greenfield. I wish I could've been there to send her on her journey, because she was always kind to me. I hope you are well. Well, I know you are.*

Mrs. Greenfield always told me everything about your life, but it did not stop me from missing you every day. You do not remember this, but before we left for Africa, I cut a lock of your hair, a long braid, and I tied it with a ribbon. You wouldn't have noticed, you had so much hair that we could barely tame it. But every day I held it to my nose until it no longer smelled like your sweet scent, and then I imagined I could still notice traces of you from time to time, in the ribbon or in my mind. Your father hated that I did that. He said we had made the right choice. But I must tell you, before I continue this letter, why we left you with Mrs. Greenfield.

Your little body had recently been sick from a horrible fever, and we didn't think you would survive the journey. I thought I would die if we left you behind, but our only choices were to leave you behind or remain in chains. They wouldn't allow free Black people to stay in Mississippi, and Mrs. Greenfield had promised to take you to Philadelphia. We made the same impossible choice that so many families had to make.

But Mrs. Greenfield assured me that she would always take care of you and educate you, and that you would be free to do whatever your heart desired, and that you would have the resources to do just that. I believed her because she always kept her word.

When Mrs. Greenfield told me of your singing lessons, it brought me great joy. I wonder if you remember your father's singing. When we were all together on the plantation, his voice would lift everyone's spirits. He sang from the tobacco field, and it was a beautiful balm, and then he sang when we worshipped together on Sundays. Even though we all had a different way of honoring the creator, your father's voice connected us all. You got that from him. I would love to hear you sing one day.

Now Mr. Howell has written to me and says that you are singing concerts in America, and that they call you the Black Swan. More than anything now I want to make it back to you and to my native *land. Your father made it back to his, and he was so happy that he kissed the ground when we arrived. Now he is buried here with your sisters and his ancestors. All taken from me by African fever. I loved them until they were gone, and I will cherish their memories.*

*I am an old woman, but not too old yet. I have some life left inside me, I believe. I would like to see my beautiful singing daughter again. Maybe I will braid your hair once more and put ribbons in it like when you were a little girl. Or maybe I will sit and let you tell me all about your adventures. I hope this letter reaches you, and I hope I reach you soon.*

*Until we meet again.*
*Eternal love and Blessings,*
*Your mother Anna*

After reading the letter I am unable to form words. I am overcome with a flood of emotions. I simply fold the letter and place it back in its envelope and rise to my feet.

"Eliza . . ."

I shake my head at Mary. *Not now.* It's a mental message that I don't know if she receives, but I turn and walk out of the room. I need a moment and space to sort these feelings.

As I flee Mary's presence, the strongest message of all from my mother's letter envelops me and wraps its arms around me. It is her enduring love for me. As I read her words, my mind's eye could see her cradling the tendril of my hair. I could almost feel her slender fingers braiding my hair even now, as she promises to do when she returns.

When she returns.

I must make this happen. And now, when I thought all interest in the Black Swan had diminished, I have a concert promoter wishing to help me go to New York City and Europe. There must be a reason for these letters being placed in my hands on the same day. Perhaps to embark upon one is to accomplish the other.

Outside Mary and Isaiah's house, I stand bathing in the sunlight. And even though the temperature is frigid, I feel a warmth deep down in my spirit as a new round of snowflakes begins to fall. I spin and spin as the fresh, wet flakes commingle with my tears and make little rivulets down my face.

She says I sing like my father.

And that is the best Christmas gift I have ever received.

# CHAPTER THIRTY

*I*t took me some time to craft a response to my mother's letter. Well, I should say that I started my response as soon as I received it, but I was unhappy with every draft until now. I have finally written a letter that I feel comfortable sending and that expresses my sentiments. I had to have Mr. Howell's help deciphering the part of the address that was missing from the envelope.

Before I fold the letter to send, I read over it one last time, to make sure that it is good enough.

*Dear Mother,*

*I was so pleased to receive your letter. It was the best Christmas gift. Although I was sad to hear about my father's and sisters' passing, it brought me joy to know that my father kissed the ground when he returned to Africa and was happy to be buried there in his native land. It also warmed my heart to know that he is the one who blessed me with this singing voice. I wish I remembered him singing. I wish I remembered my baby sisters. I wish I remembered more.*

*When I found out you had been corresponding with Miss Lizbeth all those years, a part of me felt betrayed. I wondered why you wouldn't talk with me and send me letters as well. But as much as*

*I yearn for you now after receiving one letter, I know how much my heart would have bled for you as a child and as a younger woman if I had been hearing from you all along. It is probably for the best that you allowed me to grow under the nurturing and watchful eye of Miss Lizbeth.*

*I have done everything that you wanted me to do. I have gotten an education, studied singing and pursued it, and now I am about to go on a tour of Europe. I intend to bring you home to America, with or without the funds left in Miss Lizbeth's will. If I can be successful on this tour, I will not only have the funds but the influence to make this happen. There are very powerful women in the Philadelphia Female Anti-Slavery Society who can help us as well.*

*I will stop at nothing to see us reunited. Please write to me again at Mr. Howell's address or at my sister Mary's at the address enclosed, and they will forward any letters to me, wherever I am in the world.*

*Until we meet again.*
*Your daughter,*
*Eliza*

I am not usually a person who enjoys surprises. Mostly because people who do the surprising are not always aware of what brings me joy. Their surprises bring them joy, but I am usually embarrassed by the end of their moment.

But seeing Charles in the Howards' living room, bearing gifts, is the best kind of surprise. I can hardly contain my excitement as I bound down the stairs like a much younger woman. I jump into his outstretched arms and stand on tiptoe to plant as many kisses as possible on his face. I don't stop kissing him until I hear Hiram clear his throat.

I look up to see that he's entered the room and is sitting in his favorite chair. I take Charles by the hand and lead him to the love seat.

312 @ TIFFANY L. WARREN

We will, it seems, have our visit under Hiram's watchful eyes, since he is making no obvious attempt to relocate himself to another area of the house. Forever the chaperone and protector even when it isn't needed.

"How are you back so soon?" I ask Charles. I can't stop stroking his chest, so maybe I'm wrong. Perhaps we do need a chaperone.

Charles nods his head toward Hiram in greeting. Hiram peers over his spectacles and nods back, looking every bit the father.

"We finished the load early and got a bonus for our hard work. Patrick really has great ideas on how to execute these hauls for the least amount of time and money. We are thinking of starting our own company."

"You should. I know if you two put your heads together, you will be a success."

"How are things with the Black Swan?"

"She is going on a tour of Europe," Hiram says without being invited into the conversation.

"That is wonderful news," Charles says to me, completely ignoring Hiram, as he always does. "Let's go for a walk. I'll buy you lunch to celebrate."

"As long as it's pepper pot soup."

Charles beams a smile at me that completely melts my heart, and everything else. "Whatever the lady wants, she gets."

As soon as we're on our way, Charles offers his arm for me to hold. The ground is quite muddy from a fresh rain, which has stirred up odors from all manner of muck. But at least the weather is still cool, so the stench is bearable.

"I've missed you terribly, Eliza," Charles says as he brings my hand up to his lips and kisses the back of it. "The long journeys by packet boat and steamer are lonely. And don't say I have Patrick."

This makes me laugh. "I was not going to imply that Patrick is a good substitute for me."

Besides, I know that Patrick is not one to sit around entertaining Charles when there are women and whiskey to be procured.

"He isn't. I may seem too soft a man to admit this, but during my down times, I would replay an argument we had in my mind."

"Why on earth would you do that?" I laugh imagining his mental sparring.

"To try and convince you with different versions of the same argument."

"And are you ever successful?"

Charles chuckles and shakes his head. "No, I never win."

"I am glad that your imaginary version of me is as skilled at debate as I am in real life."

"Tell me about this European tour. Has Colonel Wood somehow made amends for his abysmal behavior?"

"He has done no such thing. He didn't even pay me for that concert in Toronto." I shake my head in disgust thinking of that man. "I worry about running into him when I am out and about. Worried that he may try to exact some sort of revenge."

"If you weren't well known, with many patrons and sponsors, this might be a concern. I do not think he would trouble you with anything except a new opportunity. Me on the other hand . . . Well, he'd turn me over to the highest bidder. He might even offer me to the lowest bidder out of spite."

"I think by the end of it all, he would've sold us both off. Old money-hungry demon."

"Well, if it isn't Colonel Wood, then who is your new manager?"

"His name is Edward T. Norris, and he is a relation of Barnum's. He was able to book my concert in New York City using Barnum's name."

Charles gives me a skeptical look. "Did you check his references?"

"I asked Hiram to, and he enlisted the mayor of Buffalo to be safe. They found nothing to cause alarm in his background or in the contract."

"The mayor of Buffalo?" Charles's eyes stretch wide with surprise. "He was serious about this."

"Well, he feels terrible about what happened with Colonel Wood."

"That's understandable. Where will you be performing in New York?"

I wiggle my eyebrows with excitement. "The Metropolitan Opera House."

Charles's reaction steals all my enthusiasm, though. His countenance falls into a heavy frown.

"They do not allow Black patrons in that concert hall, Eliza. I am surprised they are even willing to host a concert for you."

"Mr. Norris assures us that the concert hall manager agreed to allow anyone to attend the concert as long as they can afford a ticket."

Charles stares straight ahead, brooding as usual. I know he doesn't trust these men to do the right thing, or even inquire about the things we want. But why does he not have more faith in my dedication to the cause of freedom?

I snuggle in a little closer to Charles as his irritated stride quickens. "He's already doing things differently than Colonel Wood."

"How so? If I've learned one thing from transacting business, it is that white men do things quite similarly, and most often in their own favor."

"Well, for one thing, I am going to sit for a portrait to be used on the concert program."

I am not sure why I mention this to Charles, because I am not at all excited about this drawing that Mr. Norris has commissioned. The idea of sitting still for hours for someone, a supposed artist, to create their rendition of my face is not very appealing. But it is less costly than the daguerreotype image and engraving. Perhaps I would feel better about it if I could at least choose the artist. I do not trust a white artist's opinion or interpretation of my features. I am sure a Black artist would do a better job.

"I like that idea," Charles says. "The world needs to see how beautiful you are."

"Flattery is very effective at getting what you want."

"And what is that, Eliza? What do I want?" Charles teases as he tips my chin upward and grins.

"Sometimes I am not sure, but whatever it is, keep complimenting me and you shall have it."

"I am not sure what I want, besides success in business and freedom. Beyond that, it is a mystery."

I wonder if Charles's future is really a mystery or if he's just uncomfortable sharing it with me. Because if he wants the same things Lucien wanted, I may disappear like vapor. What a man to invest his time and heart and to put up with the likes of me. I dare not travel too far down the path of the future. I cannot fathom things that may happen years from now.

I change the subject to safer things in my future that have nothing to do with us. "I got a letter from my mother. In Africa."

Charles stops walking and hugs me right in the middle of the street. I love that no matter how plump I become, Charles makes me feel light as a feather. "Oh, Eliza, that is wonderful news."

"She wants to come home, and I am going to help her get here," I gush when he sets me down again. "This tour will help me do that. Even if my inheritance continues to be delayed, I can do it with my savings plus the money I'll make on this tour."

"And it's a better split than with Colonel Wood?" he asks, still looking doubtful.

"Yes. I get a guaranteed thirty dollars per show, no matter the receipts. And while I'm in Europe, I get five dollars a week whether there is a concert or not. This is to pay for my living expenses, including maid and manservant."

"Manservant?" Charles asks. "And what need have you for a manservant?"

I press my lips together mischievously. "I will have to dream up a few appropriate tasks, but it is in the contract."

"I volunteer for the job. Would you like to check my references?" Charles asks. "I promise they are impeccable."

I'd thought Charles would be insulted by a request to act as my servant, so I hadn't dreamed of asking him, but there's no one I'd want on that steamer with me more than Charles.

"You won't mind riding over in servants' quarters while I have a first-class ticket?"

"No, I won't."

"Well, what about Patrick and the shipping business?" I ask. "Won't he feel like you abandoned him?"

"He has lots of other partners besides me. He will understand."

"Well, Darla is going to be keeping an eye on Ruby and William's children, because Ruby is traveling with me as my maid."

Charles's eyes nearly pop out of his head at this news. "William is allowing this?"

"Yes, only because I begged. I don't want to be in Europe with some young girl who doesn't know anything. I want Ruby. Besides, Ruby's never done anything in her life remotely exciting."

"If Ruby is coming, then things between us will certainly remain . . . chaste," Charles says with an eye roll. "I can't think of anyone more adept at blocking."

"Oh, did you think you'd get me over to England and have your way with me?" I ask.

"Only if you beg me."

He could wish on every star in the sky and that would never come true, but I smile and shake my head at him, and squeeze both his hands.

"I'm excited about this," he says. "I hope I get to see you onstage in New York, but I may need to finish one last job with Patrick before we leave. After that, I'm all yours."

"Thank you, my love."

"And the news about your mother. I hope you keep me around long enough to meet her," he says with a mischievous gleam in his eyes and a boyish grin on his face.

I grin right back at him and try to capture this moment and hold it close to my heart. I am going to Europe. My mother is coming home. And the man I love loves me despite every restriction I've set before us.

So why is there an unsettled feeling in my spirit? Why do I feel as if I am once again setting out upon troubled waters? As always, my faith must sustain me. And again, I must do a thing when I am feeling afraid.

## CHAPTER THIRTY-ONE

*New York City, New York*
*March 1853*

Spring has arrived on the calendar, and if I was home in Philadelphia, I would be enjoying the first of our blooming roses on the bushes in front of the house. But I am not home where there are plenty of trees and flowers to behold. I am in New York City, where nothing is green, and everything is filthy. Where there are people on every corner, and many of them are as grimy as the cobblestone streets.

Even with the grime and crud, I feel the buzz of excitement. Mr. Norris has reported that thousands of tickets have already been sold for the concert. This will be my most lucrative show yet, and the profits will be more than enough to raise the funds needed for the voyage to Europe.

Mr. Norris and I are lodging at the Astor Place Hotel, where I am overjoyed to see more than a few free Black people in the dining room for lunch. It also pleases me to see a waitstaff of young Black men. Though I will never share these fears aloud, I am always nervous to have my food served to me by a white person. My fear is that I may do or say something deemed disrespectful and that my meal will be poisoned or somehow tampered with.

A young man, no more than twenty or twenty-one, approaches my table with a smile and well-oiled skin. As he stands before me all shiny and coiffed, I feel proud of him just like his mother must be.

"Good afternoon. My name is Timothy, and I will be serving you today."

"Good afternoon."

"Miss Greenfield, we have a wonderful roast beef on the bill of fare today," he says, very serious and businesslike. "Would you like to try that, or would you prefer another selection?"

"That roast beef sounds delicious," I say. "Is it slathered in gravy and is there lemonade to wash it all down?"

He presses his lips together to try to hold in his laughter, but he is unsuccessful. I am glad I was able to pull a moment of joy out of him. A young man his age should be more fun than serious, even if he is earning a living.

"There is no gravy, I'm afraid, like there would be if you had it at my mother's house for dinner. There is au jus. I'm told it's French."

"Well, aren't you knowledgeable? I will have that, and a slice of apple pie for dessert."

"And the lemonade to wash it all down?" he asks.

"Yes, sir."

Timothy bows and turns to leave, but then he stops in his tracks and turns around. He takes a few steps toward me, this time getting a little closer than when he offered me the gravy-less roast beef.

"Is it true, Miss Greenfield?"

"Is what true?"

"I heard some of the bellmen talking about how they aren't going to allow Black people to come to your concert."

I blink a few times as if that will help me better hear what he said. "What did you say?" I ask.

"They said it's in the *New-York Tribune*. Irish been protesting outside the Metropolitan Hall since you got to town, and they're threatening to riot if you proceed with the concert."

This cannot be happening. Not when I am so close to reaching my goal. And not when I have dedicated myself to the cause of freedom.

"Don't worry. Your mother will get to see my concert. I promise. Will you do me a favor and find my manager, Mr. Norris? I want to talk to him to make sure everything is arranged. And would you mind also having someone bring me a copy of that newspaper? Don't worry about the roast beef for now. I will have that later."

"Yes, ma'am."

Timothy scurries off, and I hastily finish my glass of water, since I suddenly feel parched. If this is true and Mr. Norris knows about it or worse is complicit, then I don't know what I'll do or feel.

I sip my water again. And wait.

* * *

"Eliza, there is nothing that can be done. I have spoken with the manager at the Metropolitan Hall. These men are threatening real violence."

Lunch has been delivered to Mr. Norris's suite of rooms, so that we can converse behind a closed door. I sit at his dining table staring at a plate of food, chicken and potatoes, but I am no longer in any mood to eat. Neither, it seems, is Mr. Norris. But he's already a thin and frail-looking man, his large beak of a nose taking up most of his narrow face, so he can't afford to skip meals.

"Of course, I don't want violence, but I don't understand the protest," I say, although it is the same as always. "They're protesting to keep Black folk from seeing a Black woman sing?"

Mr. Norris rakes his hand through his thinning hair. A nervous gesture he does quite frequently. He never seems comfortable or at peace. There always seems to be something for him to fret about. He paces the room, with a copy of the newspaper in his hand, but I'd wish he'd sit down. He's making my nerves bad too.

"They're protesting all of it. The concert with a Black prima donna. Black people being entertained alongside whites. And they are threatening your safety."

"But we need this concert to proceed, so that we can go to Europe for the rest of the tour," I say, stating the obvious and causing Mr. Norris to rake his hair even more.

"Can't go to Europe if you're in a pine box, Eliza." He tosses the newspaper onto the table, and I pick it up, scanning the article to read the words for myself.

"So, what they said in the newspaper about not allowing Black patrons, is it true?" I'm irritated now after seeing the words in black and white. "Is the manager of the concert hall really going to enforce this?"

Mr. Norris gives a woeful nod. "He's offering refunds to anyone who comes to claim one."

I feel myself becoming flustered. This is more of what I've encountered in every other city, except here, I'm on my own, because Mr. Norris seems too timid to try to compel the concert hall manager to uphold the contract.

"Aren't you even going to try?" I ask with disdain, as I shoot daggers across the room at him with my eyes. "This doesn't bode well for our future relationship."

"Well, Miss Greenfield, you let me know when you have an idea." He is clearly as frustrated as I am, his nostrils flaring as he stares right back at me. "This entire city is angry. Can't you feel it as you walk down the street?"

"What are those Irishmen so angry about?" I scoff. "They're free."

Mr. Norris's arm drops to his side, and he stares helplessly at me, like he doesn't know how to respond. It is a valid question. The Irish may have their difficulties, and they might be treated poorly by other white people. But they are still white. And still free.

"Eliza," Mr. Norris says, some of the heat in his voice dissipated, "won't you consider, this one last time, performing the concert for an all-white audience?"

"I cannot." I slam my fist on the table, punctuating my words. I am not willing to do this, not even one last time.

Mr. Norris shakes his head and sighs. "Eliza . . . I must ask you to reconsider."

I rise from my seat and push the plate of food away. I am so weary of this. Concert hall managers agreeing to one thing, and then angry poor white men who can't even afford to buy a ticket to the concert bullying Black people into cowering inside their houses instead of seeing me perform.

And every time I allow this, I feel that I lose more power. Every time I say yes to another all-white crowd, it gives Black people the message that I do not care about our struggle.

"If I refuse to perform here, do you not have patrons in Europe who could assist in finalizing the plans for the tour?" I am desperate for a solution. To save my reputation here, to make it to Europe, and to bring my mother home. It does not seem as if I can have them all.

"If you refuse to perform here, then my name is tarnished, and the very delicate connections that I have may come undone. I am pleading with you to trust me, Eliza. Soon, we will put all this foolishness behind us." Mr. Norris's begging eyes seem sincere, and though I am not inclined to trust anyone, he has given me no reason to think he has anything but the best interests of this tour at heart.

The massive sigh I exhale is heavy from my having to repeatedly navigate the same treacherous waters and be concerned about what the *Frederick Douglass' Paper* will have to say about me this time.

Then I have an idea.

It will not fix the problem with the Irish protestors outside the concert hall or even the all-white crowd at the Metropolitan Concert Hall. But it will offer a solution that my conscience can live with.

I walk from around the table, and Mr. Norris's eyes anxiously follow my every move, waiting, I assume, for my decision. But I am not going to give it to him yet. He and the manager at the Metropolitan Concert Hall are going to wait. Unlike Colonel Wood, he doesn't try to strong-arm me into submission. That is, at least, an improvement.

"I am going to retire to my room," I say wearily. "All of this has been too much, and I'd like to lie down."

"Please let me know if you have need of anything. I will make sure it's provided."

I hear the anxiety in his tone, but I am not going to do anything to assuage it. Let him feel worried. Let him wonder if I am going to comply. I should not be the only one feeling discomfort at the hands of these protesters, when so many others are simply going to make a profit.

"Rest is all. Thank you."

When I leave Mr. Norris's suite, instead of going directly to my room, I go back down to the dining room. Timothy is on his way out, so I hurry to catch up with him before he leaves the building, but the boy walks much faster than I can manage in a corset.

"Timothy!"

He stops and then rushes back to where I stand, still wearing the same bright smile. "Miss Greenfield. Do you need something?"

I take Timothy's hand and pull him to me, so we can talk privately. He seems surprised at the sudden contact, but I need this to happen quickly. "Yes, you told me your mother has a ticket to my concert, correct?"

"She sure does. She's looking forward to hearing you sing. It's all she's been talking about since she saw it in the newspaper that you were coming to town."

"Does your mother also happen to attend church in the city?"

Timothy narrows his eyes a bit, as if he's wondering where I'm going with my questions. "Our family attends Abyssinia Baptist Church," he says. "It's the biggest Black church in New York City."

"Perfect. Will you please tell her to inform her pastor or the church's secretary that the Black Swan would like to perform a concert for your members and any others who want to attend on Sunday evening." I try to let him hear excitement in my voice, because I want him to share this with his mother like it's the biggest event New York City's Black community has ever seen.

"Will there be a cost to attend?"

I shake my head. "It will be free of charge. But make sure your mother gets there early to get a good seat. I suspect that there won't be enough room."

"All right, Miss Greenfield." Oh, good. Now his eyes are wide with enthusiasm too. "I would be happy to carry this message. Is there anything else I should say?"

I hesitate to ask this last thing, but I'm going to anyway. "If there is a church musician who can play the pianoforte or organ, I would appreciate their assistance."

"There's a young man who attends our church who is classically trained. I'm sure he would be honored to play for you."

I want to hug this boy, but I resist the urge, because even though he is a boy to me, he is every bit a man. I wouldn't want to do anything to cause him trouble at his job.

I settle for a bright and encouraging smile. "When you find out all the details, do you mind leaving me a note or sending someone to my room?"

"It won't be any trouble at all, Miss Greenfield. In fact, I will be back after I have dinner with my lady friend and her family. I have a meeting here at the hotel."

"A meeting? That sounds very important."

"It is." He leans in and whispers as if we're coconspirators. "The waiters are planning to strike."

"The Black waiters?"

"Black and white. We're striking together for higher wages. It's a good thing you're here this week. In a couple weeks our guests may be eating cold crusts of bread and apples for dinner."

Timothy hurries off, leaving me standing there in amazement. He seems like a responsible and upstanding young man, but now

I am proud of him for another reason. At his young age, he is not afraid of standing up for a cause. This is what free men do, and free women too.

The whole city may seem angry, but some of us have damned good reason to be.

## Chapter Thirty-Two

*I* didn't think it possible, but the citizens of New York City have become even more restless in the two days since we've agreed to a concert for only white people. I have not mentioned my concert at the church on Sunday to Mr. Norris. Any donations (since there will be no ticket sales) I have decided will be given to an orphanage run by the church. There will be no proceeds for Mr. Norris to collect, so he should not care one way or the other.

In my dressing room, I await my call to come onstage. The clock in the corner of the room tells me that it is past time for the concert to begin, but not yet tardy enough for me to worry that a catastrophe has taken place. It doesn't stop me from imagining a good many horrible scenarios.

There is a knock on the door, and I rush to answer, thinking that a stagehand has been sent to collect me. Instead, it is a worried-looking Mr. Norris.

"What is the matter?" I ask. "You look troubled."

He rakes his hand through his hair. That nervous tic. "Well, the crowd is . . . I am not sure how to describe them. A little rowdy, perhaps."

"Rowdy?" Now his nerves are starting to wear off on me. "What type of performance are they expecting?"

"That is what concerns me," Mr. Norris says, and winces. "It appears this is the sort of audience who visits Barnum's American Museum."

"I don't know what that means." His words or his facial expression, and I don't know which worries me more.

"That museum of curiosities draws a crowd looking for strange freaks of nature."

"Is that what they think I am? A freak of nature?" My voice makes a screeching sound from the panicking, so I breathe deeply to calm myself. I cannot allow myself to lose control in front of this large crowd of white people. There will surely be reviewers in the audience, and no matter what their expectation is, I must sur-pass it.

"I am not sure. But it is no matter. If they purchased a ticket looking for a spectacle, they will be surprised with a bit of culture for a change."

Finally, the stagehand comes to collect me. It is a white child no more than twelve or thirteen. He's dressed in a gaudy suit with black-and-white-striped pants and a yellow tailored jacket. Atop his head is a big puffy hat with a red ball of yarn on the top.

"Why are you dressed this way?" I ask suspiciously. "You look like a court jester or a clown."

He looks down at his ridiculous outfit and shrugs. "This is how we open every show with colored performers."

I look to Mr. Norris for an explanation, but he shakes his head, clearly as clueless as I am.

"Don't worry, Miss Greenfield," the stagehand says. "We always have a good amount of fun."

Since it is much too late for me to raise a complaint about this so-called fun, with much trepidation I follow the skipping, prancing merrymaker.

When we get to the curtain, the jester or whatever his role is races ahead of me and then tiptoes out onto the stage. I am not sure what's happening, but usually when I take the stage, a spotlight follows me to my mark, and the crowd is silent until after the first aria.

But when I come from behind the curtain, there is a loud horn and drumbeat to mark every step I take as if I am so heavy that my footfalls are making the sound. The crowd roars with laughter. I am not used to laughing from my audiences. Only applause, bravos, and encores.

I am not sure when to signal to the accompanist that I am ready, because the crowd is so raucous. Am I supposed to sing over them?

Finally, unsure that they will ever calm down, I nod to the accompanist, and the music begins. As I start to sing, the audience settles some, but never to the complete quiet that I'm used to. I close my eyes to shut out the activity and excessive movement and try to give my best performance under these insane circumstances.

"Encore!" Someone shouts this in the middle of a song, probably unaware of the word's meaning and not understanding that it is not the appropriate time to shout.

I ignore the misplaced exclamation and continue singing. The Italian words of the aria are lost on this crowd, as are my vocal acrobatics and trills. Still, I continue hoping that there are at least a few cultured citizens in the audience who will appreciate fine musicianship.

As I finish the aria on a high note with an elaborate run, the stagehand rushes back out onto the stage and does multiple backflips and somersaults. The crowd roars when he does a headstand in front of me and wiggles his feet in the air.

What is this? Out of sheer embarrassment, tears fall down my face, unseen by this ridiculous audience. I am almost unable to begin the next song, but I do so despite the tears. It is imperative that I make it to the end of this farce with as much of my dignity as possible.

I have no idea if Mr. Norris is complicit in this madness, but the theater manager, and whomever else decided to have the stagehand's comedic offering as a part of my concert, has turned my performance into a minstrel show without the blackface.

Four thousand New Yorkers purchased tickets to witness my humiliation. And for the first time since I started this journey, the applause stings my ears. The shouts of "bravo" and "encore" wound my soul. In the most hurtful and crass way possible, they have stolen the joy from every note being sung. I wonder if they can discern my sorrow over their boisterous behavior.

And even though Charles is probably somewhere seething at me performing once again for an all-white audience, I am glad that no one Black is here to witness my shame. This is not what my gift was meant for. I am not meant to be made a fool.

I will finish this concert and collect my payment. Then never shall I subject myself to such a spectacle again.

After the final note of the final song, I do not wait for an encore, or for anyone to escort me off the stage. I storm off on my own to the dressing room. I am on a rampage, and Mr. Norris is the first one who will feel my fury.

I don't have to wait long to see him, because he's pacing right outside my door with a horrified expression on his face. His hair is a disheveled mess, probably because of all the raking through with his hands.

He rushes forward to meet me, contrition in his eyes. "Eliza, I'm so sorry. When I saw what was happening, I wanted to rush onstage and gather you myself. I wanted to stop the show."

"I really wish you had," I say with a trembling voice. "That was awful. Just awful."

Mr. Norris ushers me into the dressing room and closes the door behind us right before the flood of tears starts. I am so angry with myself for weeping this way, but I can't help it. I feel soiled and humiliated. And somehow cheapened, as if it was my fault.

"Did you know about this, Mr. Norris?" I say as I sink into my vanity chair. "Did you know what they were going to do to me out there?"

He gasps. "Of course not! I would never have allowed such a thing. You must believe me. I even tried to stop the concert midway, but the concert manager said he would not pay. I could not allow you to go through that and not receive the pay."

I stare intently at Mr. Norris so he can understand how serious I am about what I'm about to say next.

"I will never do that again, Mr. Norris. I don't care who the management is or what they say."

"I understand."

"I will walk off the stage in the middle of the performance without a second thought."

Mr. Norris's poor limp hair flops into his face as he drops down on one knee in front of me. "Eliza, if I had known that they were going to do this to you, I would have demanded we cancel."

In his eyes, I can only see the same shock and horror that I felt on the stage, and so I believe him. That is, at least, a consolation in all this.

"There is enough for your fare to Liverpool, and for all the preparations," Mr. Norris says. "First-class cabin fare, as promised. And fares for your maid and manservant. Also, one month salary in advance and an additional ten pounds for your staff's food and lodgings. Thirty pounds in all."

He rises to his feet slowly, and I hear the creaking and popping of joints that come with middle age. He pushes the hair back so that it is no longer falling into his face.

"There are things I need to finalize here before I can join you. My associate Thomas Willcutt will meet you at the office in London. He will have explicit instructions. You will not have to worry about a thing."

I take a moment to push the dreadful performance out of my mind, allow this new reality to sink in. I am going to Europe. Finally. Everything I've worked for since I first boarded the steamer to Buffalo is coming to fruition.

I am going to Europe!

* * *

ALTHOUGH I AM still somewhat traumatized from Thursday night's concert, the funds have been collected by Mr. Norris, and he promptly secured my passage to England. Mere days after I perform my last concert at the Abyssinia Baptist Church in New York City, I will be on my way to Liverpool.

News of the chicanery and foolishness that accompanied my last concert has made its way to the newspapers. Some fault me for not participating in the merriment, even noting that I seemed out of place at my own concert, and that perhaps my talents are best suited for stuffy private parties for the elite of Upstate New York. I suppose they meant that as an insult, but I did not take it as such. I much prefer a stuffy private party to racist mayhem.

But more than anything, I enjoy taking my talents where they are most appreciated. In the Black church, where I have no fear of judgment, I can give my most spirited performances. I feel something come over me in those spaces. I don't know if it's the reverence of the gift or how moved the listeners are, but no matter the reason, Black churches feel like home.

As usual, the church doesn't have all the trappings of a concert hall, so a dressing room and warm-up space are not available. But they aren't necessary with the songs I plan to sing. These are arias and folk songs I can sing in my sleep, most without much effort even though they show the full range of my vocal abilities.

I am seated in the front row of the left section of pews, and in the center section are the children from the orphanage who will benefit from the proceeds of this concert. All dressed in clean and neat Sunday attire, and coiffed as nicely as possible. This is not just a time to collect funds for the orphanage, but to perhaps find a home for some of the children, since this event is bound to bring visitors that do not typically attend services at the church.

I whisper a prayer that any of the children who wish to be adopted by a lovely family have their wish fulfilled. I cannot imagine what my childhood would have been if Miss Lizbeth had not survived to my adulthood. And while I was not an orphan, what can two parents do from the coast of Africa for their child in Philadelphia?

There is so much business for me to attend to before I set sail midweek, but today I feel a sense of peace. And joy. Both fruits of the Holy Spirit, so it is apt that I am in a house of worship, even if there will be no preaching tonight. Only the ministry of song.

I feel a firm yet gentle hand on my shoulder, and my pulse quickens at the knowledge of whom that familiar touch belongs to.

"Eliza," Charles says, as I turn to face him. "I'm here."

"I am so glad to see you. The concert . . ."

"I heard about the concert."

"You've heard? How?"

"There was a letter to the *Frederick Douglass' Paper.*"

"Ah."

"But it was favorable toward you, Eliza. It said that in opposition to the concert hall's racist decision you scheduled today's concert to benefit an orphanage."

I let out a relieved sigh. Although I have never had the privilege of meeting Mr. Douglass, I do not want him to have a negative opinion of me.

"Is that how you knew to come here?"

"Yes, and I am looking forward to hearing the program you intended to perform at the Metropolitan Hall."

"Will you come sit next to me?" I need to feel his calming presence near me.

"I'd be honored to sit next to the prima donna."

It might seem like a small thing for Charles to share a pew with me, when we have shared dinner tables, long walks, and the stage. But it feels like a declaration in church before God and the members of this congregation.

After getting a reassuring hand squeeze and hug from Charles, I walk to the simple podium and gaze out at the attendees. There are several hundred pressed into the building, and not an empty seat in the sanctuary. Folk also stand on the walls and huddle in the back of the church. Even with the crowded confines, the spring air coming in from the open doors in back is cool and refreshing.

My accompanist from the Metropolitan Hall concert, a zealous abolitionist, joined me here for this concert at no cost when I shared with him the reason behind this additional show. As he begins to play, the rich sound reverberates off the church's high ceilings.

In a concert hall, I cannot see the audience, and so at times it feels impersonal, as if I'm singing to the wind. But in this sacred and holy space, I can gaze upon the faces of my listeners. The awe and appreciation in their expressions brings tears to my eyes. This is what I was meant to experience at the Metropolitan Hall, not the scorn I endured.

I take my time progressing through the program, singing encores when requested, and even when they aren't requested. I sing and sing until there is not a dry eye in the house, including my own. We all weep together at the beauty of the music and the sorrow of the lyrics.

Even though this concert is in response to the hatred of white men and women who would see me in chains, I am ordained to be here, standing in front of this assembly of like-minded people. These songs, offered before I set sail to Europe, are prayer and promise.

The feeling in my heart and spirit in this moment will sustain me on my trip abroad. When I travel across the same ocean my ancestors traversed to get here, I will take solace in the fact that their spirits go before me.

# CHAPTER THIRTY-THREE

*SS Asia*
*April 1853*

$\mathcal{I}$ wish I could say this voyage has been an enjoyable one. After three days on this wretched steamship, my only prayer is that this angry tossing will stop and that we might have one day of warmth and sunlight and a respite from the cold and wet air.

This is so unlike my travels up the river by packet boat and even by steamer across Lake Seneca, where the waters were mostly calm and the gentle waves were soothing. The Atlantic Ocean seems to have a vendetta against the SS *Asia* the way it's pounding against the sides of this ship day and night. And the steady, constant rain isn't helping either. I will be overjoyed to have my feet touch solid ground again, and to have my clothing and hair feel completely dry.

On this fourth morning, while I try to convince myself to overcome the feeling of seasickness for a bit of breakfast in the saloon, I take a few moments to appreciate my surroundings.

The first-class sleeping apartment that I share with Ruby is spacious, with two landscape paintings of the Great Wall of China hanging on the wall. A large window provides sufficient light that signals the passing of the days and is covered by beautiful burgundy curtains. Matching the curtains is another novelty, something I've never had in a bedroom or home—carpeting to cover the wooden floor. It has a similar pattern to the valance at the top of the curtain. Such a beautiful touch for simple travel from one place to another.

I wonder what it was like for my parents when they took a similar journey over these treacherous waters going to Liberia. And for my father when he was stolen from his home in Africa when he was a child so many years before that. They had traveled to Liberia with an entire community, but their accommodations could not have been as luxurious as these.

Ruby has already risen from her bed and has straightened it. "Are you ready for breakfast?" she asks.

I shake my head. "I don't think so."

"You've got to try to get up and put some food on your stomach, else you'll never get over this seasickness," Ruby says as she takes a damp cloth and places it on my forehead. "Here, wash your face, and then try to get up."

I let the cool cloth soothe me for a moment with my eyes closed. Then I open them again and rise. I take a few steps over to the water bowl and swish my mouth with salt water and a little piece of peppermint leaf. That is about the best I can do to keep from looking (and smelling) like death warmed over.

"I am still a bit under the weather, but I think the fresh air will do me good," I say to Ruby. "And I'm somewhat ravenous."

"Well, then, it's off to the saloon," Ruby says.

"What about Charles? What does he do for breakfast?"

Ruby laughs. "Charles and I are on this steamer as servants. We get to eat in a separate section of the saloon, but no one will stop me if I go with you."

"I don't like that you're listed as my servants," I say. "Why can't you be listed as my watchers?"

This makes Ruby holler. "Your watchers?"

"The ones who watch me to make sure I don't do something silly."

"Come on, Eliza," Ruby says, still laughing. "The sun is out this morning, and after all these clouds and rain, you could really use some sunlight. It'll make you feel better."

We step out of the cabin and onto the freshly cleaned and polished wooden deck. It gleams in the morning sun, and the view of the open ocean is simply breathtaking. It's my first time seeing the steamer on the sea with no land in any direction. It's overwhelming and awe-inspiring at the same time.

Leaning on the iron railing and getting his dose of the morning sun, Charles is a handsome sight with his traveling trousers, boots, cotton shirt, and waistcoat. He's fully dressed and waiting for me to give him some task, although the task never comes. He's free to do as he pleases, since he's only a servant in name.

"Good morning, Charles. Did you have breakfast?" I ask. "We can bring you back some of ours if you haven't."

Charles turns from the railing with a smile as bright as the sun. "I did. It was quite tasty. Your manservant is ready to serve if there is anything you require."

"There is not." I struggle to hold in my laughter. "Enjoy your morning, sir."

"You too, Miss Eliza."

Ruby elbows me in the ribs. "He's really going to play this up, isn't he?" she whispers.

"Well, he should," I whisper back. "We don't want anyone thinking or saying anything untoward about me. Everyone is watching us. I am the only Black woman in first class."

We stop at the entrance to the saloon, which is more than a place for people to listen to music and have strong drinks. It is the main dining facility on the steamship, and according to the brochure we were given when we boarded, it can hold one hundred sixty people. I haven't seen it at full capacity yet, but around dinnertime, it is certainly a hub of activity.

Ruby opens the door for me. "Shall we, mademoiselle?"

"*Mais oui!*" I say with a laugh as I walk into the bustling saloon. "And that is the extent of my French."

"Aren't you going to Paris, Miss Eliza? You need to learn a bit more than that."

"You're right. I do."

The saloon, like the sleeping apartments, also seems to have been decorated with luxury in mind. The dining tables are solid cherry wood, with gorgeous and ornate red tablecloths to match the red velvet sofas that are along the walls and the room's center beams. The ceiling has a glass dome that allows the entire room to be bathed in sunlight. The floor here is also carpeted, with a much richer texture than the one in the sleeping apartments, though I wish it wasn't. With the glass dome, marble or wooden floors would probably provide better acoustics for the pianoforte that's in the center of the room. But it sure does look stunning, even if it wasn't designed for a musician.

As soon as we're seated, our ship steward, Mr. Applebaum, appears at the table, immaculately dressed. "Hello. What would you like for breakfast this fine morning?"

I lift my eyebrows. *Fine* is a bit of an exaggeration, but since we have sunshine right now, I will allow it to stand. "I have not been feeling well at all, so I will stay with dry toast and tea. Perhaps I will try more with lunch."

"Might I suggest a boiled egg too, Miss Greenfield? I have found that keeping a full stomach helps you get your sea legs quicker."

I glance at Ruby for her thoughts. She nods. "I'd trust him," she says. "He hasn't looked ill this entire time."

"All right. And a boiled egg."

Mr. Applebaum approves with a smile and a nod. "And you, Miss Ruby?"

"I'll have a boiled egg, blueberry scone, a bowl of fruit, and a cup of tea. Thank you."

Mr. Applebaum nods. "I hope you start feeling better, Miss Greenfield."

The thing that I really appreciate about Mr. Applebaum, aside from his very clipped and proper British accent, is that he does not seem to see any issue with me, a Black woman, being here. I can detect no difference in the way he treats me and the way he treats any other passenger on this ship. Now, I have only had a few days to observe him, and I have been sick for most of those, but I simply get a good feeling about Mr. Applebaum. If his British brethren are like him, I don't know if I'll be able to pull myself back to American shores ever again.

The sun comes out stronger now, not just brightening but warming the saloon, finally making things feel like spring.

"It may get warm enough for us to walk out on the deck today," I say to Ruby. "Wouldn't it be nice to get some sun?"

"Yes. I am sick of all this gray, and I'm ready to get off this ship. Same as you."

"If I make it through all of today and this evening, I might treat everyone with a song on the pianoforte at dinner," I say as I point out the instrument.

Ruby claps her hands. "A shipboard concert from the Black Swan. That would be splendid."

"I said a song. Not a concert."

"Well, they will encore you, and like any prima donna, you will sing another song. And then another."

I am tickled by the mischievous gleam in her eyes, and by the fact that she is correct. I can hardly resist a good encore.

"You may be right, but let's see if this boiled egg will stay in my stomach first before we choose my concert program."

Ruby grins, but I can tell she's already getting her lungs ready to shout *bravo*. That's fine. The last time I sang on a steamship, I left with a benefactor. It certainly won't hurt for me to sprinkle a few seeds on my way to Europe.

* * *

MR. APPLEBAUM WAS right. The heavier breakfast, then lunch, and the sunlight all helped me feel like a new woman by dinnertime. I even took my hair out of the church bun and combed it into the Black Swan coils. It was a bit of a struggle, but Ruby and I managed.

I also chose to wear the evening bodice with my navy silk taffeta dress, to change things up a bit, and because it's fancier. Ruby and Charles both seem to approve, as do some of the raunchier men on board who have no problem ogling me even though there is nothing bawdy about my attire.

After our dinner of roasted duck and vegetables, a nearly drunk gentleman (I believe I am being generous by saying *nearly*) decides to sit at the pianoforte. I was waiting until after dessert and coffee to make my debut, and now he's beat me to the after-dinner entertainment. I'll have to wait until he's tired himself out.

"There's another performer on the ship," Ruby teases. "Perhaps you two can sing a duet."

"Let's see what he's going to sing first. Maybe he got lost on his way to the smoking room."

Ruby throws back her head and cackles. He does have two extremely large cigars crammed into his shirt pocket, so I assume he intends on smoking those later, presumably in the smoking room, or maybe out on the ship's deck. I hope not out there, because I would like to look at the night sky without being choked by cigar smoke. The water has calmed down a great deal, and this is a perfect time to enjoy it before the seas get rough again.

Our drunken musician looks down at the pianoforte keys as if they are foreign objects. But then he seems to remember them, as if they're old friends from his childhood. He lifts his hands high into the air and wiggles his fingers. Charles and I make eye contact across the room, and Charles seems to be enjoying this, even though I am not.

"Oh my goodness." I shake my head, knowing that chicanery and foolishness is soon to follow.

And it does.

The drunken musician plays a very rousing and ragged version of "De Camptown Races." A distinctly popular saloon song if there ever was one, but not very classy for those who don't frequent anything close to a saloon in their everyday life. Only a dining room being called a saloon on a transatlantic voyage aboard a steamship.

"You mustn't allow that to be the only musical selection of the evening," Ruby says as the drunken musician gives a bow to sparse applause. "Hurry to replace him before he starts another song."

"All right. He did make me think of something fun I'd like to play for everyone."

I am grateful that the ship has found calm waters this evening, so that my walk to the pianoforte is graceful. I attempt to glide over from my table, as a prima donna would, and I believe I'm mostly successful. A few of the diners view me with interest but not recognition, and that alone tells me I have much work to do. If Jenny Lind was on this ship, the clamor would be unbearable.

I make a production of swishing my skirts over the pianoforte bench, making extra motions with my arms and head, almost like a choreographed dance. Taking my time to make sure the fabric falls just so. Stretching my arms and fingers unnecessarily until I have everyone in the room's attention. Because I won't begin until they're all watching. Until I have an audience.

I glance over at Ruby, and she is on the edge of her seat with excitement. In the corner of the room, Charles stands at the ready, and he gives me a slight nod. I nod in greeting to him in return.

"Good evening, everyone," I say in a warm and appealing tone. "My name is Elizabeth Taylor Greenfield. In America, some people call me the Black Swan. I am a singer on my way to tour several cities in Europe. Tonight, I feel like playing a few songs for you. Is that all right?"

Ruby claps loudly, and then a few others join her. But it isn't enough.

"Hmmm. I did ask a question, but I didn't hear everybody's answer. The Black Swan usually gets paid to sing. But this is free. So, I'll ask again. Is it all right if I sing a little for you tonight?"

And now I hear what I wanted to hear: applause. I look around the room, and the diners' faces are ready and set with anticipation. As they should be.

I play the opening bars of "The Rock Beside the Sea." It's an upbeat popular tune that the saloon folk will be able to sing along to, and it's pleasant enough for the families dining to enjoy.

"I thought about this song," I say as I play the intro, "because today we finally got sunshine, and the sun has finally broken through the clouds."

As usual, I start songs like this in my baritone, and I hear oohs and ahhs in the crowd, like I do in my concerts. Then, in between the verses, I invite people to join in, and something new happens that I've never experienced before . . . They do.

I mean, I've had some people join in before at church, but at concert halls, the etiquette is different. So to hear a roomful of strangers sing along with me gives me a different kind of push.

Before I know it, I'm launching into the next song, and then the next. All kinds of popular tunes that are easy to play and easy to sing. This is not like Jenny Lind, or even the Black Swan. This is just me, Eliza, having a good old time on this pianoforte that's slightly out of tune (but I'm sure no one notices).

And even though Ruby and I are the only Black women in the room, for once it doesn't feel like it. There won't be a review of this in the morning or a letter about it in the *Frederick Douglass' Paper*. It's simply an evening at sea, with other seafarers who have one thing in common. Tonight, we're on the Atlantic Ocean together.

When I step off this platform, or when we get to Liverpool, things may be different, but not tonight. This evening is all about the fun I didn't even know I needed.

# CHAPTER THIRTY-FOUR

*Liverpool, England*
*April 1853*

After spending ten days on the SS *Asia*, we have finally made it to Liverpool, England. The first thing I notice about Liverpool before even stepping off the steamer is how elaborate the dock area looks compared to the dusty, filthy New York City wharf. The streets are full of people awaiting the incoming steamers and transacting business. The stench that hovers in the air is a combination of the sea, horses, and smoke. Perhaps it is the heavily overcast skies that make it feel gloomy, but I truly would like to douse the entire Liverpool dock in seawater to wash away some of the grime.

As we disembark, Charles flags down a hansom cab driver to take us to our rooms at the Adelphi Hotel. Mr. Norris has gone to great lengths to make sure my arrival is noticed, including sharing my story in the news telegraph in New York City. He says it is of great interest when celebrated Americans arrive on steamships and their names appear in the newspapers and gossip columns.

I turn to Ruby, who as my maid has the job of carrying my purse with small coins, so that I, a proper lady, don't have to handle money. "Do you mind getting a newspaper from that boy there? I'd like to read it when we get to the hotel."

"Yes, ma'am," Ruby says with a wink.

I sure appreciate Ruby and Charles getting into the spirit of their roles and not making me feel strange about it, because there is no one I'd rather have here than the two of them. Well, maybe Mary, but there is no way Isaiah would be able to care for their business and the children without her.

While I wait for Charles to get the cab and Ruby to get the newspaper, I take in more sights in the dock area. Liverpool, like Philadelphia, and like New York City, is full of tall brick buildings. The architects who designed the cities back in America certainly took some of their inspiration from what I see here in England.

One familiar thing that does *not* make me feel comfortable is the number of Irishmen on the docks. But, unlike many of the Irish in America, these seem not to be as angered by my presence.

I am fascinated by a group of Black sailors laughing and sharing a jug of something that I'm sure is a contributing factor to their merriment. Their unfettered joy is one of the most beautiful things I've ever witnessed. Un

like even the freest of Black men in America, these men are unafraid, with their heads held high.

In a week's time, Mr. Norris will arrive in England, and we will begin practice for the tour. We are set to have concerts in England, Ireland, Scotland, and perhaps a few in France. It was exciting to see all the signed contracts from the venues, to really feel a part of things, something Colonel Wood never allowed.

But I am most excited and the most nervous about the concerts in Paris. The world's finest singers grace the stages of Paris, and the critics are harsher than the ones in America, but I would not hesitate to accept an engagement there.

Ruby rejoins me with several newspapers in hand as Charles waves us over. He has procured a cab and loaded our belongings, as a light rain has begun. He helps me into the cab, then Ruby, pays the driver, and climbs into the front.

"We're lodging at the Adelphi Hotel," Charles says to the driver.

"The Adelphi Hotel?" the driver says. "That's a lovely place to stay. Some say that it is the best hotel in Liverpool."

Charles looks over his shoulder at me, impressed. "Well, I am pleased to hear that," he says to the driver.

Mr. Norris had promised that no expense would be spared and that everything would be to my liking on arrival. So far, I have not been disappointed.

The driver stops in front of a lovely three-story building surrounded by quiet and beautifully upkept townhomes. The area is picturesque and garden-like, away from the hustle and bustle of the docks, and it seems like a place to take small children on walks.

"This is it," the driver says. "Fancy, innit?"

"It sure is," Ruby says, with eyes as wide as mine as she takes it all in.

"Six pence for the ride, please," the driver says.

Charles pays him, and then helps us down from the cab. Before he can take our belongings from the back, several bellmen come to offer him assistance.

"Miss Greenfield, we've been anticipating your arrival," the first bellman says. "Please come inside out of the rain."

Ruby and I follow the bellman while Charles assists the others with our bags. I must admit that I have never seen such prompt service. Not even when Colonel Wood was at the helm.

Inside the hotel is a grand hall, with high ceilings and great Georgian columns. Marble flooring makes each of our steps echo through the cavernous space. Adding color to the grays and whites are ornate rugs with gold and maroon threading that look too beautiful to walk across, and golden vases with fresh flowers.

"Your rooms are ready, ma'am," the bellman says. "Mr. Radley, the hotelier, extends a warm welcome."

Ruby and I are quickly whisked out of the hotel lobby, even before Charles and the rest of the bellmen can get inside with our baggage.

Since I am tired and hungry, I don't raise any objections. Besides, whoever objected to attentiveness?

The bellman takes us up a winding staircase to the second floor to our apartment suite. Ruby gasps when he opens the door, and I nearly do the same. It far surpasses any of the rooms I stayed in on my American tour, and I lodged in some of the best hotels in America.

The splendor of this place is truly amazing. Green and golden wallpaper adorns the walls, and there are curtains of dark green to match. The carpeting on the floor complements the color scheme, blending in deep burgundy, giving the room a very Moorish and warm effect. I almost expect smoke and cinnamon and every other exotic scented spice to waft under my nose.

The sofa has beautifully crafted pillows, with stitching that was done by hand, I am sure. More golden and ceramic vases are on almost every available table and dresser. Wax candles scented with nutmeg and vanilla have been placed next to the grand bed in the main bedroom, and there are two smaller bedrooms for Ruby and Charles. There is even a separate enclosed room for the chamber pot.

"If there is anything you need, please have your maid or manservant fetch one of our staff," the bellman says.

"Dinner," I say, as my stomach grumbles again. "You do have a restaurant, correct?"

"Yes, but Mr. Radley thought you might prefer dining in one of our private dining rooms after your long voyage at sea. He has arranged a wonderful feast for you. When you are settled in and ready for dinner, we will provide an escort."

"Well, all right then. Thank you," I say. The bellman nods and leaves the room.

I turn and look at Ruby. "Does this feel strange to you?"

Something about this feels overly scripted. I know that England isn't America, and that slavery has been abolished for a while now on this side of the ocean, but the white people in America came from here. The Irishmen who rioted at my concert originated in this land. So I know that the hatred is less than what we experience at home, but it's not nonexistent.

"I think they're being too nice for some reason, but I don't know why."

"It's because they know you are the Black Swan," Ruby says. "That's why."

"Hmmmm . . . maybe."

Ruby laughs. "You think too much about everything. Look at this place. We are here for, what? Two nights? Enjoy it, before we go to London. Do you see this? This apartment suite is bigger than my whole house!"

"Yes, it is."

There is a knock on the door, and I move to answer it, but Ruby jumps to her feet.

"Oh no, milady, allow me," she says in a very fake British accent. "The Black Swan needs her rest."

"Do shut up!" I say in an even faker accent.

We burst into giggles and I collapse onto the sofa as she answers the door. It happens to be my trusty manservant, Charles, and another bellman with our bags.

"Where would you like for the bags to be placed, ma'am?" the bellman asks.

"Oh, I don't know. We will sort it out when you leave," I say. "Thank you."

"Remember to let us know when you'd like to have dinner. The private dining room has been prepared," the bellman says.

Charles lifts an eyebrow and looks at me, then back at the bellman. "What if Miss Greenfield would prefer to eat in the restaurant?"

The bellman gets a nervous expression on his face, as if he was unprepared for that question. "Oh, well, Mr. Radley thought that she would prefer her privacy, after her long voyage at sea."

"Miss Greenfield loves to be among the people," Charles insists.

"I will have to check into that," the bellman says. "But are you sure? The private dining room is quite spectacular."

"Check into it," Charles snaps, dismissing the bellman.

When the door is closed, I stare at Charles and shake my head. I *knew* something didn't feel right about the swift and prompt service. It was a little too perfect.

"Charles, I really don't mind being served in the private dining room," I say with a long sigh. "I actually prefer it."

Charles moves my trunk into the space in my sitting area. I can tell he's moving in order to burn off the anger that's building.

"I will not allow them to mistreat you, Eliza," Charles says, sounding very heated. "We're spending as much money here as the rest of their guests. So you won't be relegated to certain areas of the hotel to avoid the risk of offending the other people."

"Do you think that's what they're doing?" Ruby asks. "I missed it completely."

"Yes, Ruby," Charles says. "They escorted you into your room very quickly. No waiting in the common areas so that anyone could see you. And they do not want their very wealthy and important clientele to see you in the restaurant. Using the same silverware and glasses they use. Trust me, the Europeans think we're beneath them, like they do in America. They've just moved beyond the slave trade."

"Okay, I understand," I say softly, trying to calm Charles down. "But I also don't want to do anything newsworthy on my first day here."

"She's already in the newspaper," Ruby says, pointing at an article. "'Miss E. T. Greenfield, a vocalist known in America by the condescending sobriquet the Black Swan, is set to arrive today on the *Asia*. Formerly a slave, she was freed by her mistress and has proven to have unique vocal abilities. The mistress left Miss Greenfield a very sizable legacy when she died, but it is currently in dispute. The maid is arriving here with the view of obtaining advanced musical instruction and performing concerts. After a brief stay in Liverpool, she will continue to London.'"

Charles snatches the paper from Ruby and reads it for himself. "Mr. Norris gave that much information to the press?"

"I'm sure they added some of their own," I say. "I don't think he would've called my stage name condescending."

"The press here will be watching your every move," Charles says, "waiting for a scandal."

"I know. Like causing a scene at the Adelphi Hotel on my first night in Liverpool. I think perhaps the private dining room is best."

Charles closes his eyes and clenches his fists. I know how heavily the cause of freedom weighs on him. It weighs on us all.

"Let us go and eat all of their beef roast and leg of mutton, and drink their wine and sherry," I say, trying to cheer him.

"I agree," Ruby says. "And anything they have that's French. I want it. Every baked soufflé and roll and loaf. Give them all to my stomach."

"Indeed. Every poached apple, and poached pear, and poached fig," I add.

"Glazed pheasant, glazed pigeon, and glazed peacock," Ruby says.

"Glazed peacock?" Charles asks.

Ruby shrugs. "Do they eat that?"

"I don't think so," I say with a laugh, "but it sounded decadent anyway."

Charles sighs. "I see what you both are trying to do, and I appreciate you for it, but we shouldn't abide by these things. They make me so angry. To experience the disrespect and to be forced into silence and inaction is the most frustrating part about it all. We're not even allowed to have human reactions to these things."

"I understand." I stroke his back, again hoping to relax his agitated spirit.

But he breaks away from my touch. "I'm sorry, Eliza, but you do not."

He leaves the hotel room in a huff. I hate feeling powerless in helping Charles deal with these feelings, because I have them too. Daily, every Black man and woman experiences some form of disrespect at the hands of a white person.

"I don't think I helped," I say to Ruby as I slide down onto the gorgeous sofa, its colors now looking somehow less vibrant. "He thinks we don't understand his anger, as if we are not also angry."

"I have the same problem with William," she says as she sits next to me. "He only wants to defend you. You see white men all the time dueling over offenses and waging wars, all because of women."

"I can stand up for myself."

"Of course you can. And so can the white women. But the difference between our men and their men is their men can raise holy hell and live to tell about it. They get to go home to their wives and children. Hell, some of our men don't even get to claim their wives or raise their children. Not if their massa don't want them to."

My sigh is forlorn and weary. We try everything in our power to calm our men and help them find peace. Not because we don't feel as disrespected as they do. Not because we don't deserve to be treated fairly, and not because we aren't under the same duress. But because we want them to come home to us.

"I hate it when he leaves infuriated like that. I'll be on edge until he returns."

"He shouldn't have to be angry, and you shouldn't have been disrespected. That hotelier knew exactly what he was doing," Ruby says.

I close my eyes and nod. "You're right, you're right. And so is he."

"But let's not allow this to spoil our time here," Ruby says. "We're in England for the Black Swan to be a sensation and for you to learn, right? So let's get everything you came for."

Ruby gives me a sisterly hug, and I so need it. Thank God for her. Because I intend on doing that tomorrow. But tonight, we are going to eat leg of mutton, glazed pheasant, puddings, dumplings, and every poached fruit they bring us.

In our richly appointed, private dining room.

* * *

AFTER TWO NIGHTS of being hidden behind closed doors at the Adelphi, Charles, Ruby, and I take a hansom cab to the London North and Western Railway station to take the train to London. We have already reserved tickets, but I do not like the looks of the third-class train car that has been reserved for Ruby and Charles, as my maid and manservant, by the bell staff at the Adelphi.

The third-class car is at least covered but looks cramped and uncomfortable for a six- to seven-hour journey. There are two very tiny windows on either side of the car, and from what I can see, the seats have so little leg room that Charles's knees will bump the seat in front of him for the entire ride. He would probably be better off standing. Not to mention, several of the people waiting in the ticket line have wet, sickly sounding coughs. It is never a good thing to be in close confines with that kind of illness.

"Come on, Ruby," I say. "You and Charles are going to ride in the first-class car with me. If we must wait for the next train, we will."

Ruby and I go to the ticket counter, and it is no problem at all to trade in those third-class tickets for first-class. If we're going to be on a train for seven hours, at least we can enjoy it with lovely food and drink, comfortable seats, and a nice window to take in the sights. Besides, we could use the luxury to lift our spirits after that stay in Liverpool. I need to feel like a prima donna this morning.

Since we're all first-class passengers, I urge Charles to let the porters fuss over the bags for once. He can be a gentleman on this trip, traveling with his two companions. We can discuss the particulars of the tour and the things we might encounter along the way.

Ruby has several newspapers for us to peruse on the ride tucked under her arm. "Let's see what the London press has to say about the Black Swan today. They are quite taken with you, Miss Greenfield."

"The summer music season is set to begin, and they are looking for a novelty," Charles says. "Why not an American?"

The porter takes our tickets and leads us to a little compartment at the front of the first-class section.

"These smaller sections only hold three people, so you'll have it all to yourself," the porter says.

I tentatively glance at Charles to see if he minds this separation, but he smiles at the porter and gives his thanks. He helps me and then Ruby onto the car, and then finally hoists himself up the two steps.

The seats are covered with red plush cushions, and the table is the perfect size for dining or reading. The large windows on both sides will give us a picturesque view of the countryside as we travel.

"So, Charles, you didn't mind the porter separating us from the rest of the white people on the train?" Ruby asks, beating me to the question.

Charles laughs. "No. But only because everyone wants the private seats on the train."

"Some people happen to like the private dining room at hotels too," I say. "That's the reason they have them."

"I suppose," Charles says. "What will we do when we get to London?"

"We will meet with Mr. Norris's associate Mr. Willcutt for further instructions," I explain.

"Do we know where we will lodge while we're there?" Ruby asks as she opens one of the newspapers and scans the pages. "I hope it is not another situation like the Adelphi. I enjoyed the luxury, but I would prefer Charles not be in poor spirits the entire time."

I notice Charles's glare from the corner of my eye, but I do agree with Ruby. I would like Charles in high spirits as well. "I do believe he said that I would have a house, with quarters for the both of you, but I do not have an address. This will come from Mr. Willcutt."

"All right," Ruby says. "The prima donna must have a place to rest her head."

"Especially if I am to start rehearsals in a week with a British accompanist. And there is a singing coach I am supposed to meet who has trained someone in the queen's court."

"*The* queen?" Ruby asks. "Queen Victoria?"

"I believe so. Is there another?" I ask, before bursting into laughter. "I assumed that's who he was talking about. I didn't think to specify."

"Will we have any time for amusements?" Ruby asks.

"What kind of amusements?" Charles asks as he holds his hand out for the newspaper. "Let me see that."

"Hold your horses, manservant. I'm not finished," Ruby says playfully. "There's some sort of theatrical presentation called the Black Swan at the Royal Strand Theatre in Westminster. Do you think it has anything to do with your arrival?"

"I'm sure it's just a coincidence."

"Me too," Ruby says. "But I think we should see it anyhow. It sounds like something we'd enjoy."

"What about you, Charles? Would you like to go to the theater with us?"

Charles leans back into the cushion on his comfortable seat as the train finally leaves the station. "I think we should consider how that might look to the people Eliza is trying to impress. I'm sure she is not going to want to be seen attending social events with her maid and manservant."

"You're probably right, and I don't know anything about their social etiquette," I say, feeling worried. "I am sure to make some critical error at some point."

"Remember, you are not here to become British. You're here to be the Black Swan," Charles says while giving my hand a reassuring squeeze.

"Well, I can't bungle that, can I?"

Both Ruby and Charles laugh, but I do not. The worry hasn't quite left me. For some reason, I think of the crowd in New York City and how I was unaware of and unprepared for who they were. I feel the same way about these Britons. They are as foreign to me as those uncultured brutes in New York.

When I showed up as the Black Swan in New York City, I was unsuccessful. Unfortunately, I do not have a different version of myself for Europe. This uncultured American version of me will have to be enough.

# CHAPTER THIRTY-FIVE

*London, England*
*April 1853*

$\mathscr{I}$t is late afternoon by the time we arrive in London and navigate our way off the train and onto the platform. Thank goodness for Charles and his ability to move the baggage and procure the cabs. There was a moment as he was gathering our things from the train platform when I imagined having to do this alone. And I shuddered. Cross-continental travel is not for the faint of heart, and it is not for me to do by myself.

Even though we are dressed well and emerged from the first-class train car, it does take some time for Charles to procure a hansom cab for us. In fact, he cannot do it without enlisting the help of the white train porter. This is a stark reminder of home, but the difference is, in America we have friends and loved ones to call upon when we arrive in a place. And even if we don't, we know how to find Black people. We will need to build a community here, same as at home.

"Where will I be taking you today?" the cabdriver asks, after we are finally settled.

I peer down at the notes I have from Mr. Norris. "Twenty-nine George Street, Hanover Square, please."

"Oh? That will be a lovely drive."

It is an unseasonably warm day for early spring in London, and I will take it. The middle of April can bring terrible, chilling cold and rain, sometimes ripping blossoms from trees before anyone gets to enjoy them. But it is quite warm and sunny today, almost balmy. If not for the angry storms, spring might be my favorite season, because everything is new and green. Having not been trampled by pedestrians and horses and other vermin, the landscape looks exactly how it was intended.

As we traverse the busy streets, I see many young ladies and young gentlemen taking advantage of the fine weather, promenading and courting. They probably have marriage on their minds, when there are so many other things the world has to offer. I wonder if anyone has asked the young women if they'd like to do anything else besides marry.

Up ahead on the right is a spectacular park with, it seems, every kind of flower and tree in bloom. There is a burst of color and spring beauty all in that direction, and if we weren't in such a rush to go see Mr. Willcutt to finalize our housing, I'd want to stop there first and spend the rest of the daylight hours there. Especially if there's a rose garden, because it would remind me of Miss Lizbeth.

"What is this park called?" I ask the driver with great interest. "I must come back and visit it when I have a spare moment."

"That's Regent's Park. It's the biggest park in London, ma'am. And you must do the flower walk in Kensington Gardens if you're a nature lover. Gardens are a bit of a passion here."

Charles has turned to face me, and I see how amused he is by my admiration of the park. I suppose I am on the edge of my seat like a little girl seeing a pony or a fireworks show. But I do love parks and gardens.

"I hope our rented home is somewhere near here," I say. "I would love to be close enough to walk to that garden."

The driver laughs. "If it is, it'll sure cost you, and if I might be frank, it could be difficult for you to procure a lease here. If I were *you*, I would try Canning Town or St. Giles."

"Are those nice areas?" Ruby asks, although I think we can all tell by the driver's tone that they are not.

"I am only being forthright," the driver says, his voice hitching a bit as Charles gives him a silent but ill-tempered scowl. "Those are the places where you'll find other colored families."

"I wondered where we were," Charles says. "Because I sure didn't see us out enjoying the lovely weather. Did you notice that, Eliza?"

I close my eyes and take a deep breath. I hadn't noticed that all the couples promenading were white. I had not paid attention to the fact that all the cabdrivers were white. Everyone everywhere in London seems to be white. In Liverpool we saw many more Black people, although they were certainly not there in large numbers. But here, in London, particularly where we find ourselves now, it's as if someone came and asked any Black people who might be milling about if they would go plant themselves elsewhere.

"Oh, there are colored people in London," the driver says. "Many of them work for the nobles in their homes, like whites, and in shops, restaurants, and what have you. But you won't see them lollygagging about like the rich, promenading up and down the street. They'll be on the omnibus home soon to their families for supper. Working hard like the rest of us, for their living."

"Well, the lady you're driving is—"

"Sure that we'll find somewhere pleasant to live," I say, stopping Ruby midsentence. She cuts her eyes at me, and I cut mine right back.

We don't know this driver, and he could be a huckster or a charlatan. He doesn't need to know anything more than what he already knows. That I am clearly someone of status with a maid and a manservant and I am going to conduct business with someone on Hanover Square is more than enough.

"Here's your address, ma'am. Twenty-nine George Street, Hanover Square," the driver says, keeping one eye on Charles the entire time, though Charles seems more disgusted than menacing.

Charles climbs down from the cab. "I will go and inquire about Mr. Willcutt, Miss Greenfield. You wait here and enjoy the lovely weather."

"Thank you, Charles."

"It'll be another three shillings if you want me to wait," the driver says, but he lowers his eyes as Charles pays him from his bag of coins.

Twenty-nine George Street is a nondescript office building with no external signage or markings to let me know this is Mr. Norris's place of business, or anyone's for that matter. Perhaps there is a good reason for that, but I don't know what it could be other than to confound passersby.

After a few moments, Charles jogs back to the cab with a perplexed expression on his face.

"What's wrong?" I ask as he stops right next to my side of the cab.

"Are you sure this is the correct address? Twenty-nine George Street?" he asks.

I look down at the note again. The numbers and letters are spelled out plain, and there is no ambiguity there.

"Yes, I'm sure. Was Mr. Willcutt not inside?" My heartbeat starts to quicken, and my palms begin to moisten.

"Not only was he not inside, but the business here, a small book publisher"—Charles clears his throat and gives me a grave look—"has never heard of Mr. Willcutt or Mr. Norris."

"Do you have another way of contacting him?" Ruby asks, the panic in her voice echoing what I feel.

"I have an address for his office in America. I will write to him there, and I will write to Hiram."

I sound calm when I say this, because there is no need to let the driver see me go into hysterics. Besides, it may not be time for hysterics yet, although he's just told us the only area of town where we'll be able to rent is far from here and sounds quite unsavory.

"How long will that take?" Ruby asks, her hands shaking. "The post will take at least two weeks to get to Hiram and then another two weeks to get a response. What will we do until then?"

"Hush now, Ruby. Either way we will be fine. Driver, might you recommend a nice hotel for the next evening or two, until we have had time to contact our business associate?"

The driver reaches under his cap and scratches his head as if he's unsure how to answer. "I suppose that depends on how much you have at your disposal to spend."

Charles walks back around and quickly climbs up into the front of the cab. "I believe the lady asked for a recommendation for a nice hotel. Preferably nearby. She'd like to visit the park."

"Might I recommend Morley's Hotel on Trafalgar Square?" the driver asks, pulling his horse into action. "It has very nice accommodations for families, and their restaurant has lovely meals."

"That sounds perfect," I say. "Let's try there."

Charles smiles at me and winks as the driver, sufficiently chided, gets our ride under way. Ruby covers her mouth to keep from laughing, but I would much rather her laugh at the driver than have a nervous fit.

Morley's Hotel is only a few minutes away, and I am pleased with the recommendation, because Trafalgar Square is another lovely sight for a spring day. I feel like quite the traveler on vacation, and if not for this new anxiety regarding Mr. Norris, I would enjoy visiting these landmarks.

The hotel is right next to the square itself, which contains a tall stone monument with a bronze topper, and fountains. The fountains seem to be running, but the water is a weak trickle, taking away from some of the majesty. But with the flowers blooming, and the wonderful weather, it is as interesting to look at as the park from earlier.

"Thank you," I say to the driver as Charles removes our baggage from the cab. "You have been helpful."

I hope that I sound pleasant, since Charles has been cross with him more than once on our ride from the train station. Some of it was his fault, but a good portion of it was Charles having some leftover anger from the hotel manager in Liverpool.

"You're welcome, ma'am. If I may, I'd like to offer one more bit of assistance."

Charles perks up at this and stops removing bags. He takes a few steps to the front of the cab again, and the driver eyes him warily.

"It's all right," I say. "Please, go ahead."

"Well, I might be better inclined to remember the details of this assistance if I had another two shillings."

"Two shillings?" Charles asks angrily.

The driver blinks rapidly. "One shilling?"

I nod at Charles to give him the money. Charles shakes his head and places the money in the driver's hand. The driver's nostrils flare as he smiles.

"If you continue to have problems with your business associate, there is a Lord Shaftesbury, a member of Parliament, to whom you may plead your case."

Charles's scowl has returned. "What is it that you're trying to say, man?" Charles asks.

"Lord Shaftesbury hears all sorts of complaints from commoners looking for help with legal matters," the driver says, "if you can gain an audience."

"And how might she go about doing that?" Charles asks.

The driver reaches under his cap and scratches his head again. "I used to know how to go about it. Let me see if I can remember."

I nod at Charles, and he groans but places another shilling in the driver's hand. The driver grins at me, pleased that I understand his language.

"Lord Shaftesbury is indeed known for intervening in these sorts of affairs. But you must write a letter that will be reviewed by his staff. You see, they receive countless letters with this trouble or that emergency. Yours must stand out somehow among all the other requests. And then you will be summoned."

"That is all?" Charles asks.

The driver nods. "Yes. Good luck to you."

Charles finishes removing our bags from the cab and then finally helps me and Ruby exit safely. The driver leaves eight shillings richer, and we're on to our next challenge.

"I don't know how helpful that advice was," Charles says as the hotel bellmen approach us. "How will you get a British noble to select your letter from among all the letters of his British citizens?"

That is a good point. "And I don't really have much time to wait for him to discover it, so perhaps I will deliver it in person."

Charles shakes his head. "Eliza, you'll never make it inside a British noble's home without an invitation."

Perhaps he's right, and I may be inclined to agree with him. Miss Elizabeth Taylor Greenfield of Philadelphia might never get past the security at Lord Shaftesbury's home without a formal invitation, nor get her letter considered.

But what about the Black Swan?

# CHAPTER THIRTY-SIX

*I* cannot wait very long to put my plan into motion, because for all three of us, a private room and meals at Morley's Hotel will cost over a pound a day. This is not economical, and while I have brought some of my own savings in addition to what was provided in advance by Mr. Norris for the tour, I must also think of my future and bringing my mother home. I cannot spend frivolously, even if I am enjoying my stay here as a traveler. I am here to work and to study my craft.

Charles has been silent about his thoughts on the plan. But he paces back and forth in the suite, brooding, as Ruby helps me prepare.

"Will you go and make yourself useful?" Ruby snaps at Charles as she styles my hair. "Go find her some tea and honey. I'm sure it won't be too hard. We're in England. There is more tea here than there is any other beverage."

Charles looks up from his deep thoughts. "What is it?"

"Tea and honey. She needs tea to warm up her voice," Ruby says. "I'm fixing the Black Swan's hair, and you can procure the tea for her voice, manservant."

He puts his hands on his hips for a second, pushing back his waistcoat with irritation. But he must decide that she is right, because he chooses to comply. He quickly leaves the room.

Ruby kisses the back of her teeth with her tongue, making a sucking sound. "What a worrisome man," she says. "I understand now why you won't marry him."

My laughter is loud and immediate. "Who says I won't? Does Charles say that?"

"No, but it is what William and I have always assumed. That he asked you and you said no, like you did with your other fiancé, Lucien."

"Charles and I have never courted with marriage in mind, and no, he has never asked," I say without emotion. "So I've never declined a marriage proposal from him."

"Would you marry him if he did propose?" Ruby asks, now getting to the heart of the matter.

"Maybe years from now, if he does ask. But he may never, and I would be fine with that as well."

"I see."

She seems satisfied by the sincerity in my voice. If he never asks me to marry him, I would be content with only his friendship.

"But those things are so far from my mind, Ruby. Today I can think only of convincing Lord Shaftesbury to pay attention to me. I did not come all the way to England for nothing!"

"And he will, I just feel it. For some reason, I think it was supposed to happen this way."

"Oh! I was supposed to be abandoned and left to my own wits in a strange land?"

I say this with a laugh, but the reality of it makes my stomach drop.

"No, not that at all," Ruby says, as she smooths down the sides of my hair with pomade. "But if you didn't do it this way, then that man, Mr. Norris, would be somewhere proclaiming about what he did for Elizabeth Taylor Greenfield. I want you to be able to tell *this* story. It's so much better this way, I think."

"Yes, if I succeed."

"*When* you succeed, Eliza. When. You keep waiting for someone to tell you that you're ready. But who will say that? Some Parisian vocal coach? Some Italian? A concert reviewer? Who?"

She puts the mirror in front of me, and I am pleased as usual when

Ruby does her work. I am transformed. I rise from the chair and hug her tightly, and she hugs me back.

"Thank you, Ruby. I needed that so much. You're right. *When* I'm successful, Lord Shaftesbury is going to take me inside his palatial home and invite me for tea. With three lumps, because I like my tea sweet." I snap my fingers on this last part, as if I'm reminding the servant to add the last lump of sugar.

"Exactly. And he's going to tell all his noble friends about you, and you are going to tour all over Europe."

We spin in a circle of excited celebration as Charles comes back in with my tea. He stops and stares at us, then sets the tray down.

"What are you two dancing about?" he asks, still as glum as he was before he left.

Neither of us respond. We grab Charles and pull him into our circle and make him spin with us. He doesn't need to understand the reason to experience our joy, because we don't need to hear his doubt or his disbelief.

Let him be grumpy once I've finished this mission. Until then, I need to hear only expressions of joy.

* * *

LUCKILY, THE DAY I've chosen is perfect. It's warm, the sun is high, and the only clouds in the sky are the white and fluffy kind that are drawn in children's storybooks. It is exactly the kind of picturesque scene required to execute my mission.

When the horse-drawn carriage arrives to take me to Lord Shaftesbury's estate, I am wearing full concert attire. A navy dress and gloves and a lace-embroidered bonnet, since I will be outside. I was tempted to wear my all-white ensemble but decided against it. I do not wish to stain that beautiful gown with the malodorous mud that lines London's streets.

The driver helps me up the two steps into the back of the cab, and, with my guitar in tow, we are on our way. As we ride through the early afternoon marketplace, I prepare myself for nothing but success. This must work.

"This is it, the home of the Earl and Countess of Shaftesbury," the driver says. "Are they expecting your visit?"

"Yes, of course," I say. The lie sounds rather convincing and rolls easily off the tongue. That should maybe concern me, but it does not.

I confidently descend the steps of the carriage with my guitar in hand, but when no one comes to greet me, the driver gives me a skeptical look.

"Would you like me to wait until you . . . gain entrance?" the driver asks.

"That won't be necessary," I reply as I press the coins into his hand. "No need to worry."

The driver shrugs, then climbs back into his carriage and leaves me standing in front of the home. Perhaps I was being hasty with sending him away.

No, I cannot start to doubt myself now.

Lord Shaftesbury's London home is beyond impressive. There are three stories, eight pillars across the front, and two sets of doors. But what most interests me are the rows of windows. Sixteen windows on the front of the house that I can see, and hopefully an equal number on the back. On a warm and balmy day like today, at least half of the windows are cracked to allow a breeze.

Today, the windows will carry more than cool air. They will also carry the song of the Black Swan.

I get as close to the house as possible, standing left of the central doorway and hopefully out of the sight of Lord Shaftesbury's butler. I do not want to be chased away before I have an opportunity to be heard. I *must* be heard; else all this is for naught.

The first song I choose is the beautiful and intricate aria from "Casta Diva." An American folk song will not do for this audience.

I strum along on my guitar, making the already melancholy song sound even more sorrowful.

As I get to the final verse of the song, no one emerges from the house, but many people stop on the street to stare and listen. They seem stunned to see a Black woman on a noble's lawn singing opera but are too riveted and perhaps too enraptured by the music to look away. So I perform for the meager audience that has gathered behind me. I give them a concert they may never be able to afford to see in a concert hall.

I launch into my next song, another aria that has me doing more trills, turns, leaps, and embellishments. I like this one, because it is, for lack of a better description, noisy. I sing it during concerts to wake the audience after lulling them with quieter, more somber pieces.

I notice a shadowy figure appear at a window. Have I managed to get someone's attention? Is it Lord Shaftesbury or a woman? I cannot tell from this far, but my stomach tumbles a bit, knowing that I've been noticed. There's no turning back now—I must press forward.

The third song is yet another Italian aria. I can hear Miss Bella's voice in my mind saying her famous words: *Bel canto! Bel canto!* She would approve of this plan, I'm sure. Why not show how gifted I am in the context of what Europeans consider giftedness? If I may dazzle them with my perfect diction and exquisite range, perhaps they will hear my plight and offer aid.

Midway through the third song, the front door of the house opens, and a suited older gentleman with white hair marches down the stairs looking gruff and stern. My heart nearly stops at his demeanor, and my eyes stretch wide. Is he angry? Irritated? I wonder if my presence has pulled him away from something he'd much rather be doing. Have I overplayed my hand?

As he approaches, I allow my singing to come to a natural pause at the end of the second verse. He looks surprised at my appearance, as if he expected the voice to be coming from a different body. A petite prima donna body perhaps, and not this short, plump Black body?

"Miss. Are you aware that this is the home of the Earl and Countess of Shaftesbury?" His tone is as stern as his glare.

I do not allow him to fluster me, however; I remain completely composed. This has become my stage. "Yes, sir. I am aware."

"So then the singing is intentional?" he asks, still glaring.

I lift an eyebrow but remain poised. "I cannot think of a time when singing is unintentional."

The gentleman sighs wearily. I wonder if there are a great many individuals who come right up to this house to plead their cases.

"What is it, then, that you want?" the gentleman asks, now losing *his* composure. "Or do you intend to stand here singing until nightfall?"

"My name is Elizabeth Taylor Greenfield, a performer known in America as the Black Swan. I am in the midst of a legal emergency and was told to seek an audience with Lord Shaftesbury."

The man closes his eyes and sighs again, and this time he clenches and unclenches his fists in frustration. He seems so very tired of me this afternoon. But I am feeling quite energized and can sing a few more songs if necessary.

"The proper way of requesting an audience is by sending a letter, as I am sure you've been informed. Yes?"

"Yes. But time is of the essence, and I feel my unique set of circumstances are much better presented in person."

"Wait here, Miss Greenfield."

The gentleman starts to walk away, and even though on the outside I look cool and unperturbed, my stomach roils with nervousness and uncertainty. He hasn't sent me away, so that is a good sign, but he also has not invited me inside, which means that a determination is still being made.

Once he disappears inside the house, I start to sing again. Mostly out of nervousness and not even knowing how to stand without feeling uncomfortable. And the small crowd that has gathered outside cheers me on. This makes me smile and gives me strength to continue. The people are on my side, at least. Hopefully, Lord Shaftesbury has also heard their support, and it has helped soften his heart if he was thinking of denying me an audience.

After only a few moments of singing, the gentleman reappears. His expression has not changed as he approaches me. He's still all lemons and olive brine—not even a smidgen of sweet.

"Lord and Lady Shaftesbury are entertaining guests for tea, but he will grant you a brief audience," he says without emotion. "You must state your matter quickly and be prepared for a swift and perhaps unfavorable response."

"A brief audience is all I require."

I try to contain my excitement, but I think he sees it anyway, because he shakes his head as he half snatches my guitar out of my hands.

"Follow me." His words come out on a breathless, tired sigh.

I hope I haven't bothered him too much with my stunt. The last thing I want to do is make an enemy of the servants. Lord knows, they are the ones who make things happen in the house, and they can be one's greatest ally or one's most daunting enemy. I'd much prefer the former.

"Are you the butler?" I ask in a friendly tone as we walk side by side down an enormous hallway.

"Yes, I am. You may call me Mr. Ludgate."

"Thank you, Mr. Ludgate, for not chasing me away, when you very well could have."

"I happen to love the opera," Mr. Ludgate says, his tough exterior softening a bit, "so I wouldn't have asked you to leave until you'd exhausted your repertoire."

"We would have been there for hours, then." I give him a chummy bump with my elbow, and we both laugh.

"And I would have asked for at least one encore," Mr. Ludgate jokes. "Your voice is quite remarkable."

"So I've been told. Thank you."

Mr. Ludgate stops in front of a set of ornately decorated double doors. He opens one of the doors to reveal a stunning and well-lit parlor. For a moment, I am awestruck. It is simply one of the most magnificent rooms I've ever been inside. This parlor is decorated with shades of yellow and gold, and every piece of furniture looks more costly than my entire life. My whole inheritance from Miss Lizbeth couldn't purchase the items in this room. Every chair, chaise, ottoman, table, vase. Everything is trimmed in gold, and every flower is expertly placed.

Even the tea service is all white China with gold trimming and little yellow flowers on every cup. The details are amazing. Each of those yellow flowers has a gold dot at the center. I want to touch the cups and sip my extra-sweet tea from them.

Lord Shaftesbury is seated in a lovely cream armchair at the end of the coffee table. Three women share a long gold-and-blue velvet sofa. One I'm sure is his wife, Lady Shaftesbury, and there are two I cannot place, but I hope they are nobility and have the power and influence to help me.

The last woman, who sits opposite Lord Shaftesbury in a matching armchair at the other end of the coffee table, is a familiar face from home. Mrs. Harriett Beecher Stowe nods in my direction with a warm smile. A wave of relief washes over me, as this is the most spectacular display of providence. I nearly burst into tears at the sight of her, but a prima donna wouldn't do that. The Black Swan wouldn't break down into a puddle on the floor.

"Miss Elizabeth Taylor Greenfield of . . . erm . . . America. Miss Greenfield, this is the Duchess of Sutherland, the Duchess of Argyll, the Earl and Countess of Shaftesbury, and Mrs. Harriet Beecher Stowe, also of America."

I make a grand curtsy as I was taught in primary school in Philadelphia. I am unsure if it is correct, but I doubt that anyone will take umbrage with an American's curtsy. There isn't a seat for me, but since I have not been invited to tea, I do not expect to be offered one. Standing is fine.

"Thank you, Ludgate. That will be all," Lord Shaftesbury says in a kind tone. "Miss Greenfield, let us hear your concern."

Thank goodness, the man sounds benevolent. With slow and measured steps, I move across the room to be closer to the tea party group. I believe it is a good sign that Mrs. Beecher Stowe is here. If she has been invited for an intimate tea party, then she may have influence with Lord Shaftesbury.

The two duchesses bear a striking resemblance to each other. They have the same brown hair, swept into a bun, and the same droopy eyelids. One is very young, and close to my age, and the other a woman in her fifties, perhaps. They must be mother and daughter. They both are dressed in elegant silk gowns in matching shades of soft green. The mother's has hints of gold, and the daughter's has flower embellishments of cream and orange. Both are perfect for afternoon tea, and maybe for an early dinner. The countess has a pleasant face, and a plump body not unlike my own. Her tea gown is much more forgiving, with less corseting than the duchesses' but no less pretty with its pink crinoline and lace trim. I can tell that Lord Shaftesbury was a very rakish man in his youth. Even in his middle age, he is still quite handsome and has a certain gleam in his eye. Mrs. Beecher Stowe almost seems out of place for the occasion, but I am not surprised at her all-black attire. She was always modest, almost Quaker in her appearance.

"My lord, thank you for seeing me without a previous appointment," I say. "I know that my approach is unorthodox."

Mrs. Beecher Stowe gets up from her seat and walks over to me. She takes both my hands in hers. "No need for such formality with me, Eliza. Did you receive my gift?"

"I did. Thank you very much."

"It is divine providence that you would be here in London while I am promoting *Uncle Tom's Cabin*, since examples like yours are what inspired me to write the book," Harriet says with sincerity as she squeezes my hands like an old friend. Then she looks back at her tea companions. "I knew Miss Greenfield's guardian before she died, and she raised this young woman to utilize her natural God-given gifts. It's a marvel how far she's come, with all the adversity she's had to face in America. Do you know she could find only one instructor to provide her musical education, and that was woefully insufficient, but still she has managed to be invited on a twenty-city tour in America, and now she's here on tour as well? Is that right?"

"Well, yes, but . . ."

"Oh, I read about you in the newspaper," Lady Sutherland says, now very interested in this dialogue. "The Black Swan."

Harriet returns to her seat next to Lady Sutherland. "Yes. I do not very much care for that moniker," she says, her voice dripping with disdain. "It was done, in my opinion, to compare her negatively to Jenny Lind. I find there is no affection in this name they call Miss Greenfield."

Lady Sutherland tilts her head, considering this. "I suppose anyone can turn a thing into a negative or a positive. If Miss Greenfield wishes to be called the Black Swan, I think she should embrace it. Swans are lovely creatures. And she is . . . well . . . Black."

"Her talent stands on its own," Harriet quips. "It does not need a qualifier. It is not Black or white or anything. It belongs to her. To Miss Greenfield. And that is how she should be announced, not by some denigrating alias."

Lord Shaftesbury clears his throat, thankfully interrupting this volley of pontification. "I am sure Miss Greenfield did not travel here today merely to witness another one of your epic debates. She came here to request my assistance in a legal matter. Please, Miss Greenfield, how may I be of assistance to you?"

"Yes, my lord. I recently finished a tour in America. My last concert in New York City was attended by over four thousand people."

"Four thousand!" Lady Argyll exclaims.

"I read about the concert in the newspaper," Harriet says. "There seemed to be a bit of controversy surrounding your appearance. Is that true?"

"Yes. Several protestors threatened to douse the concert hall with kerosene and start a fire if I was allowed to perform and if Black people were allowed to attend."

"Brutes," Lord Shaftesbury says, shaking his head with disgust. "We were quite enjoying your impromptu concert. You certainly captured my attention."

I smile and give a polite nod. "That was the idea, my lord."

"You are here in London now," Lady Shaftesbury says, finally adding her voice to the conversation. "Will you be in concert here soon? I would love to hear your entire program."

"That is why I am here today, my lady. I am afraid I have been taken advantage of by a concert manager. His name is Mr. Edward Norris, and our contract dictates that I will perform several concerts across Europe. All was well on the voyage over and when I arrived in Liverpool, but when I arrived to the address he provided for his London office, no one had ever heard of him or his associate."

"Had he provided references?" Lady Sutherland asks, her eyebrows now furrowed, her entire expression questioning.

"He did, and my patrons back home assured me that his references were impeccable. Of course, I believed him after he was able to schedule a concert in New York City, procure a first-class ticket for my voyage, show signed concert venue contracts, and provide a salary advance. I thought we had thoroughly covered every possibility."

"This *is* unfortunate." Lord Shaftesbury's facial expression is grave. I hope this means he agrees with me.

"This is why I have appeared here uninvited." I release a heavy sigh. "I have run out of options, I am afraid."

"But what can she do to enforce a contract that was drawn up on American soil?" Lady Shaftesbury asks him. "This seems to be a concern for American courts to decide."

"Perhaps the answer is not enforcing the contract," Lady Sutherland says thoughtfully. "She only needs new patrons. Your voice is extraordinary. I believe we might replicate the success you had in New York City here in England. It could prove quite lucrative."

The younger duchess pipes up. "It is the beginning of the summer musical season, and we do not have an anchor for our troupe. Miss Greenfield could make quite a splash."

"Agreed. Your other manager was not going about things the correct way, Miss Greenfield," Lady Sutherland explains further. "A new musical sensation must be presented to society at the beginning of the season."

I tingle with pleasure at these words being used to describe me. *A new musical sensation.*

"Perhaps we should present her in a private concert at Stafford House," Lady Argyll suggests. "And, of course, the rest of our troupe will be there to lend support. It will be the perfect showcase of our summer concert fare."

Lady Shaftesbury nods with her approval. "That would be perfect. Especially with Mrs. Beecher Stowe there to speak about her abolition work, and Miss Greenfield being an example of why we should continue down that path. It all ties together so nicely."

Lady Sutherland puts her teacup down and rises from her seat on the sofa. She starts to pace the room, the silk of her gown swishing behind her.

"Mother has begun to strategize now," Lady Argyll says. "This may go into the late hours of the night."

Everyone laughs except me. Perhaps because they're all seated and I'm standing, but they haven't noticed that, so I slightly shift my weight from one foot to the other. Thankfully, my boots are comfortable, and they haven't begun to pinch my toes.

"And then we will quickly follow that up with a morning concert in the Queen's Concert Rooms at Hanover Square," Lady Sutherland says, as she continues to pace. "That will be your public debut, Miss Greenfield.

"When that concert does well, the newspapers will spread your success all over Britain," Lady Sutherland says as she claps her hands together with excitement. "You'll be touring from Scotland to Ireland to Wales and back. I hope you're ready to spend your summer on the train."

"And are you to be my new patrons?" Hardly able to contain my excitement, I ask this just for clarity's sake. They have launched into a conversation about me that I do not fully understand.

"Yes, dear, I thought that bit was obvious. We are your new patrons," Lady Sutherland confirms, with a satisfied nod. "We will provide an apartment for you while you are here. Do you have servants?"

I swallow hard, thinking of Charles and Ruby and referring to them as my servants. "I have a maid and a manservant."

"All right," Lady Sutherland says, "then your contract and wages will also include payment for their services, and lodging."

"Thank you, Lady Sutherland." I try not to gush, but I cannot help it. "This is more than I ever expected to accomplish here today."

"Well, you can thank providence indeed," Lady Sutherland tells me with a wry smile. "I nearly declined this invitation today because I was feeling unwell."

"She can thank her own tenacity." Harriet nods in my direction. "Your dearly departed guardian would be proud."

Miss Lizbeth would be proud, but I am prouder of myself. For trusting the gift, believing in its power, and walking through an open door. Or, more specifically, singing in front of a closed one.

# CHAPTER THIRTY-SEVEN

On the morning of my private concert at Stafford House, Ruby wakes me extra early to begin our grooming rituals in our little cottage near Hanover Square. I count it a miracle that our accommodations are here, however modest. Ruby and I have separate bedrooms and a large area for living and cooking, and a small, enclosed space for the privy. Charles has a separate but attached one-room apartment.

We're surprised that Charles is already awake and has already come over from his separate manservant quarters to prepare tea and a light breakfast of biscuits, sausage, and dried apples for us.

"What has gotten into you?" Ruby asks the question before I do, so I just laugh, because he is not an early riser.

Charles gives a half grin. "There was an early morning delivery, and the driver woke me. So, since I was already up, I decided to be productive. I hoped that it would be appreciated and not mocked."

"It is appreciated Charles," I say with a gracious smile. "Thank you. But what was delivered so early?"

Charles steps out of the room and comes back with a carefully wrapped bundle. "A package for you, with instructions to open right away."

I take the package from Charles's hands, wondering what it could be. "There's a note, here. Let me see who it's from."

I unfold the note and smile at the handwritten calligraphy. The same from my signed book. It's from Harriet.

*Good luck on your presentation to London's aristocracy, even though you do not need luck. You have talent that you have culti-vated, and that is what God will bless. I am praying that you have all you desire, especially a sweet reunion with your mother. I have enclosed in the package the bill for this dress in case anyone should question you about it. I do not wish for you to be accused of any outstanding debt. It is paid in full, and yours to keep. God bless. Yours, HBS*

It makes me smile to see that she was listening to our conversation about my mother. After the mother and daughter duchesses commenced their planning, I mentioned my mother in Liberia, and that perhaps I would meet people with influence here to help me bring her home. I did not believe Harriet was truly taking in that part of the conversation, but I wanted her to hear it, since she has such passion about the fates and fortunes of previously enslaved people.

"Let me take it out of the wrapping," Ruby says. "Is it a dress?"

"Yes. From Mrs. Beecher Stowe, one of my new patrons. For me to wear to the concert this morning."

Ruby lifts the dress out of the wrapping, and together we hold it up to examine it. The dress is truly impressive. It's black silk with a high neck and white lace sleeves. She's also included white gloves. While the dress is very well made, and I can tell she spent a large sum of money on it, I wish for something a bit grander and more eye-catching, like the gowns that Mary created for me.

"Now, isn't this genteel?" Ruby asks with a chuckle as she examines the very modest dress.

I nod in agreement. "It is, but I have the perfect earrings to go with it. To spruce it up a bit."

I've taken two steps toward my bedroom when I notice that Charles is leaning against the wall with his arms crossed and a pensive expression. I hesitate to ask his thoughts, because I don't know that I want to hear anything that might take away from my excitement this morning.

"What is it, Charles? What are you thinking?" I ask.

"No, ask him later," Ruby says as she waves her hands in the air. "Ask him after we've got your tour scheduled."

Charles shakes his head. "I'm not going to ruin anything, but none of this makes you take pause? None of it makes you suspicious?"

"No, it doesn't. They see me as a good investment. The duchess doesn't need the money, but she'd like the bragging rights of discovering me for the season."

"What if you're not a good investment? Then what?" Charles asks.

"Then I'm sure their patronage will cease at the end of the summer," I say, "and then I will have to figure out what happens next for myself."

"As long as you are aware of the risk in doing this," Charles says, pulling his arms tighter and frowning even harder.

I turn to Ruby and motion for her to leave us for a moment, and she nods and exits the room.

I close the space between us and pry Charles's arms apart, so that I can take his hands in mine. "Charles, don't you want me to be a success? Why are you being this way? Don't you think I've thought of these things?"

"I just don't want you to keep trusting white people." I can hear the concern in his voice and see it in his eyes. "The first one was practically a slave catcher and the last one stranded you in England, with no tour and no resources. I'm afraid to see what happens when this new set turns their backs on you."

"None of them are the source of my gift or blessings, Charles, so I am not worried about that. I do believe I am supposed to be here, so I am going to trust this journey and see where it goes."

"Promise me that you will leave if it no longer serves you to be here," Charles says. "Do not struggle to stay in England or Europe. This place does not love Black people any more than America."

"I promise to make my own choices about things. They are not deciding for me. I am deciding for myself. And I want to do this. Do you trust me to do that?" I search his face for a clue that he is still with me in this. I still need his support just as I need Ruby's.

He nods solemnly. "You should go ahead and put on your very modest dress, so that you can impress these aristocrats."

It saddens me that Charles cannot feel the same joy about this that I do, but I cannot blame him. After Colonel Wood and Mr. Norris, anyone would think I am a fool for casting my lot with another group of white faces who make promises.

But what other choices do I have? I have neither the agency nor the funds to book concerts here in Britain or even procure housing for myself in an area of town that isn't unsavory. I have even less power and influence here than I have in America, where at least I have friends and community.

All I can do is trust and save my earnings, so that I will never be left destitute. I will always be able to find my way home.

* * *

IF I WAS unprepared for the splendor of Lord Shaftesbury's home, I was certainly not expecting the extravagance of Stafford House. A carriage was sent for us, and perhaps that should have been a clue. Even that was luxurious. Perfectly shined, with golden accents and deep cherry wood on the outside, and inside, burgundy leather seats.

As we pull into the courtyard of the mansion, I try not to be overwhelmed. The home is enormous.

"This isn't where Queen Victoria lives?" Ruby asks. "Because if they're building even bigger houses . . ."

"This is the home of the Duke and Duchess of Sutherland," I say, "and I believe the queen has more than one home."

Charles looks out the window at Stafford House and shakes his head. "Abundant riches derived from colonization and oppression."

Ruby sighs at the history lesson, but I do not shun his constant reminders anymore. We should remember these things. Besides, it isn't history. It's still happening. We're still oppressed, here and in America. Just because Britain has abolished slavery doesn't mean that they aren't still profiting from the spoils.

"Well, that's all the more reason Eliza should take everything she can get," Ruby says.

Charles laughs. "That is one way to look at it, I suppose."

At the entrance of the home, we're greeted by a butler, who leads us through a grand corridor. Above us is a stunning crystal chandelier and below, gleaming marble floors, and on each side of the corridor are large vases full of fresh hothouse flowers that give off a strong fragrance. I cannot begin to imagine the staff required to care for this home. The cleaning and preparation alone must take an army, and yet now there is no one moving about.

"There is a lounge for the glee singers where you will be provided dinner and refreshment prior to the concert," the butler says. "Your maid and manservant may also wait there during the concert with the other staff."

Ruby leans close to me. "There are other singers?" she whispers. "Is it a competition?"

I do not believe so, but I cannot be entirely sure, so I respond with a slight shrug. I do recall Lady Argyll saying that they did not have an anchor for their troupe for the season, so perhaps the other singers they have do not stand out as anything special. The thought of a contest, however, makes me nervous, because I have not prepared with that in mind.

The lounge is abuzz with chatter from the other glee singers when we enter, until they notice we have arrived. A silence falls. Perhaps they are the competitive sort.

I almost want to turn and leave, but Charles and Ruby are whisked away to where the rest of the staff are waiting, and I am left to face this throng of mostly unfriendly faces alone.

Sir George Smart, a small bespectacled man of at least seventy years, comes to the front of the group. He may seem frail, but I have been rehearsing with him for a week to get ready for this concert, and I know otherwise. He is much heartier than he seems. He teaches at the Royal Academy of Music and is employed to prepare singers for exclusive engagements.

He starts to say something but is interrupted by a rattling cough. One of the gentlemen in the room rushes to help him, but he lifts a hand to stop him. When he composes himself, he surprises me with a warm smile.

"Welcome, Miss Greenfield. I hope you are ready and well rested."

"I am well rested, and thrilled to be here, Sir George," I say, happy to see him again but wondering about these others.

"Very good. Allow me to introduce you to some of London's finest glee singers. From left to right we have Miss Rita Favanti, Miss Ursula Barclay, Mr. Charles Cotton, Miss Louisa Pyne, Miss Rosina Bentley, and Mr. Sims Reeves."

"Glee singer?" The gentleman with side-parted curly side-parted hair, a thick mustache, and a fancy ruffled shirt that fluffs out from his jacket seems to take exception to this term being used to describe him.

Sir George shakes his head and gives a bow in his direction. "I do apologize. Mr. Sims Reeves is a celebrated oratorio and tenor. He has toured in Milan and Vienna and all over Britain."

"And with Jenny Lind. The Swedish Nightingale. Isn't that who they compare you to, Black Swan? Hmmm?" Mr. Reeves asks rudely as he comes closer to me to give me an inspection. "We will see what this American will bring that hasn't already been discovered."

Then Mr. Sims Reeves takes his goblet of whatever his hot breath smells like this early in the day and storms out of the lounge. Following that very chilly reception, everyone else gives quiet greetings before they go back to their chatter, leaving me feeling uneasy about the concert.

Sir George beckons me to follow him to the refreshment table, which I do, because I certainly don't want to be left with the enemies. And I can't go running to Charles and Ruby, who are mingling with the servants.

"Do not worry about Sims." Sir George's voice is kind and fatherly. "His feathers are simply ruffled because he thought he was set to be the star of the season. But that was only in his mind. He will warm up to you when he sees how gifted you are."

"I do not believe that. And it seems the others will follow his lead." I glance over at the other glee singers and confirm their suspicious looks.

"No, I promise it isn't so," Sir George reassures me. "Sims enjoys teaching and mentoring young singers, and you will be no different. He will take you under his wing. Today, your job is to stun the audience with your vocal gift. Lady Sutherland has invited everyone who is important."

"All right. I will remember that."

"Do not give thought to any of these other singers. They are here in support of you. And they will do well, because their reputations are also on the line. We will have an amazing day. You will be the toast of London this season. We will see to it." Sir George pats me on the hand, then squeezes. Then he shuffles off with a small slice of cake.

\* \* \*

THE CONCERT IS about to begin, and we've been told that the guests are going to be moved from the dining room to the concert room, so we are to line up on the stairs in that room. Ruby rushes over to make sure there are no flyaway hairs or pieces of food in my teeth, and Charles gives me a nod of support from his post on the other side of the room.

We are then placed in a line from shortest to tallest, and I am in the middle. Next, we're escorted into the concert room.

Here is another spectacular wide-open, bright, and vivid space, filled with chairs. Windows allow the sunlight to pour into the room, illuminating the staircase where we are placed. There is a piano on the staircase landing, where Sir George is seated, and we are told each singer will come stand next to him for their moment.

I am to sing three songs, and then do a vocal exercise with Sir George to prove that I have at least minimal music education and am not merely a circus act.

When we are perfectly arranged on the staircase, the guests begin to file into the room. Sir George did not exaggerate when he said that everyone important had been invited. It appears that Lady Sutherland has invited everyone in London with a title. The ladies are dressed in their fine silk morning dresses in every spring color, in demitoilet and bonnets. The men are in their fitted waistcoats. The only one looking somewhat drab is Mrs. Beecher Stowe in her black attire, but even she has a lace shawl and earrings today.

I am barely listening as Lady Sutherland gives her speech or as Mrs. Beecher Stowe follows up with some words about the plight of the Negro slave in America. It's not that I don't want to be attentive. I do. But I cannot concentrate on their speeches with the butterflies dancing in my stomach.

I cannot even enjoy the performances of the six other glee singers. Including Mr. Sims Reeves, who has a phenomenal baritone. I see why they have been selected as the best in London.

Finally, I hear Sir George call me down to the piano. I move slowly down the stairs, not to build the audience's anticipation but to make sure I don't stumble, but it gives the air of a prima donna who is making the audience wait for her arrival. So be it. Let them think that, even though it is far from the truth.

I make it to the central landing without incident and lock gazes with Sir George, pretending not to see the swarm of eyes staring at me from below. The crowd of aristocratic spectators ready to judge me. Poised to say if I pass or fail their test of readiness. Prepared to boot me from society on a whim.

The first song is a simple one: "Old Folks at Home." The only reason we chose this one is so I can do a bit of vocal grandstanding; the first verse is in my very highest range of soprano and the second verse in the lowest range of baritone. It has the intended effect. I hear the gasps in the crowd, and one gentleman even stands to see if there is a man being hidden beneath the piano. Everyone laughs at him, but it seems he has had more than a few glasses of wine with his dinner.

Then I move to the sorrowful aria from *La sonnambula*. I am glad we chose this one if for no one other than Mr. Sims Reeves, who sang lead parts in this opera. Sir George told me he was once supposed to duet with Jenny Lind, in London, but someone else was chosen. He had taken offense to that until he drew a bigger crowd at his show and felt exonerated. I am careful with my pronunciations, especially here where people are more likely to have heard Italians sing Italian opera. When I am done, the applause tells me that it was well received.

Lastly, my favorite song to sing, the crowd-pleaser "When Stars Are in the Quiet Skies." I wish I could see Charles so that I could serenade my love as I sing. As is my custom, I take the audience on a journey from the baritone to my soprano, and they love it, as do most of my audiences. There are times when I am singing and I am enraptured, and this is one of those.

After I am applauded and encored, and I sing another verse of the song, to the delight of the audience, Sir George does an exercise on the piano where he plays a note and I follow with my voice. Then he plays another and I follow. All up and down the pianoforte, he plays notes and note combinations and I repeat them. Until the crowd is enthralled and impressed by my skill.

Finally, Sir George nods and smiles. "Well done, Miss Greenfield," he says.

I turn to face the crowd, now able to look at them. I give a polite bow. Mission accomplished.

The thunderous applause that rises from this group of nobles and aristocrats feels like the beginning of something grand. And when I glance to my right, I even see the support of the glee singers *and* Mr. Sims Reeves, respected oratorio, who gives me a deep bow, a sign of respect perhaps and maybe an apology for his horrible behavior before. I am now sure to be the toast of this season.

I shall prepare my bags. For my summer on the train.

# CHAPTER THIRTY-EIGHT

*London, England*
*May 1854*

After almost a full year of public morning concerts, grand concerts, private engagements, and instruction from Sir George, I have finally received an invitation to sing for Queen Victoria. I thought it would never come.

It couldn't have happened at a more critical time for me in my European adventure. At the end of the summer season, the excitement over me died down tremendously. The invitations to perform have begun to wane, and my patrons, I fear, are looking for their next new sensation. My contract expires at the end of one year's time, precisely at the end of May, which will mean the end of the salary, cottage, and all other means of support.

I slide the embellished envelope across the table to Charles as we enjoy a quiet breakfast in the cottage. He glances at the correspondence and then up at me, mirroring the smile on my face. He finishes chewing his sausage and wipes the oil from his hands with a napkin before picking up the envelope.

"Good news?" he asks.

"Open it and see."

He takes his time reading the invitation, and his grin slowly spreads. "An invitation to sing for Queen Victoria. Well, Ruby would've been delighted about this."

"I can't wait to write her about it, but I sure wish she was going to Buckingham Palace with us."

At the end of the summer season, in September of last year, Ruby had to return to America to care for her children. Lady Sutherland sent another maid from her staff, a Jamaican woman named Flora, who reminds me of the church mothers back home in Philadelphia. She makes me yearn for home and for my own mother.

"Do you think this will result in patronage for this season?" Charles asks. "The winter was rough, you know."

I nod in agreement. "The winter was treacherous. If you hadn't been here with me, there's no way I would've stayed. I would have tried to voyage home."

My insides get warm and tingly thinking about the cozy winter nights we shared in this cottage. Flora was never far, so that she could always vouch for my virtue if questioned, but she made herself scarce when we wanted to be alone to talk, read poetry, and muse about our futures.

"Are you thinking about going home if you don't find a new patron?" Charles asks. "I can find work, and I also have savings. We could rent a flat near the Strand Theatre. It wouldn't be as nice as this, but it wouldn't be Canning Town either."

"Charles, we can't rent a flat together. I believe we've gotten too comfortable with this arrangement we have here."

"You are not wrong," Charles says with a wistful sigh. "But I wish that you were. We could solve all this hiding from the world's judgmental eye by getting married, you know."

I choose not to respond to this last part. All winter, Charles has been dropping hints about marriage and sharing the rest of our lives together. Maybe he thinks I've reached the height of my achievements with this time in Europe, and perhaps he's right. But I still have not found a way to bring my mother home from Liberia.

At least I have been able to send and receive letters from my mother while I'm here. Several times I have been tempted to provide her with the funds to sail to Liverpool from Monrovia and have her stay here with me in the cottage. The only reason I did not is because I am myself here on someone's patronage, and their goodwill can be removed at any time. Without knowing my future here, I did not think it was wise to uproot my mother when she is not able to travel back to America with us, no matter how desperately I wish to see her.

"This performance for Queen Victoria may or may not yield a patron, but I pray that it does. Else I really don't think we have a choice but to sail back to America for now."

"But what about Paris?" Charles asks. "The teacher you've been corresponding with? Is she not ready to take you on as a student?"

"She is ready, but I do not want to spend all my savings living in Europe when I intend on bringing my mother home from Africa. I need my savings for that, and it would be best for me to go home where the people of influence I know are willing to help me."

"They are not willing to help you here?"

I absentmindedly stir another sugar cube into my tea. "There have been no concrete offers of assistance. Only agreement that our story is tragic, and well-wishes on being reunited with my mother."

"Well-wishes?" Charles scoffs. "What are you supposed to do with wishes?"

"Exactly."

Even if my concert for Queen Victoria does not secure a new patron here, perhaps the publicity will spark renewed interest in my career and help launch another tour in America.

Flora appears with a pan of freshly baked bread from the outdoor oven in her arms. "Good morning, Mr. Charles. Miss Eliza, I wanted to remind you that Sir George Smart will be here soon for tea. Will Mr. Charles be joining you?"

Charles stands and wipes his hands on his napkin. "I believe that is my invitation to leave." He chuckles as Flora places her bread on the counter to cool and gathers up his dishes from the table.

"I hope I'm not rushing you out, Mr. Charles," Flora says. "Wouldn't want you to get indigestion."

"Not at all, Miss Flora. I have plenty of work to do. I will see myself out. Ladies, I will see you both at supper." Charles gives a little bow before making his way out of the cottage.

Miss Flora kisses the back of her teeth with her tongue. "If I hadn't chased him out of here, the two of you would be sitting here lookin' like an old married couple when Sir George arrives. And then how would we explain that?"

"Ladies don't have breakfast with their manservants?" I ask.

"If their manservants are dippin' in their honeypots, they do," Flora says.

My eyes stretch wide. "We don't want Sir George to think that, now, do we?"

"Certainly not. 'Tis why I chased him off," Flora says, looking quite proud of herself. "I believe that may be part of my job. I've done the same for many ladies and many of their lovers."

I don't even want to know the details Flora knows about her noble charges. "I appreciate your discretion," I say, dismissing her with a nod.

I barely get a chance to catch my breath before Sir George is ringing the bell that hangs over the cottage door, signaling his arrival. When I open the door, the spring breeze follows Sir George inside. It's cool and fragrant, making me want to take a walk instead of sitting inside drinking tea.

"Sir George," I say with excitement as I hug him, then rush him over to the dining table where Charles and I were only a few moments ago having breakfast. "I have some wonderful news."

Sir George grins. "I already know the news. Do you think that invitation made it out of the royal court without everyone knowing about it?"

Flora appears with the tea service and serves tea, first to me and then to Sir George. I pick up the beautiful invitation and hand it to him. "So you knew I was receiving this and you didn't tell me?"

"I wanted it to be a surprise," Sir George says. "And it seems to have worked."

"It did. I am genuinely surprised. But she wants me to come on May tenth, so that doesn't give us very much time to prepare. Well, what shall we sing, Sir George?" My eyebrows raise with the question, letting him know that I will leave the repertoire up to him.

"Let me explain how the concert will proceed. You and I will be brought before the queen in her private rooms. We will play maybe four of five songs for her. She will ask you a few questions. And you will say a few words," Sir George says. "She will thank you, and that will be all."

I take a sip of tea as I digest this. "I do not know why I believed there would be more ceremony to it than that."

Sir George shakes his head. "No, it's as informal a thing as there could be with Queen Victoria. She enjoys music and musicians, and I enjoy the opportunity of sharing with her my finest students, and you are one of my best. Even though, I admit, I haven't added much to what you brought with you from America. Your teacher, Miss Bella, was amazing. She equipped you with everything you needed."

Perhaps it will sound as if I lack humility if I agree with Sir George, and that is not a desired trait in a lady. But I do agree. I do not know why I believed that receiving instruction in Paris would transform me. Sir George is being modest, however; he's as good as Miss Bella, if not better, and he has helped to reinforce my confidence and encouraged me to take risks with my voice that I might have never taken. For that I am grateful.

"I appreciate everything you have instilled in me. My time in London has not been wasted."

"Will you remain here, or will you return to America?" Sir George asks. "Conditions are not improving, I fear, for Black people there. And you are welcome. Even if the invitations begin to wane, I can send you students to tutor."

"I have loved ones in America that I miss, but one of the reasons I am here is that I'd like to bring my birth mother back home to America."

"Is she here in London?" Sir George asks, seemingly ready to spring into action. "I did not know your mother was here. Why haven't you introduced us?"

"My mother is in Liberia. She was once a slave, but now she'd like to come home."

"Lady Sutherland has resources," Sir George says. "I will make sure she helps."

My eyes moisten with tears, overwhelmed at this kindness. "Thank you."

"And then, after we rescue your mother from Liberia, you will go back to America?" Sir George asks, speaking as if it's already done, which I appreciate.

"Yes. Well, hopefully. I believe my inheritance will be released soon."

Mr. Howell promises that we are down to our last hearing, and it will take place in July. All his arguments have been successful, and this is just a formality. I will not believe it until it has been finalized.

"An inheritance is a blessed thing," Sir George says with a knowing chuckle. "It allows one to pursue the desires of one's heart without fear of hunger or homelessness. I pray you have this freedom soon."

I know that Sir George does not mean for his comment to sadden me, but it does, because it makes me think of all the Black people I know with gifts and talents and heart's desires. They do not have the freedom to pursue them, because they were not fortunate enough to have a wealthy benefactor, or to fall in league with aristocratic patrons. They may be trapped on a plantation, with a voice. Like my father, who sang only to lift the spirits of the folks on the plantation with him. He could've been a world-famous oratorio like Mr. Sims Reeves if his freedom hadn't been stolen from him. It is not fair that in this society, and especially in America, when we are either in chains or in danger of them, that only a tiny number of us get to have or live a dream. Why should that be?

"I think I know what I would like to sing for Queen Victoria," I say to Sir George.

"Should I prepare some of our regular songs?" he asks. "She is quite fond of some of those American folk songs we've been singing on tour."

I stare off into the distance, thinking only of my father singing between the rows of cotton and tobacco on a plantation in Natchez, Mississippi.

"No," I reply somberly. "I think I'd like it to be a departure from my normal repertoire."

\* \* \*

WE ARRIVE AT Buckingham Palace on the morning of the concert, and already at the outer gate, I am amazed by the splendor. The gate is trimmed in gold, with two golden embellished crests on the entry. Several stories high, there are long rows of windows, and the palace sits far enough from the street that one can easily see out, but any passersby are not able to see in.

My eyes dart from side to side trying to take it all in. From the guards in red suits , to the elegant horse-drawn carriages within the gates, to the ladies in full petticoats and hoops. Of course, my eyes linger on the perfectly manicured gardens and spring flowers in full bloom. I will miss spring in London, and I will especially miss the pride these aristocrats take in their gardens. That is a love I will take back with me to America.

"Can you believe this?" I ask Charles as he sits beside me in the carriage. "We are really at Buckingham Palace."

"I believe my life has been full of adventure since we met, and I am blessed because of it." He takes my hand and kisses it tenderly. I know him well enough that he has a cynical comment in mind about the wealth of the royal family and Queen Victoria but is keeping it to himself to avoid spoiling my moment.

We are led from the carriage into the palace entrance to await further instructions, and again my senses are overcome by the grandeur. I can conduct an entire concert in this grand hallway with its marble floors and stone walls that reach up to the heavens. Surely, the angels will be able to hear my voice from here.

A beautiful young Black woman approaches us. She is one of the servants and wears red like the guards, but her dress has embellishments that are white instead of gold. She smiles and gives a slight curtsy as if Charles and I are royalty. I curtsy back and Charles nods.

"Miss Greenfield, welcome to Buckingham Palace," the young woman says, an excited gleam in her eyes though her voice trembles nervously. "There is a room prepared for you with tea and refreshment, if you would like. You will be collected when the queen is ready."

"What might we call you?" I ask, grinning back at the young woman and lightly touching her arm, hoping that she might relax a bit.

"Oh," she says with a sigh. "My name is Benita. I am one of the queen's maids."

"Thank you, Benita. This is my friend Charles. We would like tea and refreshments."

She looks at Charles and lets out a small gasp. Since it is only the three of us, no harm in calling him a friend instead of a manservant. I appreciate the freedom of not having to say that for a change, and I know Charles appreciates not having to *be* that for once.

"Then please follow me," she says.

We start to follow her down a long corridor, but then she stops. She turns to face us, and she looks as if she might burst with enthusiasm.

"May I say something, Miss Greenfield?" she asks.

"Yes, of course," I say. "Go right ahead."

Finally letting her guard down, she exhales. "Well, I am so excited that you are here. I wish to sing like you. The queen promises that if I show potential I can take lessons with Sir George."

My eyes widen with pleasure at her news. "That is wonderful. I'd love to hear you sing."

"Oh no. I couldn't. I'm not ready."

"I bet you are better than you believe. Try something. Sing me your favorite song."

"All right. I'll sing you my favorite lullaby."

Benita closes her eyes and sings a tune that I've never heard before. The clarity and tone of her voice, the way she pushes the sound from her chest, and the emotion that she imparts in only a few notes tell me that she has the potential to be an amazing singer.

I give her wild applause, and Charles joins me. "Bravo, Benita! Bravo!" I exclaim. "That was beautiful. I was nowhere near as advanced as you are at your age. You will get your opportunity with Sir George. I will make sure to tell him about you."

"Will you, truly?" Benita asks, tears rimming her eyes.

When I nod, Benita throws her arms around me and hugs me. "Oh, I have almost forgotten that I'm taking you to the refreshment room. I'm sorry. Please follow me."

"No apologies needed," I say as I smile at her excitement.

I understand feeling seen and hoping that this person can somehow change everything. Sir George can get her the education she needs, and Queen Victoria can be her patron. If Benita practices hard enough, and the stars align, I pray that she can pursue this vocation.

She shows us into a room with two sofas and a table and chairs. On the table is a tea service and a buffet of sandwiches, miniature cakes, cookies, tarts, and treats. I pour myself a cup of tea and sit on the sofa. Charles joins me with a cup of tea and a sandwich.

"Sir George will come to collect you when it's time for you to go to the queen," Benita says. "Do you need anything else, Miss Greenfield?"

"No, you may go. Thank you, Benita."

The way the girl beams at me as she backs out of the room makes me proud to have made the choices I've made. Even the ones I've made afraid. I may not ever give birth to children of my own, but perhaps I can claim young singers like Benita as my progeny.

"She's gorgeous and gifted," I say to Charles. "If they are careful to train her well, and to keep her chaste and away from the snares of romance, we may see her touring the world one day."

"'The snares of romance.'" Charles laughs. "You are humorous, Eliza."

"You know these are facts." There is no humor in my tone as I relay this inconvenient truth. "If she falls in love and marries, she may have a wonderful life, but she will not be a prima donna."

"Well, everyone's life manages to unfold differently," Charles says. "You are far past the age that anyone thought something would come of your singing career, but it did. Sometimes you have to leave room for the unexpected."

Before I can respond to the remark about my age, Sir George is standing in the doorway with his eyebrows raised over the tops of his spectacles. He's dressed to perfection in his fitted black waistcoat and trousers.

"Are you ready, Miss Greenfield?" Sir George asks.

I set down my cup of tea and glance at Charles. "It is time."

"Do not keep Queen Victoria waiting," Charles says. "She's going to love you."

I follow Sir George and the attendants who have been sent to collect me. I descend a large staircase and walk down another long hallway. This one is covered in a thick red carpet. Queen Victoria's guards stand on either side of the carpet all the way into the drawing room where the queen awaits our presence.

We stop in front of Queen Victoria, who is seated on a large red velvet chair with a gold trimmed back. She is a petite woman, but after having had many children, she has a very robust and curvy woman's body. Though she is not especially pretty, a matching emerald brooch and bracelet give her a very elegant and regal look.

The queen's day dress is a breathtaking rose-colored silk, and she wears a blue sash over her shoulder that is tied at her waist. The ladies-in-waiting that sit on either side of her in smaller versions of the same velvet chair also wear silk day dresses in pastel colors. None of them are as beautiful as the queen's dress, however. Her dainty hands are encased in white gloves as they lay across her lap. She sits in anticipation of greatness, and I intend to provide her heart's desire.

"Your Majesty, I present to you Miss Elizabeth Taylor Greenfield, the American singer," a court attendant says.

I curtsy deeply, as Lady Sutherland has taught me in preparation for this moment. Sir George takes his place on the pianoforte. I position myself where I can see both Sir George and the queen's reactions.

"Miss Greenfield, I am quite looking forward to this," Queen Victoria says warmly. "You must know I have had a love for singing and opera music since I was a child."

"Thank you for the invitation, Your Majesty." I am surprised that my voice is not shaky, because I am nervous. "It is an honor to be here."

The first two songs I sing are songs that the queen is sure to love: Italian arias displaying the vocal acrobatics I am known for in England and in America. My full three-octave range is evident. My beautiful singing, my trills, my runs, and the tremendous vocal control is here for her to enjoy. I may not be a new sensation, but I am a prima donna.

On the final song, "Vision of the Negro Slave," a very gifted flutist joins Sir George for the introduction of the song. I close my eyes as the sweet whistle notes of the flute transport me. It is hauntingly beautiful and adds the perfect amount of melancholy accompaniment to the lyrics, which are tragic and heartrending.

I open my mouth to sing the first note, and Queen Victoria's eyes stretch with pleasure, but I hope to evoke a different emotion by the end of the song. Compassion, or perhaps empathy. Ideally, a desire to give hope to the hopeless and help to the helpless.

When I am done, I take a deep bow, and then I wait for her remarks or dismissal.

"You could have chosen to sing anything, and to close you have selected a song that depicts the conditions of the slave in America," Queen Victoria says, then purses her lips and raises an eyebrow.

Nervous about her reaction, I nod slowly. "Yes, Your Majesty."

"Why did you make that choice?" Her clipped tone is not angry or annoyed but simply demanding of a response.

I take a deep breath. Then I stand tall. "As a reminder that while I have been freed from bondage, chains, and the scourge of the whip to pursue a higher calling, there are many still bound, their talents unknown and unknowable. And even those who have been freed still move about with the ever-present threat of enslavement hovering a split second away. Even I cannot escape that threat and burden with notoriety and an inheritance."

"And how, pray tell, does the burden of slavery trouble you still?" Her tone continues to demand a response, but it sounds more like a thirst for information than annoyance or ire. "I heard Mrs. Harriet Beecher Stowe speak of your being manumitted as a small child, when she was here to speak about her wonderful book."

"Yes, Your Majesty, that is true. However, my mother, who went to Liberia when I was a child, is not allowed back in America to be reunited with me because of the slavers' fear of freed slaves. And then there are the slave catchers always lurking, with their threat of kidnapping manumitted people and returning them to plantations. How is it freedom if our movements are restricted?"

The queen thinks on my words for a moment. She probably is not used to being on the receiving end of questions. She is the one who asks questions, and people give her answers, not the other way around.

"Well, Miss Greenfield, that is not freedom at all," Queen Victoria says decidedly. "No one should be able to tell a mother that she cannot have her child to care for her in old age. I am a mother, and that does not sit well with me."

"I am glad that you agree with me, Your Majesty, but I do not sing just about my own situation. The evil institution of slavery touches me personally in that way, but I am not truly free while others are in chains. It is my prayer that America follows England's lead and abolishes slavery."

"You are brave and proud to use your voice in this way, Miss Greenfield," Queen Victoria says. "I have enjoyed your presentation. Thank you."

Her nod indicates finality, and so I curtsy again and exit behind Sir George. As we leave the queen's performance room, I notice that Charles has attended my performance without my knowledge. He joins Sir George and I as we walk toward the grand entryway.

"And that is all," I say quietly to Sir George. "I hope I did well."

He nods. "You did very well. You made your mark, I suspect."

"But the summer season?" I ask. "Am I still unlikely to find a patron?"

"That remains to be seen. We will receive a note from the queen's offices in a week or two. And then we will know what to do," Sir George says. "But patron or not, you have triumphed. You do know that, don't you? No other Black woman has done what you have done in Britain."

"Yes, I know that."

"And I think Frederick Douglass himself would be proud of what you did in there before Queen Victoria," Charles chimes in. "I am too."

I tilt my head to one side and grin. "Perfect. Now, when we get back to the cottage, will you be sure to prepare an editorial letter to the *Frederick Douglass' Paper* and tell them all about it? It's about time I get a nice article about me in there for a change."

"I'll think about it," Charles says while laughing. "I have a reputation for submitting scathing editorials. I don't know what they would think if I sent in a wonderfully complimentary article."

Sir George leads us to our carriage, which is waiting to take us back to our cottage for what may be the end of our time in Britain. If it is, I wonder what adventure providence has in store next. And if providence has no adventure, then I will have to go and find one.

# CHAPTER THIRTY-NINE

*July 1854*

While Sir George thought we'd hear from the queen in a couple of weeks, two months go by before we finally receive a visit from him with word from Buckingham Palace. I've invited him inside, but I don't want to hear his news without having Charles here with me.

"Flora, please go and get Charles so he can also hear the news from Sir George," I say to my maid. "I will set up the tea service. Hurry. Sir George may have somewhere to be."

"I am not in a hurry," Sir George says. "Take your time."

Flora rushes out of the cottage anyway to go find Charles. Sir George looks at me with amusement as I prepare his cup of tea and hand it to him.

"I have never seen someone so concerned about their manservant hearing their news," Sir George says, and then sips his tea.

"What are you insinuating, Sir George?" I ask.

"Insinuating?" Sir George shakes his head. "I would never. I might wonder or suppose. I would never insinuate."

"Humph. Charles has been a trusted member of my inner circle since my very first tour and has acted in many capacities. Manservant is one. He is also a gifted musician, which I am sure he has told you."

Sir George nods emphatically. "Yes, he has told me how you met when he was an organ player at a church in Buffalo."

While I do not have to correct Sir George's supposition, I choose to make sure he hears my entire cover story, for any other gossiping hens who may question my virtue.

Flora returns with Charles in tow. He nods in greeting to Sir George and sits on the sofa, knowing that if Sir George is here, then it is time to learn our fate for the upcoming season.

"All right," Sir George says. "Are we ready now?"

I nod. "I suppose."

Sir George reaches into the inside pocket of his waistcoat and pulls out an envelope, which he hands to me. It is addressed to me, and is from Colonel Parker, Buckingham Palace.

"Who is Colonel Parker?" I ask. "I don't remember meeting anyone by that name."

"He's one of the palace guards," Sir George says. "Not someone you would remember."

I open the envelope, and inside is a very pretty piece of stationery with a note and a check for twenty pounds. I unfold the note and read it.

*By the command of Her Majesty, the Queen, Colonel Parker forwards this check for twenty pounds as renumeration for her singing for Her Majesty on 10 May 1854 at Buckingham Palace. Additionally, Her Majesty wishes to relay to Miss Greenfield that her mother, Anna Greenfield, has been located in Monrovia, Liberia, and will be brought to London. Her Majesty's secretary is in talks with authorities in America to resettle Anna Greenfield in her native land. You will be contacted when a decision is made.*

*Her Majesty, the Queen, would like to thank Miss Greenfield for her services.*

"We're going home," I say to Charles with the biggest smile on my face.

Charles looks confused. "So there isn't another patron?"

"Not that I can tell." I shrug.

I pass Charles the letter, which he quickly reads. He chuckles.

"So, the Black Swan is going back to America?" he asks.

"No," I correct him. "Elizabeth Taylor Greenfield, an American singer, is going back home. With her mother, Anna, in tow."

So, as this adventure ends, it gives way to another. Back to America with my mother and to the people I love, to live out a life I never knew possible. Perhaps I will dream new dreams and love new loves. Or instead hold the ones I cherish close to my heart, so that I may behold their wildest imaginations becoming realities.

# EPILOGUE

*Philadelphia, Pennsylvania*
*May 1863*

The courtyard of the brownstone is our favorite place to chat, to read, to have tea, and to remember. Between my mother and me, we have enough precious memories here to invite visitations from our loved ones on occasion. Spirit to spirit. And that brings us both joy.

Today we sit in the balmy warmth of spring. Eating tea cookies Mary prepared and drinking lemonade, because it's a little bit warm for tea.

Even though I know it's real, I am filled with a bit of wonder as I sit across from my mother. I see myself in her. My short stature, my prominent nose, and of course my heavy, long hair all come from her.

Mother is tiny, though, and thick around neither the waist nor hips. Nor does she have a heaving bosom. There is not one place on her body that I would call curvy. She is muscular, lithe, and agile. Daily, she is up working in her garden of herbs and vegetables. She has displaced some of Miss Lizbeth's flowers, but that is okay, because we consume what is in Mother's garden in soup, stews, and medicines.

And yes, I have my inheritance. Finally. But Mother doesn't care how much money we have. She doesn't trust it. So she grows everything and sews, and keeps and hides and hoards. Since we did not have to use the money allocated to my mother to bring her home from England, it is in a bank account for her, to be used for her needs.

She does not have many of those, living with me, but if she does, the money is there.

Mary sits in the rocking chair on the other side of Mother and pours a glass of lemonade. I am happy to share Mother with Mary and my nieces. Mother doesn't have grandchildren and they don't have a grandmother, so it is another beautiful union.

"It is hot out here," Mary says. "Does that mean it's gonna be a hot summer, Miss Anna?"

Mother nods. "All the fruit trees flowered early this year, all the way through. I think it is going to be a hot one."

"Here comes your wants-to-be husband," Mary says with a chuckle, as Lucien marches up the street with his still pretty but now over-weight from all the babies wife in tow.

"Shhh, Mary, don't say that too loud," I hiss at her. "We don't want his wife to hear you say that."

"Well, you don't think she already thinks it? Whose husband goes running up and down the street plucking someone's flowers?" Mary asks.

"That's his way to honor Miss Lizbeth," Mother says in her always peaceful yet firm tone meant to end foolish conversations. "She was good to him too. Just like an aunt."

"What do you think about it, Eliza?" Mary asks.

"I have no thoughts about it one way or the other," I say bluntly.

But then the one I do have thoughts about, all-consuming thoughts, trots up the walk past Lucien to the patio. Lucien looks up and sees who I see: Charles, wearing the military uniform of a Union soldier in the Union Army. I cannot say that I am pleased with his apparel. Charles and I, as is the case on many issues when it comes to the cause of freedom, do not see eye to eye when it comes to this war. Frederick Douglass has called upon Black men to volunteer to fight alongside white Union soldiers, because he believes that the

Confederate Army needs to be taken down, and with it the institution of slavery.

While I do want the institution destroyed, I do not have confidence that the Union is going to support the Black soldiers. I don't believe our men will have guns that work, or, if the guns work, then they won't have bullets. Somehow, I do not believe most of the Black soldiers will survive this war.

Including my Charles.

But I cannot stop him from going off to join the Union forces no more than he could stop me from getting on that steamer to Buffalo. Or from going with Colonel Wood on tour. Some choices we feel like we must make, and no one can turn us around from them.

"Hello, ladies," Charles says. "Do you think a soldier might get some lemonade on this hot day?"

"I think we might be out," I say. "Sorry."

"We are not out of lemonade," Mary says. "Come have a glass. Someone is unhappy about you leaving and going to war."

"I don't know who you're talking about," I say. "Aren't the troops fighting to free the slaves? Why would anyone here be unhappy about that?"

I get up from my rocking chair and go inside, mostly because I feel my eyes begin to water, and I do not wish to make a scene in front of Lucien and his wife. Lucien has stopped tending the roses to see what he can see, with his nosy self, although his wife looks as if she's ready to leave now that the gathering seems to be more intimate in nature.

Charles follows me inside the brownstone and into the kitchen. "Aren't you going to tell me I look good in my uniform?" he asks, with his arms outstretched for a hug.

Since I cannot resist his arms, and I do not know if this is the last time I might feel one of his loving embraces, I greedily reach for him. As he encircles me, I try to memorize everything about him. His masculine scent, from his soap and his shave cream. The way his beard scratches my face. How his hands press the small of my back when he holds me.

"You look like a freedom fighter in your uniform," I tell him truthfully. "I am proud of you, my love."

"I need you and all the ladies at Shiloh Baptist to pray really hard that we defeat the Confederate slavers, because I have plans for us, Eliza," Charles whispers.

I look up at him and smile. "What plans, Charles Monroe?"

"I might put a baby in you."

I snatch a towel from the sink with a free hand and playfully whack Charles with it. "Now stop this foolishness."

"Maybe we'll get married, like your friend outside who looked so fondly at me when I walked up," Charles says as he laughs good and hearty from his belly. "Wonder if he'll be my best man."

"You just get home, hear? Then we can discuss all that."

Charles kisses my forehead. "Now, you know you aren't the marrying kind."

I rest my face on Charles's chest and sigh, because he is right about that. I am not the marrying kind. And after the war, when the North is victorious, America may need another song or two from the Black Swan.

And she must be able to take flight.

# HISTORICAL NOTE

Even though *The Unexpected Diva* is a work of fiction, I have attempted to share the life of Elizabeth Taylor Greenfield, the first Black prima donna, by creating a world for our heroine using the few available facts. As with many enslaved Black people in pre–Civil War America, certain details about Eliza's life were either not documented at all or the records are incomplete. Thus, some specific dates, names, and individuals are fictional. However, in writing this story, I leaned heavily on not just the facts of Eliza's life but also the rich history of free people of color in America at that time.

It is documented that Elizabeth Taylor Greenfield was born on a plantation in Natchez, Mississippi, between 1809 and 1826. That is a huge stretch of time, but for the purposes of this story, we start with a much younger Eliza, around the age of twenty when the events in the novel begin. She was manumitted and then raised by her former mistress, Elizabeth H. Greenfield, who died in approximately 1845.

Elizabeth H. Greenfield was an abolitionist who freed all the enslaved persons on her plantation after her husband died and relocated them to Liberia. She then moved to Philadelphia with young Eliza and raised her in a community of Quakers and abolitionists. When she died, Elizabeth left Eliza a sizable inheritance that was disputed for many years.

The reason for Eliza's parents leaving her behind with Mrs. Greenfield is not listed anywhere in the historical record. It was noted, however, that the only way the judge would accept the mass number of slaves being manumitted from the plantation in Mississippi is if they were immediately boarding a vessel to Monrovia, Liberia. I created a cause for Eliza's being left behind, but it could've been any number of reasons. Her parents were unfortunately faced with the impossible choice to get on that ship or remain in captivity, so whatever reason they left her, it was for freedom's sake. But Eliza was left in good hands!

While there is nothing documented about Eliza's childhood and early life, there is a great deal of information available about the free Black population of Philadelphia. Pre–Civil War and Reconstruction, their community was a vibrant one with wealthy and middle-class business and property owners. A young free Black person in Philadelphia would be literate, educated, and have a life enriched by the arts.

The main sources of information for Eliza's life were a biographical sketch called *The Black Swan: At Home and Abroad* and a great deal of newspaper articles, reviews, and clippings from America and Great Britain chronicling Eliza's tours. I used the tour dates and reviews of Eliza's concerts to build a timeline for the events in this story (1850–1854).

Since the biographical sketch was for the public's consumption, it certainly does not delve into Eliza's personal life, nor mention any friends or lovers. It does include many letters from Eliza's various white patrons, who spoke highly of her and provided monetary support and letters of reference when needed.

These patrons were real people, like Electra Potter, who met and heard Eliza perform on a steamship to Buffalo, New York, and presented her to Buffalo's elite. Hiram E. Howard, then president of the Buffalo Musical Association, was not only an employer and sponsor, but he continued to write Eliza and advise her through many difficult legal battles.

Another such patron was the historical figure Harriet Beecher Stowe, author of *Uncle Tom's Cabin*. It is unclear when Eliza first became acquainted with Harriet, but it is documented that she wrote letters to Eliza and assisted her when she was stranded in Europe by an unnamed promoter. The Earl and Countess of Shaftesbury, Duchess of Sutherland, and Duchess of Argyll were all listed as patrons of Eliza's European tour.

Though there is no documented evidence that the two prima donnas' paths ever crossed, there is much mention in this story of Jenny Lind, also known as the Swedish Nightingale. She toured America at around the same time Eliza began touring. Eliza could not escape comparisons to the white prima donna. In positive reviews, Eliza was heralded as America's answer to the European star. In negative reviews, it was often suggested that Eliza seek more musical education in Europe to perhaps one day rival her Swedish counterpart. In one of the widely shared drawings of Eliza, it is noted that she fashioned her hair in the same style as Jenny Lind's, perhaps leaning into the chatter to generate buzz for her concerts.

The Black Swan toured many of the same cities as Jenny Lind; however, the disparity of pay between the two women is almost incomprehensible. When Miss Lind toured with P. T. Barnum, she secured a payment of one thousand dollars per performance (which she mostly donated to charity). Eliza's concerts, where tickets were priced fifty cents to a dollar in most cities, netted her a fraction of what Miss Lind received. So much so that, even after an American tour and a concert at the Metropolitan Hall, she was nearly penniless when she was stranded in Europe in 1853.

Since Elizabeth H. Greenfield was an active abolitionist, she would have certainly been aware of the Quakers' shuttling enslaved persons through stops on the Underground Railroad. A Philadelphia Quaker meetinghouse is one of the documented stops. All throughout the novel, there is mention of the railroad and its various conductors, particularly because Eliza is touring the country during a perilous time for Black people. The Fugitive Slave Act of 1850 empowered hunters of enslaved people to accuse and capture anyone *suspected* of having escaped a plantation. Unfortunately, there were times when free Black people, even those who were never enslaved, were ensnared and sold into the Deep South.

Missing from the historical sketch are any friends, supporters, or loved ones who were in the free Black communities of Philadelphia and Buffalo where Eliza appeared to spend a great deal of her adult life. When searching for who the movers and the shakers were in the Black community at the time, I was excited to come across the Forten family and, in particular, Hattie Forten Purvis—one of the founders, along with her mother and sisters, of the Philadelphia Female Anti-Slavery Society (PFASS). PFASS was a multiracial group of badass women who were leading the charge of abolition work in Philadelphia. I have amassed a small pile of research about them as well, and my fingers can't fly fast enough typing story ideas about these incredible women.

Eliza did not have any documented spouses or children, which makes sense due to the times that she lived in. In nineteenth-century America, a woman simply could not have it all. There was no such thing as a working mother. There was also no reliable birth control or abortion rights.

The prime directive of most women in that society was to marry and procreate. Eliza's choice to pursue a career as a prima donna was indeed unprecedented and inherently risky. This makes her choices even more groundbreaking.

Aside from Eliza's concerts, I also leaned heavily on historical events that were taking place in the Black community during the rise of Eliza's career as the Black Swan. Eliza was mentioned in *Frederick Douglass' Paper*'s editorial section on occasion, mostly in op-eds admonishing her to use her platform to help the abolitionists' cause.

In many of the cities that Eliza visits on her tour, I looked for free Black historical places, figures, or events to incorporate into the story. For example, Eliza's New York City concert took place around the time that Black waiters were planning their first strike for better wages, so in the story she meets a waiter who is involved with the cause. Another real figure in the novel is William F. Johnson, a blind lecturer and abolitionist who was popular at the time and worked closely with Frederick Douglass. The churches Eliza attends in Buffalo (Michigan Street Baptist Church) and Philadelphia (Mother Bethel AME and Shiloh Baptist Church) are historical Black churches, and in real life, Eliza made Shiloh Baptist Church her home in her later years.

When Black people were banned from Eliza's concert at the Metropolitan Hall in New York City, Eliza was encouraged to perform the same program for Black people at a church in Philadelphia. In the novel, she performs this concert at Abyssinian Baptist Church, which was at the time the largest Black church in New York City.

During this period in America, an unmarried woman with a lover or companion would have been deemed scandalous, and the biographical sketch written about Eliza goes to great lengths to paint her as the picture of virtue and gentility. But, since Eliza is a woman in her twenties during the novel, I had a great time creating her two fictional male paramours, Lucien and Charles. Particularly Charles, who was an active abolitionist and often acting as Eliza's voice of reason.

One of the things that drew me to this story was Queen Victoria's invitation for Eliza to sing in Buckingham Palace. With a slew of patrons from the British nobility and her teacher, Sir George Smart, in attendance, this must have been a very exciting and joyful moment for Eliza. It came at a time when she might have been concerned about how the rest of her life would play out, especially if her inheritance never materialized.

Last but not least when talking about the Black Swan, I can't ignore the music. Although there are no surviving recordings of her voice, many reviews mention Eliza's three octave range and her ability to sing a low baritone up to a high soprano. The biographical sketch mentions many of the arias and folk songs Eliza performed in concert. In the beginning of her career, Eliza performed some of the same songs as Jenny Lind, which undoubtedly fueled the comparisons. One in particular resonated with me: "When Stars Are in the Quiet Skies" (Bulwer-Lytton). In the novel, Eliza sings this song at pivotal moments in her journey. Also, there was a distinct time in Eliza's career when she started to include songs about the plight of enslaved persons as part of her repertoire, and that is also highlighted in the story.

One plot point that was completely fictional but that made my heart sing was reuniting Eliza with her birth mother, Anna Greenfield. This idea came simply from the real-life fact that Mrs. Elizabeth H. Greenfield did leave Anna fifteen hundred dollars in case she wanted to come home from Liberia. That fact blossomed into the reunion storyline, and I am so glad to have imagined them sitting together enjoying each other's company years later at Mrs. Greenfield's home.

In real life, after Eliza came home from Great Britain, she reunited with Colonel Wood (yes, *him*) for another tour. This was still prior to the Civil War, and nothing much had changed as far as discrimination against Black concertgoers. Eliza, however, had changed and had become much more vocal in not accepting the status quo. She refused concert halls that wouldn't admit Black patrons in favor of those that would.

Colonel Wood did tell the media that Eliza had been in Britain, and of course the reviews credited any improvements to her voice to having been trained by Europeans. A high point of her career is that she got to mentor lesser-known singers Mary Brown, Thomas Bowers, and Sarah Sedgwick by bringing them on tour stops with her. Toward the end of her life, Eliza was training and coaching many young singers and even had a group that was called the "Black Swan Troupe."

In the late 1850s and in the years leading up to the Civil War, the reviews and newspaper articles about Eliza became more and more racist and tinged with anti-abolition politics. Some of the reviews of her 1855 tour used very racially explicit language, especially after it was known that she had associated with Harriet Beecher Stowe while in Britain. There were even minstrel shows produced with the Black Swan as the subject matter.

During the Civil War, Eliza continued to tour and sang songs more aligned with the cause of freedom. Songs that I'm sure Charles (if he had been a real person) would have wanted her to sing while he was on the battlefield. As a matter of fact, Eliza sang at churches all over the northern states and some in the South from the time she returned from Britain through the Civil War.

Also, after she came home from Britain, Eliza became involved in many philanthropic efforts. She sang a widely reported-on benefit concert at Boston's Twelfth Street Baptist Church to support abolition efforts and was a huge financial supporter of her home church, Philadelphia's Shiloh Baptist Church, for many years. She fellow-shipped with Shiloh Baptist for the rest of her life.

Aside from assisting churches in raising money for a plethora of ministries and charities, Eliza also supported just about any cause that helped Black people. She sang for orphanages and for the controversial Liberian immigration efforts. Eliza even triumphantly assisted in raising funds for the Union soldiers during the Civil War.

By the end of her touring career and her philanthropic efforts, Eliza had finally started to be mentioned favorably in the *Frederick Douglass' Paper*, where she was oft criticized early in her career. There is historical evidence that Eliza performed during a lecture series that featured Frederick Douglass as a speaker in the years immediately following the Civil War, marking a triumphant rise in her status among the Black elite intellectuals of her time.

By sharing this delightful story of a tenacious Black woman, when tenacity was often a very dangerous thing, when the phrase "Black Girl Magic" could get one burned at the stake, and when the lives of most people of color were downtrodden and weary, we can celebrate Black joy where it exists in America's history. Our stories did not begin on the shores of America, but when we were empowered and allowed to flourish, often greatness ensued.

# AUTHOR'S NOTE

𝒢ive us the Black Swan!

I think the question on many of my reader's minds will be why I chose Elizabeth Taylor Greenfield's story as my first (but not last) foray into historical fiction. Like Eliza meeting Electra Potter on that steamship to Buffalo, much of the reason is serendipity and providence.

I stumbled across Eliza when I was researching another story (*A Wedding in Harlem*) about the marriage of Yolande Du Bois (daughter of W.E.B. Du Bois) to Harlem Renaissance poet Countee Cullen. I learned that W.E.B. Du Bois was involved with a very short-lived record label called Black Swan Records, which was a tribute to Elizabeth Taylor Greenfield, and then I just had to know who this woman was.

Elizabeth's story, what little there is documented, captured—no, demanded—my attention. The idea that a Black woman could tour the country singing opera music *before* the Civil War was mindblowing, as was the fact that I had never heard of her. And neither had most of the people I asked. I'd heard of Marian Anderson, the famed American contralto who was the first Black singer to perform at the Metropolitan Opera, in 1955, but not Elizabeth Taylor Greenfield, who was the first Black singer to perform at the Metropolitan Hall more than one hundred years earlier, in 1853. Why haven't we heard of the Black Swan?

Convincing my agent that this was a story that anyone would be interested in publishing was another matter entirely, but out of all the other historical proposals I wrote in 2022, Eliza's story was clearly the most compelling.

The biggest thing that struck me about Eliza's journey was that aside from the question of reproductive freedom (Eliza had none), the trials she faced pursuing a career in the arts are eerily similar to those of modern-day Black women in music, television, and film. Every review of Eliza's shows included some form of microaggression about her clothing, her body, or her virtue. She was doggedly compared to her white peer, Jenny Lind, who was by every report overpaid, while Eliza struggled to make ends meet with her craft. Eliza's story speaks to every plus-size diva, every underrated singer, and every actress passed over for the lighter, thinner, prettier version.

But even with those insurmountable odds, Eliza's gift made room for her.

I hope the Black Swan's story will spark conversation about these similarities and highlight the uncomfortable truth that while progress has been made, there is more work to do.

# ACKNOWLEDGMENTS

When I typed "the end" on this novel, my first work of historical fiction, I felt an amazing sense of accomplishment. I never shy away from reinvention, but this was on every account a daunting challenge. As with many new things that I've tried in life, I charged ahead despite a little fear.

The constant refrain as I wrote this novel is the book's theme, "your gift will make room for you." That theme was not just the lesson Eliza learns in the story; it is a lesson for me in this phase of my life. After more than two decades in publishing, and having received many bumps and bruises along the way, I am now charting the course for my career.

While charting a thing might happen alone, the execution of a thing is another matter entirely.

I must thank God first and always—the giver of gifts. And then my husband, Brent, who always supports these ideas and cheers me on to the finish line. My adult children. Wait. Let me pause on that for a moment of reflection. When y'all first met me in 2005, signing books at Joseph-Beth Booksellers in Cleveland, Ohio, you may have noticed wet spots on my very nice Tahari suit. I was still nursing my youngest, who is now in college. Where did the time go?

How could I have done any of this without my bomb agent, Latoya Smith? She is just as driven and motivated as I am, and when I sent her my list of career goals, she didn't try to talk me out of any of them. Let's see what unfolds next.

To my editor, Rachel Kahan, thank you for believing in this story and falling in love with Eliza as quickly as I did.

Also, I want to thank my tribe of friends and writers who push me to greatness. I am blessed with an abundance of prayer partners, supporters, and force multipliers. But there are a few sister writers who *really* held my hand through this one. Victoria, ReShonda, Renee, and Piper, how could I have done this without you? Thank you, thank you, thank you.

Finally, there would be no books or a career without the bookstore owners and readers who keep me in print and have continued to support me for more than two decades in publishing. Thank you for your tweets, comments, posts, reviews, invitations, and kind words.

Here is another one for you all. I hope I make you proud!

*Tiffany*